ENEMY
OF MY
DREAMS

Also by Jenny Williamson

Enemy of My Dreams

To learn more about Jenny Williamson,
visit her website, jennywilliamsonauthor.com.

JENNY
WILLIAMSON

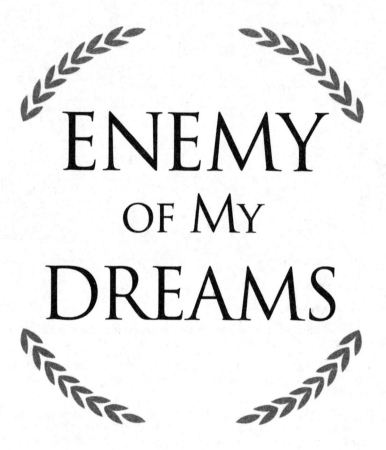

ENEMY
OF MY
DREAMS

CANARY STREET PRESS

CANARY
STREET
PRESS™

Recycling programs
for this product may
not exist in your area.

ISBN-13: 978-1-335-08051-6

Enemy of My Dreams

Canary Street Press
22 Adelaide St. West, 41st Floor
Toronto, Ontario M5H 4E3, Canada
CanaryStPress.com

Printed in U.S.A.

For Mom. I got back on the horse every time. You'd be proud.

PROLOGUE

Frigidus River, Julian Alps
September 9, 394 AD

Three days after the last battle ended, the mighty *bora* still stalked the floodplain. It shrieked and murmured amongst the broken war machines and sent dust spirals walking amidst the dead. The men were saying it was the wind that won them this war, that the gods had sent it to drive the enemy's arrows back in their faces. Alaric of the Goths set his back to the battlefield, the *bora* snapping his cloak around his heels.

Someone should tell the gods, then, that the thrice-damned battle is over.

Before him, the usurper Eugenius knelt on the ground. Even kneeling, he was thin and stooped as an overtall reed. The wind filled the executioner's stained cloak like a tattered sail and snatched the words from the condemned man's mouth.

Ten thousand of his own dead to achieve this. Half the *foederati*. And the Romans had barely scratched their breastplates.

A heavy hand clapped down on Alaric's shoulder.

"Well done." The general Stilicho smiled, jovial as Saturnalia. "Without you, we never would have taken that valley. You have covered yourself in glory these past days."

Glory. Alaric felt a muscle in his jaw clench. There had been nothing glorious about what happened in that valley. He'd walked out covered only in blood, his men's as much as his enemy's.

The emperor Theodosius stepped out of the crowd below, swollen with his own importance. He interrupted Eugenius's last words with a speech about the Christian god who'd brought them victory. Mercifully, the wind obscured most of it.

"The emperor will want to see you," Stilicho said. "He will want a count of your dead. And if you play it right, there will be a reward."

"You mean the homeland he promised?" Alaric could not keep the bitterness from his voice. For years Theodosius had been promising land. Always after the next great victory, and the next. His people were still landless and homeless, and now half of them were dead. If that was a coincidence, he'd eat his own boots.

"*Must* you do this every time?" Stilicho let out an aggrieved sigh. "The emperor owes this victory to you. But you must be *politic*, Alaric. You stand to gain much, given time."

Alaric shook his head grimly. If there was one thing his people did not have, it was *time*. He remembered the Huns sweeping down from the eastern hills, lines of homesteads burning. It was an old memory, one from his childhood, but it was still happening.

Stilicho glanced at his battered, bloodstained cuirass and frowned. "Be sure to clean yourself up first. Cut your hair, for God's sake—try not to look so much like a barbarian."

Down below, Theodosius had finished with his talk of God. He gave an impassive nod to the executioner.

The *bora* stopped just as the axe fell.

The Imperial tent was full of rich fabrics and rare wood, all the comforts the emperor could not do without on campaign.

Theodosius sat with his head bent over a solid oak desk, making scratch marks on a wax tablet, his scalp pink with sunburn. Alaric thought of the bent backs, the sweat and suffering, that had brought the emperor's desk this far.

At length, Theodosius spoke. "Your report?"

"By my reckon, we lost ten thousand."

The emperor's hand stilled. "Tell me how you managed to lose half of the *foederati*."

"The scouts told us that the rim was clear. It wasn't. The archers picked us off like turtles in a bucket."

"And you lost ten thousand of *my* Gothic troops." Theodosius set his stylus down and regarded him coldly, eyes narrowed like a merchant who suspected weevils in the grain. "Stilicho says that without your valor, we would all be meat for the crows. But I know that God won us this war. He was the one who sent the wind."

"Emperor. With *respect*," Alaric said flatly. "Your god did not suffer and die to win you that valley. And it serves you to credit him, since he asks neither payment nor land in return."

"You have a lot of nerve." Theodosius frowned. "Perhaps you do not realize you are speaking to your greatest ally, Alaric. I've defended you before the Senate, and you've done nothing to make my work easier. Your people are ungovernable. They pillage when they should be farming. I visit your camps to find women and children wandering about in a war zone. If I granted your people land now, how would I know they would farm it, rather than simply using it as a base for plunder?"

"They would not have to follow my army if they had land of their own. If the women and children had somewhere safe to go—"

"I've offered to settle them in camps."

Over his steaming corpse. "People die like rats in those camps."

"How do you think it will look to the Senate if I settle ten thousand armed Goths in the Danube Valley so soon after Eugenius turned? If your people turn to pillaging honest Romans, I'd expect to be stoned in the streets." Theodosius paused to pour himself wine, offering none. "Eugenius was part Frankish, you know."

"My people are Tervingii. That isn't even the same tribe."

"You know that, and *I* know that. But to the Senate and the people, you are all the same." Theodosius picked up his stylus and resumed his scratchings. "You are dismissed. You will keep your current position, but only because the *foederati* are loyal to you. Be grateful for my generosity."

Alaric felt his teeth clench. As if it were not abundantly clear how the Romans saw his people. *Barbarians*, all of them. The Romans could give them the trappings, but in the end, it was his people in the valley, fighting more of his people, and the Romans reaping the reward.

Stilicho would want him to bow and scrape, to make a conciliatory gesture toward the emperor's god. But he would fear no little man in a tent. Not after what he'd lived through.

"How long do you think I can keep the *foederati* loyal, Emperor," Alaric said quietly, "if they are not paid in full?"

Theodosius's eyes snapped up. "Is that a threat?"

"When I make a threat, you will know it."

For a moment everything stilled. In the emperor's face was the usual calm disdain. Something made Alaric glance at his upraised hand. It trembled.

The emperor feared him.

Suddenly Alaric understood. Theodosius had known he would walk into a slaughter. And Stilicho had given the order. To thin out his numbers against future rebellion.

They *both* thought he'd be next to turn.

Deliberately, Theodosius put down his stylus. "You'll do well to remember whose camp you are in," he said evenly, "and whose guards are just outside."

"And you will do well to remember exactly who the *foederati* are loyal to." Alaric bared his teeth in an expression that was nothing like a smile. "Pay my men what you owe them, Emperor. Otherwise you had better pray to your god for another wind."

Stilicho thought he would turn. It would be a shame to disappoint the great man.

Chapter One

Imperial Palace, Ravenna
Fifteen Years Later

Julia Augusta, daughter of the late Theodosius the Great, cracked an eye at the blazing, pernicious dawn shining through the window and immediately shut it again.

There had been opium in the wine last night. Julia knew, both from the peachy glow that had transformed her triclinium into a gleaming wonderland and the viciously pounding headache that was now pulverizing her skull. She had known what the Blue Lotus would do to her in the morning and she hadn't cared. A grave miscalculation.

She was lying on her bed, her head pillowed on the soft, breathing stomach of her best friend Verina, the niece of Rome's most illustrious general. Her limbs splayed across the torso of a Senator's son. Several others slept tangled in the huge bed, and on the cushion-strewn couches, and on the floor.

"Verina?" she murmured.

"Mmmfff," came the reply.

Julia sat up. The sun streaming through the courtyard stabbed at her eyes; even the water trickling in the *impluvium* fountain aggravated her pounding head. Her elegant bedroom was in extravagant disarray: wine spilled on white marble, couches overturned, and cushions scattered in the wreckage of last night's bacchanal. All around lay the sleeping bodies of the young and decadent of Ravenna: sons and daughters of Senators and statesmen, philosophical luminaries and handsome stage actors, most in a state of undress that would appall their parents. A man in a satyr costume sprawled on a saffron couch, drooling into a silken cushion. The miasma of stale wine in the air was thick enough to intoxicate all over again.

Julia pushed a hank of sweaty red hair out of her face and pulled a swath of near-transparent silk up over her breasts. It barely concealed her gilded nipples. The crown she had worn last night as Queen of the Maenads, Mistress of Revelries, was somehow still on her head and decidedly askew. Beside her, Verina curled up around another cushion, pulling the same silk over her own shoulders. It appeared to be a curtain yanked down from one of the windows. Images of last night came intruding on her thoughts—the music, the mad dancing, the opium in the wine. Julia shut her eyes. She needed a bath. A bath, then a drink, in that order.

A shrill voice sliced through her skull. "Julia Theodosia Augusta Filia."

Julia winced. It was Olympius, her late father's favored minister, standing in the doorway. He wore his usual joyless cassock, his expression drawn into the sour frown of a man constantly smelling his own foul scent.

"Dismiss your friends, Augusta." His gaze flicked over the piles of half-naked, slumbering bodies with bone-deep disgust. "You and I must talk."

Julia sighed heavily. She had known this was coming.

"You heard the man," she said grandly to the still-slumbering group. Slowly her friends hauled themselves up and stumbled around for their clothes. Verina righted herself reluctantly, with a look of supreme annoyance at Olympius.

"I'll find you later," Verina whispered. "After you've had his blood cleaned off the floor."

Julia smirked. At a signal from her, an army of soft-footed servants entered and began discreetly putting the room to rights. Julia maintained an air of casual unconcern, watching the blotchy red spread from the man's face to his neck. By the time the group had thinned out, she was fairly certain Olympius would burst a vessel.

"I hardly expected to find you so improperly dressed this late in the day."

Julia stood with as much dignity as she could muster, wrapping a robe around herself as if it were an empress's gown. She was very aware of what he saw—her red hair trailing down her back, the smeared black kohl ringing her eyes. The gilded nipples under the silk. But the way his face flamed, she rather thought *he* was at the disadvantage.

Since the age of fifteen, she'd been aware of the effect she had on men; she was not above using it to make an uptight zealot uncomfortable. And she would walk over hot coals before she would let Olympius think he had any power to discomfit *her*. Julia had been playing this game for a long time, and the first rule was to never let him see her rattled.

Despite the vicious pounding in her head, she maintained an air of casual ease as she sauntered over to one of the couches. "On the contrary. Receiving guests in this manner is all the fashion now." *Of course, one wouldn't expect* you *to know that* went unsaid. She gave him a cutting smile; with Olympius, she kept everything transparent and sharp as glass. "Please." She gestured to the lumpiest sofa, the one the satyr had been drooling on. "Sit."

Olympius settled onto the saffron-yellow sofa. He'd gotten thin since her father's death, his already-lean features edging toward gaunt. His eyes had always bulged; now they seemed to fairly pop out of his face.

Her chamber slave, Agathe, arrived with a pitcher of the low-quality wine from the Vatican Hill that had been foisted upon her last week. It flowed red into Olympius's cup.

"You were missed last night at the mass for your father."

"I spent forty nights at vigil." Forty nights bending knee to stone in the dusty basilica, and she'd die if they made her do it for one more miserable hour. "I cannot imagine what else you want from me."

"It is not what *I* want from you, Augusta. It is what is best for the realm." His frown deepened. "When your brother ordered you to keep to your rooms when not in the basilica, he meant for you to be *at prayer* with your women. Not involved in— clandestine orgies with Ravenna's most degenerate. By now everyone will know that last night, instead of attending the mass for your father, you hosted a party at which there was opium, prostitutes, men dressed as satyrs, and the lowest kind of debauchery."

Julia let out an elaborate sigh. How could the headache throb so hard behind only *one* eye? "There was only one satyr, if you must know." His gaze, she noticed, had drifted distinctly south of her neck. She raised a cool brow. "Does it keep you up at night, Olympius, contemplating my *debauchery*?"

His face darkened to purple. "Since your father's death, you have embarked in a headlong descent into depravity," he said stiffly. "Spending time with people below your station, reading and discussing the works of the philosophers *with men*. You take opium, become inebriated, and have had at least one very public affair." He drew a swath of parchment out of his robes and rattled it in his hand. "Your brother has entrusted me to give you this—"

Fear and fury shot through her. *Honorius*. "Give me that." Julia snatched the letter and unrolled it with undue haste. Two words stood out like they'd been excised in gold leaf. *Treason* and *exile*.

"Read it," Olympius said. "Aloud."

Julia drew a breath. "'It is hereby decreed that any exhibition of debauchery, consumption of wine, fraternization with those below her social class, reading of unseemly tracts of literature, or the ingestion of opium on the part of the emperor's sister shall be considered an act of treason against the Augustus himself.'" The paper crinkled where she gripped it. "'Punishable by exile to—to Pandateria.'"

Her eyes darted to the bottom of the page. She knew she would see it there, but she still felt its presence like a physical blow. Her brother's seal.

By the time he reached Ravenna, Alaric of the Goths was goddamn sick of the swamp.

You didn't see Ravenna from far off, like Rome. You trudged through the swamp, soaking in your own sweat, pushing horse carts out of muddy tracks, suffering the heat and the flies, until suddenly there it was. Thick walls coated in grubby plaster, the underlying brick exposed in long cracks. A rotten tooth in a rotten mouth.

His big black horse, Hannibal, tossed his head and dislodged a fly the size of a fat raisin. Alaric twisted in his saddle to look down the line. Fifty hand-picked warriors at his back, and beyond them, armor flashing in the trees and generally failing at stealth, lurked half a cohort of Roman soldiers. They'd been keeping a close eye since the *campagna* and hadn't offered a shred of help with the carts.

Even so, he was in uncommonly good spirits.

"What the hell are you smiling about? You've led us down into the Empire's stinking arsehole." His second-in-command,

Ataulf, raised a forearm to wipe sweat off his brow. "That invitation is a trap. How many times do I have to say it?"

"You don't have to say it." Ataulf had been singing this song all the way from the mountains. "I know."

Fifteen years it had been since Stilicho had sent Alaric down into that canyon to die. Alaric had persuaded the *foederati* to turn on the Romans, and then had come war and savagery, two failed attempts to carve a homeland out of the Empire's stinking carcass. After the second time—the doomed siege at Milan—his people had fallen upon Greece and Dacia, staying alive through pillage. Three years, Alaric had held them together with plunder and oaths and his own sweat and blood. Now the land was picked clean and his chieftains were starting to rebel; Alaric had begun sleeping in his chain mail to ward off assassins.

And in the midst of all this had come the missive from Stilicho. Characteristically terse. *Theodosius is dead. Come soon. The new emperor may be agreeable to giving you a homeland.* He still had that missive tucked under his chain mail, burning against his skin like a fallen star.

"I wish you luck, then, negotiating with your own assassins." Ataulf's tone was sardonic. The fly lifted itself lazily and landed on his neck; he cursed and slapped at it. A trickle of blood smudged his skin. "What do you have to negotiate with, if not our men as soldiers? I am pained to remind you that if you return to Noricum with nothing to show for it, the chieftains are likely to hang you on your own walls."

It was an old argument. One they'd been having since they left Noricum. "The chieftains will let me in readily enough if I bring them a homeland," Alaric said. "But not if it comes with an agreement to send our men as grist for the Roman war machine. I will not pay one *nummus* for land already owed. Not in alliance and not in service."

He did not mean to negotiate. He meant to bleed the Romans dry.

"If you do not give the Romans what they want, it's likely you'll die here. Why keep you alive if you cannot be negotiated with?" Ataulf cursed beneath his breath. "We don't have to choose between two paths to death, Alaric. There are still lands ripe for the conquering in Hispania—"

Alaric shook his head grimly. It was too late to run off to Hispania. It had been too late since the killing fields of Frigidus, when he had sworn to follow this road even if it led to death. That oath hung ominously close now, death before him and death behind, dogging his steps all the way from the mountains. The only way out was to accept the invitation of a man who had betrayed him. A man who'd once been as a father.

"I will not go to Hispania. Ataulf, if I'm not there to hold the Goths together, they'll splinter—and be picked off by the Huns and enslaved by the Romans." Alaric gathered his reins and tried to soothe Hannibal's anxious attempts to break into a trot. Even the horses' nerves were raw. "If I fail to get us a homeland, there won't *be* a Goths by winter."

They were almost within bowshot of the walls. Alaric gave Hannibal his head; the horse tossed his skull and broke into a bone-jarring canter, outpacing the rest of his men. As he approached, Alaric could feel the guards' hostility. He knew what they saw: fifty ragged Goths on horseback, armed and tattooed, visibly out of sorts from the swamp. *He* wouldn't want to let them in either.

A self-important centurion shouted down from the battlement. "State your purpose."

Alaric leaned his forearms on the high pommel of his saddle and answered in Latin more polished than the other man's. "You know our purpose. Your men have been keeping an eye on us all the way from the *campagna*." He gave a sunny smile, just this side of murderous. "We come under a flag of peace."

"I see no flag. Peaceful or otherwise."

"Surely the great Empire holds no fear of our sorry band, Centurion!" Alaric amused himself by calculating the force and trajectory he'd need to put one of his throwing spears in the man's throat from here. "We come at the general Stilicho's invitation."

The centurion frowned even deeper, then his head with its bristling crest disappeared from the wall. After a short time, a small porthole in the gate opened and the centurion's face appeared. "Prove you are Alaric of the Balthi."

Impatience pricked his skin. Alaric hadn't ridden hundreds of miles, the last few through a miserable swamp, only to be halted by a little man behind a door.

A bloodthirsty smile curled his lips. "Open the gate before I tear it down."

"Forgive my rude companion. He is not famous for his manners." Ataulf halted by Alaric's side, hands spread, reins dangling between his fingers. "Who else would we be? Perhaps you will explain to the general Stilicho why you left his guests waiting in the hot sun while you asked questions you already knew the answer to."

The window snapped shut. There was a clipped voice beyond the wall, one Alaric recognized. A considerable amount of shouting commenced.

"And you consider yourself the diplomatic one," Alaric said drily.

"*You* threatened to tear the door down." Ataulf leaned in, speaking low in the tongue of the pine-tree island, their long-dead homeland. "This *is* a trap. I can think of half a dozen examples of rebel leaders slaughtered at feasts in their own honor, senses dulled by drink and flattery," he muttered. "Let me do the talking at dinner."

Alaric spoke low, watching the door. "You're not coming to the banquet. We may need to go quickly. I'm leaving it to you to have the horses ready and the way clear."

"Then who *is* coming?" Ataulf glanced behind them disapprovingly. "You cannot possibly trust your life to these miscreants."

Alaric followed his gaze, eyes falling on tall blond Thorismund, last prince of the Batavi. Thorismund was an army all by himself, none better to help him cut his way out of a hostile city. Near him rode the Hunnic mercenary, Riga, eyeing the walls as if planning to scale them with a brace of arrows at his back and a blade clenched between his teeth. Riga knew all the smugglers from here to Sicily. If he needed a secret way through the swamp to evade Roman capture, Riga could find it.

Behind them, the twins slouched on their Hunnic warponies, blond hair spiked up with animal fat, wolf-teeth necklaces gleaming around their necks. Their father, Gaufrid, had been first among his chieftains, first among those who followed him at Frigidus; he had died at Pollentia with an arrow in his gut. Alaric had made him a deathbed promise to take care of the boys, made an oath to right the Empire's wrongs if it killed him. They were fifteen now, and more seasoned than warriors a decade older. Alaric sighed. Back in Noricum, he had decided to bring Gaufrid's sons along, rather than leave them to face an insurrection on their own. But now he was questioning his judgment.

No. He would lead Gaufrid's boys this far, but not down into the Frigidus canyon.

Before him, the gates swung ponderously open. Stilicho stood waiting. A wind kicked up at Alaric's feet.

The first time he'd faced Stilicho as an enemy, it had been fourteen years ago on the plains of Larissa, each side dug in deep and daring the other to blink. They had met next on the frozen coast of Corinth; he had fled across black ice to the jagged mountains, with Stilicho's army in swift pursuit. Then had come Verona, hemmed in on every side, his men starving and deserting all around him. Stilicho had blocked the road north and Alaric had fortified a hill over the city and bargained for his life and the lives of his men. Made it out with his army in shreds.

Now all that separated them was a few dozen muddy strides. Time and hardship had carved long runnels down Stilicho's cheeks, and there was more iron in his close-cropped hair than brown. His eyes were the same, though. Still that flat stare, as from across a frozen wasteland. Daring you to blink.

"Alaric." The old general cast a disapproving eye on the ragged group he'd brought along. "I sent you a personal invitation. It appears you responded with an invasion force."

"Just fifty of my closest friends and family."

"Bring ten and follow me."

Alaric urged his horse forward, straight into Stilicho's trap.

Pandateria. Of all godforsaken places.

Julia stalked through marbled hallways, the hated missive clutched in her fist. Pandateria was a barren island where the Imperial family sent troublesome women. Those who refused to be quiet, who would not stop taking lovers, who transgressed some stupid rule. A quiet assassination wasn't long in coming after. Strangling, for the lucky ones. For the unlucky, they simply stopped sending food.

Olympius *must* have put Honorius up to this.

But when she arrived at the door to her father's chambers— her *brother's* now—she found it firmly shut.

"I am sorry, Princess," his guard said. "The emperor is praying for your father's soul."

"Rubbish. My brother mourned that overbred bird of his that died last week more than he did our father." Julia knew the guard would not lay a hand on her. She was already past him, pushing at the door. *If Honorius even* breathes *the word* treason *at me*—

Julia stopped on the threshold. Gone were the maps of far-flung territories, the storied old desk that loomed like a battlement. Honorius had remade it into something like a throne room. Extravagant murals. Plush rugs from Persia. Lapis lazuli everywhere. If this had been *her* study, she'd have filled every niche with books. But it wasn't her study. It would never be her study.

By all the gods, she needed a drink.

Honorius lounged in a silver chair, swathed in an Imperial toga. Purple did not favor him; the color only made his teenager's livid spots look angrier. A throng of his boyhood friends vied for his attention while his beloved cockerels gabbled at his feet, picking seeds out of the carpet. His eyes were fixed toward the far end of the room, and it was only when she strode forward that Julia saw what he was looking at.

A naked man hung by his arms. It was her father's steward, Atticus. An older man, dignified; he'd helped her rescue a kitten from a storm drain once. Julia halted in horror as Honorius's huge Germanic bodyguard, Praxis, brought a knot-ended whip down on the man's back with a wet *thwack*.

The man screamed, and Honorius's boy companions giggled as if this was a bawdy play.

She must be careful. If it seemed she cared too much, Honorius would whip the man harder just to antagonize her.

"Honorius." Another of those dreadful *thwacks* and her stomach attempted to claw up her throat. *"Honorius."*

Her brother startled. "What are *you* doing here?"

"What on earth did he do?" Her tone carefully calibrated. Not *too* much concern.

"He overfed my cockerels again. Roma has a terrible stomachache."

"How on earth can you tell that a bird has indigestion? Really. This is in poor taste." Julia frowned. "You there, cut him down."

The man with the whip looked at her brother.

"Forgive me. I forgot about your delicate sensibilities." Her brother made an imperious gesture. "That's enough, Praxis.

Clean up this mess." The man banged a fist on his chest and began to fiddle with the steward's manacles. "What do you want, Julia? I did not summon you."

Her head gave a vicious throb and Julia gritted her teeth. After Olympius left, she'd napped for hours to try to calm the headache in preparation for confronting Honorius. Clearly it had not worked. "You sent your minister to interrupt my prayers this morning instead."

"You are the only person I know who refers to the eighth hour of the day as morning."

"And you are the only person *I* know who would have someone whipped half to death because of a chicken." Julia stalked to Honorius's chair and slapped the crumpled parchment on the desk. "Do you recognize this?"

"Of course I do. I wrote it."

One of his friends snickered. "*Told* you she wouldn't be happy."

Julia flicked a glance at the assembled throng. "Was it your idea, or did the Senate here put you up to it?"

"Calm down, Julia. You're being hysterical." Honorius's friends were laughing openly now. "Out," he snapped. They obeyed, thank the gods. "You were always Father's favorite," Honorius said when they were gone. "He used to let you run wild. I cannot."

Julia bit back a bitter laugh. "You think *I* was his favorite?" How could he remember their history so wrong?

"You were the one he used to show off at parties. Remember?"

"Until Mother died and I got sent to Capri. *You* got to stay." Julia crossed her arms over her chest. "I will not be sent off to an island again, Honorius."

"Then, you will behave." Honorius said it with exaggerated patience, as if he were the elder and she the wayward younger sibling. "I've inherited chaos, Julia. The provinces on fire, the treasury drained, and usurpers circling my throne like sharks contemplating a meal. What will they think of my strength if I cannot even control the women in my own household?" He frowned. "Alaric of the Goths is in Ravenna right now, taking my measure like a city wall he means to crack."

That name froze the breath in her lungs. *Alaric of the Goths.* It carried images of fire and death, bodies on stakes outside crumbled walls. It was practically family lore; the man had turned at some nameless battle fifteen years ago, over some sublimely petty insult, and hadn't stopped terrorizing Rome since. "Honorius, what madness has seized you that you'd invite *that* villain into our city?"

"Are you not listening? The provinces are on *fire*. Stilicho thinks he can bring Alaric into the *foederati* again, if we make the right offer. But we must not send a message of weakness. Otherwise he may just decide to try his luck at another invasion." Honorius gave a heavy sigh, and suddenly he could have been her father's beardless ghost. "Alaric would have had us all roasting in a bonfire three years ago if we hadn't moved the capital to Ravenna. But that sent a message of weakness, and now you would have me send another."

"Would the message of weakness *I'm* sending be louder than the one *you're* sending, by running to Rome's greatest enemy for help in the first place?" Julia gave a derisive snort. "Or perhaps threatening the women in your house with exile to keep us in line?"

"Julia, I don't *expect* I shall have to exile you. I *expect* you to behave as a proper Roman woman. Chaste, obedient, and not any trouble."

Chaste. Obedient. Not any trouble. Her father's voice, thundering down a tunnel of years. "Exile me then. Do it."

"Sit down, Julia." A flinty look came to Honorius's eyes. "Praxis, make her sit."

Meaty hands landed on her shoulders and the burly man

pushed her down onto a low stool. Julia gasped, shocked by the transgression. No one *ever* laid hands on her without permission.

"You turned twenty-two in April, Julia. That's too old to be unmarried."

Too old! "Seventeen is too young to be emperor," she shot back. "I hear you still wet your bed during thunderstorms."

Honorius flushed. "Olympius is in need of a wife. I think it should be you."

She was on her feet again in an instant. "*No*, Honorius. Spend me on a rich foreign ruler whose loyalty you need. Not a vain little cockroach like—"

"You calling someone else vain. Now, *that* is funny." His laughter had no humor in it. "Praxis. Make her sit."

Praxis slammed her back down on the chair. Hard enough to hurt this time.

"I never understood why you two couldn't get along," her brother continued mildly. "This marriage solves two pressing needs for me. I replenish the Empire's diminished treasury with Olympius's wealth, and I solve—*this* problem." He waved a hand to indicate her entire self. "If you don't like it, Julia, go and get your own army. Otherwise, you will marry Olympius. You will do it because you value the lives of your friends—that corrupting influence Verina, for example. But that is not the primary reason. Is it?"

Praxis's hands tightened on her shoulders. A sick fear twisted in her gut. "No, Honorius."

"What is the reason, Julia?"

She knew the answer. Her father had drilled it into her years ago, when he'd sent her away at fourteen. "Because it is my duty, Augustus. To you, and to the Empire."

Honorius *would* send her to an island to die. He would do even worse without blinking.

CHAPTER TWO

Julia's mother had taught her about the Divine Cleopatra. Her father had taught her *latrones*.

She rested her chin on her hands and stared at the *latrones* board that stood in her bedchamber. It had been her father's, made of Luna marble and porphyry. Game of brigands. Game of soldiers. Before she knew it, she was moving the stones through the patterns, lightning fast. Her hands remembered.

She shut her eyes tight. The thought of her father in the basilica nearly undid her. It led to thoughts of her mother, who had died in childbirth seven years ago; the child had died too, strangled by its own cord. Ripped from the gory mess between the empress's thighs.

She had been fourteen. Not long after, her father had told her she must give up childish things. She must stop playing *latrones* in particular, because Honorius had no mind for the game. How would his generals respect an emperor who could be beaten in games of strategy by his own sister? So he had sent her to Capri to prepare for her purpose in life—to marry for the good of the

Empire, and produce children. Later she'd discovered it had been at Olympius's urging.

The betrothals had come. But they had never lasted. At fifteen, Julia was engaged to a rising general. At sixteen, to a foreign king. Her prospective husbands were killed on the battlefield, or thrown from horses, or choked on chicken bones. Or the alliances simply shifted.

In his neglect, her father had given her freedom to choose her tutors, and so she had summoned the best Greek and Alexandrian scholars, just as Cleopatra had. She'd studied diplomacy and city planning and literature, philosophy, agriculture, and engineering. If she could make her father remember she had a mind that he'd once been proud of, perhaps he would restore her place in the family.

For years, Julia had thrown herself into ruling the tiny fiefdom of her villa. She had repaired the irrigation; changed the cycle of planting to get better use of the earth. She'd even overseen the construction of a small aqueduct across the property, to supply the nearby village.

The aqueduct had been her pride. When she'd shown it to her father, he had patted her head gently. "You are growing into a beauty. That pleases me more than any aqueduct." She had been seventeen.

It turned out he hadn't been *proud* of her skill at *latrones*, exactly. He had found it amusing. Like a dog doing tricks.

So she'd sent her tutors away and found refuge in hedonistic pleasure. She'd surrounded herself with new friends, those dedicated to staying up all night and debating until dawn. She had learned how much liquor she could hold and still beat a conceited son of a Senator in a debate. She'd learned the pleasures of pharmaceuticals from Egypt. What life was there but the life of today, when tomorrow she might be married off to some inconsequential husband and then die in childbirth, as her mother had?

It had been the parties that made life bearable. And now Honorius would sell her to a man who would rob her even of this. Imprison her in some joyless villa until she was pregnant, and then dead. Julia let the pieces fall. Where was Agathe with the wine?

"Playing *latrones*, I see. Things seem to have taken a dire turn." Verina slid into the seat opposite her, black hair in a tower of curls, niece of the general Stilicho and her oldest friend.

"Verina, what are you doing here?"

"I told you I'd find you later. Don't you remember?" Verina cast a sanguine glance over her tired eyes, her hair coming loose from its rather modest braided coiffure. "You look terrible, darling."

"I feel terrible." Tears prickled behind her eyes. "He could have married me to anyone else. *Anyone.* Some small-minded foreign prince or a portly general who smells of sour wine. Instead he chooses to marry me to—to—"

"Are you betrothed already?" Verina's eyes widened. "You must tell me everything."

Somehow Julia managed to recount the story of her betrothal to Olympius without vomiting. But when she was finished, Verina only laughed. "Oh, Julia! I never thought I'd hear you speak as though you expected to love your husband."

Julia rolled her eyes. "Of course not. Everyone knows you don't fall in love with your spouse." Love made one easily ruined and easily led. *She* was not that stupid.

"Do you remember what you told me last year, when I wept on that couch about marrying Septimus? You said no husband would stop us from drinking too much and debating with philosophers and shocking the world."

Julia smiled through her tears. "Husbands for children, lovers for amusement—"

"And each other for everything else." They spoke the last part together, like an oath. "This isn't the end, Julia. Olympius has so many villas that you can always take up residence where he isn't. You'll barely see him once you give him an heir."

An heir. Suddenly she felt nauseous. "Verina, I can't."

Verina took both her hands. "Then you know what to do."

"Get my own army." Her brother's advice. Impossible.

"No, that is a horrible idea." Verina looked scandalized. "I mean *play their game.* Be soft and sweet and make him happy. In a few years—"

"Stop saying *years.*" Panic choked her throat. "I won't last a month."

"You *must.* If you think Honorius won't send you to Pandateria—"

"I know he will. And you should be on your guard too. Honorius thinks you're a bad influence." Julia drew a shaking breath. "I'm sorry I dragged you into this, Verina."

"I'm Stilicho's niece, in case you forgot." Verina waved a hand airily. "The emperor only rules at the pleasure of the army. And the army is loyal to Stilicho, which means your brother cannot touch us. No matter how they vex each other."

Julia tried to imagine the unflappable Stilicho *vexed.* He could have an attack of the bowels at his own triumph with no one the wiser. "What is your uncle like angry?"

"A little muscle twitches, just here." Verina tapped a spot below her left eye. "It's been doing that rather a lot since this morning."

"What happened this morning?"

"You don't *know?*" Verina's eyes widened. "Alaric of the Goths arrived. He's here *now.*"

"Oh. *That.*" Julia sighed. "Honorius told me. If you ask me, inviting that man into our city is rather a stupid idea."

"Except this time he's fighting *for* us, if my uncle can persuade him." A pleased smile curved Verina's lips. "Stilicho redeployed the guards to keep an eye on the Goths camped outside. Everyone is afraid of Alaric. It makes him doubly intriguing." Her smile turned wicked. "There'll be a banquet. Perhaps we could interest him in a party *after* the party."

"Some Gothic barbarian with his rough hands? *Never.*" The very thought had her reaching for her wineglass, despite having long since emptied it. "Besides, he's a traitor and a war criminal." She stopped, her glass half raised to her lips. An idea suddenly pounding in her head in time with the headache.

Get your own army.

"Julia?" Verina watched her carefully. "That look on your face worries me."

It would probably be healthier for her friend not to know what she was thinking.

"I'm afraid my headache is getting the better of me," she murmured. "Let us meet again tomorrow, Verina."

Chapter Three

Cornelius had been the darling of the Imperial court when Julia first lured him into her arms, in the last throes of her father's illness but before he'd died, when she'd been desperate to feel anything besides grief and hadn't cared how. Underneath his polished manners, Cornelius was sweet and philosophical and a little shy.

And his family had their own legion.

His mother, Lucretia, had come to her in the basilica not a week ago, as Julia was ostentatiously following her brother's orders to pray for her father's soul. She approached as Julia knelt before his body, laid out on its plinth.

It had taken him so long to die. So long, after the bloody sieges of Milan and Verona, after watching the armies of Alaric of the Goths pillaging the countryside with no ability to stop it. Julia had been in Rome during the sieges, but she had seen what they did to her father.

Now he was dead. It was hard to imagine a world where that could be true. Julia knelt and pressed her forehead to the cool stone of her father's plinth, shutting her eyes to the smell of the perfumes someone had doused his robes with to rout the smell of death. *Why am I so angry with him?* For leaving her—no. For leaving her before she had a chance to prove herself.

"Princess Julia. Augusta. My dear. Have you heard what I said?"

Lucretia spoke in the appropriately hushed tones of a penitent, kneeling beside her at her father's corpse. There was a note of strained impatience in her voice.

"I heard you perfectly, Lucretia." It was far too early in the day for this conversation.

"Forgive my insistence, Princess. But times of transition are the most dangerous. We must forge alliances for our own safety."

"I had hoped to drink my way through the transition, actually." It was her age-old tactic for avoiding unpleasantness—simply drink until things were pleasant. "Tell me again why I should marry Cornelius."

"How bad could it be, my darling? He still pines for you, you know."

That was hardly a reason to marry. "Everyone knows you don't fall in love with your spouse, Lucretia. It's *embarrassing*." Her own mother had warned her that her husband would most likely smell like a goat shed, and not to expect to love him.

Lucretia smiled. Older than Julia by decades, her skin was still flawless. Whispered rumors claimed she kept it that way by sacrificing virgins at the moon-tide and bathing in their blood, and Julia was half-certain those rumors were true.

"You are correct, of course. We cannot afford to be sentimental. Now least of all." Her voice took on a hard-edged practicality. "Our family holds a manor near Noricum and a small marble mine, out of Stilicho's reach. It is lawless there, of course, but we have a legion to defend it. We could provide you with safety and shelter, should the worst happen."

The worst. She could surmise what Lucretia meant. Her father had left behind plenty of discontents, and if one overthrew her brother, Julia wouldn't give a copper *aes* for her own life. It would help to be tied to a powerful family with holdings outside the Empire.

She had extricated herself from that conversation without making promises. But now, if Cornelius was amenable, she would make her promises directly to him.

Now, in the sanctity of her rooms, Julia prepared her battle armor. She called for a bath of scented rose petals, had her nails trimmed and filed, summoned a cream of crushed pearls for her skin. Julia bade her women carefully arrange the thick crimson fall of her hair. She chose a white silken nightdress edged with pearls; knowing how her body would be silhouetted through the diaphanous fabric. Cornelius would fall to his knees.

She sent away all of her women. All but her head chamber slave, Agathe, who she could trust implicitly. Spies were everywhere, but she would maintain an aura of silence over what passed in her bedroom this night. "Send him in, Agathe."

"Apologies, *domina*. He is not here."

"Not here?" She had sent her message hours ago. "He's not here *at all*?"

"No, *domina*." A pause. "Perhaps I should send another message—"

"No." How embarrassing that would be. "Just fetch some wine."

Three glasses later, Julia heard a noise at her door.

Quickly she straightened from her messy slump on the couch just as Cornelius walked into the room, golden-haired and lightly muscled beneath his snowy toga. He stopped, his eyes on her.

Speechless. That boded well.

Julia straightened, wineglass held thoughtlessly to her lips. "Cornelius! Whatever are you doing here at such a late hour?"

"You sent for me. Apologies for my lateness."

"Ah. So I did. I quite forgot." She waved a hand airily. "I suppose you might as well stay."

"Forgive me. You are so beautiful I'm having trouble forming words." His smile fell. "Is it true? You're pledged to Olympius?"

"Until I can figure a way out."

He hastened to her side, knelt by her couch. "What took you so long? You haven't sent for me in ages. Why?"

Because Father died, went the answer. *Because Father died and there was no room for anyone else.* She would never apologize, of course. He wouldn't be here if he did not forgive her.

"You're too thin." He drew her into his arms as if she might break. "At your father's funeral you looked so *thin*. I wanted to—"

There was too much emotion in his tone. It made her slightly panicked. Julia slid a hand into the close-cropped curls at his neck. "Cornelius, stop talking."

She pulled him to the couch and kissed him.

Cornelius groaned in the back of his throat. His arms tightened around her, and Julia felt the old, familiar urge to pull back. To halt things before they went too far.

But why should she? What was she saving herself for? She had always known that her virtue belonged to whoever her father chose. But now her father was dead and her brother had given her far too cheaply to the man she despised most.

Wouldn't it enrage them if she gave herself to a man of her own choosing? It was like stealing herself back.

Cornelius's toga was off now. His torso gleamed, pale and hairless against the white linen of his undertunic. Julia let her breasts brush his bare chest; let him curl his hands into her hair. She could feel his arousal pushing at her stomach and she knew she ought to feel something. *He* certainly felt something.

"Marry me, Cornelius."

He blinked at her, astonished. "What?"

"I know it sounds rather mad. But I've thought of nothing else since my brother made his wishes known." Julia sat up, shoulders bared to the moonlight. "Don't you want to?"

She drew a finger idly down his chest and he tilted his head back. "God—keep doing that." Julia let her mouth follow her fingers down his slender torso. Down to where his arousal tented the cloth that covered his hips. "Julia. *Yes*—"

Abruptly she batted his hands away and rose, wrapping a silk robe around herself.

Cornelius sat up, frowning. "Where are you going?"

"Pouring wine, silly. Aren't you thirsty?" She went to the table and poured for them both. "You'd be second in line for the throne if you married me. My brother has no heir. And the public likes you better than him."

He propped himself up, his toga draping down to his waist, arousal still very much in evidence. "Is this some joke?"

"Not at all." Julia handed him his wine, a cool smile curving her lips. "I hear how the people cheer when you go out. And your family has its own claim to the throne. My brother is *not* popular, not like that. His advisors see you as a threat." She took a sip of wine. Not *too* watered, thank the gods. "Do you not know your history? Remember what happened to Germanicus. You'll be their first target once they consolidate power. Unless you act before they do."

"Germanicus." He said it slowly; as if he gave her words less credence than an old folktale. "And marrying you will neutralize this threat."

"Marrying *me* will be taking your fate in your own hands. My brother is weak, Cornelius. Stilicho has barely the troops to hold Ravenna; he is overextended at the borders. He is turning to that villain Alaric of the *Goths*, of all people, to help defend the Empire." Another sip of the wine. Courage seeped into her limbs. "How would you like to be emperor?"

Cornelius lay back on the couch, arms crossed behind his

head, looking every inch the darling of the Imperial court. "I am going to pretend that was an outrageous joke," he said drily, his eyes traveling over her silken-clad form. "Come back."

Julia stayed where she was. "With Alaric here, everyone will be distracted. We'll meet outside the city, at that temple to Dionysus outside the eastern gate." It was fitting. God of wine and revelry; god of revolutions. "We marry, and then flee to your parents' estate where it's safe."

"My God, you really are serious. You must be *trying* to get me killed." Cornelius sat up straighter. "You realize the seas are terrible this late in spring, do you not? And what about my parents? If your brother doesn't murder me, they will."

"Your mother *begged* me to consider you as a husband. She wants this."

"Then I should ask her—"

"It is far better to ask forgiveness than permission, Cornelius." Julia strolled to the garden, aware of the moonlight's fall upon her shoulders. The way it lit her hair. "Are you content to be under my brother's thumb all your life? *I'm* not. Pannonia might as well be lawless Germania for all the good Stilicho's legions can do there. Where is your spine?"

Silence. She took a long sip of the wine. *Four—three—two—*

Footsteps at her back, and then Cornelius drew her into his arms from behind. "I would marry you in an instant, you know. But your brother would have me garroted."

"Not if you have the courage to take what is yours." Julia turned to face him, and Cornelius kissed her. It was easy to feign an answering passion. She could not understand how he could be brought to his knees by the same embrace that left her cold. *I am above it*, she told herself.

"We do not have much time. I could be married to Olympius by month's end. And if we don't flee, my brother will simply dissolve our marriage. We must be beyond his reach."

Cornelius stared down at her; his eyes glowing. "Do you love me, Julia?"

The words brought her headache roaring back to life. It was what she *had* to say; she knew that. The words that would make Cornelius bend.

It wasn't quite a lie, was it? She was fond of Cornelius. He would be an ideal husband; he would not impose on her. Fondness was a kind of love, was it not?

She drew a breath and tried to *mean* it. "Cornelius," she said quietly, gazing into his eyes. "I have not stopped loving you since the day we met."

Cornelius's arms tightened until she could not breathe. "May God protect us both."

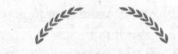

CHAPTER FOUR

Despite granting Alaric entry into the Imperial Palace, it turned out the emperor was content to make them wait.

After two days cooling their heels in a forgotten corner of the palace, his men were bored enough to try picking fights with the guards. Alaric had a feeling they'd all end up in some pit beneath the palace if this went on much longer.

And then, late at night, another message from Stilicho. Delivered in secret, as was their habit when they were at war.

Alaric waited until just a few hours before dawn. The last watch. The worst time to stay alert and the best to stage an ambush. Only then did he escape his rooms and slip into the sleeping city.

Ravenna was a maze of flimsy bridges spanning foul-smelling canals. By the palace, there were manors and churches, white marble slicked with algae. But not in this end of town, where wooden houses stood on pilings and scraps of cloth hung over the doors. Alaric could feel eyes on him from alleyways and darkened doorways; cutpurses sizing him up and deciding he wasn't worth the trouble. Wise choice.

The journey offered a perfect opportunity to assess the city's defenses. Far from the main gate, the walls were crumbling and undermanned. It wouldn't be hunger that brought Ravenna to its knees in a siege; it would be thirst. People would drink from the fetid canals, and disease would spread. All he had to do was cut off access to the beaches and block the ships that brought fresh water from the countryside. Easier said than done.

The eastern gateway was barely more than a door in a crumbling wall. It stood unguarded. No wonder Stilicho wanted to meet here; it was the gate nobody watched.

Outside the city, the swamp closed oppressively around him. Ahead a dirt path led under a thick canopy of trees, and he followed it until he couldn't see the walls. If Stilicho chose to ambush him, it would be easy enough now. But then, if Stilicho wanted him dead, he would be dead already. This skullduggery was unlike him.

A small temple loomed by the path, a Christian cross nailed to the door above a scratched-out carving of a thyrsus, symbol of old Dionysus. A shape emerged from the dark.

"You look disreputable enough to frighten the cutpurses off." Stilicho used the Vandal language. Formal and ponderous, not well understood in the Roman army, except by the frontier cavalry. "Are you certain you weren't followed?"

"Certain enough." Alaric answered in the same language. "Perhaps you'll explain the subterfuge."

"I have enemies in the palace. Some of whom would paint this conversation in a light that's less than flattering."

Alaric crossed his arms over his chest. "You going to follow the usual script? The one where you ask me to come back into the fold?"

"And then you can tell me to go hang. Again." Stilicho's mouth thinned. "No, Alaric. I simply want to prepare you for tomorrow. The new emperor is ready to grant you a strip of land alongside the Danube. Good, arable land. This will be the best chance you'll ever get."

"And what will he ask in return?"

"The Empire is crumbling at the borders. I need your help to hold it together."

Anger rose up in his chest. "I will not allow the Tervingii to be used as shields against the Empire's enemies," he growled. "My people stay *mine*."

"Is it war you want, then? Can you truly not envision a better life? I offer you peace, Alaric."

"No. You offer us endless war along Rome's borders." In a breath, he was back at Frigidus, down in that bloody cut of a valley. "That land is coin already owed. I will not ask my people to pay for it with their lives."

"My spies tell me that last winter was brutal for you. You would not be here if you weren't desperate." Stilicho's gaze turned shrewd. "How much longer can you hold the chieftains' loyalty if you return empty-handed? One month? Three?"

"Interesting line of argument for a man who insisted we meet in disguise so as not to alert his enemies." Alaric shrugged lazily. "What surety do I have that you can keep any promises you've made me? We both know the boy emperor favors your rival."

"I have no rivals."

"The son of Theodosius pledged his sister to Olympius yesterday morning. Did you offer for her too?"

Surprise flickered across Stilicho's face, quick as lightning, and Alaric stifled a grin. It was rare that he surprised the old man.

Then Stilicho let out a sudden, joyless bark of a laugh. "I assure you, the hand of the princess Julia is more punishment than reward. Whoever marries that girl will be far too busy chasing after her to bother giving me trouble."

But a muscle twitched, just beneath his left eye, and Alaric would wager there was more to the story.

"Why have you bothered to meet me, Stilicho?" he asked.

"You make the same proposal you always have—land paid for in lives. Your emperor had better make a more compelling offer than *that*."

"There is more than one path to a homeland, Alaric. The only way out of this endless violence is trust."

Trust. The word filled him with rage. "My trust died at Frigidus."

"I know," Stilicho said gravely. "I sent you into that valley to save your life at Frigidus. Theodosius wanted you executed on some invented charge because he feared the *foederati's* loyalty to you. I persuaded him to send you into that valley instead, thinking he was sending you to your death. But I knew you'd fight your way out, and once you did, he would have no justification to refuse you a homeland. Of course, you rebelled before any of that could come to fruition." He paused, shoulders rising in a heavy breath. "I loved you like a father, you know."

Alaric tensed. *Fuck* Stilicho for pulling this string. Fatherly affection was just one of his weapons, and the fact that he meant it only made the blade sharper.

"You're not my father, Stilicho," he said, "and you can go hang."

He turned and was six strides down the path when Stilicho spoke at his back. "Alaric."

He didn't have to stop. Didn't *want* to stop. But the old man's voice had worked its way into his bones long ago; even now it was snapping his spine straight. Alaric turned back, furious with himself—and halted. Stilicho had moved into a fall of moonlight, and suddenly he saw the old man more clearly. When had Stilicho's shoulders begun to stoop? When had he begun to look so haggard? Alaric couldn't explain the wild grief and raw, furious rage that rose up in his heart.

"The boy favors your rival," he said shortly. "And your rival has painted a target on your back. If you don't see that, you're slipping."

A small, faint smile crossed Stilicho's lips. "I can handle Olympius."

"That kind of thinking will put you in the ground." Suddenly Alaric could see Stilicho's death clear as daybreak. "Come into *my* fold," he said, knowing Stilicho would refuse; not knowing anything else to do but offer. "The Vandals are your people as much as the Romans. There are many such in my army. Fight for *them*."

"You ask me to bring ruin to an Empire already ravaged." Stilicho shook his head. "No."

"It is not for you to die with a knife in your back in some dusty palace." He would not abide it. Stilicho was one of his own, his teacher and nemesis and the great granite cliff face he'd broken himself against for so long. "Come die on the battlefield, under the open sky where you belong."

"So now you wish to dictate the manner of my death. You should have been a Caesar." Stilicho smiled ruefully. "I will be on your side at the banquet, Alaric. Whether you believe it or no."

Alaric shook his head. At the end of everything, Stilicho was only ever on the Empire's side. "Watch your back until then, old man."

But Stilicho was gone, striding into the swirling mist.

"So, what exactly is the plan?" Bromios asked.

Julia glanced up at him from beneath her woolen hood. Bromios was her favorite freedman—the one who would help her pull off a caper, escape from her guards, or bring her drugs. Tonight he was less than his usual adventurous self—and she was disappointed he wasn't egging her on.

She was in a mood to be egged on. It was almost dawn, and the darkness didn't make this part of town any lovelier. It was a cesspit, crisscrossed with channels of sluggish water.

It was a lovely cesspit. The most stunning Julia had ever seen. Exhilaration lightened her steps. She was seizing freedom. Maybe power, if she played things right. Which, of course, she would.

"You should wear cowled cloaks more," she murmured. "You look like an outrageously handsome pirate."

"Julia, I *hate* to ruin your fun, but are you certain this is a good idea?" Bromios glanced uneasily at the alleyways. "Have your intended's parents approved this marriage? How do you know they won't simply pack you up and send you back on the next tide?"

"Don't be silly. His parents will erupt in joy once they realize I intend to sweep into this town with their legion and make their son emperor."

"What?" Bromios halted and pulled her into an alleyway. "This is treason," he hissed. "You had better explain yourself. Otherwise *I* might drag you back to the palace myself!"

"Don't be such a bore." But the freedman's glare did not let up. Julia sighed. "Lucretia tried to persuade me to marry him. And Cornelius is sweet and biddable and will do everything I say. If his parents don't have the fortitude for the more daring part of my plan, well—legions can be bribed."

She twitched her cloak aside to show him what she was wearing. All the jewelry she owned. Bromios cursed and rushed to close her cloak. "You *also* failed to mention I'd be dragging you through the roughest parts of Ravenna wearing the entire Roman treasury. Are you out of your *mind*?"

"Bromios, dear. Stop worrying. It will give you wrinkles." Julia glanced around the corner. "Is that the gate?"

"Yes." He followed her gaze. "I don't see him."

"He's probably hiding."

"Or he changed his mind." Bromios turned back, his face taking on a hard, angular expression. "Stay here." Then he was gone, and she was alone.

Julia drew back into the alley, her back against the damp wall. A rat scampered by in the dark. Her doubts multiplied. *What if Bromios was right?* What if Cornelius changed his mind? What if Honorius found out? The possibilities crashed down on her. Exile. The long, long wait for death. Watching for a ship every day, praying it came with food and not her assassin—or perhaps, after some time, praying for the assassin. And no wine. No wine ever. She'd go mad.

A shape at the alley's mouth. Bromios. Julia nearly jumped out of her skin.

"He's not here, Julia. Perhaps he had a change of heart after all."

Impossible. "Perhaps he went to a different gate."

"*What* different gate? The nearest is a mile from here." Bromios cursed beneath his breath. "Wait here, Princess. *Do not move a muscle.* I'll never find you in this warren."

And then he was gone again, leaving her alone with her panicked thoughts.

A black mood settled on Alaric as he made his way back to the gate. Bend his pride—bargain his people back into conscription—*trust* the old man indeed. He hadn't come to bargain on trust. He'd come to wring concessions like blood from a severed limb.

But at least he hadn't wasted the trip. This wasn't the only meeting he had to keep. He passed through the gate and slipped into the yawning alleyway where he'd promised to meet Riga's liaison.

Shit. No spy.

This was the more important reason to risk escaping his confinement. He needed precautions taken. A map of the smugglers' ways through the swamp if things went to hell at that banquet— assuming he could get them all out of the palace alive. Alaric cursed beneath his breath. If the time came, he just had to be sure his boot on the Empire's neck held firm.

A sound at his back. He turned, his hand going to the dagger at his waist.

Riga hadn't told him his contact was a woman.

She turned, startled, the hood of her rough woolen cloak falling to her shoulders in her haste, and something about the look of her made him halt. High, graceful cheekbones. A full, red mouth. Eyes heavy-lidded and tilted like a cat's; an arresting blue-green.

"Bromios. You have no idea how—" That voice, redolent of smoke and sex. "You are not Bromios."

And she was not his spy. Alaric knew this woman's kind. A perfumed, pampered lapdog. She belonged in a soaring atrium, surrounded by fine statuary and marble columns—not here, amidst broken cobblestones and gutter trash.

One such as her would just as soon raise the alarm as look at him.

He could silence her now, before she breathed a sound. For a moment he weighed the worth of that carnelian at her throat, the pearls in her ears. Those could buy grain enough to see a hundred people through another starving time. A hundred of his own against this silly woman's life. His hand strayed to his blade, and stopped. The death of a highborn woman would not go unnoticed and he didn't need this kind of trouble.

Besides, she didn't want attention any more than he did. Perhaps he could frighten her off without bringing the guards into it.

"You mistake me, woman." That ring on her finger could feed a small village for a season, by his reckon. "Go home to your soft bed and your soft husband."

Her sharp little chin came up. "I see your master never taught you manners," she shot back. "I am no man's wife."

"And I am no man's slave." Temper became her. A pretty

flush spread across her rising breasts; her eyes flashed at him from out of the dark.

Lust rose up in him so hard and fast it was almost painful.

He wanted her. This laughable confection of a woman. It angered him enough to make him want to teach her fear.

"Go," he said, stalking closer. "Your kind does not belong here."

"My *kind*?" Of all the insolence. "Just what exactly do you mean by that?"

A moment ago, only his outline visible at the other end of the alley, Julia had taken him for Bromios. Now she saw that he could only be mistaken for Bromios if you were half-blind and entirely deaf. He was dressed plainly, but his bearing was faintly military and his Latin too educated for his clothes. A kind of leashed ferocity rolled off him like heat from a forge.

She was being very stupid, just by standing here. But she couldn't leave. What if Bromios found her gone? She'd miss Cornelius. She'd miss her *chance*.

He came closer. "The kind that has never been hungry. Never cold. Never slept on a bed not made of silk and feathers."

"You know nothing about me," she snapped. Although technically, he was right.

"I know you are the sheltered pet of some powerful man." His eyes were vivid blue, bright enough to catch the moonlight. "What would he do if he knew his pet had been lurking in secret alleyways, I wonder?"

"This is my alleyway. I found it first." This was getting ridiculous. "Don't make me call the guards."

"You won't." A pirate grin flashed that made Bromios's look like a cheap imitation. "You wouldn't be here if you didn't have secrets to keep."

His hair was burnished bronze and long enough to brush his shoulders. She felt an urge to run her fingers through it, to start at the temples. To rip it out by the roots. "If you get any closer, I will scream so loud the whole city hears."

His laughter curled around her like a soft caress. "I can think of much better things you can do with your mouth."

How dare he? A thousand retorts rose to her tongue as his blue eyes locked to hers. She felt the jolt of it all the way to her toes.

"Julia?"

The voice was faint, but near. *Oh thank the gods.* "Cornelius? *Cornelius.*"

He was waiting at the other end of the alley. Julia ran to him, yanking herself out of the stranger's spell. Cornelius's arms slid around her and she almost fainted from relief. "Forgive me. It took forever to find you." Cornelius spoke against her hair. "Who were you talking to?"

"No one." Behind her, the alley stood empty.

Had that just *happened*? Perhaps it had been some god, descended from on high to toy with her. That sort of thing was always happening in stories. Julia pictured the strong line of the stranger's jaw, the mocking turn to his mouth. A voice that could call the sin from a holy man. She must have dreamed it. "Where's Bromios?"

"Waiting by the gate." Cornelius wound an arm around her shoulder. "My priest will meet us at the ship, and then we'll be married."

"Yes. Married. Wonderful." The sun would rise any moment, and the watch would change. But the gate was in sight now. Soon they would be free. "Let's go."

They had almost made it to the gate when the soldiers flooded the street.

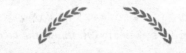

Chapter Five

So this is what fear is.

Real fear. Julia felt as if she was floating above herself, watching the guards march a stiff-backed woman to her quarters, cloaked in middling wool. Walking as if going to her death.

The guards escorted her into the palace and locked her in her chambers. Julia paced to keep from collapsing in fear. They had Cornelius. She could only hope Bromios had escaped.

Perhaps they'd rounded up that villain who'd nearly accosted her in the alley. Perhaps she could blame it all on him. She could say he'd kidnapped her—that Cornelius had happened by and rescued her—in the middle of the night, alone without his entourage, in a part of town he had no reason to go to—no. It would never work.

What would her fate be? A messy public garroting? Rape before that, since it was against policy to execute virgins, and *technically* she still was one. Julia sagged onto the couch. *Stop thinking such things. It doesn't help.*

Perhaps if she took a nap, she'd wake up and find this was all a bad dream.

She slept for hours, until a crashing at the door woke her. Her brother's soldiers. Honorius had summoned her.

Of all the terrible punishments, Julia never imagined Honorius would subject her to the Games. How diabolical.

She had always, *always* hated the Games.

Honorius wasn't even here yet. Julia slumped in the Imperial box, wilting in the afternoon heat. She wanted it over with. The public sentencing, the garroting, the exile. Surely that would not be as bad as this horrid anticipation. She pulled the hood of her fine embroidered cloak up over her hair as the weight of twenty thousand gazes settled upon her. The whispers hit her like a wave.

She would *not* let them see her rattled.

Down in the arena, someone had tied a man to a stake, his paunch hanging white and pillowy over the rim of his loincloth. Three lionesses paced around him in eerie silence, underfed but gloriously lethal. One raised a paw in a leisurely swipe. A red line opened in the man's ample stomach. A loop of glistening pink innard fell out.

Suddenly her stomach was doing its best to claw its way up her throat.

A trumpet blast made her start. A stream of wine pourers and fan bearers entered the box, followed by Honorius in a snowy-white toga lined in Imperial purple. The crowd roared and Honorius held up a hand in acknowledgment.

"Dear Julia. Forgive my lateness." His lips curled in a cold smile as he settled into his chair. "I hope you are enjoying the special games I arranged for you."

The man below was still alive; shrieking like wind through a keyhole. Julia maintained a careful, tight-lipped mask. "It's hardly a mystery how I feel about these things."

"Perhaps I see your point. The man knows he's going to die. The least he could do is refrain from being dramatic about it."

Honorius raised a finger and one of the slaves handed around chilled wine. "Have some refreshment. This heat is vile."

Thank the gods. Now at least, there was wine. Julia took a cup, trying to seem unbothered. Under no circumstance could she show fear, or concern about her friends. He would hurt them only to hurt her.

"And what about the next act?" Julia asked, as if this was all some light amusement. "Am I to be thrown to the beasts before the whole city?"

"Give me some credit. I am not so uncivilized as that. Besides, if you died in the arena, you'd miss my banquet tonight." Those words struck her with an unreasoning fear. *What would happen at this banquet?* Honorius gave her a direct look. "I'm in a bind, Julia. My advisors are warring over their place as the true power behind the throne. But *I* wish to be the power behind my own throne. Stilicho has the army, and armies can be bribed, but Father depleted the treasury to fight his endless wars. Olympius is very rich. I need that money to turn the army's loyalty to *me*. Then I will be untouchable." He frowned. "You almost ruined that for me."

Below, the man had finally met his fate. Slaves removed his body and tried to beat the lionesses back into their cages. One took a swipe at a slave that sent him screaming and reeling across the arena; the crowd howled its delight. A troupe of men with rakes turned over the bloody sand.

There was a fanfare, and a man stepped through the doors of life, holding a long spear. A heavy helmet hid his face.

"I hope you enjoy this next act, Julia. At first I thought lions, but there were lionesses in the act just preceding. Then I thought bears, but bears are terribly slow and boring. And then I had an inspiration." Honorius glanced idly at her. "I hardly need remind you of the symbolism."

A door opened and five wolves came bounding out, tongues lolling. The man began to run, the crowd howling. A wolf nipped at his heels; he gave an unbalanced swipe with the spear. The oversize helmet tumbled into the sand.

Cornelius.

Julia's hands clenched. "Honorius, please. Don't do this." Her throat was a desert; no amount of wine would help. "It was all my idea. He didn't even know. Show mercy."

"This is mercy, Julia," Honorius said mildly. "By all rights, you both should be dead. Many will believe me weak for sparing your life. Perhaps even Alaric will, which is why I've waylaid all his spies." He glanced at her, gray eyes hard beyond his years. "But I will not be the emperor who executed his own sister just weeks into his reign. Father would roll in his grave. You will not make me regret that decision, will you?"

A sob broke in her throat. "No, Honorius."

"I think it prudent that we move up the date of your wedding. Say, to the kalends."

A week away. Julia felt her options narrowing to a single terrifying point.

"Are you watching? I went to great effort to arrange this for you. Praxis, make her watch." The burly slave put a hand on either side of her head, pointing her gaze down at the scene below. "Watch," her brother said in her ear. "Watch *everything*."

Her rooms were empty when she returned. Her women had vanished. Julia knew why. She was a sinking ship, to be abandoned or die.

She stalked on trembling legs through the soaring rooms. Past the marble-edged pool. Past the perfumed gardens, tall braziers staining the mosaics in light. She fell to her knees beside a low silken sofa, pressing her hands to her eyes as if she could tear them out.

Cornelius had died screaming, his throat ripped open, his blood soaking the sand.

My fault. All my fault. She rose and her hand closed around the long, iron stem of a brazier; sent it tumbling, glowing coals skittering across the floor. A priceless vase went next. Red Hercules fighting the hydra against a background of black, sailing into the marble wall. Julia felt exactly like the vase. Like a thousand sharp, tiny pieces of something that used to be whole.

There was wine on the side table. Her slaves had abandoned her, but at least the wine had stayed loyal. Julia poured herself a cup and flung it at the wall. The sticky mess at her feet was gory and expansive. She'd never be able to look at anything red again.

She drank the next cup, though. And the one after that, and the one after.

After drinking the rest of the wine, she went to the bath.

Everyone knew there was a proper order to the baths, cold then tepid then hot. Julia wanted scalding always, first to last. Her grand, columned private *caldarium* was big enough for a hundred and all for her. She sat alone in the hot water, steam rising up to drift among the columns, filled with a sort of weightless calm. The kind that only came after she'd cried herself dry and broken everything within reach that would shatter.

If Agathe was here, she would offer a massage. Scented oils. It was just as well. Julia didn't want to be petted and soothed. Didn't want to emerge from this bath the same. Cornelius was dead and she was the reason; that was real, and she couldn't drown it or drink it away.

If she had been born a man, she'd have inherited an Empire. Instead Honorius had given her away like so much cheap currency. She was nothing but a *latrones* piece, pretty and powerless, to be moved or sacrificed at the player's whim. The thought made her curl her hands around the beveled edges of the bath in anger, fingers pressed white into stone.

It was time she became a player.

Her attendants hadn't taken the linen, but they had taken the silk—*all* of it. Her wardrobe, her shoes, the golden statue of

Cleopatra her mother had given her. Not the *latrones* board—it was too heavy to carry—but they had stripped the silken sheets from the bed. *Thieves.* They hadn't taken her jewelry, only because she'd been wearing it. Julia opened her jewelry cabinet and probed for the compartment, heard the click of the little latch—and a hidden door gave way.

Julia thrust fingers in and gave a sigh of relief. It was still there. Her little golden box.

All emperors had them, and everyone in the Imperial family if they had any intelligence. Insurance in case everything went to hell. Julia opened the box with trembling hands, and saw the little green bottle inside. Aconite, distilled to its most potent state. A drop would kill an ox.

Cornelius and red, rending death filled her sight. It *had* to be done. She wanted to feed this spark of fury until it became fire and burned to ash everything in her that was soft or scared.

And she knew exactly who she could call on for help.

Chapter Six

The party was a careful reflection of power and taste; swan-shaped lanterns floated in the *impluvium* and a thousand lamps turned the ceiling to white sky. Rome's wealthiest lounged on ivory couches. Julia raised her eyes to the dais where her brother sat.

Even now, she was shaking with rage.

Honorius's guards had all but dragged her to the banquet hall. They'd made her wear the green silk she'd tried to slip out of the city in; rumpled and stained. And all her jewelry. Honorius meant to make an example of her. He'd put her on a couch just below the dais, where everyone could see her. "*I* know you plotted against me," he hissed. "Now everyone will know you failed at it. Make a scene and I'll humiliate you further."

Already she could feel every eye on her, flaying her bare.

At least Honorius was not having any more fun at this party than she was. Above on the dais, he looked pinched and annoyed in his ill-fitting purple toga. His taster sat next to him, a man with a bald pate, dutifully taking bites from every plate offered her brother.

It had taken a great deal of effort to make contact with the one person who wanted her brother dead as much as she did. Atticus, her father's steward, his back still sliced to ruins. He had reassured her. Killing Honorius was *necessary*, he'd said in his hushed, pained whisper. Honorius would be a tyrant.

Atticus had known exactly which of her brother's bed slaves had the spine to help. Artemisia—a slim, dark-haired girl from Dacia who was secretly married to one of the guards. *She* wanted freedom, and this was the way to get it.

Artemisia would serve at her brother's table. The poison was slow-acting; her brother would take it at the banquet and be dead by sunup. No one the wiser. Julia drew a breath. But where *was* Artemisia? She ought to be here by now. Meanwhile Stilicho sat at the other end of the table, bolt upright when he ought to be lounging, while Olympius worried at a plate of cheese. Julia stared at his pale, spindly fingers, his little pile of cheese, and felt a blind hatred.

"My poor little pheasant. Drink this." It was Verina, pressing a small flask into her hand. "It is, ah—a bit *augmented*," she said in a hushed tone. "To take the edge off."

Julia took a sip and felt that peachy glow of the Blue Lotus take hold; another sip and she could see nimbus rainbows around every torch. "You shouldn't be here. My brother—"

"Will what? Put me in chains?" Verina laughed. "I have more freedom than the rest of these spineless cowards. I couldn't watch you waste away without a drop to drink." She grinned. "It's ridiculous how tragedy agrees with you. Soon every well-heeled trollop will be wearing her hair half-undone and smudging her kohl. By the way, if you're wondering why Honorius is out of sorts, it's not you. At least, not entirely." She paused significantly. "He's late."

"Who is late?" Belatedly, Julia remembered who this party was for. "Oh. *Him*." She understood how Alaric of the Goths must feel at a party like this, which was surely a sign of how far her life had unraveled. "I don't blame him. We're all here to gawk at him like a caged leopard. It's distasteful."

"At least the buzzards will soon have someone to gawk at besides you," Verina said. "They say he eats Roman babies for breakfast and bathes in Roman blood every night. Exciting, don't you think?"

"I am sure the great Alaric will be like most men surrounded by legend. Reeking of *gharum* and garlic, and not nearly as tall as you imagined." She took another sip from the flask. This evening—the rest of her life, short as that might be—would be entirely more manageable if she was tipsy.

Just then, the heavy ceremonial doors gave a *clank* and began to swing open. Julia froze, wineglass half raised to her lips.

The villain from the alleyway stood on the threshold. Julia recognized him down to her toes: the shoulder-length bronze of his hair; the proud, fierce planes of his face. He stood with an intimidating group of Gothic warriors at his back, a crimson cloak flung over one broad shoulder, gold torques snaking around his biceps. His presence was a physical force. *Everyone*—musicians and dancing girls, Senators and their wives, Honorius—fell silent at his entrance.

His eyes cut in her direction for the barest second, bright and clear as glacier water. If he recognized her, he didn't betray it. Not a flicker.

"Well. King of the Goths, at long last. Have you any idea of the hour?" Honorius's voice was a sharp stone cast into the silence.

"I was told this was *my* celebration, Emperor." An unnervingly attractive smile spread across his face. "Thus the hour is mine, whenever I choose to arrive."

"It is customary to bow to your emperor," Olympius said with open hostility.

Alaric said nothing. But his eyes shifted to Olympius, and

something murderous rose in them that made Julia break out in a cold sweat.

"Emperor, if I may." Stilicho came forward with arms outstretched. "You are well met no matter the hour, King of the Goths."

Alaric's expression didn't change. But that flat gleam left his eyes and he stepped forward to meet Stilicho, who clasped his forearms and spoke low and hurried in his ear.

Julia caught her breath. It had been Alaric in that alley. The man who had terrorized all of northern Italy; who had chased the court into the swamp and driven her father into the ground. A man who commanded armies and starved cities and hung Romans he didn't like on stakes, and who had stood in a muddy alley last night and *toyed* with her like a cat with a bit of string.

Her blood went cold at the thought of what he could have done to her.

It was that woman. The one from the alley. Amidst a crowd of smug-faced aristocrats, draped in jewels and silks, she was the only one he saw.

She was a courtesan. That was the only explanation for her lurking in alleys. And *Honorius's* courtesan, of all unlikely things. She looked rumpled, as if Honorius had bedded her already. Alaric's skin prickled. If she'd told the emperor where he'd been, there could be trouble.

"Bring this roof down around our ears and I will be *extremely* displeased," Stilicho muttered darkly. "It sends a bad enough message that you're late."

"It sends just the message I meant to send." Alaric relaxed into an easy swagger, careful not to look at the red-haired woman again. It took a surprising amount of willpower.

As he approached the dais, he took a swift inventory of the

guards in the room. Most were clustered around the platform, protecting the boy emperor; a few were by the doors.

"So you are Alaric." The son of Theodosius was pale as mutton fat; softer than his father. But the edge to his smirk said he was capable of cruelty. "The way my father described you, you were nine feet tall and breathed fire. Now here you are, and look at you." Honorius gave a light little laugh. "Just a man."

"It is men you should fear, Emperor. Not stories."

Stilicho clapped him on the shoulder. "Come. You must regale us with tales of your time in my officers' school."

"Stilicho says you once killed a bear in the arena with your bare hands." Honorius gave another of his high-pitched laughs. "I don't believe it."

Alaric's jaw tightened. For a moment the banquet hall disappeared and he was back in that place, with the bear and the crowd and the summer heat rising thick off the sand. Unearthing that memory for this boy's entertainment felt akin to pissing on the grave of his father.

But the old man expected nothing better of him than to lose his temper. Instead he could have this boy eating out of his hand if he wanted it. And then he could have anything.

So he flashed a smile for the son of Theodosius. "You are wise not to believe such a lie, Emperor," he said. "I had a spear."

The boy laughed and the entire court let out a collective exhale and he was in.

Of all the things she might have expected of Alaric of the Goths, Julia never thought he'd be *charming*.

He was trading war stories with Stilicho now. Teasing her brother—nobody *ever* teased Honorius—and flashing his teeth in a laugh that enthralled the banquet hall. Honorius was listening with rapt attention, and even Stilicho was beginning to unknit in his chair.

It set her teeth on edge, that someone so murderous could be that attractive. As if he had any right to exist without some disfiguring facial scar.

The scions of Rome had lost interest in her. Now they were watching Alaric. Some secretly—others brazenly—staring, *ogling* him, really. Most had lived through the sieges of Verona and Milan, when this man had been a figure of terror. Julia remembered the stories. The corpses tossed into the water supply. The dead prisoners lined up on stakes in full view of the walls. And always this man, King of the Goths, stalking the battle lines on his enormous black horse as if mayhem were his natural element. But now here he was, with his easy laugh and his flawless Latin and manners like a born aristocrat's, and an entire court of his enemies looked ready to swear fealty. Julia didn't trust this. Not an inch.

"Look at his etiquette." Verina sounded slightly dazed.

Julia gave a bad-natured snort. "*That* man is the reason we all live in a swamp."

She had the uneasy feeling she was the only person who could see the violence simmering beneath the surface of Alaric's charm. Behind his easy smile, he seemed to be contemplating snapping her brother in half and picking his teeth with the bones.

The great doors clanged open again, and Honorius rose from his couch. "An exchange of hostages," he announced. "To guarantee our good intent."

Soldiers appeared from behind the dais, flanking a group of Roman youths. Children from powerful families, clinging to the hands of nursemaids—children from families who had been at odds with her brother. While their parents dined, Honorius had sent soldiers to their homes to bring in their sons and daughters.

It would seem she wasn't the only one Honorius sought to bring to heel.

Bromios was among the hostages. A bruise was blossoming along his jaw. He caught her eye and gave a barely perceptible shake of the head. She kept her face blank as a still pond.

Honorius's soldiers escorted the hostages to the other end of the room, and Alaric's fur-clad warriors surrounded them. Julia could have told him these were worthless hostages. Honorius would not care a fig about them. The children of his enemies would provide no surety.

The great doors behind the dais clanked open again and another brace of Roman soldiers appeared, with the hostages from Alaric's side. There were only two of them—pale youths. Identical twins, dressed in barbarian furs, their blond hair spiked up with animal fat; identical toothy necklaces gleamed about their necks. Julia watched them walk to the front of the room, utterly ignoring the soldiers, and assume a carelessly lethal slump against the wall near the dais. Just a few dozen strides from where she sat.

Alaric was still lounging on his couch, looking slightly bored. But the blue eyes narrowed, just slightly, and suddenly the lethal tension beneath his relaxed demeanor intensified.

He'd been surprised by those hostages too. *Interesting.*

"You look positively sick with nerves," Verina whispered. "Was the wine too strong?"

"No. As a matter of fact, I haven't had enough." It would seem her brother was attempting to play Alaric of the Goths the same way he was playing *her.*

Suddenly she was very intent on what was happening on the dais.

The twins. *Fuck.*

How had Stilicho gotten hands on the twins? The boys didn't seem hurt. Not limping or favoring a side. But their gait said they were armed. At the hip, in the boot, and Horsa had one up his sleeve. Alaric held back a curse.

Stilicho was watching him carefully. It was just like the old man to pull a trick like this. Far harder to hold ground in negotiations when the other side holds a knife to the neck of your closest. But if he betrayed his fear, he'd put the twins in danger.

So he shifted his attention back to the conversation as if it didn't matter to him in the least. "And then he threw that spear from halfway across the arena," Stilicho was saying. "It skewered the bear in the heart and the animal fell down dead."

Honorius's eyes went wide as dinner plates.

"It wasn't so heroic as all that," Alaric said lazily. "That bear was sick and starving and only half-grown."

"Killing a bear of any size and condition is a feat for an adolescent boy. And I knew talent when I saw it." Stilicho smiled indulgently. "I stood up and claimed him for my officers' school."

"And he regretted it ever since," Alaric added, glancing casually across the banquet hall. Thorismund glowered by the servant's passage, the slave girls giving him a wide berth. Riga had gotten hold of a leg of mutton and seemed completely absorbed in it. Both near enough to the twins to react to any trouble. Meanwhile, there were enough of his own with the hostages to hold the doors, if only for a few minutes. He hoped it wouldn't come to that.

"I wonder, Alaric," Honorius mused, "how you wound up in that arena in the first place."

Alaric felt his skin tighten. The question brought with it the mines, the crushing darkness of those tunnels. The smell of blood and the raw sight of men's whipped backs.

"I was a slave," he said flatly. "I killed my master with a length of chain."

"That is a serious crime. Murder. By all rights, you ought to have faced justice."

"Perhaps you would have a different concept of *justice*, Emperor, if you had ever been a slave."

A sudden, brittle silence. Stilicho spoke hastily, "Perhaps the time has come to discuss what we might achieve together. Alaric, Honorius stands ready to honor his father's promises. And Honorius, with Alaric's aid, you could unite the Empire again. Let us talk in peace."

An ugly laugh rose up from the opposite side of the table. It was the one who'd told Alaric to bow. Olympius. He sat with his shoulders hunched over a platter of eel pie, hatred tangible as tar. "You'll get no aid from the King of the Goths, Emperor," Olympius said, setting his teeth into a slice of eel. "He turned on us."

Stilicho looked at him coldly. "The landscape has changed, Olympius."

"I see the same landscape as always. The one this man ravaged twice in three years. No other wades so deep in blood as *this* man." Olympius's mouth curved in an ugly smirk. "Goths do not stay loyal."

Alaric felt his hand clench around his wine cup. So this was the wealthy advisor with his hands in all the pies. Stilicho's enemy, husband to Honorius's sister. "As if your people have anything to teach mine about loyalty."

Olympius's eyes narrowed to slits. "Watch your tongue, traitor."

"Watch your own. Lest it strangle you."

"Still your talk. Both of you," Honorius said. "All this talk of honor and homelands and promises. Any more of this and I'll stab out my own eye." He glared at Olympius. "You have a lot of opinions for a man who's never been to war. And *you*, Stilicho—you created this monster and you have yet to make peace with it." He turned to Alaric. "So let us leave this conversation to the two at this table with the power to agree on something."

Despite himself, Alaric laughed. The steel in the boy was a surprise. Who would have thought he'd be *pleased* to see the ghost of that sour old fanatic Theodosius.

"Your move, Honorius," he said quietly. "Tell me how you plan to buy me."

Julia slouched on the sofa, chewing absently on a piece of fattened fowl.

Where was Artemisia? It had been *hours*. The second course had come and gone, along with a troupe of lithe acrobats and a recitation of Virgil. Through it all, Alaric and her brother passed treaty terms back and forth. They were talking infrastructure now, grain tributes and conscription. Julia listened intently. Being near Alaric was like sitting next to lightning forced still. He spoke quietly, but Julia didn't miss the way everyone fell silent to hear him.

Alaric *did* realize that strip of land along the Danube that Honorius was trying to foist on him was a war zone, did he not? Accepting settlement there would simply be putting his people between Rome and the Huns. Not that he had asked *her*.

She had a bad feeling about what might happen when Alaric finally realized Honorius would never give him what he wanted.

"The hostages seem terribly bored," Verina said, nodding at those strange twins. "That one looks like he's about to fall asleep." They didn't look sleepy to *her*. They occupied space the way Alaric did, lounging casually, inches from putting a dagger in someone's throat.

Suddenly two pairs of eyes were on her. Their faces were young, but their eyes seemed ancient, corpse-pale and empty of pity. The farther one laid a finger on his lips; a solemn warning. The closer bared his teeth and pulled his finger across his own throat.

Julia shuddered and looked away.

"That is all very well," Honorius was saying. "But I'm afraid no matter where you settle, our terms must include conscription."

"My people have already paid in blood. Choose another currency."

"We've offered you terms that include a tribute, in grain or gold. Surely you understand that I cannot simply break off a chunk of the Empire and *hand* it to you, absent any terms at all."

"I don't see why not," Alaric said mildly. "This is land taken from my people to begin with. All I ask is an allotment of it back." He would *not* bargain away his people's freedom to save his own skin. But the twins were a knife to his neck.

A glossy-haired girl appeared with a cup of wine on a tray. Her eyes fell to Alaric and she halted in her steps. The look she gave him was one of recognition. She was dark for a Tervingii, but Alaric would have to be blind not to recognize one of his own.

Honorius's cup had emptied and Alaric signaled the slave girl to refill it. A silent acknowledgment.

"Be reasonable, Alaric," Stilicho broke in. "You are asking us to allow a hostile force to settle en masse within our borders. The Senate will never stand for it."

"The Senate cannot afford to make an enemy of me, old man." Alaric let the friendly pretense drop away and the words came hard and flat as millstones. "Give my people land they can live on, and do not crush them with taxes or spend their lives in conscription. In exchange, I offer you peace in the east. A peace I intend to keep."

"Strong words for a king with no kingdom." Olympius's words dripped contempt. "He threatens us, Honorius. *He* is the reason we don't have peace in the east to begin with. He threatens to pillage if we do not deal to his liking."

"Gentlemen, please." Stilicho's warm, calming voice rolled over the sudden tension. "We are all willing to fight and die for our subjects, and for that we need each other's strength. That is why—"

"Tell the truth, Stilicho," Olympius snapped. "You've been in league with Alaric for years. Secretly splitting the spoils of war." He leaned into Honorius's ear. "Haven't you noticed how many times Alaric escaped Stilicho's justice? In Thrace, in the hills of Verona, and again on the plains of Milan? Suspicious, don't you think?" His mouth curved like a scythe.

Honorius held quiet. One raised finger from him, and they'd

be dragged off to molder in a cell. Alaric watched the emperor, waiting to see in which direction the boy would sway.

In the silence, Honorius's taster turned purple, blood foaming at his mouth.

Julia watched in horror as the taster slumped forward on the table, his face foaming into his plate of fattened fowl.

This *wasn't* the plan.

Artemisia had put the poison in the *wine*. Julia had told her to put it in the *water*; the taster would taste the wine but not the water that went in after. And she'd used the wrong dosage. *How could this have gone so wrong?*

"Arrest him!" Olympius rose to his feet, pointing furiously at Alaric. "Did you see that signal he gave the slave girl? *Arrest him.* He tried to poison the emperor!"

Chaos erupted. At the far end of the room, the great double doors slammed shut, and the room descended into panic. Amidst the mayhem, Alaric rose to his feet, and Julia saw his next move as if he had already done it. He would take her brother hostage.

She had a better idea. The enemy of her enemy would be her friend, whether he liked it or not.

"Isn't this *exciting*?" Verina's eyes had gone bright with bloodthirst.

"Verina, go under the table and don't come out until this is over." Julia took one last, long gulp of her wine—she was *not* drunk enough for this—and snatched up a silver table knife.

Then she ran up the dais steps, dodging the soldiers.

Alaric lunged, shoving the table out of the way. The guards were rushing up the stairs but they wouldn't reach Honorius before he did.

Suddenly the redheaded courtesan planted herself in his path. *Stupid.* He could have cut through her like wind through a curtain. But her interference had had its intended result. In a blink, the centurions had the boy surrounded. His chance lost.

She pushed sharp-edged metal into his hand. "I presume you know what to do with this."

Alaric looked down at her and smiled. He damn well did.

He hauled her close and put the knife to her throat. He could feel every curve of her through the gown she wore; the scent of roses and wine filled his senses. Lust thundered through him, strong and fierce as battle fury, threatened his concentration.

In less than an instant, they were both surrounded by a ring of steel.

Alaric shifted his gaze to Honorius, the boy's mutton-fat face white with shock. "Best call off your guards," he said quietly. "Else someone might get hurt."

Stilicho roared across the dais. "Of all the *stupid* things you could possibly do at a time like this, Alaric—"

Honorius waved a hand. "Take her. You've no idea the trouble she causes."

Alaric gave a bored shrug. "If that's the way you want it—"

He applied a little pressure with the knife. Just enough to make the woman flinch. The boy's jaw tightened and Alaric wondered what he'd do if Honorius didn't make his guards back off. *Cut this woman's throat in the middle of the banquet hall?* Fuck.

Then, to his immense relief, Honorius gave the nod. His centurions backed off down the dais. "Make them throw their blades in that pool with the asinine swans in it." Alaric indicated the lamplit *impluvium*. "And then stand facing the far wall. *Now.*"

Stilicho gave the orders. Then came the clank of sword belts being unfastened, metal hitting water. The silence that followed was immediate and breakable as glass.

Stilicho broke it. "You are not a villain, Alaric. You do not kill defenseless women."

"On the contrary. I believe the world would be vastly improved with one less silly Roman wench in it." There was no point in negotiating now. He'd never get his homeland on the terms he wanted. Threat was all he had. The woman, meanwhile, was resting her entire weight on his foot now. Which was outrageous, considering this had all been *her* idea. It was petty revenge that made him pull her closer, his breath fanning against the concubine's throat. "Imagine this beautiful woman is your city, Honorius, and this knife is my army." His breath raised her skin in tiny pebbles. "You've allowed me to bring fifty of my best men up to your gates. Gates that are rotting and undermanned. If I don't make it out of this palace alive, my men outside will ravage this city like a dog ravaging a carcass. And my army will sweep over the mountains within the week and wreak their revenge."

"No, they won't," Olympius spat. "Your people are starving and fractured, and hardly in shape to stand against us."

Alaric grinned. "You're right, they are hungry. They'd rip the meat off *your* bones the quickest, Olympius." By all the gods, if they wanted a barbarian, he would give them one. He dragged the blade up the woman's neck, lightly tracing her skin from collarbone to jawline, fascinated by the color that rose high and fevered on her cheekbones. "My knife is at your throat, Honorius. Just like this." The woman's pulse danced like a trapped butterfly beneath her skin.

"You will have safe passage," Stilicho said quietly. "I guarantee that. Let her go."

"I don't think so." Alaric tightened his arm around the concubine's ribs, drawing her down the steps. "She comes with me. If anyone looks at us wrong, I'll slit her throat myself."

"You'll be dead in a day, barbarian," Olympius spat.

"I doubt that." He laughed—pure, reckless bravado—as his own men surrounded him. "I hardly need a weapon to grind you down, Honorius. Surrender your arms and hide."

CHAPTER SEVEN

If anyone looks at us wrong, I'll slit her throat myself.

Julia spent the entire way from the palace in stark fear of an errant glance. Alaric seemed entirely capable of carrying out that threat. The wine and Blue Lotus still coursed through her, but the fiery courage that had inspired her to press her knife into Alaric's hand was gone. Now she felt sick and exhausted, alcohol sweating through her pores.

Alaric was up ahead, laughing with his men in Gothic as if this was an afternoon picnic. Alaric of the Goths seemed like the kind of person whose idea of a picnic involved the taking of hostages. She was starting to believe she'd made a terrible mistake.

But outside the city, his laughter evaporated and a fierce, focused look came to his face, like a man attempting to walk the sharp edge of a sword. Julia caught barely a glimpse of him before she was surrounded by a throng of men and horses. Then the wine sickness claimed her and the swamp closed hot and thick around her.

There was a cart, and then a boat. The moon shone high on stretches of watery marshland threaded through with sluggish rivers, and a heavy hand of exhaustion pressed her down flat in the bottom of the boat. Eventually she curled up in a pool of warm and brackish water and slept.

Julia awoke slung like a feather bolster over the back of a galloping horse.

For a blinding moment, all she knew was pain. A pounding apocalypse of blood in her head and the ground rushing by at terrible speed, stubbled with rocks and hard little hillocks. The animal's flank was a wall of surging muscle inches from her face and every stride sent a breath-stealing jolt into her stomach.

"Let me up." She had barely the breath to say it. "I can't breathe. Let me *up*."

A hand grabbed the back of her dress and the world righted itself with a dizzying lurch, mountains and trees and sunset-stained horizon falling into place. Julia looked down and saw thick, muscled wrists; strong, square hands controlling the reins. She recognized those hands.

Dear God, what have I done?

Alaric of the Goths guided the horse at breakneck speed over rough country. *I am going to die,* Julia thought. *I am going to die, thrown from this horse, my head dashed open on a rock.* Her stomach rebelled and whatever she had eaten last night shot up her throat. She had to get off this horse. It had to be *now*.

"Stop!" she shouted. He was either perversely ignoring her or couldn't hear her over the sound of their passage. The beast gave another lurch and suddenly there was no more time. Julia leaned over and retched.

The horse came to a bone-jerking standstill. She was on the ground and there was a stream. The water was very clear; little fish darted among colorful stones as the remains of last night's dinner came up her throat.

Behind her, the ground shook beneath the hooves of galloping horsemen. Julia shut her eyes, up against the hard wall of her own sobriety. The night before assembled itself in her memory. The taster falling forward into a plate of roasted swan. Herself, pressing a knife into Alaric's hand. What a joke. The one thing she'd succeeded at since she'd decided to *become a player* was getting kidnapped by Goths.

A hand touched her shoulder. She nearly jumped out of her skin.

It was Bromios. He stared down at her grimly, the bruise on his cheek turning yellow. He looked positively like a villain.

Julia had never been so relieved. "What on earth are you doing here?"

"Saving my skin. *Someone* had to guide Alaric of the Goths through the swamps." He glanced at the surging knot of men and horses kicking up dust behind them. "I overheard them talking. I'm concerned our reward will be a gash to the throat."

"That monster! I *rescued* him from that banquet!" But what should she expect? Alaric was a lawless barbarian. "I will handle him," Julia said calmly. "I shall speak to him like one royal to another." Her brother set the bar low; no doubt he'd be grateful simply to have his status honored as King of the Goths.

Bromios's expression was carefully bland. "I think I'd better do the talking."

Then he glanced over her shoulder, his face going pale.

Alaric of the Goths stood behind her, leaning on his spear. Watching them. His eyes sharp slices of blue beneath heavy lids.

With deliberate calm, Julia rose and turned to face the screaming calamity her life had become. She inclined her head regally. "I owe you my thanks, King of the Goths. I am in your debt."

The polite answer would be to acknowledge that he was equally in *her* debt, considering it was her quick thinking that had saved his life. He did not offer the polite answer. Instead his gaze drifted down in a lazy perusal that was nothing short of insolent.

She gritted her teeth. He wasn't even *pretending* at civility now.

Bromios shoved in front of her—elbowing her hard in the ribs—and threw himself at the warlord's feet. "Please, King Alaric! It was I who led you out of the city through the smugglers' ways, and now I beg that you take me with you. I can be useful! I know all the secret ways from here to the mountains—I can play the lute—I can find you the *best* wine and opium. Only don't leave my poor carcass here, I beg you—"

One of Alaric's men wandered up in the midst of this tirade. He was barely taller than Julia, his hair golden, loose, and brushing his shoulders. He and Alaric exchanged a glance as Bromios continued his pleading tirade. The other man said something in rapid-fire Gothic; Alaric's reply was curt.

The blond one spoke in Latin. "Can you sit a horse?"

"Of course I can!"

Julia snorted. What a lie. Bromios had never ridden a horse in his life.

But the man swung up on his horse and pulled Bromios after. Julia could only stare, outraged, as the two of them galloped off, Bromios waving goodbye with a mouthed *good luck*. Leaving her alone with Alaric.

That little brigand.

Alaric was still watching her, amusement gleaming in his eyes. "That's an impressive weight of metal on you." There was a Gothic edge to his Latin that wasn't there last night. "I'm surprised you can stand."

"I brought it for you, King of the Goths." She would *not* avert her eyes like a slave. "I wish to propose an alliance."

He laughed softly. "Perhaps I should tell you that among my people, it's the man who offers the dowry."

A bright heat rose to her face. *Blushing!* What was *wrong* with her? He said nothing, only raised a hand and Julia flinched back, almost putting herself in the stream. *Oh good God, he's going to throttle me and toss me in a ditch.*

But instead he reached behind her hair and undid the clasps at her throat.

Julia fell utterly silent as he bent to his task, bronze hair falling forward, each brush of his fingertips sending bright shocks down her spine. His fingers were deft at her neck, undoing the clasps of a dozen necklaces as if he had infinite practice denuding ladies of their jewels.

When he pulled back, she was breathless.

"Your rings?"

She flushed hot. "Oh. Yes. Of course." She slid off the rings— seven of them, all heavy gold and delicate filigrees and gemstones worth a kingdom—and gave them into his hands without a thought.

Only then did she realize she'd given him her mother's ring too.

"There is an opal ring among those you took. I'd like it back." She drew a careful breath. "It's worth nothing to you, but a great deal to me."

"Too late, woman. What's yours is mine now. Consider your debt paid." He grinned rakishly. "Ravenna is sixty miles to the southeast. That way." He pointed. "Good luck."

And then he turned on his heel and strode off into the churning dust.

Julia stared after him, open-mouthed. This could not be happening. He could not simply *leave* her here, to be scooped up by some passing patrol. She hitched up her torn skirt and plunged into the mob of men and horses, barely avoiding being trampled to death.

She found him holding the reins of that enormous black mountain of a horse, his head bent in conversation with another of his men. "A word, if you please, King of the Goths."

He turned, and something in his ice-blue eyes made Julia step back. *What the hell was she doing?* Bodies impaled below the walls. Starvation in the streets. She would be *lucky* to have this man release her to her fate. *Grow a spine,* she admonished herself. "You cannot *possibly* leave me here. I am far too valuable to simply leave by the side of the road like a—"

"Valuable?" Amusement flashed across his face. "I doubt I'd get more than a quarter talent if I tried to ransom you."

Julia's jaw dropped. *A quarter talent?* "Just who do you think you've abducted? Some expensive Greek house slave?"

Alaric swept her a glance, coolly evaluative; she could practically feel him weighing the value of her like a sack of wheat. "You think you are worth more?"

She had a terrible feeling he was *toying* with her. "I'm worth more than your entire two-cent army. You've never *seen* as much money as I'm worth."

He was laughing now; a warm, powerfully infectious sound she could sink into like a bath—if only it wasn't *at* her. "Woman, you're smeared in filth and you reek of wine and vomit. If I left you by the roadside in this state, not even the swineherds would touch you." Beside him, the giant warhorse stamped an impatient hoof. "Now go, and do not test my mercy. The boy emperor misses his concubine." And then, in one fluid motion, he was up on his big black horse.

Julia stared, speechless. *Concubine.* The man had no blessed idea who she was.

Alaric nudged his horse forward, thinking that would be the end of it. The woman had other ideas. She lunged for the reins. Hannibal reared up, all black muscle and flying hooves.

"I'm not a concubine, you idiot," she shouted. "I'm Honorius's *sister.*"

Hannibal didn't like people messing with his head. Alaric fought to control his furious horse before he stove her skull in with his hooves. *"Let go,"* he barked at her, but she didn't. Her fist was clamped on the rein as if her life depended on it.

Only then did he realize what she'd said.

He managed to calm Hannibal, stroking the bunched muscles on his quivering neck. "You are the emperor's sister." It beggared belief. *"You."*

Even from this distance, she smelled like a winery. But he watched her draw herself up, her face smoothing into a proud, flawless self-possession that could credibly be Imperial, despite the ruin of her clothes and the wild, sunset wreck of her hair. A neat transformation.

"I am Julia Augusta, second child of Theodosius and the empress Galla. Sister and daughter to emperors," she declared.

Well. This changed the calculus. Twice before, he'd tried to carve a homeland from the Empire's stinking corpse. Maybe this time, with an Imperial hostage in his pocket, it would all end differently. And this way he would not be going back to his people empty-handed.

Alaric grinned in a way that made her back up a step. "Princess, it would seem your ransom value has just shot up tremendously."

Then he reached down and hauled her up before him on the horse.

CHAPTER EIGHT

The brothel was the seedy kind, in the disreputable section of town where cutpurses swarmed the streets. Stilicho counted himself lucky getting to the place alive.

The madam was a buxom woman of indeterminate age, dressed in a cheap red toga. She smiled cheerfully, displaying a row of broken teeth, as she showed Stilicho to a narrow room flooded in oily light. A thin mattress was tossed over a rough stone shelf; little protection for bouncing hips and spines. She left a jug of cheap wine and two clay goblets when she went.

Stilicho settled into a chair to wait. As he had many times in the last forty-eight hours, he turned his thoughts to the boy in the arena.

The boy had been barely fourteen, not yet grown into his frame. An escaped slave, ragged and bruised; he had fought like hell when he'd been caught and the signs of that were all over his body. Alaric had laughed at the banquet, called it luck and the bear's sickness. But Stilicho had seen the boy's steady hand, his cool resolve. There'd been nothing of luck in that shot. When the boy stood victorious over the heaving carcass, Stilicho rose to his feet with the rest. Made sure he shouted the loudest. *Bring him to me*, he'd said. *That boy is mine.*

He never dreamed one day he'd face that cool, determined gaze from across a bloody battlefield. Meet him over and over, on frozen ice and howling plains, surrounded by bloating corpses in the heat of summer. Trying to save the boy in the arena from the man he had become.

The door swung open and a towering giant from the primeval forests of Thrace strode into the room. "It's about damn time," Stilicho said. "Could you not have chosen someplace clean?"

"You requested privacy. This is one of the few brothels in the city not infested by the Empire's spies." Calthrax slouched into a chair by the door. "Lettice is an old friend."

"Yes. I thought I'd recognized Thracian tattoos." Calthrax poured himself some of the rotgut wine. It seemed incongruous, all that hulking muscle sitting still, pouring wine; every inch of Calthrax seemed built for violence. "That stuff will kill you," Stilicho observed drily. "They keep it flowing, the better to rob you later."

"It's no worse than we had on campaign." Calthrax grinned. "And any who tried to rob me would regret it, I think. What do you want, old man?"

"Surely you can guess." Stilicho raised his cup to his lips; caught a whiff of the contents and winced. "You have ears in every corner of the palace."

"You must be referring to Alaric of the Goths pulling the roof down around your ears." Calthrax's eyes turned hard. "Are you surprised? You offered him everything he wanted on a platter and he still couldn't bring himself to take it."

"Alaric has kidnapped the emperor's sister."

"Yes, so I heard. And you let him."

"I had no choice. Alaric would have cut her throat." He could not let it happen. The princess Julia had been a joy, once; a bright, sharp girl who could beat anyone in the palace at *la-*

trones. "I suspect he will try to ransom her, but we cannot allow ourselves to be extorted. Not without sending a signal to every tin-pot usurper in the Mediterranean that Rome is ripe for the taking. Our only real recourse is war, and we cannot afford war. Not with the northern provinces in revolt." He sighed. What he had to say next pained him deeply. But so many lives had already been lost. This was the only way that did not lead to mass bloodshed. "I need you to hunt down Alaric, kill him, and bring back the princess. Alive or dead, but I would *strongly* prefer alive."

Calthrax went still. "I never dreamed to hear that from your lips."

"It cannot be helped," Stilicho said. "Alaric travels with fifty men. I've already blocked the ports, but he may aim for the mountains. My patrols will be thin on the ground and they do not have your tracking skills. You will need to assemble your best."

"My best will cost you."

Stilicho took out his purse and counted out a measure of gold—enough to outfit a small mercenary group, with plenty left over for bribes. "This should be enough."

Calthrax examined the money. "If you had asked me to do this years ago, the north of Italy would not be in ruin."

"I know." How many had died for his wish to preserve Alaric's life? He'd tried everything. Tried reason and military force; tried giving him what he wanted. Nothing else had worked. And now he was left with no other option.

Unbidden, the boy in the arena rose up in his mind. Hand steady on the broken spear, incandescent with the will to live.

Stilicho spread a worn leather map on the rickety table. "If Alaric is heading toward the passes, here is where I believe he will aim. Start your search in this direction."

This was the best course, he told himself. Even if they went to war and won, Stilicho would be damned if he'd let Alaric be paraded through the streets and strangled at the foot of the statue of Mars. Instead he'd aim Calthrax like a spear at the heart of his enemy, and ensure he died a warrior's death. He owed that much to the boy in the arena.

CHAPTER NINE

Julia's muscles felt like tenderized meat after riding until dark. By the time Alaric let her off the horse, she wanted to curl up and die.

They stopped in a dry gully under a low rock overhang. After hours of riding through trackless wastes and burned-out fields, avoiding the main roads and inhabited towns, she had no blessed idea where they were. Julia hoped Stilicho would be similarly confounded.

Alaric seemed unconcerned about capture. He left her in a tent at the edge of the camp, in the hands of those pale twins who followed him around. He gave them quiet instructions in Gothic and looked at her exactly once. An ice-blue glance that sliced through her like wind. Then he left.

The twins regarded her with ghost-pale eyes, rimmed in red. Julia glanced between them uneasily. They were wood from Alaric's tree, but at least Alaric's brutality had a reason behind it. She had a feeling these two just wanted to watch the world burn.

Even so. She was an Imperial Princess. She would not be afraid of two teenagers in a musty tent. "Well?" she demanded. "What did he say just now?"

One of them gave a devil smirk. "He said not to kill you unless the Romans attack."

"But don't worry," the other added. "You are gently born, so we would do it quick."

"Don't go to any trouble on my account," Julia muttered. She glanced around the tent. Unfurnished and plain, it appeared to be a simple cavalry tent. "Is this how Alaric always entertains his high-ranking hostages?"

"Sometimes he lets us have fun with them. Finger breaking. Eyeball gouging. That sort of thing." One of them grinned, his canines strangely sharp. "We send bits of you back to your people, to encourage them to pay ransom."

Julia eyed the long knives at their waists with trepidation. She wasn't entirely sure they were joking. But even if they were—they were right that Alaric would ransom her back to her brother. She was a windfall dropped in his lap. It was what *she* would do, in his situation.

Alaric *must not* ransom her back. Going back to Honorius might as well be a death sentence. Instead she must persuade him to provide her with the army she needed, so she could go back on her terms.

Of course, that was easier said than done.

Seduce him, Cleopatra whispered in her mind. A strange, deep thrill shot through her— *No*. The very idea was beneath her. Besides, she could offer a homeland. Surely that was more beguiling than momentary pleasure.

The boys settled in front of the doorway. Julia crouched on the floor, drawing her knees up to her chest, trying to control her rising impatience. Alaric could be making plans to get word to Honorius even now. She *had* to get to him.

The boys unrolled a scrap of cloth. It was a portable *latrones* board, stitched into a scrap of old leather. Julia edged closer. "Is that *latrones*?"

One of them slanted her a speculative glance. "You play?"

"Will you teach me?" Boys loved teaching things to girls.

"All right." Soon they were talking over each other, explaining the rules. There were a few differences from the way she'd learned the game, but Julia could adapt.

As they spoke, Julia pulled out the flask Verina had given her. Pure Blue Lotus, in unwatered wine. The boys looked at it with curiosity. "It's from the banquet."

One of the boys took the flask without hesitation, taking a long, hard pull. He frowned. "This doesn't taste like wine."

"It's Caecuban. A rare vintage. Very special."

The boy shrugged and passed the flask to his brother. Eventually they passed it back to her. She took a small sip. Just enough to dull her fear. She would need all her courage for the conversation with Alaric to come.

They had names, these barbarian twins. And they were not quite as identical as they seemed. Hengist was slightly taller, with a quiet, introspective air about him; Horsa, the one with the chipped front tooth, seemed the more wild. Julia examined the tooth necklaces that circled their necks and wondered if those were wolf teeth and whether they'd had to kill the wolves themselves. She decided not to ask.

She watched them drink and listened to them launch into further explanations of the rules, trying to look vapid as empty sky.

The play began. Outside, horses snorted; men walked by with weapons jangling. The world shrunk to the sixty-four squares in front of her and the cool, soothing click of the stones in her hands. She'd forgotten how she'd loved this, once. There had been a time when her father used to call his generals in to try to defeat her. And beam with pride when they failed.

Meanwhile, she drank herself, just a little, and watched the boys carefully. She would take only enough to assuage suspicion, and dull the jittery anxiety that swept through her as she contemplated spending time in Alaric's company. She would *not* enter his presence afraid.

The boys were not inured to this drug. They would crash into sleep, any moment now. And then she would go seize her destiny.

What Alaric remembered most about his childhood was the starving time.

It had begun with the Huns. He had an old memory of them lined up on the north bank of the Danube, hulked over their tough little ponies. A line of houses blazing, a smell like cooking meat. Then the river's overwhelming current. Clinging to a hand and losing it.

Those who made it across the river were warehoused in camps. The emperor had sent food, but the Roman guards had stolen or sold it. He promised land, but year after year, the refugees stayed trapped on the river's south bank until parents were selling children into slavery for the promise of a full belly. Even his proud father had been reduced to taking the deal the guards offered: one child for the slaver's block, one dog for the roasting spit. At least, his father explained to him, his new Roman master would feed him when his parents could not.

That princess was now his people's only chance at avoiding that again.

Alaric strode through the camp, on his way back from checking their boundaries for threats. A thing he did compulsively. This gully was well hidden, a haven for smugglers. They'd gone sixty miles today, avoiding the villages and main roads, in a direction Stilicho would not anticipate. They had seen no riders following them; that meant Stilicho was probably using his limited troops to block the ports.

They would have to be very careful indeed to avoid being spitted on a Roman sword.

"Alaric." It was Riga, the Hunnic mercenary, stepping into his path, laughing as if at some private jest. "You'd better come to your tent. You have a visitor."

★ ★ ★

Alaric thrust aside the door flap with one arm, staring with no small measure of astonishment down at the princess Julia.

She was staring up at him, swaying slightly on her feet and looking surprised to see him in his own damn tent.

Alaric glanced at Riga, speaking in Gothic. "How the hell did she get in here?"

"Mystery to me. I think she's drunk."

That much was certain. There was a fresh scent of wine on the woman's breath, and an unfocused look to her eyes that spoke of something more. Opium, maybe.

He switched to her own Imperial Latin. "Hello, Julia."

"Send your men away, won't you?" She looked at him beseechingly. The pitch-perfect tone of a manipulator in distress. "What I have to say concerns your ears alone."

Alaric gave her a particularly nasty smile. "No."

Clearly people didn't tell her that very often. Julia's delicate jaw clenched and her eyes lit with temper. "Have it your way. I'll say it right here." She raised her chin. "You were talking to the wrong child of Theodosius at that banquet. I'm here to give you an empire."

If Julia was capable of one thing in this world, it was holding her liquor.

She'd drunk only enough to drown the fear. But now, craning her neck to meet the barbarian king's gaze, she realized too late that it hadn't worked. She was terrified.

His eyes slid to her lips and suddenly she was *very* aware of his nearness, in a way entirely different than fear.

"You have my attention, Julia." He gave her a mocking smile—he knew exactly the effect he had on her, damn him—and crossed the tent, taking a seat in a battered camp chair. At his signal, one of his men brought her a three-legged stool. "Sit." She did. "What is it you want?"

So blunt. *If I was a man, I would be given all the courtesies.* She needed wine, of the nondrugged variety; that would calm her nerves. "I believe it's customary to offer refreshment to a royal guest before negotiations."

"So, we are to negotiate now," he said softly. But to her surprise, he acquiesced. At another of his wordless signals, someone handed him a wineskin. Alaric poured some onto the ground, speaking in Gothic. Then he drank, muscles moving in the golden column of his throat. "A tradition among my people," he told her solemnly, offering her the wineskin. "We drink to Woden, that he may grant us wise and fruitful conversation."

Julia eyed what he offered with trepidation. She'd never drunk to honor a barbarian god. She wasn't sure such an action was entirely sanitary.

But there was challenge in Alaric's eyes. He didn't think she had the nerve.

Julia snatched the wineskin with firm resolve. "Wise and fruitful indeed," she said, smiling through her teeth. Then she put the wineskin to her lips and drank deep. Searing fire streaked down her throat. "Bloody *hell*," she managed, bent in half by a fit of gasping coughs. "What in all that's holy *is* this?"

"*Ealu.* A liquor made from barley." He watched her struggle with cool dispassion. "If it is too strong for you, we have water—"

"A *pox* on your water." She took another swallow. The bright, burning line lit up the inside of her throat again, but this time she was ready.

The drink was good. The drink was what she needed.

"Does she know she's supposed to sip it?" Riga asked, sitting cross-legged on the floor.

"Perhaps we should tell her," Ataulf mused, looking not the least inclined to do it.

"We can't let her drink *all* of it. That's the last of the batch."

Thorismund sounded distinctly irate. "If you piss-weasels won't stop her, I will."

"No." Alaric held up a hand. "Let her dig her own grave."

Whatever she wanted, she seemed intent on making a fool of herself in getting it. Maybe she'd come to seduce him to her cause, he thought, eyes lazily tracing the fine lines of her collarbones. Maybe he'd let her try. "You've had your drink." Custom demanded they pass the skin back and forth between them, taking small sips as offer met with counteroffer. Julia gave no sign she intended to pass it back. "Now, speak."

Her voice dropped low, the affected purr of a gifted seductress. "You plan to ransom me, but I have a better proposition. We share the same enemy—my brother. Put me on his throne, and you can have any land you want. Point to a place on a map, and it's yours."

Not a chance. He had been betrayed for the last time by Theodosius and his children. "Put you on the throne." Alaric struggled not to laugh. *"You."*

She frowned. "You laugh because I was born a woman."

"I laugh because you were born a lapdog. Perhaps I should let my people bleed and die to raise one of your brother's peacocks to the purple. It makes just as much sense."

The look she gave him could freeze fire. "They're *cockerels.*"

"I wonder," he mused lazily, "what would drive an emperor's sister to slip me a knife in the middle of a battle and engineer her own kidnapping?"

"You've met my promised husband. Olympius," she said coolly. "I loathe the very ground he stands on."

She meant it well enough; the venom in her voice was real. So, the woman was running away from her engagement. "And what is this to do with me?"

"Honorius *ordered* me to marry him. The only way to argue with Honorius is with an army at my back." She raised her eyes, blue-green and fierce as a cat in a trap. "Your army."

Julia took another hard slug from the wineskin. If she just kept drinking, she could *be* Cleopatra. "You will need allies when the time comes," she informed the barbarian warlord who was currently glaring at her in an intimidating fashion. "No one knows the snake pit of Roman politics like I do. You cannot hold Rome by force of arms alone. Take it, maybe, but not hold it."

"Who says I want to hold it? Maybe I just want to see it burn." He bared his teeth in a brutal smile. "Grow up, woman. What does it matter if you hate your husband? Marriage does not follow love; it never has. You'd be less of a fool to lie on your back as you were made to do."

Julia bristled. A searing flush swept across her body—bright heat just beneath the skin. Outrage choked her throat. *The nerve.*

"How far down the peninsula do you think you'll get without support from at least *some* of the people?" she snapped. "Not everyone in Rome is happy at my brother's rise. I could lend your next invasion legi—*legi*timacy." Somehow her tongue got tangled over the word. "And beyond that, money. I have a fortune in villas all up and down the coast. All yours, King of the Goths." She let out a hiccup. When had there become *two* of him? "I think I should sit down."

Alaric's reply seemed to come from the bottom of a well. Julia barely heard. Slowly she slid off the chair and onto the bearskin rug.

Alaric watched the princess slide off the stool and list onto the bearskin like a sinking ship. That last pull from the wineskin had been the one that broke her.

He could not trust a thing she said, of course. She was a daughter of Theodosius; she'd shred any agreement the moment it suited her.

Even so, he wanted her. Even now.

"You're already sitting." She ignored that. He knelt beside her and offered her water, which she regarded with scorn.

"I'd be emperor already if I were a man," she declared accusingly.

"Certainly," he drawled. "Drink."

She took the waterskin. Up close she smelled of *ealu* and sweat and beneath it the intoxicating scent of roses. She took a sip and grimaced. "This is *water*."

He laughed. "And what else should it be?"

She stared up at him as if just realizing he was there. Eyes green as gemstones one moment, dark blue the next, like the sea over a vast crevasse. "What else do you want from me, King of the Goths?" Her lush red lips curved in a drowsy, knowing smile. Her hand rested boldly on his arm. A scorching burn.

Fuck. He'd put her in the farthest tent from his. He'd been scrupulously careful. "Do you even know what you're offering, Julia?"

"I—" She let the sentence fall away, her mouth a breath from his, begging to be plundered. *Fuck it.* He could send his men away, then press her back on this bearskin and take what she offered. He would make her *sob* for him. It would be his own kind of revenge.

"I believe I shall take a nap," the princess Julia announced to the room at large, fingers curling in the bearskin. "I am indisposed. You may all come back later. Come back tomorrow." Then she lay down on her side on Alaric's bearskin rug and let out a particularly loud *snork*.

For a breath, quiet reigned in his tent.

"Well," Riga said cheerfully. "Now what?"

"Let's have a bit of fun with her," Thorismund growled. "Show her the consequences of drinking the last of a man's batch."

"Maybe tie her to a stake outside," Riga said agreeably. "Leave her for the beasts."

"Not one of you touches her." Alaric spoke softly but with a force that shut them up.

The edge of her *stola* rode up her perfect leg and he took off his cloak to cover her.

There was a thin line of drool dangling from her mouth now. *Drool.* Alaric shook his head in disgust. He didn't even *like* this woman.

"We cannot take her," Ataulf said. "She's a distraction."

Alaric glanced pointedly at Ataulf's new lover, the Gothic ex-slave with the calculating eyes, who had stayed conspicuously quiet. "As if you don't have your own distractions."

"Do you honestly think the Romans will bargain for her? She's defied her own brother."

"They'll bargain," Alaric said. "The boy emperor can't afford to look so weak as to have his kin kidnapped out from under him." He lifted his eyes to the twins, who had come bursting into the tent just now. He hadn't the patience for whatever elaborate excuse they'd no doubt invented to explain their failure to keep the princess confined. "Take her back to the tent," he ordered them before they could say a word. He would deal with them later.

Then he called his men around him and bent over the maps, the plan for their escape already building in his mind.

CHAPTER TEN

Alaric's plan was simple enough. The Roman army was over-taxed by rebellion in the north, and Stilicho couldn't withdraw those troops without losing the provinces. Alaric would bet that with as few troops as he had, he would try to draw his net tight at the border. All they had to do was slip through. Which was easier to do in bands of five or ten.

And while on their way, they could shut the door behind them. The mountains were full of tribes with shifting loyalties. Alaric's men would take different routes through the mountains and renew alliances with the hill tribes. If Stilicho's thoughts did turn to war, the allies would hold the mountain roads. They could not hold it forever, but that would at least buy them re-prieve.

An hour before dawn, Alaric watched his men ride off into the war-blasted landscape. Remaining with him were a small band: the Batavi prince Thorismund; the Hunnic mercenary Riga; and Gaufrid's twins. And the princess, who'd clearly never ridden a horse in her life.

Alaric knew these lands; among these hills, he and Stilicho

had stalked each other years ago. He'd memorized the maps, knew every village and garrison. He stuck to the secret paths, the thicker forests, stayed away from ridgelines and populated areas.

By day's end, his men could barely stay in the saddle. He stopped in an isolated grove and let the princess down off his horse, then tramped up to the top of the ridgeline to keep watch. Once he was alone, he took out his leather satchel and spilled the princess's treasure in the dirt.

Sixteen necklaces, seven rings, and a pile of looping bracelets. Most of it gold—white gold from mountainous Anatolia; green gold from Lydia; and the purest, softest yellow gold from the mines of Sicily. And that opal. Trash rock that would have been tossed aside in the mines. He almost tossed it himself. But then he remembered the princess's face, that guarded look as she asked for it back. Maybe it could provide some kind of leverage over her.

Horsa and Hengist approached, Horsa swinging his *seax* at the undergrowth.

"Put your blade away, Horsa. You'll dull the edge." Alaric sighed. "Sit." The boys did, eyeing the jewelry with avid curiosity. "Have you ever seen green gold before?" He held out one of the rings. "That's from Lydia. Ten times the value of ordinary gold." He picked up a bracelet with emeralds the size of his thumbnail. "This is from Dacia. I could feed an army for a month with that." Alaric shoved down a memory, an old one, of crawling through some crack in the earth, searching out veins with his fingertips. Those days were done. Now he could tell Dacian gold from Spanish at a glance, and the boys would have that knowledge without paying the price he had.

Hengist let out a low whistle between his teeth as a strand of pearls spilled out over his hands, each one worth a castle. It was the pearls that were the most valuable. The boys passed the jewels between them, admiring their glow.

"How did you come to be taken hostage?" Alaric asked it with deceptive mildness. "Horsa?"

"It wasn't my fault," Horsa said, just as Hengist insisted, "It was *my* fault."

"Hengist, quiet." Alaric raised his eyes to Horsa. "You, speak."

Horsa launched into an elaborate tale in which he and Hengist had gotten too close to the walls, through no fault of theirs. As usual, Hengist backed his brother up. Alaric knew them well, knew them both inside out. Horsa had dragged his levelheaded brother into it, as he usually did.

He interrupted the litany of blamelessness. "It's clear enough the capture was Horsa's fault. And I saw you stab that guard at the banquet, Horsa. If not for that, we might have walked out with a deal." As soon as he said it, he knew it wasn't true. There would have been no agreement, not then or ever. "But there's also the matter of both of you letting the princess escape her tent last night. Which of you is responsible for that?"

"There was something in that drink! It wasn't our fault—"

"Of course there was something in the drink, and of *course* it was your fault. She isn't your friend." Alaric glanced between them. "You are both old enough for a man's blame and a man's punishment. I won't tan your backs, despite you deserving it. I can't have you diminished in a fight." He drew a breath. "Don't twitch a muscle without my order. Understand? Otherwise it's the Romans who'll dole out your punishment. Now go."

Riga and Thorismund strolled up just as the boys stalked off.

"Your royal guest is mad enough to cut your throat," Riga said cheerfully in Hunnic. "I see she's falling prey to your legendary charm." Riga was always cheerful, and it did not lessen his brutality an inch. Alaric had seen him merrily flay a man alive once.

"That woman wants to drag us all into a war over her siblings' squabbles," Thorismund muttered, settling beside him with his back to a tree. "I don't trust her."

"I don't need to trust her to ransom her, Thorismund."

"It won't be worth the trouble." Thorismund snorted derisively. "Better to knife her, drop her in the sea, and be done with this cursed business."

"I like her," Riga said. "She stood up to our fearless leader, and him in a surly mood."

Thorismund shot Riga a glance of disgust and deliberately changed the subject. "Which route will we take through the mountains, Alaric?"

"Through Brisca's territory."

"You must be fucking mad. Those passes almost killed us last time."

"We must take the risk," Alaric said. "Brisca is our strongest ally there. If Stilicho no longer holds that road, he can threaten war all he likes but the eastern passes are closed to him."

"Let's see what the gods have to say." Thorismund untied the pouch of oracle bones at his waist and cast them into the dirt, speaking an old Batavi incantation. Eventually he fell silent, blond brows knitting together. "I hate to tell you this, but we're fucked no matter which way we take through the mountains."

"Better ask my gods. They're far more optimistic," Riga said.

Alaric began to sharpen his *seax* as the men fell into a debate over the merits of their gods. He himself gave little weight to religion. But Thorismund was not wrong to worry. The Empire had the relays and the fresh horses, and all the roads were watched. They would need whatever help they could get.

"I better ask the gods again," Thorismund muttered. "They were nothing but doom and gloom just now. Perhaps a sacrifice—"

"No sacrifices," Alaric said firmly. "No hunting, and no fires."

He stood, sliding his *seax* back in his belt, and descended the ridgeline to their temporary camp. On the other side of the clearing, the twins were arguing over an obscure *latrones* rule and Julia sat as far from everyone as she could, knees drawn up to her chest, seething quietly in his direction.

He supposed he could take pity on her.

He found a piece of smoked deer meat and a full waterskin in his pack, and crossed the clearing to her. Even now—eyes smudged with kohl, coppery hair an irredeemable tangle—she held an arresting, wrecked beauty as if he'd already bedded her.

It took a moment to realize he was simply staring at her. Devouring her with his eyes. Meanwhile she was looking at the deer meat as if he had offered her a dead rat.

"No thank you, King of the Goths."

Alaric felt a stab of irritation. Not a man among his own hadn't eaten bark and dirt to ease the hunger pangs, and here she was, refusing perfectly good food. "Go hungry if you wish," he growled. "But trust me. It won't take many days of it for you to start boiling your own boots."

She said nothing to that. He felt her eyes on him all the way across the clearing.

Lie on her back as she was made to do indeed.

Julia would admit, in the interest of fairness, that she had drunk far too much last night. And she'd perhaps overestimated her own ability to hold the foreign liquor, which did *not* agree with the Blue Lotus. She'd vomited twice this morning.

But nothing about the situation had required him to mock her before all of his men. The man wasn't just a terrifying warlord; he was *rude*. And for no good reason! She could give him everything he wanted, if only he would help her with the pesky little problem of not currently being empress. Why wouldn't he take what she offered?

Why wouldn't he take what she offered?

Julia sat with her back to a tree, watching the men roll themselves in their cloaks and prepare for sleep. She didn't have a cloak. They all expected her to sleep on the ground and eat shoe leather. Her body still ached in places she didn't know existed from the long day spent on the horse. In Alaric's arms.

A slow flush heated her cheeks.

That man had no right to be so beautiful. Just *looking* at him made her angry. What right had he to be so tall? And so perfectly built? She couldn't stop staring at the swell of his chest beneath his tunic, the chiseled strength of his arms. But looking at his face was perhaps the most dangerous of all. Clean-shaven and arrogant, skin tinged with gold as if he spent all his time in the sun. And those *eyes*. The shock of meeting his gaze was enough to make her forget her own name. She could hate him for that alone.

He was across the clearing now, rubbing his horse down with a handful of grass; Julia couldn't help but stare at the way his back muscles shifted beneath his tunic. The way he placed a hand on the horse's haunch, speaking low. She sucked in a furious breath.

He *hadn't* touched her last night. She'd woken up in the tent that morning, freezing on the hard ground and her head pounding worse than it ever had in her life, thoroughly untouched. She'd been at his mercy and he hadn't touched her.

He did *want* her. Did he not? Had she imagined the heat that seemed to scorch her skin whenever he looked at her?

If he ransomed her back to Honorius, she was done for.

Julia felt her hands clench into fists. He had refused her alliance; all that was left was seduction. She could admit last night hadn't been her most elegant attempt. But since when did a woman have to be *elegant* to seduce a man like that? He was a barbarian, was he not? Accustomed to taking what he wanted.

She would have to try again. Sober this time.

Dark had fallen by now. Alaric was still awake, sharpening that wicked curved sword of his while he kept watch; he looked like everyone's nightmare of raiding barbarians in the night come true. She felt a slash of fear. A man like that wouldn't be gentle. He would take what he wanted, use her as he liked.

A hot, explicit pulse bloomed between her thighs. Julia shifted uncomfortably on the ground. *Stupid body.*

It would work, she told herself. Did men not fall at her feet? Cornelius had.

And he had died for it. Julia felt a stab of sudden, crippling guilt.

She shoved it away. *Think*, she told herself. *How should it be done?* She was a princess of Rome. She would not simply crawl under his cloak like a camp follower. But—there was a river, between the trees. It would be the perfect place for a seduction. Moonlit and private.

Julia rose to her feet. Alaric's gaze fell to her and for a moment she couldn't move as he lazily perused every inch of her. She *felt* it, a wave of heat that ignited an answering burn beneath her skin.

Oh yes. He wanted her. He did. This would work.

She turned and started walking through the trees.

The water broke the moon's reflection into a thousand shards of silver. Soft mosses cushioned her footfalls. It was a very *mythological* place. She would have chosen a perfumed bed for her first time, piled high with silks and cushions. But this would do.

Her throat was suddenly dry with terror.

Julia had always been aware of the effect she had on men. They blushed and stammered and averted their eyes, made fools of themselves to gain her favor. Of course, her body would be pledged as her father willed, and if she turned up pregnant before marriage, *that* was a dire offense. In addition, her mother's death in childbirth still gave her screaming nightmares.

None of that prevented her from taking lovers, of course. But she had always chosen very carefully: men like Cornelius, sweet and biddable and easily controlled. Men so grateful for her favor that they would never dare transgress beyond what was offered.

Which was to say that the princess with the reputation for or-
giastic revelry was still, technically, a virgin.

Alaric was completely unsuitable to share her bed, of course.
If she'd ever met a man like him at court, she'd run in the opposite direction. But now she needed *his* favor. It was all so terribly unfair. Would it hurt, the first time? Not with a considerate
lover, but Alaric would surely be a brute.

Stupid. What did it matter if it hurt? Starving on Pandateria
would hurt worse.

Julia eyed the sluggish water with trepidation. There were
probably snakes and bugs and *eels* in that water. This was the
furthest thing from her seduction of Cornelius. There was dirt
under her nails and her hair was long and loose and tangled,
crusted with something she shuddered to name. Her gown was
a torn, soiled wreck. She had no *armor*.

Julia sighed. She knew what had to be done, and she did not
want to. Did not *want* to go into the river and rise from it nude,
hair streaming wet down her back. She would keep her gown
on. It was silk; it would cling.

Julia dipped a toe into the water and flinched. It was *freezing*.
Hopefully the barbarian warlord would at least concede to do
the deed on the bank.

The bottom of the river was thick with mud that squelched
between her toes. Julia waded into the river up to her thighs.
Then—missing *nothing* in the world so much as her clean, *heated*
baths at home—she sank into the water, up to her breasts, and
waited.

And waited.

Really. Julia gritted her teeth. She was shivering violently
now. Was it possible he had misinterpreted her blatant invitation? Who did he think he was to make her wait?

Something cold and slimy brushed her feet. Julia leaped up
with a yelp.

When she looked back, he was leaning against a tree on the riverbank. Watching her.

"Is this elaborate performance for me? I'm honored."

Casually she stood, wringing out her hair like she'd seen Aphrodite do in a famous portrait. "What performance? I'm simply having a wash. You gave no orders not to."

He smiled faintly. "You don't strike me as the kind who follows orders."

"Very perceptive. I prefer to *give* the orders." Julia let her voice drop to a suggestive purr. "I will only obey a man worthy of commanding me." Slowly she began to walk toward him, trying not to slip on the treacherous river bottom.

His eyes were on her with the fierce attention of a wolf watching a wounded deer. Suddenly she was *extremely* aware of how her wet clothes stuck to her body.

"Is this what you want, woman?" There was a harsh edge to his voice.

He was so *direct*. Her face heated. "Does it matter what I want?"

"Yes, it damn well matters, *Julia*." He purred her name, a mocking edge to his voice.

Then he pulled off his tunic and stood before her, naked from the waist up. Her face went up like a bonfire. Julia had seen plenty of men's naked torsos before, but with the exception of gladiators, those had been very different from Alaric. In her circles, the smooth, slim perfection of youth was the ideal. No hint of vulgar excess.

Excessive wasn't how she'd describe Alaric; *magnificent* was more fitting. She saw a broad, muscular torso, hard from a lifetime wielding sword and spear, crossed with scars that only made him more breathtaking. The only thought she could summon was that everyone she knew had been wrong about male beauty. Completely wrong.

Suddenly she wasn't cold at all. She was burning in her own skin, and he hadn't even touched her.

Then he looked at her with a mocking turn of his mouth and tossed her his shirt. "Since you're down there, wash this."

She caught it on instinct. It smelled of man and horse and sweat. His laughter curled her toes in the riverbed and she had *never* hated anyone more.

"You—you *bastard*." She made as if to rip it in half.

"I wouldn't if I were you." He turned and started back to the camp. "And wash yourself while you're at it, Julia. There's vomit in your hair."

Alaric sat with his back to a tree, sharpening his blade while his men settled into sleep.

The image of Julia was burned into his mind, rising from the river like a ravaged goddess. Rich red hair tumbling down her back, just asking for a man to bury his hands in. Wet silk clinging to spectacular curves. He'd had to admire her commitment. That river *stank*. She'd slipped in the mud in her attempt to glide effortlessly to the bank.

He'd wanted her so much he *shook* with it.

How stupid did she think he was? Clearly she expected no better of him than to allow himself to be led about by his cock. It was insulting to the core. He'd been enslaved. He knew *exactly* what it was to offer his body to get what he needed. He would not be a target himself.

What a fucking lie. If Stilicho had marched his army along the riverbank behind him right then, he wouldn't have noticed. At least he'd had a good laugh, deflating that enormous pride of hers. The expression on her arrogant face when he'd tossed her his shirt had been worth a city's ransom.

Thorismund sat up in his cloak. "My watch, is it?"

"No. Keep sleeping." It was Thorismund's watch, but Alaric didn't mind. He wouldn't be able to sleep anyway.

After a while, Julia came crashing back, loud enough to wake the dead.

He smirked. "Well. Look who it is. You look like a drowned cat."

She held up his soaked shirt as if it were a dead animal. "I'm afraid I couldn't get the stench out, King of the Goths." She balled it up in her hands and tossed it at him.

He caught it lazily and stood to hang it on a branch. "Given up on seduction, I see." He couldn't resist stalking closer to her. Letting himself loom. "It looks like you used it to clean a latrine floor."

It was the air of quiet menace he used to put the fear into upstart warlords who needed a reminder of their place. Julia stared him down as if he was a recalcitrant servant. "And will I be allowed dry clothes? Perhaps you haven't noticed, this dress is silk." He'd noticed. "I've been wearing it for days. I tried and failed to *insurrect* in it. I saved your miserable life in it. And now, as you can see, it is soaked." Her shaking, he realized, wasn't all from fury. She was cold. "You will not make me sleep on the ground, wet from washing *your* shirt, in this ruined dress. Unless your grand plan to secure your homeland involves letting me die of cold before you can ransom me." She looked at him expectantly. "Well?"

Alaric's jaw clenched. There wasn't a single thing about this woman that didn't set his teeth on edge. She was in a temper now; her eyes flashed mercurial fire and a red flush spread down her neck. Perfect breasts pushed up against wet silk. Nipples hard through near-transparent cloth.

He sucked in a breath. *Fuck.*

"Hengist," he snapped over his shoulder, in Gothic. "Give her your extra shirt."

"I don't think it will fit."

"It'll serve," he said grimly. "Horsa. Your spare trousers."

When the boys handed her the folded clothes, Julia thanked them quietly. It surprised him. He didn't think the woman had an ounce of thanks in her.

She turned to him with one aristocratic brow arched. "That is a start to an apology. Now make me a bed to sleep in."

Did she just give him an *order*? Behind him, Riga and Thorismund were snickering. He was well within his rights to drag her into the woods and teach her respect with a stout switch. It would even be expected.

But there were other ways to do this. More amusing ways.

He crossed his arms over his chest and grinned. "Make *me* a bed, Julia."

"I'll do that when the Capitoline Hill turns into a giant dormouse and scampers off into the sunset."

"If that's how you want it." Alaric gave a bored shrug and crossed the clearing. As he passed, Riga grinned widely and Thorismund muttered something about the balls on that woman being the size of a Bactrian bull's. Alaric reached his pack and pulled out a length of rope.

Julia eyed him warily. "What are you planning to do with that?"

"One guess, woman." He turned back to her, rope coiled in his hand. "Annoying prisoners sleep bound."

How dare he?

There was nothing for it but to curse. Julia did so loudly and at length as she stomped off into the woods. And to think she'd been planning to offer him her virtue on a platter!

That man's half-naked body was a blight on coherent thought.

Julia gritted her teeth. *He didn't want her.* That made everything so much worse. *He* should be the one stunned to silence before *her*, as was the right and proper order of things. The rude barbarian rendered speechless before civilized beauty. Instead the world was upside down and he'd made her his *washerwoman*.

How *dare* he reject her? He'd ruined everything.

Julia stripped off the dress and pulled on the barbarian tunic and trousers, and almost wept in relief. They were warm. Dry. Not a day ago she'd have been scandalized to wear such garments. But now she felt nothing but relief to be clad as a barbarian boy. How far she had fallen already.

She hoped Alaric galloped into a thornbush and got himself impaled.

She set herself to gathering up boughs for his bed. The branches were heavy. One slid out of her arms, then another, rough bark scraping her hands. "Pluto's *stinking ass*," Julia announced to the trees. The very *idea* that she would have to make a bed for this man—that he would make her *touch* his *bed*—scorched her pride to ash.

His bed. Her skin flushed hot. She'd been shivering, but now she was uncomfortably warm, just thinking about herself in proximity to this man's bed. As she bent to retrieve the branches, her hand brushed against something that sent stinging pain up her arm. She yanked her hand back and peered into the shadows. A silvery-green clump of spiky leaves trembled in the undergrowth.

An idea took shape in her mind. A very stupid idea.

Everyone was awake now. Alaric gave the wildly giggling twins the next watch, and turned his attention to sharpening his sword. There wasn't a chance he would sleep.

His mind was full of Julia's hardened nipples under wet silk.

He tried to distract himself by cataloguing all the things that could go wrong from here to the mountains. They could be spotted at a checkpoint or rounded up in a Roman patrol. Speared on stakes along the Appian Way. And then what would happen to his people? Scattered and enslaved. The twins dead, or in servitude. Meanwhile the princess was crashing around in the forest, loud enough to scare away game for miles. At least he'd hear her if she tried to run.

Finally she strode into the clearing, arms full of bracken and a rebellious set to her jaw. The twins' oversize clothes did nothing to lessen her allure. With a glance, he indicated where she should arrange his bed; she kept her eyes lowered and did as she was told.

So she'd finally learned to fear him. *Good.* She'd walk all over a man she didn't fear.

The bed she had made was surprisingly comfortable. Alaric settled into it and folded his arms behind his head, watching the moving lace of branches overhead.

Sharing a horse with that woman all the way to the mountains was going to kill him.

Her body had been a soft, yielding temptation pressed against his own for the torturous length of a day. All he could think about was pulling her off the horse and laying her flat beneath him, burying his hands in all that bright hair and thrusting hard into her until the Romans came to put him on a cross. He let out a strained curse. Now he was aroused and ready as a gang of barbarian thugs about to sack a town. He could either put a stop to these thoughts or drag Julia into this bed with him. He rolled over onto his side, no closer to sleep.

A line of burning pain streaked up his arm.

Alaric leaped to his feet with a roar. In the fading light, he could see the stinging nettles woven among the darker green of birch and oak. *Treacherous woman.*

A twig snapped and he turned to see Julia standing at the edge of the woods, her delicious little mouth curved in a smug smile. *I did it*, that smile seemed to say. *What are you going to do about it?*

Alaric bit back a curse as he strode in her direction.

Julia stood rooted to the spot as Alaric stalked toward her, all towering, muscled fury. Her momentary satisfaction was completely erased by her terror. Of all her stupid ideas, this ranked as the stupidest.

He caught the front of her tunic in his fist and hauled her up against a tree. "I have been gentle with you, woman." His voice a lethal whisper, his hand curling around her throat. "I could stop."

He could break her neck with that hand and he looked like he wanted to. Julia held his gaze and tried not to show her fear. "I am worth more to you alive than dead and you know it."

"Are you?" His grip tightened, making her gasp. "I'm starting to believe you are far more trouble than you're worth."

Julia licked her lips and his gaze fell to her mouth; something savage gleamed behind his eyes. "Well? What are you waiting for?" she snapped. "If you're going to rape me, get it *over* with."

For an instant the air crackled between them and Julia knew for a fact he'd leave her bleeding and broken on the forest floor. Then he dropped his hand from her throat. His gaze raked over her with palpable contempt. "Woman, I wouldn't touch you with a barge pole."

He dragged her back to camp; then let her go abruptly and she staggered and fell, skinning her palms in the dirt. Julia looked up to see Alaric stalking toward her with a length of rope coiled in one hand.

She scrambled to her feet. "Don't you *dare*." Her eyes darted to his men. No rescue there; they'd nail her to a tree if he asked it. His hand closed on her wrist, and panic rendered her witless. She lashed out, barely striking a glancing blow before he had her spun around, her back pressed against the battle-hardened length of him. She twisted in his grip and he clamped one arm down across her rib cage, pinning her arms to her sides.

Julia trembled, overcome by the sudden closeness of his body. She could *feel* his heartbeat, thundering through her as if they were already joined. He was standing rigid as well, every muscle taut. Both of them breathing hard. "Don't make this difficult." His voice a lethal growl in her ear. "You'll only hurt yourself."

He started to loop the ropes around her wrists. It was the final insult. She'd been humiliated and rejected, manhandled and laughed at. Rage burned all sense to ash. "Eat filth and die, you *vermin*."

She lashed out with the panic of a cornered beast. Hands and legs and feet. A fierce battle, and they were falling in a tangle of limbs. Alaric twisted so he would hit the ground first; she landed flush against his chest, and his body was no soft landing. The force of it knocked the air out of her lungs and he rolled her beneath him. In an instant, Julia found herself on her back, Alaric straddling her hips; wild shadows streaked his face, beautiful as some avenging god come down to ravage the earth.

There was a furtive struggle. Everything she had, in a single burst of strength. He put an end to it quickly, locking her wrists to the bare ground above her head. "You brought this on yourself," he grated, tying her hands with quick, efficient movements. "I offered you freedom. I was merciful. You threw yourself at my feet and begged me to take you."

Her face went white-hot. "I didn't *throw myself*—"

Alaric's hand clamped over her mouth. He leaned down, the heat of his breath sending little shocks down her spine. "I don't give a damn if you find me *worthy* of obeying. You will obey me anyway. Understand?" Only when she gave a resentful nod did he take his hand from her mouth. He tightened the ropes at her wrists and ankles. When he was done, he rose and looked down at her, a pitiless glint in his ice-pale eyes. "Sleep well, Princess."

Humiliation had a *taste*, she realized. Hot and astringent at the back of her throat.

Alaric stalked to the other end of the clearing in a seething rage. His arm felt like it had been flayed to the bone, and a savage, violent lust still thundered through him.

If you're going to rape me, get it over with. It was a dire insult. Alaric had waded up to his neck in blood, for the Empire and against it, but he had never forced a woman to his bed in his life. Even so, there had been a moment when her little pink tongue had darted out to wet her lips and his control had come dangerously close to slipping.

He rummaged in his pack for his salve and spread it over the reddening rash, then ripped off a length of cloth from a spare tunic to wrap it.

Only when he finished did he glance up to see his men staring at him. *"What?"*

Thorismund spoke first. "We just watched you wrestle a woman to the ground and truss her up like a feast-day heifer."

"What did she put in your bed?" Hengist's eyes had gone moon-round. *"Nettles?"*

Horsa cracked his knuckles. "How will you punish her? Can *we* do it?"

"Nobody touches her. No one even *looks* at her. Is that clear?"

"You bungled your chances by that river," Riga said, slinging an arm around his shoulder. "Next time she makes an offer like that, try *not* tossing her your shirt to wash."

"Bring her a freshly killed rabbit," Thorismund added blandly. "It would work on me."

Now everyone was off in gales of laughter. Alaric didn't find it funny. "Since the lot of you would rather cackle like demented old women than check our perimeter, I'll do it myself." He rose to his feet. "Try not to bring our enemies down upon us with your laughter."

They were audibly ignoring that advice when Alaric tramped off into the woods, his mood blacker than ever. He traced a rough circle around their camp, moving swift and silent, then spiraled it outward. Nothing in the forest moved.

He made his circuit back to their camp, halting at the edge of the trees. His men had curled themselves up in their cloaks and gone to sleep; all but Riga, who had taken the next watch. Julia was still awake. Weeping. The muffled sound filled the clearing.

He didn't know how she'd managed to manipulate things so that he was the one with the burning arm and he still felt like the scoundrel.

It wasn't his watch yet, so he spread his cloak on the ground and tried to sleep. Julia lay with her back to him, and he couldn't stop staring at the long sweet curve of it; the high, tight rise of her ass. He wanted his hands on that ass, gripping hard enough to bruise as he spent all his violence inside her. He wanted to quiet her tears this way, surging endlessly into her, one hand fisted in her hair and his mouth at her neck. Alaric shifted uncomfortably on the ground. This was *Theodosius's daughter.* She didn't deserve even his own brutal form of comfort.

Alaric didn't mean to listen so closely for the fade of her weeping into silence, or to rise to his feet when he was sure she slept. He certainly had no intention of crossing the clearing to stand over her, staring too long at the vulnerable curve of her body on the ground, before spreading his cloak to cover her.

CHAPTER ELEVEN

Julia woke with her cheek pressed to the ground. Her entire body was stiff; her ribs felt bruised from the inside out. Her arms were tied at the wrist, and her legs at the ankle. She wrenched herself to a sitting position, and only then realized why she hadn't frozen to death in the night. A thick, warm cloak had been draped over her.

Alaric's cloak. It smelled of him; leather and pine trees and wide-open spaces.

It was hideously early. The day had that cursed gray dimness of dawn not yet risen. No one should be awake now. The men were already up and readying their horses. Alaric was across the clearing, adjusting the straps on his saddle, the burnished bronze of his hair glinting like barbarian treasure, despite the sad lack of sun. She hoped he fell in a ditch and broke his stupid, gorgeous neck. She rubbed her forehead with her bound hands.

Too bad Alaric was the only person who could save her from exile and certain death. That meant she *must* find some way to win him over. She had to. It was a matter of survival. This war of attrition had to end.

He hated her. And he had reasons. Her brother *did* try to arrest him at the banquet, and there was bad blood from his time as a *foederati* leader. Of course, her father had always been the soul of charity and Alaric was a treacherous, grasping bastard. Julia sighed. Seduction had not worked; she would *not* humiliate herself again.

What she needed were allies.

Julia watched the men saddling the horses. There were four, besides Alaric. The tall blond one, tattooed to his fingertips; the two dead-eyed boys. And a black-haired man with a patchy beard and a bowlegged roll to his step. A Hun. The very name sent a chill down her spine. The Huns were even more terrifying than the Goths.

One of these had to be the soft one.

Alaric started toward her, and Julia was once again struck by the sheer force of his masculine beauty. It was starting to feel like a personal insult, the way her body reacted to his. She kept her eyes resolutely focused on a spot beyond his shoulder as she braced herself for more contempt. But he only knelt beside her and offered a waterskin and another strip of dried meat.

"Best eat something," he said quietly. "You'll not get a chance again until nightfall."

This time she did not refuse. The strip of dried meat was surprisingly flavorful—but just as tough as the bottom of a boot. As she ripped into it, Alaric took out a knife and cut the ropes at her ankles. Then he stood, ice-blue eyes gleaming down at her. "Get up."

Rude. Julia rose to her feet, the blood rushing painfully into her cramped legs. He turned to walk away and she stared after him incredulously. "You forgot something, King of the Goths." She held up her bound hands.

He turned, and the smirk that flashed across his too-handsome face made her want to open his throat. "As long as my arm burns, your hands stay tied."

They rode hard. Alaric led his men through the lowlands, avoiding the port cities and the Roman roads. They passed towns burned out and crumbling, crops dead in the fields. Julia curled in his arms, her wrists tied in front of her. His arm throbbed through his shirt, but he gritted his teeth and ignored it. He had more important things to worry about.

Like the fact that they were being followed.

They weren't bandits or refugees. And they didn't sit their horses like the Roman cavalry. A lifetime at war had taught Alaric to trust his instincts; now every one was on fire. He'd roused them all before dawn; it felt dangerous to stay in a place so undefended. He veered west through thick forest and overgrown fields, circling back through a marsh and then making good time on a track leading due north that twinned the Roman road. Finally he tacked northeast and lost the pursuers behind a ridgeline.

Julia slept through most of it.

She was sleeping now, her cheek pressed into his chest, and Alaric gritted his teeth. He hadn't known sleeping on a horse was *possible*, let alone at a gallop. Her body pressed warm and trusting against his, her hair rising up loose in his face. Smell of roses and intoxicating woman. Making a mockery of his resolve.

It was taking every scrap of will he had not to reach up a hand to cup her breast, press his lips to the pulse at the base of her throat. She was a distraction past bearing, but he would have to bear it. Alaric had ridden countless miles with blood seeping into his shirt from some wound, fought and killed at the end of it. He knew how to block out pain. This was just another thing he could learn to block.

This time they wouldn't camp in the open.

It was only midafternoon, but the horses were blown and the men dog-tired. Alaric knew well enough that to lose a horse out here would be a death sentence. He chose for their resting place a tumbledown watchtower on a small hill. It was more visible than the deep-woods clearings, but also more defendable. Julia woke only when he cradled her down, more gently than she deserved.

She stood staring up at the ramshackle structure. "What happened here?" The diamond pattern of his chain mail was still livid on her cheek. "Was there a fire?"

"There was a war." The watchtower had been torched while they'd fought for the ridgeline three years ago. He'd been in the thick of it then, leading his infantry into the teeth of the Roman defense. He could still smell the blood in this place.

Julia glanced at him with open dislike. "So you did this."

Her gaze was a level ocean green, and for an instant he felt the dizzying pull of her, strong enough to sway him on his feet. Some devil made him give her a sharkish smile, all teeth and deadly promises. "I burned whole cities. This I left to my men."

"Civil of you, King of the Goths." Her tone was one of scathing courtesy.

This time he let himself lean close, his hand planted on the wall by her head. "It must be a strain on you, being so polite."

His attention caught on the delicate bones of her wrists. The skin beneath the ropes.

He caught her wrist in his hand and turned it. "Let go." Alaric ignored her. Instead he cut the ropes and cursed himself for his carelessness.

The weals were red and livid. He turned her wrists over gently, examining them. Soft, warm skin, delicate veins streaking beneath his fingertips. "Why did you not tell me?"

"There was a very good chance you'd make it tighter."

"Don't be a fool, Julia. Even a small wound like this can kill if the blood turns." He took out the stone jar; spread yellow salve on her wrists. He kept his touch perfunctory; still, he couldn't stop his body rising to the feel of her skin. "In future, you will tell me if you are hurt." Julia's eyes flashed and he bristled in annoyance. "The proper response is *thank you*."

"I don't need you to teach me manners."

His mind assailed him with vivid images of all he might teach her. "Someone should."

"Was there something else you wanted?"

You have no idea. "When I want something else, you'll know." He let his hands drop from her wrists; a clear dismissal. "Go."

She swept off into the tower as if she owned it. Alaric watched her thoughtfully. Those welts were deep and she must have been in pain. But she hadn't said a word of complaint.

His men were watching. Riga with a kind of knowing grin, Thorismund with barely concealed incredulity. "Something to say?" Alaric asked coldly.

"No." Thorismund took a slug from his wineskin. "Fuck no."

Riga kept his grinning mouth shut, which was its own kind of mercy.

"Thorismund, you've just volunteered to help me backtrack our trail." There was still plenty of daylight left. "You saw them?"

Thorismund nodded grimly. "Not bandits, by my reckon."

"No. I wager they're not long behind." He turned to Riga. "Keep the twins and the woman out of sight until I return."

The tower had half a wall missing and no ceiling. Julia wrapped Alaric's cloak around herself, still shaking from the brush of his fingertips against her wrists. She'd never thought a touch so light could be so searingly erotic. Never thought he was capable of gentleness.

Julia set her teeth. She did not have time for fantasies. The man would rather kill her in her sleep than look at her. She had allies to win over.

The twins had been avoiding her ever since that night in the tent. The other one—the Hun—seemed an improbable target. If there was anyone on earth who matched Alaric's own fearsome reputation, it was the Huns.

The tall blond one, then. Tattooed to his fingertips, long blond hair tied back with a leather thong. He was formidable-looking, kept to himself, and carried a huge double-sided axe. Julia couldn't believe that *he* was her likeliest bet. But moments later, he rode off with Alaric, leaving her alone with the murder twins and the Hun, who was building up wood for a fire.

Perfect. Her least likely targets.

After a few moments, the Hun glanced at the boys. "Is he gone?"

One of them checked through a doorway. "Long gone."

"Excellent." He set a spark to the kindling he'd piled on the cracked stone floor, and the boys sprawled loose-limbed beside him. "We'll have to kick this out when we're done. He's been impossible about the fires." He took out a leather bag and passed it to the nearest twin, who unscrewed the top and drank.

Julia perked up. "Is that wine?"

Three pairs of eyes turned to her. Her skin prickled.

But then all three broke into applause. "The woman of the evening!" The Hun laughed. "Well done with the nettles. I haven't laughed that hard in *years*."

"Did you see the look on his *face*?" One of the twins giggled. "I thought he would *kill* you."

"So did I." Her death seemed to strike them as hilarious. She looked at the twins. "I'm sorry I drugged you."

"You should be. Alaric will kill us both once we're back in Noricum." They seemed rather lighthearted about it.

"Come. You look like you need a drink." The Hun held out his wineskin. "Milk wine. We make it from our mares." It tasted slightly sour, but with a kick to it that warmed her limbs. Julia took a second sip, then a third.

The Hun's name was Riga. He was a mercenary, he told her

as he poured a handful of dried seeds into a metal plate set over glowing coals. He had joined Alaric on promises of plunder. Alaric had delivered on those promises many times over. Especially at Milan.

"I wasn't in town for the siege of Milan," Julia said, shivering. "But I heard about it. Bodies on pikes and severed heads in ball games. That sort of thing."

"A severed head makes a terrible ball," said Hengist. The quieter twin. "Too squishy."

"Only after a few days," his brother Horsa loudly contradicted him. "When it's fresh it has bounce."

"Did you hear of the impalings? That was me. I can make them live for days now." There was a gleeful note in Riga's voice—the tone of an expert craftsman, eager to share the machinations of his work. "I make the tips of the poles round, not sharp, so it moves the organs aside rather than piercing them. And then I send it up along the spine, so it won't—"

Hengist broke in with something quiet in Gothic.

"Nonsense. Any woman who puts nettles in Alaric's bed wouldn't be scared off by a few old corpses." He looked at her approvingly. "I've never *seen* a woman get under his skin like you do. Already I like you the best of all his women."

"I'm not one of *his women.*" Then—because she didn't want to know *at all*, but somehow she did—"Just how many women does that man have, exactly?"

Horsa and Hengist began a rapid-fire conversation in Gothic that involved multiple attempts to count on their fingers, and ended with Horsa turning back to her and saying triumphantly, "Countless."

"Impossible to count," Hengist added. As if that cleared it right up.

Julia rolled her eyes. "Numberless as the tall grasses. Boundless as the stars." *I'll bet they can't count past five.*

"Keep making him angry." Riga grinned. "Not because he likes it. Because *I* do."

"So long as the three of you promise to protect me from his wrath." Julia laughed.

Riga had been assembling a small metal stand as he spoke; now he stood it over the fire and rested the little dish upon it. The smoke turned white and pungent. Riga leaned over and wafted it toward himself with his hands. The boys followed suit with a practiced air. They all looked at her expectantly.

Well. If she couldn't get Blue Lotus out here, she might as well try the barbarian drugs.

Hours of laying false trails, riding past ramshackle towns and crops rotting in fields. No sign of pursuers. Alaric almost regretted it. He could have used a good fight.

When he returned to the tower, it was well into afternoon. Julia was laughing with the twins and Riga as if they were old friends. There was a kicked-out fire in the corner, and the tower smelled of the Hunnic leaf.

Fuck. They'd have been sitting ducks for anyone who'd bothered to attack. Julia barely glanced in his direction when he walked in; for some reason, that made him grit his teeth in irritation. *He* couldn't stop looking at *her*. He watched Julia laugh at something Hengist said. She lifted her hair off her neck, and he imagined striding across the tower and fisting a hand in that hair, tilting her head back, and devouring her whole.

He found a place on the other side of the tower and took out his spear to sharpen it.

"If you sharpen that spear any more, there won't be anything left of it," Riga remarked drily. The Hunnic mercenary sat cross-legged, stitching a repair into his worn scabbard.

Alaric looked down at the spear in his hands, the edge gleaming wickedly. Sharp enough to part skin like a sheet of silk. "Look to your own damn business."

"I wouldn't let her near anything sharp," Riga said in Hunnic, following his gaze. "She's mad enough to cut your throat, since last night."

"She wouldn't know which end of a dagger to stick in me."

"Oh? How is your arm?" Riga slid him a sidelong look, grinning.

Something behind him interrupted the conversation. It wasn't a sound; more a sound *beneath* the sound. A disruption in the tapestry of moving branches and birdsong and wind from the valley. For an instant Alaric went still, hands tight on the haft of his spear. Riga tensed with him, and across the tower the boys straightened, every sense alert.

Julia kept chatting merrily away, oblivious.

"You might as well stop lurking in the doorway, Thorismund." Alaric went calmly back to sharpening his spear.

A curse preceded Thorismund over the ruined threshold. "One of these days I'll take you by surprise."

"I can't even sneak up on him and I'm good at it." Riga grinned.

"My people have a long and proud tradition of sneaking. You insult my honor." Thorismund sat between them. "I followed the road south. There's nothing in that forest except us and feral pigs. If you want my opinion, that boy still hasn't figured his arse from his pisshole." As he spoke, Alaric's eyes strayed to Julia— arrested by the silvery chime of her laugh, bantering with the twins as they spread out bread and cheese on Thorismund's massive shield as if it were a table. Thorismund followed his gaze. "Little shits. They're eating food off it now."

Alaric suppressed his irritation. "I noticed you still haven't settled that."

"Do not shame me. I know it already. I have forsaken my

shield. I am no longer fit to stand beneath the halls of my fore-fathers."

"If it helps, the halls of your forefathers are nothing but glowing coals," Riga said.

"Same as all of ours," Alaric added.

"The two of you haven't an ounce of tact between you." Thorismund glanced darkly at the twins. "They can't even lift it, let alone fight with it. They're keeping it just to spite me."

Alaric rose to his feet. They couldn't afford these honor games. "I'll step in, then."

"No. *Wait*." Thorismund gripped his arm. "If my men get wind of it, they'll laugh into their tankards as I pass. They'd even compose songs about it. *Hilarious* songs. Completely at my expense."

"They already do that," Riga remarked.

"Get your shield back however you want, but get it back," Alaric said, his patience at its limit. "You're no good to me in a fight if you're underequipped."

Julia felt the weight of Alaric's gaze on her all the way across the tower.

It seemed advisable to ignore him. *What* murderous Gothic warlord in her tower? There was no murderous Gothic warlord in her tower.

A shadow blocked out the sun. It was the tall blond one with all the hair: Thorismund. "Get lost, Roman." He spit out the word like a mouthful of bloody teeth. "You little hooligans let me win back that shield. Or else."

Horsa grinned. "But I haven't carved my initials in it yet."

"You do that, and I'll skin you slow and make a coat of your weeping hide."

The three of them exchanged more warlike words and then

Thorismund stalked off, visibly enraged. Julia stared after him. "Is he always that eloquent?"

"He's found a new tongue since we won his shield," Hengist said darkly.

"He was *so drunk*." Horsa laughed. "He challenged Riga's horse to a duel."

"Can you fight with it?" Julia glanced curiously at the shield balanced on Horsa's knees. Elaborately carved, with the detailed image of an oak tree in the center.

"Not the point. We won it fairly. Besides, he's funny when he is angry."

"His face gets red as a slab of meat." Horsa smirked.

"You provoke a man twice your size who threatens to skin you alive, because it's *funny*?" They nodded, identical toothy grins on their faces. "You really are fifteen," she muttered.

It was easy to forget. Something ancient lived in the twins' eyes; it shocked her to think they were two years younger than Honorius. Julia tried to picture Honorius in the same room with Horsa and Hengist, trying to dredge up conversational topics while the twins picked at the sweetmeats. The thought of it made Julia laugh. The twins would slit her brother from throat to sternum, if Honorius didn't have them jailed for their insolence.

"Thorismund wouldn't skin us," Horsa was saying. "Not really."

"Riga would," Hengist added darkly. "Once he—"

The butt of Thorismund's spear crashed onto the ground before them. Julia gave a surprised little squeak. "Alaric's orders, pigshits," Thorismund said. "Play me, or fight me."

Thorismund couldn't play *latrones* worth a goddamn. Julia sat with her knees curled up to her chest, watching him make mistake after obvious mistake. At first, she tried to help, quietly making suggestions; he brushed her off like a fly until she went.

Fine, she thought, retreating to her corner, wrapped in Alaric's cloak. Alaric was engaged in a low-level argument with Riga, and the twins were busy batting Thorismund around the board with predatory glee. She fell asleep and when she woke, the sun was setting and everyone was wrapped in their cloaks on the broken ground.

Except Alaric. Alaric was gone.

Julia sat up. She'd fallen asleep with Riga's wineskin under her head like a pillow, and there was still alcohol in it. Gratefully she took a swig. Warmth pooled in her limbs and she rose, looking automatically for Alaric.

She couldn't say why she felt uneasy in his absence, as if she were safer under his fierce blue gaze than away from it.

Alaric stalked the rim of the tower. Below, a small boy was herding a flock of straggly sheep. Dark-haired and of indeterminate parentage, he couldn't have been more than six, kicking dirt clods as he walked, not bothering to hide himself. Alaric barely remembered his parents, but he knew he'd have been beaten bloody for being this careless. Even at this boy's age.

Aside from the boy, nothing moved on the horizon. Alaric didn't like it. Stilicho ought to be breathing down his neck right now.

Scrape of boot against stone behind him, and a whispered curse. *Wonderful.* "What do you want, woman?"

Julia came to stand next to him, leaning against the parapet. She smelled of liquor, and under it, roses. It was strange, that haunting scent; beneath the sweat and mud of travel and the brackish water she'd bathed in, it seemed to live in her skin.

She took a swig from a wineskin. Riga's. Apparently she was pilfering liquor from *all* his men. "Do you never sleep?"

"Someone has to keep watch."

"You'd be in a better mood if you slept." She proffered the

wineskin. He declined. "Suit yourself." She took another swig and gazed at him as if trying to read the future in his face.

"I am not some curiosity to boggle at. What is it you want?"

"Are you this damnably rude with everyone, or am I simply blessed?"

"Do you always find your courage at the bottom of a wineskin?"

Her eyes flashed green. "It's really quite remarkable. You've been cursed with an *excruciating* personality. No wonder you're such an unpredictable element at parties." She took another drink. "This liquor is truly a marvel. Did you know the Huns make it from their mares?"

Irritation tightened his jaw. "You asked me to kidnap you at that party."

"It *was* getting rather boring." She looked at him through her lashes. "I was the one who tried to poison my brother at that banquet, you know."

She said it as if imparting a secret to a chosen friend. So *she* was the one who'd nearly gotten them all killed. Strangely, he wasn't angry.

There was an invitation here. Intrigue warred with irritation. A tiny smile played at her mouth and he felt a sudden, ruinous urge to lean over and kiss it off her.

He would regret opening this door. "Why?"

"You met Olympius. You saw how odious he was."

"I saw a man sick with want for you. One of the richest men in the Empire. If you had wanted to be empress, why not persuade *him* to use his riches to bribe Stilicho's legions?"

"I'd rather put out my own eyeball than ask Olympius for anything," she said bitterly.

"So you attempted insurrection because you didn't like your engagement."

"As if *you've* never wreaked havoc to preserve your freedom.

You've done rather a lot of it over the years. We've been riding through your wreckage all day, after all."

His temper rose. What right had *she* to judge his actions? "Do you honestly think we haven't tried anything else?" he growled. "It's because of your father that my people haven't had a permanent place to live in a generation. It was *your* father who put us in refugee camps, hoping to starve us down to nothing. Who enslaved us wherever we tried to sit still. Those of us who survived learned that the only way to live was to be the strongest. So all my people know how to do is pillage. All *I* know how to do is pillage. That is who I am."

"And so your people slaughter mine, and mine slaughter yours, and there's no hope of stopping it." She glanced away, across the moldering countryside. "Have you noticed what we've been riding through? Farms ruined and abandoned, the countryside emptied. It's almost summer and hardly anyone has bothered planting. And it's unseasonably dry." She stared out into the dark, her brows drawn down; suddenly serious. "I could *fix* this, you know. I could shore up the infrastructure and increase the grain dole and actually *do* things. I could help your people and mine, if we could only trust each other."

He gritted his teeth. She sounded—almost fucking *earnest*. For a moment he was assaulted by a wave of something strange and powerful—lust, but something else beneath it. *Protectiveness*.

That urge to kiss her became almost too strong. He could do it now—kiss her and kiss her and never stop.

He curled his hands into the edge of the parapet. "No. My answer is final."

"Nothing is final, King of the Goths." She pulled the hood of her cloak—*his* cloak, damn it—up over her head. "I'll be waiting if you change your mind."

And then she was gone, picking her way down the crumbling stairs.

CHAPTER TWELVE

As the moon rose, Alaric led his group across a bare, muddy field at a flat-out gallop, crossing trackless wastes with the night sky wheeling overhead. Lonely grain silos and tumbledown farmhouses cut haunted outlines against the stars.

I could help your people and mine, if we could only trust each other.

It had been five days since then and Julia was feigning sleep again, pliant in his arms as they sped across the wasted countryside. Alaric could not stop a single thing he felt. Not his body's ferocious reaction to her, nor the protectiveness that came roaring up just as fierce as his lust.

He'd been careful to avoid conversation with her since that night on the tower. He didn't need to know that she hated her brother as much as he did. Didn't need to understand that she'd tried and failed to live under Roman law, as much an outlaw as he was.

It almost didn't matter, though. She seemed to lose interest in him after that night—turning her attention to his men. The past few days, Julia had set herself to winning them over like a general on campaign. With the twins, she was playful and free with her laughter; to Riga, she offered rapt attention and smiles that could melt stone. All while setting her back to him, turning her face from him, speaking with reserved formality when she spoke to him at all.

Whatever she was doing, it appeared to be working. Alaric couldn't take his eyes off her now. The little glimpses of skin, the hot little glances when she thought he wasn't looking. In the end, it *wasn't* his men that worried him. No; what worried him were his own feelings. The wild, possessive, violent feelings that ripped through him whenever she laughed like that, free and unguarded and never for him.

Only Thorismund remained unwon. Thorismund whose people, the Batavi, had found their end under Roman rule, after long decades of service. He trusted the Romans less than Alaric did.

"She's trying to get under your skin," Thorismund growled one night, following Alaric's gaze across another clearing as he sharpened his axe in the fading light. He'd noticed Alaric's staring problem. They all had. "Watch yourself."

Alaric gritted his teeth. Once he reached the mountains, he'd take up with Brisca again. Or whatever willing woman would have him, if she wouldn't.

At some point between dark and dawn, it rained, soaking them all to the bone. Alaric was wet and exhausted and *angry* at his body's unrelenting response to Julia, while she slept blissfully on, unknowing.

And then Hengist's horse turned up lame.

Terrible luck. Alaric pulled them to an abrupt stop at a wide place in the trail. This was one of the most dangerous stretches of their journey. Aquileia thirty miles north. A military road not a hundred paces east. The city ahead was overrun with bandits, and that meant these woods would be too. But that wasn't the only reason Alaric didn't like this place. Three years ago, it had been a killing field. The past was thick on the ground here, like fog.

Julia stirred in his arms. "Must we stop? I was having a pleasant dream."

"I'm sorry to interrupt your nap." He helped her down off the horse. "Some of us have more important things to concern ourselves with. Such as keeping us all alive."

Hurt flickered across her face just before the mask of self-possession snapped into place. "Perhaps it escaped your notice that it rained last night and I didn't get a minute of sleep."

"Perhaps it escaped *your* notice that it rained on all of us." She still wore his one goddamn cloak and *he* was soaked to the skin. "You got more sleep than anyone else. Sleep appears to be the only thing you're good at."

There was no mistaking the hurt in her eyes. Immediately he felt like a villain. He was cold and exhausted and on edge from the constant vigilance and the unrelenting, ferocious lust that held him in its grip; none of that excused what he had said.

"Impeccable manners as usual, King of the Goths." She was looking at him with the cool impassiveness of a marble wall. An apology was ready on his tongue, but he couldn't quite make himself say it.

"Stay here," he muttered, securing his horse. "Don't do anything stupid."

Across the clearing, Hengist stood next to his tough little Hunnic mare, Bura. "How long have you known she was lame?" Alaric asked.

"Maybe a mile back."

"Then, you should have told me a mile ago." Alaric cast a worried eye over the sturdy brown mare as Riga examined her left front foreleg.

"It's a stone bruise," Riga said, straightening. "She needs rest and a poultice."

And I need a saddle-broke harpy to fly us to Noricum. "Can she make it to the mountains?"

"She's a Hunnic pony. Tougher than old hide. She'll go far, if we don't run her into the ground."

Alaric let out a low curse. "We don't have time to coddle her."

"Better make it quick, then." Riga took out his curved knife.

Hengist went rigid. "Wait, Riga," Alaric said, pulling the boy aside. "You knew what might happen," he said quietly.

"We don't have to kill her. Leave her here. Give her a chance."

"A chance to be eaten by wolves or captured by the Romans? Death would be kinder."

Hengist kept his eyes stonily on the ground. "Better I do it, then."

Alaric's jaw tightened. He could almost hear Gaufrid at his back, cursing him for letting it come to this. Hengist had his knife in his hand now and was looking over his shoulder at the mare he'd taught to come running when he whistled, a resigned steel in his face.

"Put your knife away, Hengist." Riga could have done it cleaner anyway. "You'll ride with your brother, and we'll take her riderless as far as the mountains. Then we'll see."

The sound of Julia's laughter ripped through him. He glanced across the clearing to see her talking to Horsa over Hannibal's back as his horse nuzzled at her pockets.

Alaric gritted his teeth. Hannibal was a vicious warhorse, an animal who crushed the heads of the enemy beneath iron-shod hooves. Hannibal did not *nuzzle*.

Julia reached into her pocket and fed his horse a wrinkled apple, she and Horsa speaking low and easy as old friends. It was irritating past bearing; Hannibal seemed to be attempting to climb *into* her pocket at the moment. Her eyes skated over to him from beneath lowered lashes, and there was a calculating gleam amidst all that blue and green.

She knew exactly what she was doing.

From the corner of her eye, Julia watched Alaric place a hand on the mare's haunch and run it down her leg to check for lameness, speaking to her all the while; low and tender and hypnotic.

She was suddenly, *blindingly* jealous of a horse.

"I'll only be a few moments," she said in an urgent whisper to Horsa over Hannibal's broad back. "Please."

Horsa looked skeptical. "What for?"

Julia sighed. Was it too much to say she wanted to be somewhere, just for a moment, where Alaric was not in her sight? Last night when exhaustion had gotten the better of her, she'd leaned against him; his arms had closed around her, drawing her in. She had never felt so safe. She'd laid her cheek against his beating heart and fallen asleep to a fantasy where Alaric of the Goths *cared* whether she fell off a horse and dashed her head open on a rock.

She blamed herself. It was entirely stupid to entertain such fantasies. He'd made that clear this morning.

Hannibal crunched his apple happily, torquing his neck around to nuzzle at her pockets as he did—smearing a thick froth of green foam on her hip.

Of course, there were plenty of other reasons to want privacy. *To wash.* She could smell her own filth. There was a stream not far back in those trees; they'd ridden through it. "*Woman* things, Horsa. Do I have to be specific?"

"You realize Alaric will put my head on a pike if you go wandering off. He's still angry at me for letting you poison me."

Julia rolled her eyes. "He's a tyrant."

"I *know*." For a moment they looked at each other in shared exasperation. Horsa glanced uneasily across the clearing. "Just as far as that tree over there. Hurry."

The tree wasn't far enough, and the stream was farther back than she remembered, across an overgrown road. Julia washed her hands and face and neck, and did her best to clean her hair.

She was just about to go back when she spotted the blueberry bush. Her stomach gave an emphatic growl.

Alaric was in a terrible mood already. If she lingered too long, he'd make her regret it. *Maybe not if I bring him some.* He'd give his share to everyone else out of sheer perversity. But maybe the freeze in his eyes would warm, just a little.

It was her last coherent thought before she fell upon the bush like a starving wretch.

When she'd stripped it bare, she sat back on her heels. She hadn't been planning to eat *all* of them. But she'd had nowhere to put them so she'd just put them in her mouth, and then her hands and shirt were stained purple and her arms were scratched to the elbows. She wiped at her face and only managed to make herself stickier. She could not go back like this. Everyone would know what she'd found, and that she hadn't shared.

Julia went back to the stream; plunged her hands in and scrubbed. She was almost done when she noticed the berry stain on her shirt. Hurriedly, she stripped it off. Soon she wore nothing but the barbarian breeches and the strip of silk she'd ripped from her gown; a makeshift *strophium* to hold her breasts. She put the shirt in the water and began to scrub furiously.

The stain wasn't coming out. She needed a stone to beat it against. The closest thing was a pale, round one by the bank, about the size of a melon. Maybe if she washed the moss off it—

She picked it up, then dropped it with a stifled scream. It fell and rolled, landing face-up; a plump worm crawled through one gaping eye socket. Julia gave a yelp and staggered back, tripping on the rough ground. She landed in a cluster of curved sticks that were not sticks.

Then she began to scream in earnest.

The scream made Alaric's heart seize in his chest. His war spear was with the horses, but his blade was in his hand. He ran down the wooded slope as he had three years ago, the forest thick with enemies, his weapon drenched in blood.

The sight of Julia, lying on the ground and wearing almost nothing, jerked him back to the present. She scrambled to her feet as Alaric slid to an abrupt stop. Her little pink nipples pushed up against a transparent shred of binding silk; above it, the swell of her breasts begged to fill his hands.

Slowly he closed the distance between them. *Gods*, he wanted her. Wanted to push her up against the nearest tree and trail hot, open-mouthed kisses across the tops of her breasts, then unwind that silken band and take each of her nipples in his mouth. One and then the other.

When he got close enough, he leaned down—careful and deliberate; holding himself in absolute check—and picked up her shirt. Their eyes met when he handed it to her. An intense, kinetic hush fell between them and he knew. She felt it too.

She took the shirt and turned away, striking him utterly silent with the sleek, pale sight of her naked back. "Spying, King of the Goths?"

It was the last insult. Once she had *invited* his presence. "What do you fucking *think*, Julia. You screamed loud enough to bring a forest's worth of bandits down on our heads. Do our lives mean *nothing* to you?" He sucked in a ragged breath. "What the hell were you screaming at?"

"That." She pointed to a scraggly pile of bones. "It's a skeleton," she informed him, as if he couldn't see well enough for himself. "And there's a skull. I'm afraid I *touched* it."

"That's to be expected, since you went frolicking off in the middle of a battlefield." He was in no mood to coddle her. "Look around you. This place is full of the dead."

She did, with dawning horror. Gape-mouthed skulls, neat lines of vertebrae; tangles of ribs and jawbones covered by a mossy scrim. "You could have *warned* me."

"And when would I have done that? Before or after you went blundering off like a damn useless fool?"

"Useless!" Fury colored her cheeks. "I got you out of Ravenna alive, with a king's ransom. I'm *hardly* useless."

"You need a legion's worth of slaves just to wipe your arse, woman!"

"And you worry about *me* bringing bandits down on our heads. You'll bring a whole legion with your shouting." A hard, hurt little smile curved her lips. "You truly hate me, don't you? Just say it."

"I don't—" He drew a ragged breath. "I don't hate you, Julia."

"Liar," she spat. "Everything I do makes you angry. When I'm quiet and when I speak. When I keep to myself and when I don't. I even irritate you when I sleep."

Tears glinted in her eyes. Alaric's instincts demanded that he make it right in any way he could. It took every shred of control to keep his hands to himself. "And so?" The words were bitter on his tongue. "You hate me just as much."

"No," she said quietly. "I don't."

That was a fucking shock.

A noise at his back. Sound beneath the sound. Disturbance in the air.

He pulled her into his arms, clamping a hand on her mouth and dragging her behind the nearest tree just as a long line of men came marching around the bend in the road. Julia went utterly still. Her scent was roses and blueberries, sweat, and under it, a heady mix of desire and fear. It filled the whole damn world. Meanwhile death marched past, close enough to hit with a lazy spear-throw.

He could have lost her. Would have, if she'd screamed a moment later. If he'd been just a breath too slow.

The wave of intense, possessive lust that came roaring up in him this time almost put him on his knees. Stronger than when he'd first seen her in that alley and wanted her *now*, up against the nearest building, any way he could have her. Stronger than that night when she'd offered herself to him on the riverbank, while he fought off his instincts with everything he had. He couldn't resist it anymore. There was no point in resisting anyway.

Alaric gave in and laid his lips against the smooth column of her throat.

His touch was whisper soft, like his fingertips on her wrists but far more potent. His mouth against her neck turned her blood to smoke.

Julia shut her eyes. At her back, an avalanche held in harrowing check. A predator, caressing her jugular with its fangs.

"Suppose they found you before I did." His body so close and his voice so low that she felt the words rather than heard. "What do you think would have happened to you, had I not reached you first?" His hand clamped down hard on her mouth, silencing her answer. "There are no princesses in these woods, only predators and prey."

With agonizing slowness, he traced a fevered line up from her shoulder with his lips. Every so often he breathed in as if devouring the scent of her.

"I'd kill every one of them who saw you naked by that stream."

Then he laid his mouth against the place where her jawline met her neck.

Her body gave a hard, insistent pulse and Julia tilted her head to give him better access. A clear sign of acquiescence. Alaric made a sound like a satisfied *thrum*, deep in his chest, that drew an answering heat from between her legs.

Then his arms dropped away and her back hit rough bark.

Alaric stood above her, watching the last of the soldiers disappear around the bend, as if he hadn't just reduced her to tears one minute and helpless, insensible desire the next; murmured death threats in her ear in between. He flicked a glance over her and his eyes turned a shade cooler. The look she gave him back was perfectly calibrated: irritation mixed with boredom. "If you're done slavering on my neck, King of the Goths—"

"Where did you find the blueberries, Julia?" He slid his hand along the line of her jaw and closed his fist in her hair; tilted her head to the side. "You missed a spot."

He put his mouth on her neck again, and suddenly there was nothing in the world but the scorching drag of his tongue on her throat and the sweet, aching pain of his hand in her hair. Julia lost herself. Arched up to him and tilted her head back and made a desperate, mewling noise that made him laugh against her neck.

She was beside herself by the time he was done with her. Practically crawling out of her skin with desire.

He drew back, his thumb tracing the place where lips and tongue had been; his lightest touch sending little shocks of pleasure through her. "The next time you find those, you'll share."

CHAPTER THIRTEEN

That patrol had been no accident. All the roads were watched now.

Alaric suspected that Roman patrol must have doubled back and found some sign of them. He counted the *ifs* as he moved through the ravaged countryside. If the horse hadn't gone lame. If they hadn't stopped so close to that road.

If Julia hadn't been so damn *distracting*.

The land was parched as death here; all the springs had run dry and the rivers moved sluggish in their beds. Alaric rode through plains of brittle grass that rattled against his horse's legs like finger bones. All he had to do was keep them out of Roman hands for another few days. But the closer they drew to the mountains, the harder that became.

And sometimes, on the horizon, he caught a glimpse of riders following. Riders who weren't bandits and weren't Roman patrols.

It took three more days to reach the temple sanctuary.

The place was exactly where Alaric remembered it, on a rise at the foot of a cliff. Three terraced levels of porticoes, all of it sacked and left to rot. Already the forest was taking it back; ivy blanketed the tumbled marble statues, leaves dry and rattling in the wind.

They tied the horses at the foot of the sanctuary, where a spring overspilled a marble trough. Alaric let Hannibal drink deep, as the men stripped their horses and rubbed them down. They moved slower than they should; the horses' heads hung low and their ribs moved in and out like bellows.

"We should've kept moving," Thorismund grumbled as he wrung out a damp cloth on the back of his neck. "We'd reach the mountains in two days if we ride hard."

"Thorismund, we've got one lame horse and the borders are heavily patrolled. If we tried to slip through now, we'd never make it."

Riga shouldered his recurved bow down from his saddle and tested the string against his thumb. "What if they come to us?"

"The enemy can only approach from south or east," Alaric said, pointing with his sword. "We'll see anyone approaching from miles off."

"Plenty of shelter for sniping," Riga said.

"I'll have the boys pile up slingstones." He reckoned two deadeye slingers could hold this place against a *contubernium*, at least. He picked up his *seax* and war spear.

"You're going to lay false trails, aren't you?" Thorismund frowned. "Don't be a fool. You're as dead on your feet as the rest of us."

"Someone has to do it."

"You're of no use to us if you get skewered on the end of some Roman pike."

Alaric sighed. This argument was recurring. "Stay here, Thorismund. I need you and Riga to keep unrelenting watch." A moment of inattention could be their death out here. "I'll be back before dark."

Julia huddled in the shadow of a crumbling temple, trying to keep warm in the wind.

Alaric had said that it would take two days' hard riding to get to the border. But now they were taking shelter, and Julia was impatient. She wanted to be free of Italy. Free of Stilicho. Once those threats were gone, she had only one—the threat of Alaric sending her back.

If only she knew how much progress she was making with him. Since Hengist's horse had gone lame, Alaric had barely spoken to her beyond basic commands. *Eat this. Get up. Go to sleep.* Even so, Julia was primally aware of the weight of his gaze, hot and hungry on her wherever she went.

Was she winning, or not? The man was mercurial as a war elephant.

In the past few days, their travel had turned even more brutal. Alaric had them moving fast over rough ground at night, stopping only for brief rests during the day. There were times Julia felt they were doubling back or waiting for something to happen. Sometimes Alaric would hold up a hand and listen; once he made everyone veer off trail and take a route that was near invisible. Once Riga disappeared into the trees and returned hours later with blood on his knife.

Now they had stopped in this mysterious place, with no explanation, and Julia felt the bite of impatience. She did not have endless time.

Riga was nearby, tending the mare that had gone lame. Her ears were delicate, her eyelids fringed with long, curved lashes. "Will she be all right?"

"Perhaps." Riga straightened. "How is your campaign progressing, Princess?"

Riga saw everything. "Am I that transparent?"

"Not so transparent as Alaric is. This is the most entertainment I've had in years."

Julia resisted the urge to roll her eyes. Riga struck her as the kind of person who would gleefully watch a chariot crash just to see the mangled limbs. Still, he might have knowledge she could use. She smiled, conspiratorial. An invitation. "If I *really* wanted to get under his skin…"

"Solve a problem for him. *That* will grate on him."

He was right. Alaric thought her useless; if she could prove him wrong in a way that would make him grateful—he would hate it. But he would be beholden to her. Perhaps she could use that against him. It *was* rather diabolical.

Now if she only knew *what* problem—

A bellow caught her attention. Across the temple, Hengist and Horsa sat atop an ivy-covered wall, Thorismund's massive shield between them, giggling wildly. They appeared to be trying to carve their initials into it.

Thorismund stood at the foot of the wall, bellowing. Julia winced as he swung his massive two-handed axe and threw it in their direction. The boys ducked and fell over laughing.

"Is he *trying* to kill them?"

"If he can get his hands on them," Riga said blandly. "He lost prestige by losing his shield to them in a bet, and he loses more by failing to win it back. Alaric doesn't like these honor games. He thinks it's a needless distraction." His eyes gleamed mischief. "If you solved *this* problem for him, it would be a kick in the teeth."

Thorismund was now trying to climb the wall. Julia shuddered. "Do you think he'll kill *me*?"

"Maybe." Riga produced a wineskin. "Drink?"

Julia took a swig and suddenly she wanted to see the look on Alaric's obnoxiously handsome face when she succeeded. Which she would, of course. She sucked down more of the milk wine and then slapped the wineskin back into Riga's hands. "Hold this for me, will you?"

Then she was off, striding toward disaster.

Thorismund in a rage was all muscle and menace, his torso a rippling wall of tattoos and battle scars. He roared something murderous in Gothic as the boys jeered with their teeth bared and knives gleaming, and then he leaped at the wall. His fin-

gertips just barely brushed the bottom of Hengist's boots. He
fell back, fury in every line of his body.

Julia had no idea where she found the courage to place herself between them.

"Stop it. *Stop.*" She put her hands on her hips and faced down
Thorismund, who eyed her like an insect he wanted to stomp
flat. "What are you going to do if you reach them? Hack off
their heads? What do you think Alaric will say about that?"

"He'll say they had it coming."

"He'll be angry. He's insufferable when he's angry." She drew
a breath. "Let me win back your shield."

His face reddened to the neck. "My honor will not allow it."

"Are you under the delusion that you can win it back yourself?"

"My honor will not escape the stain if rumor spreads that I let
a Roman win my battles. A *woman* at that." He spat the words.
"And they will. The twins won't keep their mouths shut."

"What about the stain to your honor if you fail to win your
shield back from a pair of shrieking hooligans?" Julia asked
mildly. "*I'll* spread a rumor myself that I did you a favor because
you saved my life in a courageous fashion."

"That would be a lie."

"Yes, Thorismund. That's the idea." Julia turned to the twins.
"The two of you will play *me* for that shield. If I lose, keep it.
Carve your names in it for all I care." She turned to Thorismund. "As for *you*, you can ride home with your shield on your
arm, or not. Your choice."

Thorismund's expression darkened. He appeared to be reaching for his knife.

She gave an unflappable shrug. "Suit yourself. I look forward
to seeing your further humiliation. It *has* been quite entertaining." She walked back toward Riga, who was openly laughing.

Three. Two. One.

"Wait," Thorismund said at her back.

The land was crawling with patrols. Alaric barely avoided being caught. It was after dark when he returned to the ruined temple by one of the hidden ways, in case he was being followed. But as he approached, he saw that all of his caution had been for nothing. All the patrols had to do was look up.

Despite his commands, the idiots had lit a fire.

Alaric halted among the broken columns and watched the smoke drift into the darkening sky. What he ought to do was berate them for not keeping careful watch and this needless indulgence of a fire.

But then he caught sight of Julia, and didn't feel at all like doing what he ought to.

They were gathered around the twins' *latrones* board—and Julia appeared to be *playing*. She had her chin in her hands, concentrating fiercely. Riga said something that made her burst into laughter—not the hard, brittle laugh of the Imperial Princess, but guileless and clear as wind chimes. It ripped right through him. He couldn't take his eyes from that guileless girl.

Perhaps he would let the fire go. Just this once.

Despite his better judgment, Alaric propped his shoulder against one of the columns and watched Julia play *latrones*.

She was good at it. That surprised him, because *latrones* was a military game. Good players had to see seven steps ahead, to think around corners. He'd taught the twins during a grindingly boring stretch of time while he laid siege to Verona, thinking to teach them war this way, as Stilicho had once taught him. They took to it, cutting a large swath through his army. They were legendary by the time that siege was through.

And Julia was holding her own against them.

More than holding her own. *Who the hell taught her to play?* Beside her, Thorismund hulked by the fire, occasionally emitting a disapproving *huff* or a guttural curse when the game swayed one way or another. Riga laughed and drank and taught Julia curse words in Hunnic, which she lobbed at the twins as she played. Her brittle court polish had dissolved, and what was underneath was sharp and brilliant and feverishly alive.

Hours passed and soon it was fully dark. It was taking all of Alaric's considerable patience not to shove the twins out of the way and win the game for them.

His attention was now wholly focused on the *latrones* board. The boys could've won the game three moves ago if they'd held some of their pieces in reserve. Then she'd have no recourse but to divide her strength.

Horsa chose that moment to hurl ribald invectives in Gothic; Julia parried with cool disdain in her high-palace Latin as she gutted his vanguard. He could see the shape of the pieces on the board; Julia's formation falling in from the edges like a besieging army. If the boys would only retreat three spaces to the right now, where her defenses were weakest—

But no. The boys surged ahead, as they always did.

Julia played like a Roman, in the rigid style he'd learned from Stilicho. The twins favored a more freewheeling technique popular in his own camps; it should have been the antidote to Julia's method, but not with a player at her level. The air became hushed; soon even Riga was focused on the game.

Then she began losing. The boys picked off one piece, then another. Thorismund began a steady stream of heartfelt cursing, interspersed with threats.

Deliberate losses. She was up to something.

Alaric had to stare at the board for long minutes before he spotted her trap. Neat and ingenious, a self-contained spider at the center of a web. He almost laughed aloud as she slowly opened a channel for them, lulling them into a false sense of security. Alaric was transfixed by the way her brows gathered in when she thought. Her lips curved in a tiny, secret grin that tugged at his gut like a swallowed fishhook.

Then she closed her trap.

Thorismund let out a hoarse shout. The boys broke off to confer, and for a moment they almost got a vanguard through— opening a new channel that should have had her spurting blood. That was when she flanked them. Alaric couldn't keep the grin off his face as the game devolved. Horsa and Hengist staring in identical shock while Julia scooped up their pieces in an elegant series of closing moves. She'd won.

And then she was surrounded. Thorismund pulling her to her feet, pounding her on the back like a companion in battle. Riga leaning in to tell her something that made her laugh in delight. Even the boys joined in, and Alaric had to clench his teeth against a surge of jealousy.

He wanted that laughter. Wanted to bottle it up tight and keep it for himself.

"You did well." He came out of the shadows. "Who taught you to play?"

"My father. He used to let me play his generals when I was a girl."

It was a crack in her armor he couldn't resist probing. "Why did he stop?"

"Because I beat Honorius and shamed him in front of his generals. Olympius said it was proper for my brother to win against them, as he would rule one day, but since I was a girl—"

She let the sentence trail off and shrugged lightly, as if this didn't matter in the slightest. Alaric suspected this was a thing she did when something mattered very much indeed.

He decided if he ever saw Olympius again he'd beat the man to death with his bare hands.

"Your father wasted your talents," he said quietly. "You should have been a general."

A fevered pink spread across her cheekbones. "Does that mean you'll make me empress after all, King of the Goths?"

"Don't push your luck." But he was laughing now, and she

was laughing too, green eyes outshining the glow of the fire, and the pull of her was inexorable.

Damn it. He was going to take her to his bed after all.

An arrow whizzed past him, faster than a diving hawk.

CHAPTER FOURTEEN

Alaric turned, his *seax* leaving its scabbard in a battle-mad hiss. Mistakes piled upon mistakes. If he hadn't been so distracted. If he hadn't allowed the damn fire. He cursed his own fire-blind sight.

Julia was staring at him in shock. He gripped her arm, and for an instant all he wanted was to kiss her hard, to put into it everything he felt. Instead he gave her a shove away from him, in the direction of the horses and safety. *"Run,"* he gritted. "I'll guard your back."

And she was off, running like a deer into the dark.

Movement caught his eye up the slope, at the cliff that loomed at the back of the sanctuary. Half a dozen shapes dropped in the darkness, swarming down the ruined temple.

This was the chaos that a few moments of lapsed vigilance wrought.

In minutes, Riga's arrows were flying and he and the twins were fighting back-to-back at the center of a maelstrom of whir-ring blades. He had trained the twins himself. Polished them to a killing edge; when they fought together, it was as one lethal, perfectly tuned machine. From the corner of his eye, he saw Horsa bring his hunting knife low under his opponent's defenses and overreach only slightly—but enough to make him stumble into the path of the Gaul's heavy downward blow. Alaric whipped around, acting on reflex, his Hunnic hatchet flying over the boy's shoulder. It landed with a *thunk* in the Gaul's skull.

"What a throw!" Horsa gave a mad, fevered laugh. "Hengist, did you see—"

"Shut up and watch your fucking reach." The boy was going to get himself killed, fighting like that. Alaric braced his foot against the dead man's head and yanked the hatchet out of his skull with a jerk.

There was a lull in the battle. Riga emerged from his sniper position and walked among the dead, kicking them over on their backs. *"Foederati,"* he said. "Mercenaries."

Thorismund strode toward him amidst the fallen statues and corpses. "Some are searching for Julia. I'll hunt them down."

Julia. Of course they were here for her. Alaric's instinct was to take off at a run in her direction, but something stopped him.

He felt the air change, felt the earth shift beneath his feet.

"Get her up the mountain," he said quietly. "I'll buy you time."

Thorismund's face darkened. "I will not let you lay down your life for a *Roman.*"

"That Roman will buy us back our homeland, Thorismund." There were others as loyal, but what bound him to Thorismund was the will to bring back what was lost, no matter what it took. "I need your oath. There is none but you I would ask to do this."

Thorismund cursed, low beneath his breath. "I'll stick to her like a burr to a camel's arse. That is my sacred oath."

"I accept your oath and hold you to it." The Batavi took their oaths to the grave. "If I haven't found you by morning, go to Brisca." He reached into his pocket for the finger-bone flute he'd carried all this way. "Do you remember the tune?"

"I remember."

"Good. Play it wrong and you may get your throat slit."

Now Thorismund was gone after Julia, and it could not be a moment too soon. Down the slope to the south, the moon-drenched tree line had begun to move.

Julia crouched near the spring where the horses had been teth-ered, faint with terror. She could hear the distant sounds of bat-tle, but that was a distraction. There were footsteps echoing off the ruins. Looking for her.

Someone gripped the back of her tunic and yanked her out of her hiding place.

Her scream was throttled by a huge hand clamping down on her mouth. "Quit your yelling," Thorismund whispered hoarsely. "I'm trying to save your life."

He hauled her down the slope. Julia grasped his wrist, thick with muscle. "Where are we *going*?"

"Fucking *Alaric*," Thorismund spat, dragging her along like a sack of wheat. "Sending me off into the mountains while he stays and dies. Says I'm the only one he trusts to get you to safety. *Bollocks*."

"What?" Julia tried to dig her heels in. Thorismund did not seem to notice. "Did Alaric order this?"

"Yes. The fool. He'll be dead by sunup. He *orders* us to go."

The nerve of that man. "He doesn't get to order *me*. He isn't *my* king—"

They'd reached the horses. In the next instant, she found her-self lifted and thrown on the back of the nearest. "Run," Thoris-mund growled, slapping the horse's rump. It surged forward, and Julia could do nothing but hang on as the animal plunged at a flat gallop down the hill.

She glanced behind to see six men were emerging from the

trees. Thorismund was running at them, battle-axe raised and its blade glinting coldly like a sickle moon. Going to his death.

There were hundreds. Too many to fight.

Behind a wall, Riga was readying another arrow. "How many of those do you have left?" Riga held up one hand, palm open, then another. Ten. Not enough.

They would die here. He, Riga, and the twins, who had refused to flee. Alaric had not wanted that; he wanted the boys to *live*. After Gaufrid had died, Alaric had named the boys among his most select bodyguards and kept them close so *he* could protect *them*. If the boys died, he would go with them and explain it to Gaufrid himself. Soon he would get his chance.

He could only hope Julia and Thorismund made it into the mountains. He would do his best to give them a head start.

Just then, the moon emerged from behind a cloud, and he recognized a figure leading the men below. Swathed in barbarian chain mail, face concealed by a slit-eyed Thracian helmet. Alaric would know him blind.

He stepped out from the shelter of the ruined temple and propped a boot up on a crumbling wall. "What took you so long, Calthrax?"

"You kept me busy chasing down dead ends." Calthrax produced a bundle wrapped in cloth and gave it a heave. It hit the stone wall below Alaric with a wet *thunk*. A severed head. One of his fifty, not much older than the twins. Neck a jagged stump. Eyes rolled back, rotted whites. *Fuck*.

"They put up a good fight, but I couldn't let them live for wasting my time." Calthrax's brutal laugh rang through the ruined temple. "Send the woman, Alaric."

"Over my rotting corpse."

"That can be arranged." Calthrax gave the signal and his men moved forward.

Horsa and Hengist came to stand at his right and left, looking down the sweep of desiccated grass. "Can we fight them?" Hengist asked.

Alaric shook his head grimly.

At a signal from Calthrax, an archer cocked an arrow and aimed it up the slope toward the twins. A fierce shrieking rose from the chinks in the ruined walls as the wind snatched breath from lungs and sent the arrow awry, tumbling down the mountain.

It was the *bora*. The demon wind. Alaric knew it from the battle of Frigidus.

Horsa held up a hank of dry grass, a jagged grin spreading across his face. Fire blooming in his hand.

Alaric nodded. *Do it.* The boy opened his hand and let the grass fall. Then all the world was fire.

CHAPTER FIFTEEN

The mare was mad with terror. She galloped down the mountain, no check on her speed. Behind, a fire came roaring, whipped to a frenzy by a sudden, all-devouring wind.

Julia clung to the mare's back, smoke filling her lungs. Certain she would die.

After endless time, the ground flattened and the mare slowed, moving through a blasted landscape of undifferentiated gray. The wind switched direction, driving the fire east. It was this that saved her life. That and the mare, who was limping now. Shreds of poultice still clung to her hoof. "Good girl," Julia muttered, stroking the mare's neck. The dawn was just breaking and Julia slumped over the horse's neck, waves of dizziness overcoming her. It had been hours.

Suddenly she canted to the side, sliding with hideous slowness off the horse. She lay gasping on the dusty earth, an iron band tightening around her lungs.

The world slid to black.

Julia opened her eyes to a blue sky and the mare's long, dour head, reins looped and hanging, nuzzling at her face. The smoke had cleared and the sky was a hard, uncompromising blue. Julia sat up and rubbed the mare's ears. "Good girl."

"I thought you were dead. You looked dead."

A man stood a few paces away. Bald, with a goatish little beard. "Hello," Julia said warily.

"You've nothing to fear from me." Avuncular as an uncle. "Are you alone?"

A bolt of unease shot through her. *No princesses in these woods. Only predators and prey.* "My friends will be searching for me."

"You must be from the city. I doubt a girl like you would be from the countryside."

A girl like you. She wore a boy's Gothic tunic and her hair was one long snarl; how on earth did he know—oh.

She'd been using high Latin and he'd been replying in kind.

"My name is Origenes. I once tutored the governor's son in Aquileia. Are you from there?" His eyes crinkled at the corners. "Come. You can shelter with me and my wife until your friends catch up."

Julia eyed the man, trying to discern any threat. The tutor to a governor's son would have been an educated slave, probably Greek. His Latin was fluent, and his clothes were fine, though worn. And he had a wife. *You've been traveling with the worst of the Goths for weeks*, she told herself. *Surely you aren't afraid of a little Greek tutor.*

Even so. This man could not protect her from Stilicho's mercenaries. Julia had a feeling that if he aided her, he would suffer for it.

"I thank you for your kind offer of hospitality," she said. "But—"

His smile turned wolfish. "It was not a request."

He hit her twice. Open-handed slaps, hard enough to snap her head back. Julia tasted blood as he led her and the horse across the smoky plain.

She would have fought, if she was brave. She'd never been brave.

They came to a cave in the slope of a hill. A dozen hard-looking men lounged around firepits, dicing and drinking and gnawing on stringy chicken legs. Eyes turned to her, hot with resentment and lust.

Suddenly she couldn't breathe around her fear.

A bald, bearded man came swaggering toward them, wearing a ragged red cloak with several long rents in it. Stab-holes. "Well, Origenes. What did you drag in?"

"A woman. Highborn." Origenes gave an ingratiating smile. "I was hoping you would accept her as payment for my debts."

The bandit's eyes narrowed. "Where is your family, girl?"

"Dead." The lie came readily enough. "You'll get no ransom for me. You might as well let me go."

"Someone taught you to talk nice, at least. Perhaps you'll be worth something at the slave markets." He smelled of stale beer and sweat. "You may call me King of the Goths."

Julia stared in astonishment. This man with his bulging belly and hair thinning over a sunburned scalp—she heard a high-pitched laugh and realized it was coming from her.

His eyes narrowed viciously. "What are you laughing at?"

He was looking at her like he might kill her and she *couldn't stop.* "I'm sorry. It's just that—I *know* him." Julia let out a panicked cackle. "You are not the King of the Goths."

The false Alaric gave her an ugly smile. Then he drove his fist into her stomach.

The force of it folded her in half. He watched with clinical detachment as she sank to the ground, gasping for breath. "That'll teach you to laugh at me," he muttered. "Haughty bitch." A chaos of laughter rose up behind him, his men cheering him on. "We took care of the aristocracy in Aquileia, and she isn't one of them. You ought to know better," he growled at Origenes. "Probably just some high-paid whore."

Then he was stalking back into the cave and Julia pressed her scraped hands into the earth, wracked with pain. A violent sob rose up in her throat and she put every ounce of strength into holding it back.

If Alaric was dead, he was watching. She refused to let him see her cry.

The fire had done its work, sweeping through the enemy line, sending it into chaos. Now dawn cut across the mountain, illuminating a landscape transformed. Down the slope, corpses lay blackened and twisted. Alaric and his men found their horses at the bottom of the hill, milling about beyond the tree line. Calthrax had been lucky. He was not among the dead.

Neither was Julia.

She wasn't supposed to be here. The fire had spread downhill, carried by the furious wind; Julia and Thorismund had been ordered to run farther up into the mountains. They should have been safe. Alaric had hoped they had escaped the fire, until Thorismund rose from the smoking earth, eyebrows singed but otherwise unhurt. He had last seen Julia galloping *down* the mountainside. Back into Italy.

Now they were combing the hillside, turning over burned corpses, searching for Julia's. A sick desperation rose in Alaric's chest. He put no hope in prayer, but he prayed anyway, low between his teeth. If he'd killed her, with his own lack of vigilance—

He turned over yet another charred corpse with his boot. Not Julia. An infantryman, face scorched beyond recognition. He thought of her last night—the upturned tilt of her mouth; her brilliance by the fire—and cursed. If he saw her again—if she had managed, beyond all likelihood, to survive—he would do it all differently. He hoped he got the chance.

Up on the slope above, Riga gave a shout. Kneeling on the

ground, he pointed to a line of tracks leading off to the south-east. "Galloping. Favoring its left front foreleg." He held up a shred of cloth he had used as a poultice. "She was riding Bura."

The outlaw leader declared he would have her first. But one of the others challenged him, and now they were fighting over her.

Julia curled up at the back of the cave, near out of her mind with fear.

Was Alaric dead? *Impossible.* This was *Alaric.* The man who starved cities into submission, who'd flashed a reckless grin with a dozen swords pointed at his neck and strolled out of her brother's banquet with *her* in his back pocket. A man like that couldn't just be killed.

Yes he can. It was her father's voice, corpse-pale in the basil-ica. The voice of Cornelius, a wolf's muzzle buried in his belly.

And if he was dead, she was lost.

Alaric had never laid a hand on her. Even when she'd pro-voked him. She hadn't realized how much worse it could be. Soon the false King of the Goths would come strutting over to fulfill his promise. If he touched her, she'd rip out his throat with her teeth.

"You must be hungry." Origenes stood over her, holding a plate of stew.

"Thank you," she managed. "Now, do me the mercy of going away."

"I've been too long among these brutes. I've been dying for decent conversation."

"I'd rather converse with the rats."

His face hardened and he glanced at the outlaw leader, still drinking and wrestling. "Treat him nice. Maybe he'll keep you for himself instead of passing you around."

"Yes, and wouldn't *that* be a happy ending." The words dropped like acid from her lips; she could practically hear them hissing on the floor. "Aren't you going to join this asinine fight?" Perhaps he would get himself killed.

"Oh no. I am no warrior." Origenes smiled. "Besides, I don't mind going last."

Julia's hands curled into angry fists. She'd chew out his throat too.

A watchman shouted a stranger's approach. The bandit leader strode to the cave opening, and there was a tense, interminable exchange. And then he came into the firelight shouting for drink, arm slung around the newcomer's shoulders as if they were old friends. Julia nearly fainted with relief. Because there, face smudged with dirt but gloriously, miraculously unhurt, lips curved in an easy smile and firelight glinting in the burnished bronze of his hair, was Alaric.

Someone had hit her. The side of her face had gone red darkening into purple, and there was a sharp cut across her left cheekbone.

Alaric hid his murderous rage behind a genial smile.

"So tell me, kinsman. What brings you to this side of the mountains?"

The man's breath smelled of rank ale. Alaric answered in Sicambri, with its distinctive Celtic rhythms and suffixes. The other man's home language. It had been a lucky guess. "Thought I'd make my fortune robbing aristocrats in the lawless north."

As he spoke, he cast a deceptively casual eye around the cave. A cave he knew; they had used it to store supplies during the siege of Milan. There were twisty back passages that opened on a nearby slope. Hengist had sworn he remembered the way, even in the dark.

No sign of them in the back tunnel yet. That worried him.

In a single glance, he'd sized up every man present; those useless from drink and those alert enough to be suspicious. Saw the path he'd cut through them, clear as an Imperial road. His eyes strayed to Julia again, the fear in her face beneath the mask of contemptuous stoicism, the purpling bruise. He had half a mind to start now.

"You're in luck, brother." The outlaw leader's lips stretched over gleaming teeth. "You've fallen in with the King of the Goths."

Suddenly Alaric was engaged in a very difficult struggle not to laugh. "It is an honor." He sketched an amused bow. "You fought like a lion at the battle of Pollentia."

"Not *that* King of the Goths. Although many tell me there is a resemblance." He laughed. "Soon as I can dry out this group of sorry knaves, I'll take them over the mountains and challenge Alaric myself. Two invasions and he never made it past the Po." He snickered.

You fucking try it. Alaric felt a spike of impatience. Where the hell were they? His eyes fell on Julia again, and the rage he felt nearly choked him.

He would fill this place with the dead in answer for that bruise on her cheek.

The outlaw leader followed his gaze, a pugnacious look on his face. "Don't get any ideas. I expect a good price for her on the slave market, after we've had our fun." He smirked. "She won't be so high-and-mighty once we've had her on her back."

And there, at the rear of the cave, the signal. Weak sunlight flickering off a mirror, quick as a witch-light. It was about fucking time. Alaric tightened his arm on the man's shoulder, the two of them closer than brothers. "You'll never touch her."

Then he pulled the man's knife out of his belt and stabbed him with it.

Afterward Julia would remember everything in disjointed scraps.

The long knife sliding into the outlaw's belly. Blood spurting between fingers as he clapped his hands to the wound. The unholy light in Alaric's eyes as he tossed the man aside like a sack of rags and strode into a mob that wanted him dead.

Then the rest came roaring out of the dark. The twins, their faces dark with campfire-black. Riga's sharp Hunnic sword opening bellies and throats. Even Thorismund, who'd have gone to his death for her, now miraculously alive, swinging his two-handed axe with one hand.

But Julia couldn't rip her eyes from Alaric. He killed like he'd been born to it, brutally graceful and lit with savage joy.

"Are these your friends?" Origenes spoke with a kind of horrified awe.

Then Alaric came striding out of the carnage, blood dripping from the tip of his blade. Julia sank to the floor and he knelt in front of her, eyes burning blue hellfire and his chain mail covered in gore. He caught her chin and tilted her face to examine her cheek, his thumb lightly brushing the bruise. A little jolt shot through her.

"Who did this?" His voice was chillingly quiet.

Julia's eyes slid to Origenes, who was begging now, swearing he'd been her protector. Alaric hauled him to his feet, pinned him to the wall with one hand. With the other, he took his long knife and opened a bloody grin in the man's throat.

Blood gushed hot and red. Origenes made a gurgling, drowning sound and was dead before he hit the ground. Then Alaric turned to her, blue eyes blazing out of a mask of blood.

Julia turned her face to the cave floor and retched.

There was a spring in the back of the cave. Alaric pulled off his chain mail and washed the blood off his face. Then he stood, stretching a kink out of his shoulder.

Julia had gotten over the worst of her sick and now sat slumped against the wall, her hair sticking to her forehead in damp curls, staring into some middle distance only she could see. He'd seen that look before, on the faces of women far gone in shock. *His fault.*

Then her blue-green gaze fell to him, and the world forgot to breathe. In two long strides, Alaric crossed the space and helped her to her feet, his hands on her bruised face, almost frantic with the need to touch her. "Are you hurt?"

"I'm fine." The tense line of her shoulders said that she was emphatically *not.*

He tilted her face to look at the swelling. Another burst of rage and he was fucking *delighted* that vile little shit who'd hurt her was dead and he'd done the job himself. "You're safe, Julia." He produced the salve and tended to her bruises. "Softly now. Hold still."

"I'm sorry." She was staring at him with a luminous fragility that stole his breath.

He slid his thumb across her cheekbone, and the air went hot and thick between them. "For what?"

"I didn't mean to run. Thorismund told me to, but—" A shudder passed through her, for all he tried to be gentle. "He would've died for me. Please don't be angry at him."

Alaric's hand stilled on the curve of her cheek. No love lost between her and Thorismund, and here she was defending him. A raw, bruising ache rose up in his chest that had nothing to do with lust. "I'm not angry." He slid his hand into her hair; couldn't stop himself. Fingers curling tight into damp silk. "I'm just glad you're alive."

Then he pulled her close and kissed her.

He felt the sudden tremor that shot through her at his touch, felt the hitch of her indrawn breath against his mouth and knew he didn't have it in him to be gentle. Her lips were all soft, silken heat, and he kissed her fiercely, all his careful control dissolving in a fury of teeth and tongue. In an instant, he had her crushed hard against the wall with his hand anchored in her messy braid, exactly as he'd wanted her from the instant he'd first laid eyes on her.

At first she stood rigid and astonished in his arms. Then suddenly she was kissing him back like she was *starving* for him, her mouth opening with a breathy little moan that had him instantly, savagely hard. Alaric lost himself completely to the hot glide of her tongue against his, the soft sounds she made in the back of her throat as her nails dug little half-moons into his biceps. Julia alive and safe and *his* from the tips of her toes to the ends of her long red hair. This was the only possible way it could end.

He was so lost in her he didn't even realize when it turned.

She shuddered in his arms and it was only when she gave a loud sob against his mouth that he knew it wasn't from pleasure. Her hands braced against his forearms and he tasted tears on his tongue. It took a monumental act of will to break the kiss, his breath coming harsh and ragged, lust raging through him like a flooding river. Barely held in check by its banks.

"Woman," he muttered, "I think you are going to kill me."

It almost killed him to drop his arms and step back, but he forced himself to do it. She was shaking. He wanted to comfort her any way he could—and he reached for her again. Didn't know what else to do. She flinched back. Not even a word of thanks. Fuck if he wasn't as bad in her eyes as that pasty little man whose throat had so badly needed cutting.

Alaric couldn't stand being this close to her, wanting her this much. He took a composing breath and tossed her the salve. "Use that on your bruises and be quick. We leave as soon as the men are ready."

He didn't spare her another glance as he strode out of the cave.

CHAPTER SIXTEEN

One hour bled into another and they rode like the devil himself was at their backs. Julia sat still in Alaric's arms and tried to come apart as silently as possible.

Watching him kill had made every hair on her neck stand up in recognition. All this time, she'd heard his violence whispering beneath his laugh and seen it flashing out of every grin; now she'd seen it bare. One glance from her and Origenes had died.

And then he had kissed her. Her body still tingled like the aftershock of a lightning strike. She had never been kissed like that before. She would have kissed him back until she *died* from it. She'd wanted to rip him open and crawl inside.

But then Cornelius had risen behind her shut lids. Red, rending death.

The sun was long past its zenith by the time they climbed a high, twisting trail to a meadow surrounded by towering cliffs. At one end, spilling down like a veil over black rock, was a waterfall. "It's beautiful," she breathed.

"It's safe. For now." He said it like a man who never believed he was safe, not ever.

There was a cave behind the waterfall. The twins secured the horses beneath an outcrop—Bura with them, the little mare well enough despite being kidnapped by bandits—while Alaric and Riga disappeared into it with knives drawn.

Thorismund pulled her aside. "Listen. *He* won't teach you this, but you must be taught." He offered her a small knife, pommel-first, and turned it in her hands until it was pointed at her breast. "You thrust it in here," he said, positioning the tip just under her rib cage. "Point it upward, like this. Hard and fast. Don't hesitate. You'll die quickly and with a lot less pain."

Her mouth went dry. "Less pain than what?"

"Being raped by all those men. I wouldn't wish that on a woman. Even a Roman one."

Julia took the knife and turned it in her hands uneasily. She thought of how he'd thrust her behind him and gone running toward the enemy as if he'd been an army all by himself. "Thank you," she said quietly. "For what you did at the temple."

Thorismund looked *offended*. "I was only keeping my oath."

Julia sighed. He just stood there, an irascible wall of a man, all battered leather and faded tattoos and suddenly, *terribly* dear to her. "Well, it was the bravest thing I've ever seen in my life." She managed an unsteady smile. "Now when I tell everyone you saved my life in a courageous fashion, I won't have to lie."

"Thank Alaric if you need a place to put your gratitude. *He's* done things to make my blood freeze."

Julia flinched at the suggestion. She didn't know why it was so easy to show her gratitude to Thorismund and so difficult to do it with Alaric.

"Don't tell him you have the knife," Thorismund said quietly, showing her how to hide it in her boot just as Alaric and Riga emerged from the cave. "It's designed to be hidden. More trouble if Alaric knows you have it."

Inside, the cave was barely large enough for everyone and strangely warm, a passage at the back inhaling humid wind.

The others were already curled in their cloaks. Alaric settled closest to the entrance, long legs stretching across the cave floor with his knife across his lap. Keeping watch. The only place to sit was next to him.

Julia couldn't take her eyes from him. His profile was a thing of harsh beauty against the moving backdrop of the waterfall and she found herself staring unabashed as he began to polish his knife. She was still shaking. Up until now, this had all seemed like an adventure—almost a game. It wasn't. She saw how much her life depended on Alaric's protection. He had come for her, killed for her.

She wished ferociously that he would kiss her again.

But already it seemed as if she'd dreamed it. And she'd been the one to push him away. This time she would have to *ask* for it.

How do I do this at court? The game was easy in Ravenna. All she had to do was deliver the right kind of look from beneath her lashes, along with an encouraging, secretive little smile. Lean forward *just* a little, to make her intentions known. But Alaric had cut someone's throat for her and she had no idea how to flirt with a man like that.

"You should sleep." His hands worked over the blade, even and smooth. She couldn't stop staring at them.

"I'm too cold."

He slanted her a glance. Flash of brilliant blue in the dark; it burned her eyes. "How can you be cold? This place is stifling."

Her shaking wasn't from the cold. "Can I have my cloak back?"

"It's my cloak."

"No, it isn't. You gave it to me on the first night, remember?" It felt *good*, to banter with him like this. Julia felt an urge to giggle wildly and never stop.

He was looking at her impassively. "I *loaned* it to you."

"No," Julia said loftily, her lips curved in a teasing smile.

"You *gave* it to me, because you felt guilty about tying me up and leaving me to sleep on the ground."

"You put nettles in my bower, Julia. I didn't feel guilty at all."

"You are horrible."

"So they tell me." Clearly this didn't distress him in the least. "Come here," he said then, and hooked an arm around her shoulders and pulled her in, engulfing her in his warmth and the warmth of the cloak. It overwhelmed her. Julia laid her head against his shoulder and breathed in. Leather and pine trees and wide-open spaces.

Somehow, with her head on his shoulder, she slept.

Julia lurched into wakefulness. She was curled in Alaric's lap, swathed in his cloak. Moonlight through the waterfall illuminated the cave in an uncanny glow.

Cornelius. Already the dream was fading, and she snatched at the bloody scraps.

"What is it, Julia?" It was Alaric. His voice dark silk. Endlessly gentle. "What's wrong?" It was the exact tone he used to quiet horses.

"It was a dream." A shiver ripped through her, violent.

"You really are cold." She nodded. "Come with me."

He helped her rise. Now the men were stirring, and dimly she heard Alaric speak to them, in low, rough Gothic. They settled back to their cloaks and he led her deeper into the cave.

It took her a moment to realize it was not pitch-black here. A faint blue light gleamed on the walls, and when the passageway opened, Julia halted in wonder. Tiny pinpoints of blue light covered the walls and ceiling, outlining hanging forests of stalactites. In the center was a pool, almost perfectly circular, its water a brilliant, impossible blue. The exact shade of Alaric's eyes. Steam rose from the surface in ghostly tendrils. Hot water. A godsend.

"Why didn't you tell me this was here?"

"It was more important that you sleep."

"Nonsense. *Nothing* is more important than hot water." She sat at the edge of the pool, testing the surface with one bare toe. *Hot.* She closed her eyes in pleasure.

Cornelius was waiting for her in the dark.

Alaric sat down beside her, and Julia let out a low, animal sound and collapsed against his chest. She was trembling so hard—and now she was sobbing, the tears coming rough and harsh. "I'm sorry. I must have woken everybody—even the bats in this place."

"There is no shame in it. Every one of us wakes up screaming occasionally. Hengist still cries for his mother sometimes."

"You never have, surely."

"Me most of all."

That was a shock. "What dream on earth could frighten *you?*"

"There are many," he said. "The worst is from a battle I fought fifteen years ago. By a river called Frigidus."

Ever after, when Alaric thought of the Christian hell, he would think of that place. Waterless cut in the earth, walls melting out of a red-soaked sky. He remembered letting his men off their leash, racing down into the canyon's throat. No sign of trouble until it was too late.

Julia listened, curled in the curve of his arm, and he understood now why she had reacted as she did when he'd tried to kiss her. Alaric knew well how violence could leave scars on the inside that *hurt.* He had enough of those himself. An invisible map beneath his skin of all he had lived through. He had assumed Julia's status as a princess would have sheltered her from pain and violence. He had been wrong about that. He wondered what else he had been wrong about.

She could not bring herself to talk. Not yet. So he told her the story of who had lived and who had died. He described the blood that soaked the earth as he fought, how his feet had slipped in it. The screams of men and arrows echoing off the walls.

"That's what I remember most," Julia said in a small voice. "The screams."

Her story was eating her alive. "You don't have to tell it," he said. "But sometimes these ghosts lose their power when we make them stand in the light."

As if it was that easy. As if he didn't wake up every day with the past burning a hole in his chest. He waited, gave her space to speak. Then all at once she was telling him.

He put it together in pieces. There was a man, someone she'd cared about—and that made him go tense. *Did her heart belong to someone else?* He tried to divine her feelings as the story wrenched itself out of her, this other man now jumbled with her hateful intended and her brother's staggering malice.

Then she got to the part with the wolves. *He made me watch,* she told him, wracked with sobs, and suddenly he was ready to torch that city to ash.

"I understand this burden far too well," he told her finally. "Do not pick it up when it is not yours to carry."

"You don't understand. My brother—"

"Your brother is a needlessly cruel little shit who deserves every ounce of blame in this," he said. "You were right to come to me."

"I was a fool to come to you." She turned her face into his chest as if she'd trusted him her whole life. "If I'd offered myself instead, perhaps Honorius would have thrown me in there. I didn't have the courage."

Didn't have the courage. He thought of Julia at that banquet, the vision of her lover being ripped apart still burned on the backs of her eyelids, pressing a knife into his hand to save them both. Now he understood what she had been running from that night. The raw, brute nerve it had taken to do what she had done.

"You are not without courage, Julia." The words were entirely inadequate to what he felt. "I've never seen anything so brave and wonderful as you."

Brave. He'd called her brave.

Suddenly she would walk into an arena full of wolves for him.

A princess of Rome should not lose her virtue in a cave, she told herself sternly. But oh—she wanted to. She wanted nothing more than to sink into the warmth of this steaming water, and she wanted Alaric in it with her. She didn't care what she would get in exchange.

Hastily she rose to her feet and stripped off her layers. Tunic, undertunic, *strophium,* followed quickly by her leggings. Warm air curled around her naked breasts.

The silence in the cave raised hairs on her arms. She *felt* his gaze, fierce and devouring.

Without turning, she slipped into the pool. Warm water closed over her head and she sank down, her toes grazing rock. *Relief.* She pushed up from the bottom, staying under until her lungs burned.

When she finally came up for air, Alaric stood on the other side, blue eyes blazing through the steam.

In one smooth gesture, he pulled off his tunic over his head.

She'd never, in all the days since she'd first seen it, forgotten what he looked like with his shirt off. She'd been starving for that sight ever since—the powerful, stunningly muscled contours of his chest. His stomach, flat and ridged with muscle, crisscrossed with scars. Julia's fevered gaze traveled down his sculpted abdomen to the thick, hard shape of him straining to be free of his trousers. A thrill shot through her. Anticipation mixed with fear.

Then he removed the trousers. He was *naked* now, and there it was, right in the open, as proud and perfect as the rest of him. "You just—stay over there." Her eyes fixed on an area distinctively south of his waist. "Alaric—do you hear me?"

He laughed. "Woman, do you honestly want me to stay here?"

"I'll die if you do."

She said it so low she could barely hear it herself. But of course he knew. He *always* knew. That barbarian smile lifted his lips and he slid easily into the pool.

The water came up to his chest; he strode through it until he stood before her, close enough to feel the heat rising off his skin. Trembling, Julia laid a hand flat on his chest. He felt exactly like she'd imagined. Like warm, breathing marble.

"Julia—" There was a raw ache in his voice. Then he pulled her hard against the length of his arousal and seized her mouth in a searing, soul-destroying kiss.

She'd been warm in the water; now she was scalding everywhere he touched her. And he was touching her *everywhere*, kissing her endlessly, a hand buried in her hair, clenching hard enough to cause delicious pain at the scalp. Julia buried her lips in his neck and tasted him there, sweat and salt and *him*, and she heard him suck in a sharp breath, every muscle in him tensing beneath her touch.

The world dissolved into skin sliding against skin and Julia never wanted it to stop. His hands slid beneath the curve of her ass and he lifted her. Weightless, effortless, he carried her through the water. Cool stone at her back now, and her legs were around him, his mouth on her naked breasts—*yes*—closing around a nipple. The hard, heavy heat of him was nestled right between her legs, the ridge of his erection pressing against the white-hot pinpoint of her desire.

Slowly, with excruciating control, he rocked himself against her even as he deepened their kiss. Julia pressed desperately against him as everything dissolved except sensation—the profound, drugging heat of the water, bright sparks rising everywhere under her skin. His hands were everywhere, his mouth everywhere, and beneath it all, the slow, heady stroke of his arousal against the place where her need was greatest.

A ravenous ache began to build in her. He followed her movements relentlessly, possessing her utterly with his deep, masterful kisses. Her nails dug into his back, and for a moment she twisted on a line of taut, building pleasure until a tremor ripped through her, pulling her apart. She heard herself cry out. Wordless, inarticulate sounds. His name.

Then she was water. Boneless.

He laughed softly, a sound of pure male satisfaction. The message in his eyes was undeniable. *Say yes.* It was not a question.

She turned away from him, tried her teeth on the rise of his shoulder. He growled and pressed his hand to the nape of her neck. She spoke the word against his throat. *Yes.*

She was going to do it. She was going to lose her virtue in a cave.

He pressed her up against the wall and kissed her again, the heat of him melting right through her, and he was *right there*, huge at her entrance. For a panicked instant, she didn't know if she would live through what he'd do to her and didn't care. He was whispering her name now; his free hand clenched in her hair and he groaned against her neck as he stroked against her, slow and strong, his shoulders tensing beneath her hands as he gathered himself to surge forward.

Shouting at the mouth of the cave. His name. *Fuck.*

Alaric tensed, Julia's legs wrapped around his waist and her eyes dazed with desire. Soft and willing, her lips swollen from the onslaught of his kisses, and it was *better* than he'd dreamed all those feverish nights. He took her mouth again, plundered it, pressed her up against the rock wall as if she might dissolve in his arms.

Let the enemy burn the mountain down. Let them riddle his back with arrows.

Another shout. Alaric braced an arm against the stone wall, sheltering her from view. Breathing hard from the effort of stopping. *"What."*

"Pardon the interruption, Alaric." Riga's amused drawl drifted in from the entrance. "Your presence is requested outside."

He rested his forehead against Julia's. Their breaths mingling. "Handle it yourself."

"We tried. Horsa is about to get beheaded and Thorismund is waving his axe around and bellowing. At this rate, we'll all be stuck like pigs by the time you, uh—*finish*."

"Go." There was amusement in Julia's whispered voice. "You'll regret letting Horsa lose his head."

"No, I won't." But she was shoving at his shoulders now, her silken legs sliding down his thighs. He turned, ensuring his body blocked her from sight. "Wait for me outside, Riga."

A muffled snort from the cave entrance. "You ruin everyone's fun."

Julia's mouth curved, bare shoulders slicked with water and glowing. For an instant he was overwhelmed with a feeling that went beyond protectiveness. *She* had been the one to insist he rescue Horsa from whatever trouble he was in; he'd been ready to let the boy sleep in the bedroll he'd sewn. He kissed her ferociously. "Don't come out until I send for you." The gods only knew what was going on out there.

Her husky laugh rang in his ear long after he'd pulled his trousers on and stepped out into the narrow passageway. Riga was waiting for him there, tossing a dagger hand to hand and trying to peer around his shoulder. "It's about damn time you took that girl somewhere private and showed her what's what. She's been unsubtly hinting at it for *weeks*."

Alaric threaded an arm around the other man's shoulders and turned him toward the entrance. "Riga, glance behind you again and you'll find your guts on the floor."

"Message received."

Alaric strode out of the cave into a night flooded with moonlight and the pool at his feet, a perfect lens of stars. Thorismund stood with his back to the cave, his two-handed axe in one hand. Beyond, lining the encircling cliffs, stood a number of distinctly unfriendly warriors. A dozen arrows were pointed at Thorismund's heart. Ahead three men stood in the clearing, one holding Horsa by his hair. Blade to the boy's neck.

"Alaric," Thorismund bellowed, splitting the sky. *"Get out here."*

Alaric put a hand on his shoulder. "Put your axe away before you get us killed."

"They think we're bandits. We *told* them who we are and they don't believe us," Hengist whispered at his back. "They said they'd kill Horsa if anyone moved."

Alaric took in the dark, lime-stiffened hair of the intruders, tattoos that kept count of how many they'd killed. He knew those tattoos.

"It will be all right, Hengist." He strode out into the path of all those arrows. "To what do we hold the honor, warriors?" He slipped into the language of Brisca's village. An old-fashioned Celtic, with the thick burr of the high valleys. "What did the boy do?"

"We caught him hunting in our forests." The man gave Horsa's hair a hard jerk. "The penalty is death."

"I told him no hunting." Alaric spoke to Horsa, switching to Gothic. "Apologize to the men, Horsa." He said the words in the peculiar arcane Celtic of the hill tribes.

Horsa glared balefully at him but repeated the apology readily enough. The man who held him loosened his grip, and Horsa swaggered away as if his pride hadn't been pricked. "I'll deal with you later," Alaric muttered. The men ringing the cliffs had not put up their arrows. The harm had not been rectified. "What reparation can we give?"

The tallest one's eyes narrowed. "How come you to speak our tongue?"

"I have spent much time in Acerrae." The village's name

rolled easy off his tongue. "We come to pay our respects to Brisca."

"He says you are Alaric of the Goths," the tallest said, jerking his chin at Thorismund. "There have been many pretenders these past weeks."

"I know. I killed one on my way here."

"Prove you are not one of them. Else you will share his fate."

Alaric shrugged easily. "Very well."

He glanced behind, and Thorismund handed him a small cylinder of bone, carved with birds and animals. It was no bigger than a finger bone, because it was a finger bone. He brought it to his lips and played the song Brisca had taught him. Three long notes, two short, and accompanying trills, a haunting melody.

With great solemnity, one of the archers raised a small flute to his lips and played a snatch of birdsong. Identical to his own. Only then did he relax.

The tallest spoke, and the tension seemed to evaporate like mist. "It would seem you are who you say—" He paused. "Who is *that*?"

Julia stood at the cave entrance wearing her too-large tunic and loose trousers, having flagrantly disobeyed his orders. She shaded a hand over her eyes, and even in that gesture—neat and elegant—there could be no question of who she was.

"She is my guest," Alaric said blandly.

The warriors exchanged glances. "I think you had better come with us," the tall one said.

CHAPTER SEVENTEEN

Julia gripped Hannibal's torso with her thighs and hung on for dear life.

They'd been climbing for hours. Up fearsomely steep switch-backs in the screaming wind, the night sky relentlessly clear. Alaric sauntered along at Hannibal's head, one hand loosely curled on the reins. He did not seem concerned about the men who walked with their bows half-drawn. Even Thorismund looked nervous. But not Alaric.

Julia pulled Alaric's cloak tighter with one hand; with the other, she maintained her death grip on the reins. She didn't like her tippy position, the way she kept sliding backward.

"Alaric," she whispered. "Who are these people? What do they want with us?"

"Do not worry yourself. All will be well."

As he spoke, his thumb glided across her ankle. A white-hot jolt of a touch. Julia snapped her mouth shut, her heart racing, as everything that had happened in that cave came rushing back. That pleasure, arcing down her limbs in waves of blue lightning.

Now she understood how a man could completely ruin a woman.

Her eyes strayed back to Alaric, drawn helplessly to the sway of his broad shoulders, the easy, relaxed cadence of his stride.

Julia understood such things were supposed to be pleasurable—but such pleasure had always eluded her. She always assumed that reports of such were profoundly exaggerated. She had never, in all her life, felt anything like that ruinous bliss that had ripped through her like lightning in Alaric's arms.

What had he done to her in that cave? She felt as though she'd been enspelled. The slick reins slipped in her hands. Hannibal gave another lurch and Julia slipped backward in the saddle with a little squeak.

Alaric glanced back at her, as if nothing so miraculous had happened between them, as if that feeling for him was as expected as everyday bread. "Are you all right?"

She gave a strained laugh. "Of course." Amusement glinted in his eyes and Julia wished for once he'd pretend not to see her cowardice. Her foolishness.

She gripped the pommel as they climbed into the windy dark.

Sometime in the small hours, Alaric joined her on the horse. Julia woke in his arms, sunlight stroking her face. She screwed her eyes shut, lulled by the closeness of him and the gentle movement of the horse. "Make it go away," she muttered. "Tell it to come back later."

"Make what go away?"

"The sun." She'd been drooling on his shirt. *How embarrassing.*

"I'll tell it, but I don't think it will listen." His thumb idly stroked her shoulder; a jittery heat shot through to her core. "Wake, Julia. We're here."

Julia opened her eyes to a looming wall of ashen stakes thick as ship masts, towering into a sky so blue it hurt her eyes. The ground was barren rock, tumbled steely gray; behind it, black mountain peaks sawed at the sky.

One of the tattooed men swaggered up to the gate, holding a curled bone horn to his lips. For a moment the deep, discordant note it made hung still. Then the gates swung open and the air filled with a cacophony of voices and buzzing horns.

Julia was used to being surrounded, but never like this.

She breathed in the animal tang of this place, smells of pigs and chickens and cooking food. She was accustomed to riding in litters, standing on porticoes above a sea of pressing bodies. But now she struggled to stay upright in the midst of a jostling crowd, clad in furs and rough-spun tunics, who showed her not the slightest deference.

They weren't here for her. They were here for Alaric.

Julia caught sight of him in the thick of it, flashing a grin as he greeted tattooed warriors and women in colorful kirtles. Someone handed him a tow-haired boy and he held the child casually in the curve of one arm, smiling indulgently at his beaming mother. Julia was shunted to the side, holding Hannibal's reins.

No one was looking at her. No one was paying attention to her at all.

A shouted greeting rang out and a woman strode down from the top of the slope, black hair woven into an elaborate braided crown, a pine-green cloak swirling about her heels. She threw her arms around Alaric's neck with a whoop of joy. Alaric lifted her off the ground, easily, with one arm, with an answering grin that could make the stars weep.

Both of them were looking at her now. Alaric's eyes a glacial blue, the woman's moss green and discernibly cool. Julia was intensely aware of the state of herself—hair an irredeemable tangle, clothes that could walk by themselves. She stared back imperiously. Alaric might be king in this meager scrape of a village, and this woman its queen, but neither would intimidate *her.*

Then Alaric was striding toward her, the crowd parting before him. No one extended such courtesy to *her*; someone knocked into her and sent her reeling into Hannibal's shoulder. The horse snapped at her with block-like yellow teeth and she startled back.

"Easy, Julia." Alaric's hand curled around her bicep, a teasing, sun-warmed affection in his eyes that made her stomach flip over.

"You forget yourself," she hissed. "I'm not one of your grizzled camp followers. See to your own damn horse."

Laughter lit his eyes as he took the reins from her and spoke a few reassuring words to Hannibal. "I wouldn't call them *grizzled*." He astounded her by brushing his lips against her forehead. "I must leave you alone awhile. I have much to discuss with the chieftain of this place."

Much to discuss indeed. An image of him gloriously naked with that woman punched her in the chest. "Fine," she fumed. "That's *fine*. Go *discuss* things."

He crossed his arms over his chest and looked at her with a bemused expression; the chiseled beauty of his forearms made her lightheaded. "The twins will find you a place to rest and a change of clothes and a bath. If you are hungry—"

"A bath?" Julia blinked up at him. "A hot one?"

"If you wish it, yes." His voice went warm and intimate. "I will find you later. You and I have much to discuss as well."

"We do?" There was too much meaning in the way he said it. Was *much to discuss* some filthy Gothic euphemism?

He did not elaborate further, only strolled off toward the tall woman, Hannibal walking beside him, chickens and small children scattering at his feet.

Baths, Julia decided, were better than wine. Better than *everything*.

There was no gleaming marble pool superior to this half barrel of a size to hold a man. No rare scented bath oils that could improve upon this animal-fat soap with its meager lather. She would stay in this stone bathhouse until wind and rain wore down these mountains and nothing was left but dust. Or at least until the water cooled.

What was the matter with her? Ever since Alaric had rescued her from those bandits, she shook when he looked at her. She'd nearly given him her virtue in a *cave*. And just now, she'd watched Alaric turn the dazzling force of his smile on another woman, and the jealousy had eaten her alive. Then he'd come swaggering up to her as if nothing was wrong in the world, kissed her forehead like a wayward little sister, and flashed his forearms at her, and Julia was suddenly, acutely aware of the trouble she was in.

She sat up in the bath suddenly. Water sloshed on the floor. *Oh good God, no.*

She was in love with him.

This was intolerable. *This* was the feeling that had gotten Cornelius eaten by wolves.

She seized the soap and began to scrub herself vigorously as if she could scour the feelings off her body. A determined pounding shook the door. Julia started, the soap slipping through her fingers. *"What?"*

"What are you doing in there?" Horsa's voice. "Hengist thinks you drowned."

"You know perfectly well what I'm doing. Go away."

"Finish up or we're coming in after you!"

"Don't you dare!" Julia squeaked, ducking to rinse herself. She wasn't entirely sure they *wouldn't*.

After the bath, the twins took her to a guesthouse unlike any that Julia had seen. A mushroom of a building, with a thatched roof pitched at a steep angle to the ground. The door was a leather flap of indeterminate origin. Her old self—not a month ago— would have fainted dead rather than sleep in such a place. But it was a far improvement from sleeping on the ground.

Inside, it was surprisingly pleasant. A single room, with a floor lined with springy moss and a firepit. A sturdy table stood along one wall, made of scarred blond wood. Dried herbs hung from the ceiling; it smelled fresh and clean.

Was this the home Alaric imagined for himself? She could believe his wants would be this humble. In one corner, there was a low platform bed piled with furs, and Julia's thoughts immediately went to him in that bed. Gloriously naked. With that other woman.

Stupid. Now was no time to be lovesick and jealous; what she needed was a *strategy.* Alaric had women from one side of the continent to the other. If she played this wrong, he would simply take what she offered and then send her back to Honorius with his compliments, and perhaps a Gothic baby in her belly that would kill her in the coming out.

That image of him naked flashed before her sight again. Golden and gleaming, water streaming down the muscular wall of his chest. If she shut her eyes, she could still feel the heat of his hands everywhere he'd touched her, rough and strong, *claiming* her.

She wanted him so much she could *sob* from it. She could not—not *ever*—give any hint of her real feelings.

A change of clothes had been laid out on the bed. A light woolen dress dyed pale blue, and a creamy-pale underdress to go beneath. There was a woven belt and a pair of soft felt boots. There was even a small, bone comb, carved with horses' heads. Julia dressed hurriedly, combed her hair, tried to gather her thoughts.

She still needed Alaric's army. He *must not* send her back to Honorius. And she could not let him think she had such little value as to offer herself in a cave, or a field, or a ditch. She would *not* lie with him again unless it was on her terms. It could not be a thing he took lightly.

In the meantime, he might have women from one side of the continent to the other, but *she* would be the one he couldn't have.

She went outside in the sunshine to find Hengist and Horsa talking in Gothic with a tall young warrior. The warrior's hard, kohl-lined gaze shifted to her and Julia stopped in her tracks.

The warrior was a woman, surely not older than twenty. Her hair was very dark, shaved close to the skull on one side, on the other in long, narrow braids. She wore leather trousers and a fur-lined vest and two curved swords at her hips.

Hengist waved her over. "This is Ehre. My future wife." Ehre's immediate laughter said that this was an outrageous joke. "The last time we came through, Ehre was seventeen and I fought a duel with Horsa over her. I won."

Horsa gave him a black look. "*I* won, braggart."

Ehre ignored them both. "So this is the woman who travels with Alaric of the Goths." She gave Julia a hard little threat of a smile, and said something in Gothic that sounded less than complimentary.

"Excuse me," Julia said, politely. "The only things I can say in your language are *piss*, *fuck*, and *your mother is a whore*."

Hengist laughed. "She said she wasn't expecting you to be skinnier than a new calf."

Julia shrugged. "Running from the Roman army will whittle you down, I suppose. My figure has been the least of my worries."

"Our princess has not dishonored herself," Horsa said. "One time she put nettles in Alaric's bed. *That* was a laugh."

Ehre glanced skeptically at Hengist's arm slung casually over her shoulder. Julia could just see her making the calculations. The twins' good opinion was apparently strong currency.

"I do not believe you did that. You'd be dead."

It was Hengist who smiled, seeking to smooth the sudden

spike to the conversation. "Ehre is sister to Brisca, the chieftain of this place. And Julia—"

Sister to Brisca. The black-haired chieftain currently warming Alaric's bed, if Julia had eyes. "I saw your sister. Is it true she rules alone with no husband?"

"My sister won't marry again. Not since Alaric killed her last husband." Ehre regarded her steadily. "What about you? It isn't often Alaric takes a Roman bed slave."

Had the boys told her about the cave? Julia hid her outrage behind a thoughtless laugh. "I would rather say he is *my* bed slave."

"You must be very generous, then, allowing my sister to borrow him," Ehre said. "He lies with her whenever he comes through. The first time, she spent four nights in his tent and emerged the queen of this place. Perhaps he will lie with me and gift me a kingdom too."

Julia felt her fists clench. So Alaric was in the *habit* of lying with women and offering them kingdoms. "Certainly he will lie with you. Me, you, your sister, or a hole in the wall at the appropriate height. I wonder how many kingdoms he has to give."

"Shouldn't I find out?" Ehre laughed as if it were all an outrageous jest and slung an arm around Julia's shoulders. "Let's go and do something fun."

Alaric wasn't certain when he'd made up his mind. Perhaps while watching Julia trounce the twins at *latrones*. Or perhaps in the cave behind the waterfall, listening to her tell him of the scars beneath her skin, before she turned to fire in his arms. Or perhaps he had come to his decision the moment he'd lost her to the bandits, searching for her on the long windward slope of the mountain. It didn't matter when. He had decided.

He would not send Julia back. Not to her brother; not to anyone else.

Now, standing amidst the crowd in the fortified town of

Acerrae, with the village's black-haired chieftain, he watched the twins draw her away—and wished *fiercely* that he was the one showing her the bathhouse. He'd bar the doors and take her in his arms and finish what they'd damn well started. And then he'd tell her, under no uncertain terms, that she would not be going back to Ravenna.

She would stay with him and be his concubine.

It was what she wanted, wasn't it? He was assured that she wanted *him*; her passion had not been false. He wouldn't grant her an army, but he would give her safety. A place in the world. In his bed.

He wanted her in his bed. He would go to war if necessary to keep her there.

Alaric knew that claiming her would mean war. With the Romans, yes—but also with his own. The chieftains wouldn't like it, but he would bend them to his will in this.

And he would need the hill tribes more than ever. That meant he needed Brisca more than ever. Everything depended on holding these passes.

Not long after, he sat with his boots propped on the scarred table in Brisca's great hall, a cup of ale in his hand.

Brisca shrugged off her moss-green cloak and sauntered to the window. "Fuck you," she muttered, almost to herself. "Fuck you, Alaric of the Goths."

Alaric grinned. "I have had better greetings from you, Brisca."

"You had better have a decent explanation for bringing that redheaded portent of disaster to my doorstep."

Alaric laid it out plain. Stilicho's invitation after Theodosius's death. The unmitigated calamity of that banquet. "When I made you chieftain here all those years ago, I told you I may have reason to call upon you in turn," he said. "Now is that time. I need the hill tribes to hold the passes, and I need your help in convincing them."

"Alaric, three years ago your army came through as a cloud of locusts and stripped everything bare. I'd have better luck persuading a stone."

"We were starving, Brisca. I had to let the men feed themselves in these hills, and I kept them away from the towns."

"But not from the pastures."

"There is no inch of these mountains not chewed over by those rawboned sheep of yours. To keep them out of your *pastures*, I'd have to teach them to fly."

Brisca's eyes flicked to his boots. "Get your boots off my table."

Alaric slid his boots off the table and rose, crossing the room unhurried. He joined her by the window, propping an arm on solid stone.

"I need you, Brisca. Tell me what you want in return."

Brisca's eyes fell to his mouth. That old, familiar heat pulsed between them. "Well." Her fingers lazily brushed the laces at the neck of his tunic. "I do need something."

"And that is?"

"My cousin Black Nathan wants to marry me off to his kin, which would bring my territory under *his* control. Some among my people want to see me married too. It hurts their pride to follow a woman." She lifted her gaze to his. "Black Nathan is too powerful to defy directly. I need you to be a forceful presence beside me."

And in your bed. Alaric understood what his answer must be. Even as a pair of green eyes arose in his thoughts, flashing in rage and hurt.

He forced the thought down. If this was what he had to do to keep Julia his, then he would damn well do it. He would fuck his way across the continent if necessary. Julia used her body to get what she wanted; she had done it with him and it had *worked*. Surely she would understand that there were times when he must do the same. It meant nothing to her. She would know it meant nothing to him. If he tried to seek her permission, she would laugh in his face.

He hooked a hand into Brisca's belt and pulled her to him. He put his mouth to her neck; she leaned her head back and he heard her moan her assent in the back of her throat. An image of Julia flashed before his eyes. Hair wet and streaming down her back. Eyes green and gleaming through all that steam, *asking* him to take her.

Lust slammed into him. Hard and violent.

He pressed Brisca up against the wall, kissing her deeply. If he shut his eyes he could pretend this was Julia, her lips opening eagerly against his, the warm silken heat of her tongue in his mouth. Longing flooded him. His hands shook. *Gods*, he wanted her.

But it wasn't quite right. Brisca was taller. The leg twining around his hip now was more muscular, honed from riding horses and tramping through mountains. Not fined down from a week or more on the road, defenseless and in need of his protection. He was instantly, *savagely* hard now, just thinking about Julia's legs, and how much she fucking *needed* him. Because she did. She needed him.

Brisca's kiss was the wrong taste. What he wanted was roses and blueberries and under it the whole black sky. He opened her shirt, the laces giving way beneath his hands, his mouth closing on a nipple. Brisca gasped, arching up into his touch. In his mind, it was Julia wild for him and moaning his name, Julia with her fingers curling in his hair. *No.* Nails not sharp enough, not vicious like a little cat the way she clenched at his roots. Julia's lust was always fired by rage. Same as his.

Laughter. Starlight scattering across a lake. Alaric stiffened.

Brisca hissed between her teeth. "What is it?"

He turned to the window, cursing. Below, a crowd had gathered, drinking and placing bets as a pair of young warriors sparred. Among the spectators, her head bent and whispering with a handsome young man, was Julia.

The sight knifed through him. She was wearing a woolen dress and kirtle, pale blue, her red hair braided and falling in a thick rope down one shoulder. She looked like some chieftain's daughter whose battles were *his*.

Fuck. "Stay here," he muttered, striding to the door. "I'll be right back."

Amidst the crowd below Brisca's great hall, Julia sat with a young man whose brown hair curled to his shoulders, their heads together as if sharing some illicit secret. The sight filled Alaric with unreasoning rage and envy. *He* should be the one sitting on that bench in the sunshine, drinking with Julia and making her laugh.

It would hardly help his case with Brisca if he beat her kinsman to death in front of her.

Hengist was lolling in the grass, drinking, while Horsa diced in a circle of wild young warriors. Alaric nudged Hengist with his boot. "Get up." Then he reached out an arm and yanked Horsa out of his circle by his shirt.

"Ow! Stop!" Horsa scowled. "What is it?"

Julia had noticed him now. She did *not* look happy to see him. "You know what it is."

"Brisca's kinsman? Berig?" Horsa scratched his head. "He's a harpist."

As if he gave a fuck. Across the yard, he saw her lips curve in that smug smile. It was provocation past bearing. He wanted to drag Julia back to the guesthouse, lay her down beneath him, and show her *exactly* who she belonged to.

"Take her back to the guesthouse. Don't let her out for the rest of the day, and no visitors. *Especially* not him." The boys gaped at him. "Well? *Go.*"

Alaric watched them stride up to Julia and explain it to her;

clearly they were making him the villain. Her blue-green gaze sliced across the yard to him, seething. He had a feeling Julia's anger with him had to do with more than his orders.

And his own feelings for her had to do with more than lust. He wanted her. Not just in his bed. He wanted to sit in the sunshine and drink with her. He wanted—

"Did I just hear you order that woman confined?" Brisca's fingers curled around his forearm. "Your guest is perfectly safe here."

The sight of Julia under lock and key offended Brisca's honor; it implied that she could not control her own village. But he could not have Julia unguarded. Last time he relaxed his vigilance, he'd nearly gotten her killed.

He ran an agitated hand through his hair. "You have no idea the trouble she gets into."

"If you want my advice, you'll keep her where you can see her," Brisca said quietly. "Who would dare to spirit her off under your watchful eyes?"

"I'll think about it." Perhaps it was a better idea than leaving her with the twin geniuses. "In the meantime, we should finish our discussion."

That distracted her well enough. It didn't matter what passed between him and Brisca, he told himself. He would go to Julia after and explain his decision, and she'd agree.

And then, if he had her once—well, more than *once*, but just for the one night—he'd be free of this miserable preoccupation and could make decisions with a clearer head.

CHAPTER EIGHTEEN

Julia paced the guesthouse, furious.

Hours had passed. Day had faded, and the twins would not let her out. Alaric had put the fear in them. How *dare* he imprison her here like a dog that had slipped its leash. The message could not be clearer. She was a prisoner, and she must never forget it.

At least there was wine. Julia poured herself another cup of the robust red, just as voices rose outside and then the shadows shifted. She turned to see Alaric, framed by the sunset, lifting the door flap with one superbly muscled arm.

"Where have *you* been?" she demanded.

By way of reply, he crossed the room and pulled her into his arms, silencing her disapproval with his mouth.

He crushed her to him, his kiss hot and demanding, and suddenly she'd forgotten her anger entirely. "I'm sorry," he murmured against her throat. "I'd have come earlier if I could—" But she no longer cared. She was on fire, melting in his arms, defenseless as he lifted her onto the table. Her legs came up of their own accord, locking around his hips.

He pressed her onto her back, his mouth burning a ferocious

line to her collarbone. Her hands curled into his hair. "Don't—Stop." But she was shaking with need, and from the wicked laugh in her ear, she knew what he had heard: *don't stop.* She felt like a candlewick, lit aflame. He brought his mouth back up to her lips, kissing her long and deep, and Julia forgot everything else. This was *Alaric,* fire and war and savagery racing through her blood like fever. It had been so goddamn long.

He'd come to her warm from another woman's bed.

The thought was cold water on her desire. Dimly she realized he had her up on the table now, her legs thrown wildly around his waist, her skirt hiked up her thighs, her whole body arching up to him as if making an offering of herself.

So much for being the one he couldn't have.

"*Stop.* We have—" Her body throbbed and ached and *hurt.* "We have to talk."

It surprised her to no end when he backed off.

Julia slid off the table, turning her back to him as she adjusted her clothes, then busied herself pouring a cup of wine. Her hands shook. At her back, an intense, *ferocious* quiet. She gulped the wine—and when she turned he was leaning casually against the central pole that held up the roof, chiseled arms crossed over his magnificently bare chest. When had he lost his shirt?

"Well?" He raised a brow. "Talk."

Julia drew a breath. For a moment she could not remember words.

"If you won't, then I will." Blue eyes glittered in the light from the banked coals. "I will not send you back to your brother. Stay with me, Julia."

Julia covered her shock by taking another drawn-out sip of her wine. What was she to make of this? Was he offering Rome in exchange? Had he come from Brisca's bed to say that?

Be the one he can't have.

"You have nerve," she said lightly. "You assume a great deal. Just because I lay with you once doesn't mean I will again."

His eyes dropped significantly to her shaking hands. "Is that so."

Julia tensed. She *wished* he wouldn't drop his voice to a throaty purr like that. It was entirely unfair, when all he had to do was look at her to make her absolutely stupid with the desire to touch him. The gods help her when he grinned or crossed his arms over his chest or took his shirt off.

"Are you prepared to pay my price, King of the Goths?" Julia arched a brow. "You gave Brisca a kingdom for her time in your bed. I want an empire."

Alaric's laugh rolled through her, warm and luxurious. Julia's hands clenched around her cup. *Would she win this negotiation by throwing it at him?* Cleopatra would never.

"Julia, not three weeks ago you were a vagabond who begged me to take you. You have nothing to offer—no kingdom, no allies, no land. And you think you have the standing to demand an empire of me. For something I can have from any willing woman." His grin flashed on his tanned face. "You're the one with nerve."

Rage stopped her breath. "Laugh at me all you wish. But if you want a place in *my* bed, an empire is my price."

"So transactional, Julia." He said it softly. Hairs rose on her arms. "No."

No. Why did it hurt so much? What did Brisca have that she did not? "I suppose you don't wish to share my bed after all."

"That is not what I said." He was coming toward her now. A dangerous stillness about him even when in motion. He stopped before her, planting his hands on either side of her on the table, boxing her in. "Correct me if I'm wrong," he said quietly. "But it's been my impression that you want this as much as I do."

A hot, insistent throb began between her thighs.

Julia felt herself lean forward, almost meeting him. Close enough to kiss. Their breaths mingled, heated the air. She had the distinct feeling he was waiting for her to cross the final distance between them.

To admit he was right.

In her mind, she slid her hands up the corded strength of his arms, then greedily over his chest, feeling the hard ridges of muscle on his stomach and the lines of his scars beneath her palms. In her mind, she ran her tongue along the seam of his lips, just a finger's length from her, pressed her mouth to the strong column of his throat. Licked the scent of him off his skin. Oh *gods*, she wanted to.

The thought of him holding himself still like that—that fierce, *disciplined* stillness while she touched and licked him everywhere—made her weak with desire.

Of course she could never admit to the debilitating power he held over her. That would be a terrible mistake.

"I don't want you." What a lie. She wanted to rub herself against him like a cat in heat. "I want to rule Rome in my brother's stead."

More lies. She was lying through her teeth to a man who looked at her as if he could see down to the bottom of every lie she'd ever told.

"If that is how you want it. I will not come to you again. In fact, I'm willing to predict it is you who'll come to me." A mocking grin lifted his lips. "I'll take you then, but only when you beg."

"I'll never do that. In fact, I rather think it's you who'll beg before this week is out."

His laugh sounded against her throat. The sweet, warm vibration of it made her toes curl. "We'll see who breaks first, then."

And then—to her vast annoyance—he was gone.

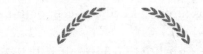

CHAPTER NINETEEN

This time, when Julia held the little flute to her lips and blew, it made a low, anemic whistle. She was rather proud she'd made any sound at all. "How was that?"

Alaric's flute was fiendishly hard to play. She sat on a bench near the sparring ring, Horsa on one side and Hengist on the other. She had spent the night tossing and turning, but now it was a glorious morning and Alaric had ridden out to hunt with Brisca and the elder warriors. Meanwhile, the younger were holding a tournament. The twins desperately wanted to go, and Julia promised to return to her prison before Alaric returned. He'd never know.

She would *not* waste time thinking of the gauntlet he'd thrown at her feet.

Horsa laughed at her efforts with the flute. "That is very bad." He took the flute, blew an agile little trill. "You purse your lips like this," he said, puckering.

"No one can do that with their lips. You are a freak." Julia snatched the flute back, examining the delicate carvings. "What kind of bone is this?"

"Human." Horsa said it just as she put it to her lips again. "It's a finger bone."

Julia nearly spit the flute into her lap. "In future, when something is part of a human corpse, you will tell me *before* it goes in my mouth," she said in a strained voice.

"It belonged to Brisca's husband. When Alaric killed him, she had this flute made in thanks, so he could find her in these hills if he ever had need of her."

"How touching." Gifts made of human body parts. They were *made* for each other.

Up on the dais, Ehre was sparring with a man. Both were breathtaking. Excellently muscled: the man stripped to the waist and Ehre wearing only a cloth wound about her breasts and long, loose trousers. Her narrow braids lashed at the air as she spun. Then Ehre surged forward with a series of aggressive slashes that made the man stumble, just the smallest misstep and her sword was at his throat. For a moment they were still, both breathing hard as the drums fell silent. Then the silence broke and the two of them clasped hands and grinned.

Horsa leaned in and spoke to Hengist. "I'll fight you for her."

Julia laughed. "No fighting over me, please."

"Not *you*. Ehre. I won last time we fought over her, remember? Three years ago when I broke your arm and Alaric had to set it."

"We were boys then. Ehre wants a man." Hengist laughed.

"Then, I will give her one." Horsa rose to his feet. "I challenge you, brother. Winner takes the girl."

"*Sit down*, the both of you. No one is *taking* anyone." Neither listened to her.

Horsa slid his *seax* out of its sheath with a slow hiss. "Last chance to save yourself before I shame the life out of you."

A feral grin spread across Hengist's face. "I'll make you weep like I did when we were twelve."

And then the boys were off, swaggering toward the platform,

swapping insults through bared teeth, just as Ehre slid onto the bench they'd just vacated.

"Did you hear that?" Julia fumed. "Fighting over you as if—"

"If those boys really wanted me, they would have to fight *me* for me. They would both lose." Ehre passed her a wineskin. *Ealu*. Julia sucked it down.

The twins climbed onto the platform, peeling off their shirts. They began a slow circle, taunting each other in Gothic. Then the drums picked up and they began to fight in earnest. Twisting and lunging, their weapons screaming through the air; Julia found herself holding her breath. She had known these boys first as pitiless child warriors, then as formidable *latrones* opponents, and finally as something akin to little brothers. But these terrifying warriors, sharp as spear points—this was what they *were*.

The fight ended at an impasse. Horsa's knife at Hengist's throat, Hengist's at his brother's heart. The boys embraced amidst the cheers of their friends, young and alive and so terribly beautiful. Julia found herself on her feet with the rest of them, laughing and shouting.

When she sat down, Alaric was standing behind her.

She knew from the way the skin on her back prickled as everyone fell silent, even the drums. *Fuck*. She had not expected him back this soon.

He stood a few paces behind her, leaning casually on his spear, his tunic a dark blue that lit up the sun-warmed gold of his skin. He said something in Gothic to the twins. Hengist responded with tight-strung deference, but Horsa was all bravado, teeth bared in challenge. Alaric gave a laughing response in Gothic. Then he reached up and pulled off his shirt.

A silence fell just as Julia drew in a sharp breath. *He should warn people before he does that*, she fumed; now everyone had heard her gasping like a landed fish.

Without glancing at her, he dropped his tunic in her lap. "Hold this."

Julia stared as he sauntered to the platform, fingers curling into the soft fabric of his tunic. *That* was on purpose. Well. If he thought she'd go to him—*beg*—he would be severely disappointed. She had dignity! She was not a barbarian. She was Roman. *Intellectual.* In control of her desires.

The drums picked up an arrhythmic beat that put Julia's nerves on edge. For the barest instant, everything went still and sharp as glass. Then the three leaped into motion, spear points dissolving in a blur of flashing light. Julia forgot her temper, eyes fixed on the ripple and flow of Alaric's muscles beneath his skin, the heavy spear weightless as wind in his hands.

It wasn't a free-for-all. The twins were working together against him, and they'd been playing in their previous fight. In this one they were faster, almost terrifying in their focus. Alaric stayed a step ahead of them, but it was a scant step; Julia's stomach clenched as a spear point went whistling by his face. A breath closer and it would've laid his cheekbone open like a book. He didn't bat an eye.

Ehre glanced pointedly at her hands. "You'll rip that if you grip it any tighter." Julia winced as a blade slashed murderously close to an exposed abdomen. If Horsa hadn't sucked in just then, he'd be dead. "You needn't fuss yourself. He's only teaching them."

The *ealu*, Julia noticed, made Ehre distinctly friendlier. "I rather think they'll murder each other."

"They can't touch him. He's slowing down for them." She leaned forward, intent on the flashing spears. "There. *That* was proving a point. I'm surprised Hengist kept his grip on that spear," Ehre said. "That thrust would have glanced off the hip bone. Alaric wants him to aim for the kidney. A killing blow."

"Yes, a killing blow. I hardly see how *that* could go wrong." Julia eyed the platform anxiously, looking for bloodstains. "Has anyone ever died doing this?"

"Calm yourself." Ehre took a pull from the wineskin. "You'll embarrass him."

"Nonsense. Nothing could embarrass that man." Julia eyed the wineskin. "If I'm going to watch this, I will require more to drink."

The *ealu* helped. Julia found herself absorbed as Ehre narrated the lesson. There was a fierce elation in Alaric's violence, his blue eyes flashing as he blocked and feinted and drew the twins on. By the time it ended—Alaric laughing, an arm slung around each of the boys' necks, pride lighting him up from within—Julia was on her feet again, some nameless ache building in her chest. *He loves them*, she realized. *Loves them like sons.*

What if he loved *her*?

Suppose he beamed with pride like that at *her*, watching her play *latrones*. *You should have been a general*, he'd said. Why did he have to *say* that? Now she couldn't stop thinking of it, enamored of the warmth in his voice and the fierce honesty in his eyes.

Ehre spoke low in her ear. "Is he yours?"

"What? *No!*" Her face flamed. Was her infatuation tattooed on her forehead? Did *everyone* see it?

Ehre grinned fiercely. "Good."

Julia could only stare as she stood and strutted toward the platform, eyes locked to Alaric's, a long battle-knife in each hand and a challenge on her lips.

"He loves the attention, doesn't he," Julia muttered acidly.

Hengist slouched next to her on the bench. "It's always like that. Chieftain's daughters and warriors and tradesmen's wives. Even Roman aristocrats." He glanced at her beneath ghost-pale lashes. "No offense."

"None taken. *I* don't care a fig for that man." Why did her voice rise to a screech when she said that?

Horsa had gone back to dicing while she and Hengist shared a wineskin and Ehre sparred with Alaric. The sunlight glinted off the sweat that gilded Alaric's muscles and Ehre's lean, fierce limbs. The rhythm set by the drums was almost *sexual.*

This time, Julia wouldn't mind seeing a little blood.

"Can I tell you a secret?" Hengist glanced at her. "I don't *want* to be a warlord. I want to be a farmer. Or a horse breeder. Maybe both."

"Who says you must be a *warlord*? It sounds grim."

"Alaric does. He says we'll inherit his kingdom, and I can't go against him. He's *Alaric.*"

"Really? I don't find it difficult at all." Up on the platform, Alaric blocked a vicious slash to his chest; Ehre barely avoided his lightning response. The air fairly *crackled* between them. *If she isn't in his bed by nightfall,* Julia thought darkly, *I'll eat my own hair.*

"Hengist, I am going to go and feed this shirt to a goat." She announced, taking a last long, blistering suck of the *ealu.*

Alaric knew the minute Julia left. Half-gone with drink, as if she'd seen something shiny she wanted to look at more than *him* half-naked for her benefit. His pride seethed.

When the fight ended, he was immediately mobbed. He *needed* these people; and so he stayed to smile and laugh and posture, let himself be flattered and fawned over. All the while his impatience grew. Julia couldn't be allowed to wander about the village unguarded. Brisca had assured him a close escort for Julia wasn't necessary; still, he thought her too trusting. And the boys had failed him in keeping a careful watch on her, *again.*

Hengist and Horsa were sitting on the rough-hewn bench, looking up at him with identical expressions of guilt and fear.

"It wasn't our fault."

"It was Julia's idea. She said—"

"There is no doubt in my mind it was Julia's fault. I'm still blaming you." He glanced between them. "Horsa, your reach is off. You overbalanced twice just now, as you did in battle the other night. You'd be dead three times over if I wasn't there to watch your back."

Horsa's face reddened. Hengist spoke up. "He's slow with his feet too."

"And *you* should've been keeping your brother out of trouble," Alaric said to Hengist. "No more children's sparring games. The two of you are well out of swaddling clothes. Every day at dawn from tomorrow until we leave, we practice."

The boys turned pale. And with good reason. The real training he put them through was far more difficult than these sparring matches. But he himself had suffered much worse under Stilicho, and keeping Gaufrid's twins alive meant never tolerating mistakes.

He nodded toward Julia, who seemed to be trying to feed his tunic to the livestock. "See that she gets back to the guesthouse. If you feel the urge to wench and drink, remember what awaits you in the morning." He paused. "What are you waiting for? *Go.*"

The twins went. He'd goaded her into her fit of temper, he knew. He had no excuse for provoking her, other than that he liked the way her eyes lit up when she was angry. Almost as much as he liked how she looked at him without his shirt. It had been—very distracting. He was surprised he hadn't gotten himself skewered, showing off for her like that.

If you want my advice, you'll keep her where you can see her. Brisca's words. Alaric considered it. If he kept her where he could see her, he could make her *want* to come to him.

He was petty enough to want her to beg him to take her. And he would then. Oh yes, he would.

She'd crack first. He would be sure of it.

CHAPTER TWENTY

The next three days could only be described as a fiendish war of attrition.

For three days, Julia was present at feasts and bonfires as Alaric flaunted Brisca before her, her hand lightly brushing his forearm as they sat on their high-backed thrones in the cavernous feasting hall. But not as much as he flaunted *himself.* Bare-chested and glorious, golden torques about his biceps and throat. Julia did not miss the way his gaze went to her, even as his hand lingered on Brisca's thigh. He was doing it on purpose, and relishing her discomfort.

So Julia retaliated. She hadn't missed how Alaric had stared the first time she'd appeared before him in a borrowed Gothic dress. So she took care with her appearance, braiding her hair as she'd seen the women in the village do. And she flirted outrageously with anyone nearby, ignoring Alaric utterly. Soon she had a throng of admirers. He did not fall to his knees and offer her a kingdom for a night between her thighs. But sometimes she could *feel* his gaze upon her; a hot, scorching need.

She would *not* crack first. She would not crack at all.

★ ★ ★

On the third night since Alaric had come to her guesthouse, Julia sat by a bonfire in the shadow of the feasting hall, the twins nearby, drinking and laughing and telling stories. She'd never had *fun* like this in Ravenna. If Alaric weren't nearby, she would be perfectly happy.

But Alaric was nearby. Ruining her happiness.

Brisca's great hall had once been a Roman villa, but its upper stories had been razed and a great, beamy Celtic hall had been built on its bones. A columned portico jutted out of one wall, a remainder of the old building. Alaric stood on the portico, in intense conversation with Brisca, smiling down at her with such bold, warm sexuality that Julia felt the force of it like a rising tide. Her famished gaze traveled from his gleaming bronze hair to the broad, sculpted beauty of his shoulders and chest beneath his tunic; the lazy violence pulsing beneath his skin.

She was positively *miserable* with jealousy.

Across the fire, Riga was coaxing a tune from an instrument stringed like a cithara, its neck long and slender, the end carved in a horse's head. No Roman instrument sounded like this, the notes dripping and sliding from his fingers in one long, eliding lament.

"Something grieves you, pretty woman." It was Berig, nephew of Brisca's late husband, the young man she'd met the day she arrived. He was younger than Alaric, perhaps closer to her own age, and his voice was—nice. Not a force of seductive persuasion like Alaric's, but sweet, with a musical lilt. "Perhaps I should try to distract you from your troubles."

"My troubles are legion, I'm afraid."

"And I would take them for you, if I could." This man reminded her of Cornelius—his kind eyes, his unthreatening demeanor. Here was a man who would not turn her heart inside out and leave it in the dirt.

Julia smiled. "Perhaps I would let you."

"I wonder if you will allow me to speak plainly, Princess."
Berig studied her intently. "I don't like seeing women kept prisoner. Is it your wish to escape him?"

Alaric was leaning into Brisca's space now, far too close. Was
he—*nuzzling* her neck? Julia gritted her teeth. *That* required
retaliation.

"How could I?" She let her fingers trail across his thigh. "I
cannot go back to Rome, and I cannot cross these mountains
myself."

Berig's lips brushed close to her ear. "I'd take you."

His sudden closeness caught Alaric's attention. Just one sharp
slice of a glance, glittering in the dark, and it was coldly murderous. Julia froze, imagining Alaric cutting Berig's throat. That
was a very real possibility.

Don't be ridiculous, she admonished herself. Alaric wouldn't
murder Brisca's kin under her own nose. Perhaps she would lie
with Berig. It was only fair.

Julia picked up a stick and stabbed viciously at the fire. Riga
was still plucking away at his instrument. "Riga, perhaps you
know a cheerful tune to play on that thing."

A grin spread across Riga's face. Pure malevolent glee. "For
certain."

Berig was touching her again. Alaric imagined cutting off his
hands.

His exhaustion made him savage. The past few days he had
been up at dawn, training with the twins, hunting with Brisca's
warriors, proving his mettle and cementing his legend—and
then awake till past midnight, listening to the men's boasting
and their tales of woe.

Through it all, Julia had been always at the edge of his vision and just out of reach. Laughing and flirting, the firelight
tangling in her hair. Alaric glanced at Julia and her paramour,

heads bent together by the fire. She looked like a young goddess in the firelight, and jealousy ripped right through him. He could still fucking *taste* her from the last time they'd kissed.

He wondered how many he would have to kill to kiss her again.

"Black Nathan sent a message. He'll arrive tomorrow afternoon," Brisca was saying. "He had some *choice words* about the last time you came through these mountains."

"He'll think better of me when he finds himself on the point of a Roman sword."

"A sword *you* brought to his doorstep for the sake of Theodosius's daughter."

"Is that how you see it?" Alaric asked her. "What will you tell him?"

Brisca shrugged. "He needs to believe you'll affix the head of any man you find in my bed to your saddle."

"You don't need to share my bed to ask for my protection. I'll kill any man you point to."

"I don't need you to actually kill anyone, Alaric. I need the *threat* of it."

Julia's faint laughter cut through the conversation. He glanced down to see Berig whispering in her ear and in an instant he was gripped by raging jealousy.

"I'll tolerate a lot from you, Alaric, but I'd appreciate if you'd not kill my kinsman," Brisca said drily. "Take that girl to bed if you must, but I won't have it keep you from doing as you promised *me*."

Annoyance gritted his teeth. "She's nothing to do with us."

The music quickened under Riga's hands and he recognized the tune. It was the dance of Ēostre, nowhere near the proper season. The way Julia had been draping herself all over Berig, he wouldn't wait for the song to finish before dragging her off into the shadows to finish the rite.

Riga was doing it on purpose, just to make him stark mad.

Hengist's hand was slicked with sweat. His hold slipped, and the circle spun faster until Julia felt she'd fly off her feet.

In Ravenna, one listened to music with remote decorum. One did not fling oneself into the dance, music thundering up from the ground like a commandment from the heathen gods. The drums were a driving bedrock beneath Riga's leaping arpeggios; sweat plastered her hair to her neck, and she was only one of many here, sticky and unkempt and *free*. She had the strongest feeling this was exactly where she was meant to be. She spun through a night sky lit with fire. Dizzy and laughing, she came down with a jolt at the edge. A shadow rose from out of the dark.

Suddenly she found herself pressed up against the palisade in the shadow of the mead hall, out of sight of the others. Alaric loomed above her. The fire sent up lazy sparks behind him and lit his hair to molten bronze.

Her face went numb, then flushed bright hot. "Hello."

"You and I must have words."

"I can't imagine what would be so urgent *now*." She couldn't keep the reproving tone out of her voice. "You've barely spoken to me in two days—"

He silenced her utterly with his thumb at her lip. Stroking, gentle as a kiss. The place between her legs was suddenly a mess of throbbing heat.

"What is it you chase with your wine and your opium? Tell me."

"Pleasure."

His eyes darkened with lust.

"Oblivion. Both."

"I'll be your damned oblivion. You'll remember nothing before me, and nothing after will ever be enough. Come to me in the dark and let us both for once be happy."

Julia raised a brow. "Are you—cracking first?"

"Maybe I am."

Words failed her as she stared up into the savagely beautiful face of this man who had conquered and killed. This man who was *asking* her now. "And my price?" His silence cut deeper than any blade. Her temper rose. Why couldn't he make it *easy* for her to say yes and save her dignity? "I see nothing has changed," Julia said icily. "What will you do now, Alaric of the Goths? Drag me off to your longhouse? It's what you barbarians do, is it not?"

"So that is what you want." His self-assured grin flashed. Glint of pirate gold at the end of the world. "Not until you beg me, Julia."

She had her pride. "I'll never do that."

She had no warning. The next instant he'd spun her around and pressed her hard against the skinned poles of the palisade. She gasped, "What are you doing?"

"Making you beg."

Oh gods, she was weak. She was *eager*, gasping a whispered *yes* as one hand clamped down on her mouth. Huge and hard and calloused, a warrior's hand. He'd killed with it, many times, and now he used it to silence her breathless moan, as his other hand slipped beneath the waistband of her skirt.

Not fair. Julia arched her back, grinding her ass into his rigid erection, and was gratified to hear him curse between his teeth as his fingers convulsed in her hair. *Yes.* She'd be the one to win this game; she—

Then his thumb brushed the white-hot center of her desire.

She lost all thought of retribution. Caught between the palisade and his pulsing arousal hot at her back, Julia dissolved into a sea of fire. Somehow he knew the exact alchemy of pressure and speed to drive her out of her mind. He kept her pleasure going, chasing that pinnacle she'd felt in the cave—that pleasure that had sent her back arching like a strung bow.

When he tilted her head back and seized her mouth with his—fingers splayed along her jawline, holding her captive—

Julia had no sense left. She kissed him back wildly—even as his fingers slowed. Became lighter. Leisurely. "Please," she whispered. *"Please."*

He made a sound halfway between a laugh and a growl. His thumb was turning slow, lascivious circles around the center of her pleasure now, and it was *torture*. He drew back from their kiss, and when she tried to chase him for more, his free hand gripped her by the hair, pressing her cheek against the wood as his other hand made her come apart. Something was building, the same huge, explosive pleasure that had ripped through her in the cave. Her fingers arched against the wall. "Gods. Alaric. *Please*—"

"I told you I would make you beg."

In the next instant, his hand was gone. He was looking down at her, both hands planted on the wall above her head, a smug grin lifting his lips. He'd left her dangling off a cliff; now he was standing above her as she clung to the edge, laughing at her plight.

How *dare* he? How dare he bring her to this precipice and then pull away, leaving her panting and aching for him? "I *hate* you."

"No, you don't." His voice so rough and soft. "I am no ravening barbarian who forces women to my bed, Julia. *You* come to *me*. Walk across that yard and come to my longhouse. If you ask nicely, maybe I'll finish you off."

Outrage flushed through her. "You bastard."

"Suit yourself." He seized her chin and kissed her once, hard and swift and possessive; his thumb dragging across her cheekbone. Then he was gone.

Julia let out a shuddering breath. Her body still ached and throbbed, the delicate flesh between her thighs swollen and hot with need. She pressed her legs together, barely stifling a moan. How could he leave her in this pathetic state! His self-assured grin flashed before her sight. *I told you I would make you beg.* Fuck him. He'd brought her to the edge, and then demanded she walk across this yard in full view of everyone to beg him for her satisfaction.

It would be a cold day in *hell* before she did such a thing.

Julia went back to the fire, trying to act as if nothing had happened. The crowd had emptied out, young couples disappearing into the dark. Alaric's kiss still scorched her mouth.

She stared into the fire, furious. She would not go running to his longhouse and offer herself up like a sacrificial virgin. She *would not.*

Except—why not? What did it matter? She was ruined anyway. Why should she not take her pleasure where she could? Just a few dozen steps, and she'd be in his arms again. Drowning in his kiss.

Fine, she thought. *I'll crack.*

Horsa sat with his arm flung around the shoulders of a wheat-blonde woman and a dark-haired young man—he seemed to prefer both. He gave her a sly grin when she rose to her feet. "And where are you going?"

"None of your business. *Nowhere.* To bed."

"I'll walk you."

"There is no need. Please don't go to any trouble. No—*sit down.*"

She was so consumed with arguing that she almost didn't notice when Brisca swept down the steps to the portico, crossed the half-dozen yards to Alaric's longhouse, and slipped inside.

Alaric paced his room like a caged animal. What was *taking* her so long? *Fuck.*

He thought of her in his arms, pressed up against the palisade, her breath coming hot and fast as he pushed her to the edge of desire. He'd thought to teach her a lesson about who exactly was in control here. Had thought to bring her to the edge and then walk away, defy her low opinion of him, and force her to make the choice herself.

It never *occurred* to him that *he* would be the one on the edge of begging. And that her choice might not be him.

Alaric bit out a curse. Fires burned in metal fire bowls next to a bed piled with furs, a bed he'd planned to put to better use than sleeping. He stripped off his fine embroidered shirt and stalked to the window, naked to the waist, staring out toward the bonfire where he'd left *his* woman. The one he'd killed for. The one he was risking a war for.

To hell with these power games. He'd drag her into his bed where she belonged. He would give her whatever it took. Armies, conquest— *No.* Then she would know the true extent of her power over him. A child of Theodosius. This game was too dangerous. It would not end well.

Alaric drove his fist into the wall. Plaster exploded onto the floor.

A knock sounded. Alaric's heart leaped in his chest as he strode to the door and ripped it open. "*Finally.* What the hell took you so—"

But it wasn't Julia staring up at him, her eyes gleaming in the torchlight. It was Brisca.

CHAPTER TWENTY-ONE

Julia sat up in her platform bed and blinked the terrible dawn out of her eyes. Last night sent a flush of shame through her. She had cracked so *fast*. She'd been about to go to Alaric, the hell with all dignity. Only to be beaten by Brisca. *She'd* been the one to spend the night being showered with kingdoms and orgasms.

Julia pressed her face into her hands and let out a raw, ugly sob.

Horsa stood in the doorway, one eye narrowed, the other too swollen to see through. "Are you *crying*? You look terrible."

"*I* look terrible?" She eyed the darkening bruise of Horsa's eye with some alarm. "What on earth happened to you?"

"We practiced. Alaric told me to protect my face if I wanted to keep it pretty. I wasn't fast enough."

"He's in a terrible black mood." Hengist came into the room, limping. "Best avoid him."

"I plan to." She'd rather fall in a sewer than lay eyes on that man. "Come here, Horsa. I think I can help with your eye." She found Alaric's jar of salve. "This *works*, whatever it is. My bruises are almost gone."

"Is that Alaric's cloak on your bed?" Horsa smirked. "Do you *sleep* with it?"

Behind him, Hengist was laying out food on the scarred table. "I'll wager she sleeps swaddled in it like a day-old babe."

"I'm going to burn it," Julia said airily, dabbing at Horsa's battered face. "It smells of horse dung." But of course it didn't—it smelled like *Alaric*, and Julia didn't think she'd mind dying as long as she could be buried in it. "Do you have any bruises, Hengist?"

"Just pass it here."

She pushed the salve toward him. "Where is Alaric?"

"Hunting. There's to be a party later. We need game for the table." Hengist sliced a piece of bread. "Eat. We brought honey."

The bread was steaming warm, and she *did* like honey. "What sort of party?"

"Not like your fusty Roman parties, with your paper lights and silly food and dancing girls we aren't allowed to fuck. The only fun part of that was when Alaric took you hostage." Horsa snickered.

"I'm so glad that amused you," Julia said acidly.

A shadow fell over the threshold, and Brisca stood at the door, wearing a blue tunic, leather leggings, and soft felt boots.

Julia's spine snapped straight. For a moment the two women eyed each other as two cats across a muddy yard.

Brisca's eyes flicked to the boys. "One of you bring us a drink. Don't care which."

"Make it a large drink," Julia said.

And then the boys were out the door, and she and Brisca were alone.

Brisca studied her and Julia studied right back. So this was the woman that Alaric *had* deigned to make a queen. Brisca wasn't beautiful, not the way the court at Ravenna defined beauty. Even so, there was a sharp, forceful clarity to her face that made it arresting.

When Hengist returned with the jug, Brisca poured a large, foaming mug for Julia and another for herself. "It's beer," she said. "We make it from barley." She shoved a mug over to Julia's end of the table. "Has he hurt you?"

Julia blinked. How on earth was she to answer that?

"Last I heard, Alaric kidnapped you at knifepoint. I come here to find your face swollen with tears. What else am I to think?" Brisca took a sip from her mug. "Alaric isn't the kind to abuse women. But he's not the kind to kidnap them either. And here you are."

Resentment rose up sharp in her. She hated the thought of Brisca seeing her as a victim.

"*He* kidnapped *me*? Is that what he told you? I kidnapped myself." Julia gave the beer an experimental sip. It tasted like a loaf of bread in beverage form. "I plotted a coup to get out of my impending marriage," she said casually. "Alaric simply came along at the right time."

"Well. Aren't *you* more interesting than I thought." Brisca's dark brows shot up. "Did you truly put nettles in his bed?"

"How did you know about that?"

"His men gossip like fishwives." Brisca regarded her over the rim of her cup. "Did you?"

Julia nodded. Brisca threw back her head and laughed—a loud, bold laugh that filled the room. "I'm surprised he didn't kill you."

"I'm surprised I didn't kill *him*." Julia shrugged. "Do you ever want to murder that man?"

"Frequently," Brisca said drily. "The worst thing about him is that he's *right* all the time. Have you ever tried to argue with someone who's always right?"

"It isn't arguing I have trouble with. It's having a normal conversation." Julia sipped her beer. "Have you ever tried to discuss the price of wheat in Tuscany with him? He'd get all grim and dreary and then try to stab things."

Brisca snorted. "He's off stabbing the wildlife at the moment."

"Yes, *after* he beat the twins to a pulp. I'll wager he turns your party into a bloodbath too." Julia shuddered. "I *hate* bloodbaths."

"I'll bet it shocks him to death every time you manage not to fall into bed with him."

Julia nearly choked on her beer.

"Have you?" The question was too casual. "Most women think him pleasing to look at."

"Yes, and he is *very* aware of that." Julia straightened. "What about you? Why haven't you married him?"

"Married him? *Me?* Oh, goodness. Julia, that isn't what Alaric is *for*." Brisca laughed. "He would only try to lord over me. I swore the day Alaric slew my last husband that I would never be imprisoned again."

There was an easy swagger in her words that made Julia love her a little. "I quite agree," she said with feeling. "Men are a rot on existence."

"Oh, but they have their uses." Brisca's grin broadened. "Alaric, for instance—"

Julia tensed. "That's quite enough on *that* topic."

Brisca finished her beer in one long gulp. "He ordered you not to leave this hut while he's away. Let's disobey."

People loved to talk about themselves. Brisca was no different.

Julia listened attentively as Brisca proudly showed her the village. The pens for baby goats. The tanner's and the brewer. The forge for smelting iron. The place was a tight, contained machine—it needed hardly anything beyond these walls.

Brisca led Julia on a narrow, treacherous trail into the mountains above the village, into the vineyards. The early summer air was unseasonably warm. There were men among the grapes, clipping and harvesting; one brought two cups of cool, crisp wine, pale as sunshine.

"You must think we're quite provincial here," Brisca said.

"On the contrary. I think it's far more intelligent to cultivate self-sufficiency than to depend on a faraway grain supply that can be easily cut off."

"That is very astute." Brisca gave another of those crooked grins. "If you rule as a woman, Julia, you will have to be more astute than any man. And meaner. If you have no husband, other men will take it as an invitation to take your kingdom—by war or marriage. There is little difference."

Questions leaped to Julia's tongue. What was it Brisca was doing with Alaric then? Was their affection simply an act, designed to drive away Brisca's suitors? Had she *really* lain with him last night? The thought of it tortured her. Julia opened her mouth to ask.

A bronze horn split the silence. Below, Alaric rode through the gates. A dozen warriors followed in his wake, the limp bodies of several deer and a boar slung on poles between them. Ehre rode beside him wearing a fine black cloak, her dark hair loose and hanging down in a fierce, gleaming mane. Julia watched them laughing together, Alaric's bronze head bent to her dark one, and suddenly felt sick.

What a fool she was, loving a man like him. Surely Brisca would see her infatuation written all over her face like an incantation in bronze.

But the other woman only rose to her feet. "There will be a great feast tonight. We must both prepare."

CHAPTER TWENTY-TWO

That afternoon, Brisca's kinsman Black Nathan arrived with his entourage—over fifty strong. Alaric leaned on his spear, watching from the high portico of Brisca's great hall as a sacrifice was made in their honor. The pure white cow lay on its side with its throat weeping blood, her legs spasming as the priestess thrust her hands elbow-deep in the animal's belly.

Below, Black Nathan stood with his bodyguards. King and warrior, chieftain and thrall, listening with all their might for the gods to speak through the bloody viscera.

Alaric was well aware of the knife edge he balanced on. Three unfavorable winters had hollowed out his alliances in these passes and an unlucky reading could undo everything he'd worked for. Even now, he could feel the nervous edge to the crowd's stillness. Alaric could see clearly his own vulnerability, his own army on the other side of the mountain and more than halfway to rebelling. No time was riper for a challenge. His gaze drifted to Julia, standing across the yard. The twins flanked her, their hands resting lazily on their weapons as if only a casual gesture, surrounded by the friends they'd been assiduously making in this village. He hoped they wouldn't need them.

Somewhere in the sky, an eagle screamed—magnifying the omen—just as the priestess stood with her arms crimson to the shoulder, the heavy liver draped across her hands.

"The readings are unclear. The gods have chosen not to speak."

In the face of unclear omens, gold could be its own benediction. And Julia's gold was a powerful one.

Alaric called for the exchange of gifts, watching as the chieftains held strands of priceless jewels to the light, their expressions baldly admiring. His allies expected certain things of him—prowess in battle, the gifts of charm and persuasion. And wealth, as much as he could wrest from his enemies. Alaric had brought his people gifts before; he'd laid cities at their feet for the sacking. But the princess's jewels were on another level entirely.

Black Nathan was barrel-chested with a bristling black beard that gave him his name, and a wily, battle-scarred look to him. He whistled through his teeth as he held up a string of carnelian beads. "You must be a wizard," he muttered. "I'd love to know how you made the Romans part with this."

"I have my ways."

Black Nathan slid one of Julia's rings onto his finger. It had a ruby that gleamed like a clot of blood. The chieftain held out a battle-scarred hand to admire it, exacting as a noble lady. "You are well met, King Alaric. Even though you come with war trailing behind and no good fortune from the gods to fill your sails."

"If I only made war when the auguries were good, Nathan, I would never leave home."

"You are a dangerous enemy to have, Alaric. But so are the Romans."

One of Nathan's men approached the high seat with a bundle in his arms, wrapped in a fortune of foreign silk. He spread it at the foot of the stairs with some ceremony. Inside was a brace of hatchets, finely wrought in ash and gold. Nathan's gift. The young man handed him one and Alaric made a show of testing its weight. Wholly impractical for battle, but sharp enough to part a floating hair.

It was the kind of gift he had to watch, lest he find it buried in his back.

That night, the fires were lit in the great hall and everyone gathered under its roof. A blaze roared in a hearth large enough to stand a horse in. Men and women strolled about, armed to the teeth, drinking from large, foaming tankards; barefoot children rolled in the straw with hunting dogs the size of small ponies.

Julia dove into the party like a fish into water. Parties were her natural element.

From one direction came a drinking horn, foam spilling thick over the rim. From another came the roasted leg of some animal, skin still sizzling. Music pulsed in the air, and she danced until she went careening out of the circle, straight into a man with the build of an oak tree. He turned, scowling; bright gold hair glowing from the firelight like a dragon's hoard, eyes gray as an axe blade; tattoos writhing across his chest. Julia took a step back.

It was Thorismund. Was he—swaying from the drink?

"Julia. I just lost my sword, my horse, and my shield at *latrones*. The only other thing I have to bet is myself." His scowl deepened, as if it pained him to ask. "Help."

He had to be *very* drunk to be overtly asking, and in front of a crowd too. Julia methodically won back Thorismund's belongings, relishing the shocked, appraising looks from the grizzled old warriors.

The twins were never far from her side. They needled and ribbed her as she played *latrones*, pulled her into dances, and pressed drinks into her hands. She was aware that Alaric had sent them to watch her like nursemaids. It made her grit her teeth in annoyance. But it wasn't the only thing to be annoyed with him about. Julia spotted Black Nathan casually looping a pearl necklace around his wrist and held back a curse. Surely Alaric could buy far more than the allegiance of one petty chieftain with that.

It didn't matter. She would get what she wanted at this party. She would make allies, discover more about Alaric's relationship with Brisca—and flirt with everyone in sight, right under Alaric's nose. Even though he seemed not to notice or care.

And that was infuriating, because she hadn't been able to stop noticing *him*. He was sitting at a high table, dressed in a richly embroidered crimson tunic, thick golden torques at his biceps and throat. He radiated a relaxed charisma that was a powerful force in itself, putting everyone at ease and laughing. Julia was drawn to him like a flower leaning toward sunlight.

All night she'd watched him flirt outrageously with every woman who came within his orbit. He occupied the ornate chair next to Brisca's—the higher one, the *chieftain's* chair, which surely wasn't his—as she leaned over to whisper in his ear, one hand resting proprietarily on his thigh.

Julia rolled her eyes in disgust. What a disgraceful hussy he was.

Across the room, music picked up again—a tune like a brook skipping over stones. And there was Berig, his dark hair curling at his shoulders. "Julia." His smile was warm; inviting. "Will you dance?"

"*Please.*" Julia stood, shaking out her hair. She threaded her arm through Berig's and let him lead her toward the music.

Alaric sucked in a breath as across the hall, Julia rose from her bench, giving her hair a hard shake that sent it shivering down to her hips. He bit back a curse.

All night he'd given her a wide berth. She'd made her choice, and it hadn't been him.

"If we aid you, we will need an infusion of men from your army. A hundred should do it." Nathan scratched his cheek through his thick black beard.

"And a hundred barrels of grain to see them through the winter," Brisca added. Her method of persuasion appeared to be teaming up with Nathan to fleece him for all they could. He was hardly in a position to refuse.

Alaric shrugged casually. "You have merely to ask for what you need." Never mind that his own were barely able to scavenge a meager dinner. Across the hall, Julia was dancing with Black Nathan's son now—the pretty one, golden-bearded; his name in the high mountain tongue translated to *handsome*.

Alaric's hand tightened on his drinking horn. Hard enough to bend metal.

Black Nathan followed his gaze. "Seems she likes them prettier than the likes of you or I, Alaric." There was a goading edge to his grin. "Let my son have her. She seems partial to him. You get a nice safe place to keep her hidden, and I get a good-looking grandbaby to bounce on my knee. Everyone wins, eh?"

"Did I just hear talk of giving women away like chattel, under my roof?" Brisca's nails dug into Alaric's thigh. "Julia may be Alaric's prisoner, but in this, she is free to choose."

"Who says she wouldn't choose my son? Most women do."

Alaric leaned back in his chair. "I have a better idea. Send your boy to me in Noricum. I'll give him a privileged position at the front of my army."

Black Nathan went slightly pale. "You do him too much honor, Alaric."

"Nonsense. Give him the chance to bring glory to your family. Bards will sing his name." Alaric's gaze shifted to the crowd, looking for the bright beacon of Julia's hair.

Julia was gone. So was Berig.

"What is it you need to tell me in private?" Julia halted in the shadows beyond the torchlight, just outside the great hall. "Hurry. If Alaric finds me gone—"

"I heard word from my friend outside the walls," Berig said, pulling her deeper into the shadows. "He can get you over the mountains. But we must go now."

Julia stared. She had not been expecting this. "I need time to think."

"Brisca's husband was my uncle. When Alaric killed him, he robbed me of my place next in line as chieftain. Since then, I've had to serve Brisca with a smile on my face, though she aligned herself with Alaric. My uncle's killer." Berig's hands rose to her cheeks. "Since the moment I saw you, Julia, I knew you were like me. Imprisoned. Let us escape *together*. Surely you would not prefer that brute."

Then, without warning, he lowered his mouth to hers. Julia stiffened. She felt the same nothing she'd felt with Cornelius.

That is better. It makes everything so much easier.

A pair of ice-blue eyes rose to her thoughts.

She pulled away as if burned. "Berig, if you think I am running off into the mountains with you, you are *daft*. Alaric will find you and make you eat your own liver."

"I know these mountains. I can protect you."

"Stop being a nitwit and let go of me." He didn't. "Berig, please let go."

"You had better listen to her, Berig."

Alaric stood just paces away, the light from the torches casting his face in shadow. His voice was quiet, but the threat beneath was clear. She felt it all the way down her spine.

"She doesn't want you." Berig turned to face him. "You're the villain, Alaric."

"Maybe so," Alaric said quietly. "But she told you to back off. So do it."

It was the same tone of voice he'd used just before he'd cut Origenes's throat. Julia *saw* the murderous glint in Alaric's eyes, the casual way his stance shifted, and his hand moved to the hilt of his knife. Cornelius in the dust was all she could see.

"You are *so stupid*," she hissed at Berig. "If I have to look at your insides tonight, I'll never forgive you. Now get out of here. *Go.*"

"If you wish it, Julia. But do not forget my offer." Berig gave her one last lingering glance before disappearing back into the longhouse.

And now she was alone with Alaric, his presence raising every hair on the nape of her neck. "As for *you*," she said, "I'm hoping if I ignore you, you'll go away."

"Fucking hell, woman. Running off into the night with Brisca's half-wit kinsman with a ransom on your head—"

"As if *you* care," Julia hissed. She thought of Brisca in his guesthouse. The glorious night they must have spent. "I'm nothing but a momentary diversion to you, am I not?"

He touched her gently, brushing her hair back from her forehead. "Is that what you think?"

His voice was whisper soft; for once there was not a trace of mockery. Julia was humiliated to find tears springing to her eyes. "Please go away."

"Not yet. There are things that must be understood between us." The quiet tenderness in his voice was salt in her wound. "Will you allow me a chance to explain?"

Julia was sullenly quiet.

"I've been working to gain Brisca's support in persuading the chieftains to hold these passes against the war I bring to their doorstep," Alaric said. "The war they believe I'm starting for trivial reasons—"

"*Trivial* reasons? You mean me, don't you?" She bristled. "You think I'm trivial!"

For a moment he was absolutely silent. Then—it was dark

but Julia could have sworn he *blushed*. "I've made no secret of how I feel about you, Julia."

"How you feel about *me*?" A raw, incredulous laugh ripped from her throat. "Let me tell you what I know about your *feelings*! You treat me with contempt, mock me at every turn, and then command me to your bed like a thrall. You came to me warm from another woman's bed to demand I be your *concubine*. And you'll send me back to my brother as soon as you tire of me, will you not? I'm too valuable a pawn to waste."

"I already told you. I will not send you back to your brother."

What a lie. Tears were already rising behind her shut lids and she *hated* herself for them.

"Look at me, Julia."

No. Oh no. Julia dropped her gaze to the fabric of his shirt, tight across the spectacular architecture of his chest. Tears burned her cheeks.

Alaric cursed under his breath and tilted her head up until her eyes met his. "You stubborn, impossible woman," he muttered. "Whether you'll have me or no, I will not send you back to your brother. Not for ransom and not for a homeland. And if Stilicho wants a war, I *will* give him one." His thumb skated over her cheekbone, brushing away tears; sending off sparks beneath her skin. "You are worth a war."

Julia let out a shaky breath. She felt a sudden rush of feelings she couldn't name, a river that left her drowned. Trembling.

He's been in Brisca's bed the last few days. He thinks he can cast pretty words at my feet and have what he wants of me. "And so that is my fate, then?" she asked acidly. "To stay with you and become your concubine?"

A charged silence. "Would that be so terrible?"

"I am a *princess of Rome*, Alaric. Forgive me if I do not leap to become one of your many *women*."

Alaric drew back, torchlight grazing his face. "What makes you think there are many?"

"I have eyes, Alaric. I *saw* the way Ehre looked at you today. And then Brisca—"

He leaned in again, bracing a forearm over her head, blue eyes pinning her still. "I have shared my bed with no one since I came here. Brisca came and I sent her away." His thumb grazed her cheek and every inch of her shot to attention. "Was she the reason you didn't come?"

As if I would have come to you. The words sat scathing on her tongue. But she couldn't give them voice. Not while he was looking at her like that, his eyes burning terrible fire. Refusing to let her hide.

"I saw her go to your guesthouse," she said bitterly. "I certainly didn't *care*. The two of you can do what you like. But what was I supposed to think?"

A bold, self-assured grin flashed across his face. "You're jealous."

"Don't be preposterous." But she was blushing, her burning face making a bonfire of all her secrets, and Julia wished she would fall over dead and end the humiliation.

But he didn't mock her. Instead his lips curved in a slow, knowing smile. "I already told you, Julia. The one I want is you."

Julia raised her eyes to his, and the heat she saw—the raw vulnerability—stole her breath like a fire stealing air.

She couldn't help herself. She threaded her fingers into his hair as he pulled her into his arms, the strength of him rising up all around her like a tide, as his kiss scorched her to ash. Julia clenched her fingers in his hair and kissed him back, frantic to pull him closer, wanting it to *hurt*. He only laughed, low and savage in her ear, as he fisted a hand in her hair in return, dragging her head back to get at her neck.

"You are mine." He spoke in a husky growl, his lips grazing her skin. "You came to *me* and you made your choice." Starbursts went off behind her shut lids as he pressed his mouth to the sensitive spot beneath her jaw. "Don't even *think* to run to another. I'll gut any man who looks at you."

Then he took her mouth again, and the world went black at the edges. Julia kissed him back wildly, clawing at his shirt. Needing to feel him bare. She felt his hands slide beneath her thighs and lift her, setting her back to the door, her legs locking around him as her skirt rode up past her knees. She'd been wrong about him. Wrong about everything. Nothing mattered in the world but this.

A sound split the air, cutting through the sounds of revelry and burning fires and music.

A Roman *cornu*.

CHAPTER TWENTY-THREE

Alaric stood atop the village wall and looked down upon a hundred men spread out on the slope below. Battle-hardened *foederati* under a Roman flag, lit by a fingernail moon.

At the head stood Calthrax. His face split into that blood-hungry grin. "Well. It looks like the traitor has found walls to hide behind."

He was speaking high Latin, just to drive the point home. "I'm not the one with the slaver's language in my mouth," Alaric drawled, in Gothic. "What is it you want, Calthrax?"

"I didn't come to talk to you. I come to parlay with the chieftains of these passes." Calthrax switched to the same language, addressing the chieftains behind him. "Send out the princess Julia, living or dead, and I will pay two thousand pounds of gold. Double if you send out the traitor Alaric with her. Refuse, and my men and I will take this place apart." He gathered his reins in one mailed fist. "You have an hour."

The great hall was timber and stone, the only building in the village that could withstand attack. Now every man, woman, and child was packed in beneath its eaves like spears in a barrel. The chieftains were in an uproar, pounding tables and shouting over each other.

Alaric cut them silent. "They cannot win," he said flatly. "The army is *foederati*, not Roman military. They have no siege engines and no supply chain. If they don't break the walls tonight, they won't at all."

"I've seen what the Romans do to the vanquished." Black Nathan cursed. "They'll enslave everyone they do not kill. I'll not see that happen to my kin. I say we send that woman out to her people."

"Are you so craven, Nathan, that you would let your courage be bought?" Brisca answered. "These walls have stood for a hundred years and they will not fall today."

"Not craven. *Realistic*," Nathan said. "I say we send out the girl and the girl alone. The three of us split the gold." He turned to Alaric. "Was that not your plan to begin with? You planned to ransom her. You simply do it sooner than expected."

Alaric gritted his teeth. "She goes out beyond the wall over my steaming corpse."

He and Nathan were toe-to-toe now, Nathan's hand on his battle-axe, Alaric's drifting to the hilt of his *seax*.

"Please. Don't tell me you *believe* those things the man in the silly helmet told you."

Black Nathan scowled through the black tangle of his beard. "Who let the prisoner speak?"

Deliberately, Alaric beckoned Julia forward, made room for her at the table. "It is her fate we are debating." He put a hand on her shoulder, wanted it very *fucking* clear that to threaten her was to threaten him. "Speak, Julia."

Julia did not seem the least intimidated. She spoke in a ringing voice, her spine straight, her hands flat on the oaken table. "Let me tell you what I would do if I was outside the walls," she said. "I would send gold. Perhaps a small amount as a gesture of goodwill, or perhaps the entire amount. It doesn't matter. Then, when you send the prisoner out, I would raze this place to the ground, take back my gold, and sell all of you into slavery. I'd make a tidy profit."

Nathan gave a pugnacious snort. "No general would risk his men like that."

"The Roman army has men in spades. And the *foederati* are especially expendable, as Alaric knows." She glanced at him. "Besides, it's not much risk. I could walk in under the guise of friendship, clean out a troublesome nest of outlaws, and empty these passes of resistance. You'd barely put up a fight."

Nathan looked scandalized. "None of you Romans have any honor at all."

"That is correct. We do not. Honor is for worthy adversaries, not slaves, or those who will soon become slaves," Julia said flatly. "That is why you must fight."

"She is not wrong, Nathan," Alaric said quietly.

"Whether the Romans turn on us after we send out our hostages, that is for the gods to know. And the gods let us know their minds this morning," Nathan said grimly. "They are against you."

"Is that true?" Julia asked. "As I recall, their answer was inconclusive."

"*Enough.* The pig doesn't get a say in how we cook it," Nathan roared.

"Actually, the pig has a point." At the opposite end of the table, Thorismund rose to his feet. "The gods' answer was inconclusive. That does not mean they hold no opinion. It just means they chose not to share it. A judicious man would ask again."

Below the dais, the air had gone taut as an unstruck lutestring.

"I know what will solve this problem. A test that none may question. Let the gods speak through our blades." Nathan turned to Alaric and grinned. "It has been long since the gods demonstrated their love of your kingship, has it not? Perhaps *that* is the question that needs asking."

So Nathan would force him to defend his kingship by the sword. *Good.* Alaric's lips curved like a *kopis* blade. "That sounds like a challenge. I accept."

"Stop posturing, you cretins," Brisca said. "If you think I'd let the two of you hack at each other in a *holmgang* within these walls—"

"Not a *holmgang*," Nathan said. "It won't be that easy. Alaric, you've been bewitched by that girl and I'll burn in *hell* before I join a war you started over your cock." He turned to face the crowd. "That is the daughter of the emperor Theodosius," he thundered, pointing to Julia with his axe. "Who wants to see what color she bleeds?"

A roar went up among the people, like wildfire through dead grass. Suddenly men were pounding sword against shield, loud enough to shake the rafters.

"There will be nine hatchets, and nine throws. A turn for each of us," Nathan bellowed. "If the gods are behind King Alaric, the daughter of Theodosius will emerge unscathed. If they are not, we'll send out her corpse for the ransom. *Nine hatchets and nine throws.*"

The throng took up Nathan's call—*nine hatchets and nine throws*—and Alaric knew in an instant what would happen if their will was thwarted. He'd seen people pulled limb from limb at the hands of crowds this ugly.

If anyone laid a hand on Julia he'd torch this place to ash.

"*Enough.*" He walked down the steps, into the seething quiet. "It is just, what Nathan has said. But the question is for *me* to put to the gods. If I harm a hair on the woman's head, give me the honor of the threefold death. Do it here, and scatter my ashes at the feet of the Roman army. No king who fails you deserves to live." Alaric let his gaze rake over the assembled hall. "If I succeed, then the gods are at our back and we *fight*."

For an instant the hall was absolutely silent. Then the warriors roared their approval, raw and deafening in a hundred throats.

Nathan gave him a black glare and Alaric knew clear as day that he'd planned to miss, to send out Julia's corpse with no further conversation. But the crowd was against Nathan now. There was nothing he could do except put one of the gilded axes in Alaric's hand.

Alaric tested the weapon's weight. It would be too easy for this to go wrong. If his hand slipped. If he failed to account for the shitty balance. If Julia flinched, even by a hair.

Across the table Julia's blue-green eyes were fixed on him. Once again, that raging protective fury ripped through him. But he could not let any of it show.

"You," he said impassively, his eyes falling to Horsa. "Tie her."

Julia had expected another cow's liver held up for inspection. But now she understood that *she* would be the sacrificial cow. And Alaric had just offered her up.

Horsa pushed Julia up against the wall with jarring force; fastened her arms with chains at a sudden cold-eyed glance from Alaric. "Horsa. Stop—don't do this!"

"Relax. It's a game." He patted her cheek. "Don't forget to act afraid."

Then Alaric stood before her, resplendent in his scarlet tunic. He held a gilded, ornate hatchet in his hand, and spoke to her in the highest, purest Latin; the language of a prince. "Do you trust me, woman?"

"*Trust* you!" She stared at him in open disbelief. "Are you *insane?*"

"Now you must." There was no mistaking the command in his voice. "Close your eyes and do not move an inch."

Then he paced to the other end of the room amidst a tense

silence. The hatchet rose in his hand, and Julia squeezed her eyes shut.

She felt the wind on her cheek from the first throw. The hatchet struck the wall beside her head with a shattering force, and there was no time even to flinch before the second splintered the wood on the other side, the cold steel kissing her cheek.

I will not go to my death pissing myself in fear. I won't give him the satisfaction. Another axe slammed into the wall above her head and Julia choked back a scream.

More axes hit the wood in quick succession. Julia held herself rigidly still and waited for the one that would split her open. For an instant the silence was absolute.

She risked opening her eyes and saw she was framed with axes, head to knees, none of them farther than a finger's length from her body. Pinning her skirts to the wall.

A cacophony shook the roof and all Alaric could see was Julia. Standing straight and tall, her body framed by his axes, looking like she would happily murder him.

He was so proud of her he couldn't speak.

"Well, *fuck!*" Nathan's voice boomed out over the crowd. "That girl has bigger testicles than my son!"

In an instant, Alaric whipped around, his own war hatchet leaving his hand in a single, fluid motion. The hatchets he'd used on Julia were ceremonial and too light for battle, but his own was a mean chunk of steel. Nathan's cup exploded in a rain of beer as the axe embedded itself in the wall.

Silence reigned. Alaric sauntered over to rip his hatchet out of the wall. He leaned close to Nathan, smelling piss and stale beer. "Do not anger me again." Then he turned to face the crowd. "The gods have spoken. We go to war." He pointed toward Julia with his hatchet. "That woman belongs to our gods. If any lay a hand on her, *I* will bring their justice."

The people crowded the dais in a kind of feverish, terrified excitement. He wanted to pull Julia down and kiss her until she couldn't stand. But the crowd enclosed him. Someone handed him a full tankard of beer, foam spilling over the rim; a woman with dark, dancing eyes pulled him down for a kiss as if this was the last of her life.

By the time he managed to disentangle himself, he could not see her.

"You didn't even *flinch*! I wouldn't have done so well." A mad grin lit Ehre's face as she undid the shackles. "They'll be singing your name for a hundred years—! What's wrong?"

Julia's knees had turned to water, and now she was sliding inelegantly down the wall. "I think I am going to be sick."

"None of that. Do you want them to see you weak?" Ehre yanked Julia to her feet. "Stride into that crowd with your head held high. That is how you cement your legend."

Cement your legend. Was that *her* name the people were shouting?

In the next instant, Alaric was standing over her, and before she could speak, he'd hauled her into his arms and claimed her mouth in a deep, savage kiss.

She kissed him back with all the fury she felt. Then she pulled back and slapped him.

A roar of approval ripped through the great hall and a rueful grin flashed across his face. "I suppose you believe I deserve that." He rubbed his jaw with the flat of his palm.

"A knife in your black heart is what you deserve." And then her arms were around him again, fingers threading through his hair as his mouth opened over hers, kissing her again ferociously. The room erupted in a cheer that shook the floor, and a raw, guttural chant began, accompanied by fierce, rhythmic stamping.

"What are they saying?"

"They are saying we go to war."

For a moment she and Alaric grinned at each other—wildly, perfectly matched in joyous disbelief. Then he was kissing her again, the scalding burn of his mouth on hers erasing everything she knew. It was only when he let her down—after endless time; Julia's toes barely brushing the ground—that the embarrassment hit her. "Everyone is looking at us."

"Do not worry yourself. There is no shame in being happy."

She *was* happy, she realized, so full of bliss she might as well burst from it. *Love.* Was this how it felt? He was staring down at her now, his blue eyes alight with pride, and she would open her veins to keep him looking at her like this.

"Don't you have a battle to fight?"

"Yes."

Julia reached up, pushing his hair off his forehead as he had done so many times to her. "Go on, then. Don't do anything stupid."

That dangerous grin lifted his lips. He kissed her again and was gone, calling his warriors to him.

CHAPTER TWENTY-FOUR

Under Brisca's direction, the villagers set up a makeshift infirmary in the great hall.

Not hours after the battle started, the wounded came streaming in. Arrow wounds and axe wounds and head wounds. Water boiled in the cauldrons and physics with herb knowledge bustled among them, tying bandages and mixing poultices. Brisca oversaw it all with the energy and focus of a general.

Julia kept busy. The healers showed her how to stop bleeding, how to mix a poultice and bind a wound. She mixed pain medicine into the poultices—she knew her way around opium, at least. All the while, battle sounded outside—ballista bolts and slingstones and arrows tipped in iron, slamming into the palisade with shattering force. If Alaric failed—she shut her eyes and an image of one of those ballista bolts punching through his chest filled her sight. *If he dies—*

No. The gods had spoken. He would not die.

Hours passed. And then she saw Thorismund among the wounded, face gray with pain as a group of healers helped him onto a bench. Julia rushed to his side, her heart in her throat. He smiled wearily. "Not to worry. I killed the man who did it."

"And the others?"

"Alive. Last I saw. But—" The healers were elbowing her out of the way now, arms full of bandages, and Thorismund stiffened as someone tried to help him into a sitting position.

Brisca squeezed her shoulder. "Do not worry. He has the constitution of an oak tree."

Then a shout went up that sent a shock down her spine. *Fire.*

If Calthrax's men had been Roman regulars, the defenders would all be dead by now. Alaric knew that well enough.

Roman regulars would have engineers to build ramps and tunnels under the walls; all these men had were ladders and grappling hooks. That was trouble enough. The defenders beat them off, dodging missiles, the air thick with lead. Then, in the blackest night, the ballistae announced their arrival when a bolt the size of a man's leg slammed into a wall just feet from Alaric's head. Brisca's walls were stout oak, but even they couldn't withstand a ballista barrage all night. If they didn't drive the attackers off before sunrise, they were dead.

Now the night was more than half-over and the attackers were by no means driven off. Alaric was at the main gate where the fighting was fiercest, his defenders dropping all around him. He prayed that the wall would hold.

"*Alaric.*" It was Hengist, climbing the ladder at his back. "It's the western gate. I went to relieve Horsa and found it hanging open."

Panic shot through him. "Where is Horsa?"

Hengist pointed down the line. There, amidst a knot of besieged defenders, was Horsa, fighting fiercely with his Hunnic hatchet and *seax.* "He heard you were losing the main gate. He came to reinforce you."

Fuck. Horsa had gone against orders, again. And now the gate was open. That meant the enemy was inside. They'd be hunting for Julia. Alaric turned, bellowing orders to the men around him. The invaders had to be hunted down. He would lead the party himself.

Fire flashed in the corner of his eyes. The roof of the great hall was in flames.

Julia streamed out of the great hall, the crowd surging around her, and for a moment she could barely keep her feet. *Thorismund.* She turned back in a panic, only to feel a hand reach out and pull her out of the crowd.

"*Julia.* Thank the gods." It was Berig, his face smudged with ash. "Alaric is asking for you. He took a nasty wound to the head—"

Her knees buckled. "Is he dying?"

"I don't know. There is not much time." Berig led her away, down a dirt-packed road between buildings. He pulled her into the shadows as a pair of men ran by, armed to the teeth. "Invaders. Looking for you. They set the fires to distract everyone."

A chill of fear shot down her spine.

Berig led her to the northwestern edge of the village, far from the sounds of battle. The houses here were deserted; frightened goats stood tethered in paddocks, calling frantically. Ahead a large barn had been set on fire, and Berig led her toward it, sticking to the shadows.

A man was standing in front of the burning barn, a shadow outlined in flame. His slit-eyed helmet was the stuff of nightmares—one side lit by leaping flames, the other in absolute darkness. It was not Alaric.

His lips peeled back over wet, shining teeth. "There you are."

Berig halted, his hand gripping Julia's arm painfully. "Give me the ransom you promised, Calthrax."

Calthrax's voice was the dark inverse of Alaric's, rolling across the yard like black smoke. "Bring her here and I'll give it to you."

"Don't be stupid," Julia hissed. "He's going to cut you in half the minute you're within reach."

"Shut up." Berig tightened his grip on her arm. "I want my money *before* I turn her over. And I want safe passage down the mountain. Guaranteed."

Calthrax took out a small pouch and tossed it at Berig's feet. "Now, bring me the princess."

Berig dragged her across the muddy yard despite her fierce objections. Julia struggled, twisting her ankle painfully. "Take her, then," he said, thrusting her at Calthrax. Julia staggered, almost falling to her knees.

When she glanced up, it was to see Calthrax thrusting his sword into Berig's belly.

Berig sagged to the ground. Calthrax kicked his twitching body off his sword. Then he turned to Julia, the fire throwing stark shadows across his bronze helmet.

"You've no idea the trouble you've caused, Princess."

She took a step back. Hot wind whipped at her hair.

"Thinking of running, are you? I wouldn't." He wiped his bloody sword and shoved it back in his scabbard, striding toward her with a smile vicious as a slit throat. "Stilicho wants you back unharmed. But the reward is the same if you're dead."

Then he grasped Julia's hair in his fist, close to the scalp.

Julia screamed as he dragged her across the yard. Her ankle twisted again and a bright, hot pain shot up her leg. Thorismund's dagger was in her hand. She slashed wildly, the blade glancing off knucklebone. Calthrax roared in pain and backhanded her into a stone wall, the world exploding into light. Then he stood above her, an enormous curved weapon glinting in his hand, a snarl leaping out of his face. She watched the huge arced blade descend from the spark-filled sky.

A ringing clash and Alaric stood between her and death, his *seax* upraised to catch the heavy blade.

Calthrax's weapon was the terrible Thracian *rhomphaia*, long as a Celtic sword, affixed to a heavy oak spear shaft. Alaric had seen teams of Thracians take down war elephants with them. He caught its weight on his own upturned blade, shock resonating down his forearms.

Calthrax's lips peeled back in a feral grin. "Took you long enough."

"Seems you've taken to fighting women in my absence." The image of Calthrax striking Julia was burned into his mind. He would die for that. "Let's see how strong you stand against me."

They orbited each other, blades held low. Assessing. Alaric's focus narrowed to a deadly point. Beneath the surface, everything tense as a primed catapult.

"Give me the woman. I'll tell Stilicho you slipped through my fingers."

Red rage rose up in his sight. "You've already made that offer. My answer is still no."

Alaric raised his blade and lunged forward. There was no more talking after that.

In Stilicho's officers' school, Alaric and Calthrax had been evenly matched. Not more skilled than the other boys so much as *angrier*, rage burning the same hole in both of their bellies. One night, they'd gone up to the roof to settle which one was better, fought to broken ribs and split lips, swollen knuckles and black eyes. Emerged at breakfast with no clear winner, sixteen years old and looking like they'd been to war.

Even now, fighting Calthrax felt familiar as an old grudge. Together they had been drilled to breaking in the finer points of the deadly *armatura*, forced to fight in the hot sun with wooden weapons twice the weight of a real sword. Been beaten and starved for every misstep.

Now they each pulled out every trick in lethal earnest.

Alaric held the disadvantage. His curved *seax* was of patterned steel, but he was missing his axe and had lost his spear on the wall. Calthrax's deadly *rhomphaia* was designed for a man on foot battling mounted cavalry. He could only last so long against it.

Even so, Alaric knew every line of Calthrax's body, every shift of weight and what it meant. It was keeping him alive. He kept light on his feet and his defenses drum tight, watching for openings as he traded punishing blows with the only man who had ever been able to mark him. The fire rose up behind them both, their shadows stretching long across the yard, and he breathed in soot and murder.

"Is she worth it? Theodosius's thrice-cursed daughter?" Calthrax laughed. "Every man in Ravenna has spent himself between those thighs."

"I thought you came to kill me, Calthrax. Not to gossip."

"I came for four thousand pounds of gold. I've spread news of that ransom all over these mountains, Alaric. By the time you get to Noricum, even your own chieftains will have heard. How soon before your own betray you for that money?" Calthrax's bared teeth gleamed. "Will it be before Stilicho arrives, I wonder? He's marshalling his armies now. He'll be in Noricum before the snows come in the mountains."

So Stilicho *would* make it a war. And it would be soon. Their blades clashed and held. The sound of metal on metal careened off the walls as the fire blasted them. *There.* An opening. Alaric *lunged—*

Calthrax aimed a vicious thrust and Alaric barely twisted away, a bright-hot line opening in his side. He hissed through his teeth, his arm rising automatically to block the downward swing of Calthrax's killing blow.

His sword shattered in his hand.

Julia crouched in the doorway and watched as Alaric's blade shattered.

If he dies, I'm doomed.

Thorismund's dagger was lying in the dirt. She snatched it up with nerveless fingers. *How did Thorismund say to do it? Think.* The point of the dagger found the place just beneath her ribs. Her breath came hard in her chest. It would *hurt*. Did she have the courage?

Better this than going back to Ravenna.

Julia tightened her grip on the knife's hilt and prepared herself to die.

A grin split Calthrax's face and Alaric *knew* that grin. It was the one they'd exchanged dozens of times in Stilicho's practice yards, the two of them utterly ruling the melees, fighting back-to-back with wooden weapons in their hands.

Alaric raised his sword and caught the weight of Calthrax's immense curving blade in the crux of his hilt. If his own broken blade slipped a finger's length, he'd be cut in half. His feet shifted for purchase, muscles straining. Both of them sweating in the smoke and fire.

His grip slipped and Calthrax's blade bore down on him like a judgment from the gods. Alaric let his weapon drop. Calthrax stumbled. Only the barest mistake, but it was enough. Alaric angled his body, letting the other man's blade pass as he stepped inside his guard.

Then he drove his broken-off sword into his enemy's neck.

CHAPTER TWENTY-FIVE

Brisca's people had taken to the rooftops, quenching the great hall fire and then raining down projectiles on the invaders until they broke and fled.

Julia returned to the great hall at dawn, Alaric holding her up, to find the yard littered with broken tiles and rocks and corpses. Alaric said something laughing in Gothic, and Brisca's answer was to hurl herself into his arms—and then pull Julia into their embrace, all of them blazing with triumph. *They were alive.*

Pain shot up her ankle, making her gasp.

Alaric steadied her, and he was smiling; the beauty of it made her lose her breath. "Come with me," he said, taking her hand. "I'll take you to the healer."

The village healer was an old woman with a cloud of white hair floating over a sunburned scalp. She stood with her hands on her hips, giving Alaric a *very* thorough dressing-down.

Alaric stood with his arms crossed over his battered chain mail, his expression one of bemused respect. There he was, this man who had ridden the battle line at Milan with his horse stomping the severed heads of the enemy—standing in this yard with garden herbs growing up to his knees and an old woman giving him a tongue-lashing that would make the skies weep.

In that instant, Julia fell a thousand feet standing still.

"She says she's too busy for the likes of us. She had *very* strong words for me causing this wreckage in the first place." His blue eyes lifted to her. "But her hut is that way. We can make use of what she has. Can you walk?"

"Of course I can walk." Julia took a step and her ankle gave immediately. In the next instant, she was swept up in his arms. "*Will* you put me down?"

His answer was no.

The healer's cottage was a cobwebby place out of an old tale about *strigas* and spells. Julia sat beneath clusters of dried herbs as Alaric searched through bottles and clay jars, unstopping them, staring fiercely down at the contents as if each one presented its own battle.

"Let me see those." He handed her a blue jar and a green bottle. "This," she said, holding up the blue. Tincture of comfrey. Bone-knit. "You'll need to boil water."

He lit a fire in the little hearth with brisk efficiency as Julia sat at the healer's scarred table, preparing a simple poultice that the healers had shown her. She opened a waterskin and added a few drops of water to her mixture, then looked up to see him watching her intently.

"Brisca says you comported yourself well among the healers."

"I know my way around poison. One has to in the courts of Ravenna." Julia shrugged. "Most poisons can also heal, in the right doses."

It was no great thing. But the glow of approval in his eyes made her dizzy.

"Let me see your ankle." He sat next to her and pulled her injured foot into his lap. Suddenly Julia felt oddly shy. He slid off her boot and probed with long fingers, that cloud of intense concentration gathering around him.

Pain lanced up her leg. Julia hissed through her teeth. "Ah."

"That hurt?" His fingers moved, and suddenly there was no pain. A tingly feeling swept up her calf. "What about here?" She shook her head. "You are lucky. It is not broken."

Julia watched, transfixed. Calthrax had been the most terrifying man Julia had ever encountered, and Alaric had killed him. That would make *Alaric* the most terrifying man she had ever encountered. And yet he was endlessly gentle with her as he spread the poultice on her ankle, then wrapped it in a bandage.

He did not lift his eyes from what he was doing, but his tone changed.

"Where did you get the dagger, Julia?"

Deceptively casual. Yet it sent a chill up her spine. "Thorismund gave it to me." It seemed impossible to lie.

"Let me see it."

Reluctantly, she slid the blade out of her boot and handed it to him. He turned it in his hands, frowning, and then shoved it into his own belt. "You should not have this," he said flatly.

"Why not? I need to protect myself—"

"I saw what you were doing. It was not protection." He did not look up from his task, but she *felt* the sudden tension in him. "Is that your plan if I fall? To send yourself out the same way? I will not allow it."

Julia hissed. "It isn't *your* choice."

"Yes, it is." He was looking at her now with a fierce intensity that turned her insides into a trembling riot. "I will *not* fail you. You will never need that dagger."

He was *afraid*, she realized. Afraid of failing her. Afraid of what she'd have to do if he did. "You cannot always protect me."

"Can't I?" He brushed a strand of hair from her eyes. "I'm beginning to think I must swaddle you like a babe and watch you every second."

The sunlit affection in his eyes brought her up short. "*You're* one to talk. You're the most reckless person I know." There was a long slash down his cheekbone. It wasn't the only one. He was cut and bruised all over, she realized. From defending *her.* She sat up, pulling her ankle off his lap. "Take off your tunic."

She thought he might refuse her, but instead he only did as she bid, standing and pulling his tunic off, wincing as he raised his arm. Julia held in a gasp. His left side was one great bruise. He did not wince when she touched him; the muscles in his jaw tightened only imperceptibly. He was used to pain, used to carrying it, used to pushing on despite it. She hadn't missed the rough edge of exhaustion in his voice; he wasn't just tired. He was dead on his feet. And yet he would not sleep, not for days.

It was so *like* him, to put everyone else's needs before his own, no matter how tired and battered he was.

"I don't think it is broken," she muttered. "Pass me your salve." He held himself still, lashes lowered as she rubbed the ointment into his skin.

The air went quiet between them.

Eventually she looked up to see him staring down at her with a fierce tenderness that scorched her where she stood. She stopped with her ministrations, struck utterly silent.

She loved this man. *Loved him.*

Alaric's huge hand curled around the back of her neck as he pulled her in to him. Julia pressed her cheek to the warm, breathing planes of his chest.

Alaric insisted on carrying Julia, despite her protestations, back to her guesthouse. He lowered her onto the bed as if she was breakable as glass.

She pulled him into bed and wound her limbs around him.

Alaric gritted his teeth. If she thought he could stay in this bed with her and do nothing but sleep, she was out of her *mind.*

But Julia seemed to have no such problem. She dropped off immediately, her head on his chest, every warm, delicious inch of her pressed tight against him.

He felt himself stirring instantly, savagely to life.

But it was not the time or the place. Her breathing was even and deep, her dark lashes fanning her cheek, and he found himself transfixed, simply watching her sleep. The way the light set her skin aglow like a sunbeam in alabaster. She was so fucking *fragile*. And yet so brave.

He lay in her arms and categorized all the acts of bravery Julia had shown in the past hours. Facing down his axes without twitching an eyelash. Shoving reality down the throats of the chieftains. Lending her hands in the great hall with the healers.

That image of her pointing the knife at her own chest would not leave his mind.

Suddenly his heart was racing and his breath coming fast. He did not doubt for a moment that if he'd fallen, she would have died in that doorway by her own hand. He must *never* let her feel unsafe, never let her *be* unsafe. She had the resolve to do it. And if she did, it would be because he had failed her.

How long would it be until someone else tried to rip this woman from his arms?

The ransom is the same whether she's alive or dead. So Calthrax had told him. Alaric tightened his arms around Julia and coolly considered what the dead man had said. The size of that ransom would have his chieftains warring among themselves to turn her over to Stilicho. The thought of the old man made Alaric curse beneath his breath. He had thought to buy time until next spring, but if Stilicho could marshal his forces to be over the mountains before winter—if he could make it through the passes despite the alliances—

It was early summer now. There was not enough time. And fear of Stilicho's swift arrival would only motivate the chieftains further to make themselves rid of Julia. She would be in danger every minute she was in Noricum. Until he made the city safe, she must remain under strict, unceasing guard.

There was one thing he could do to keep her safe. His chieftains would assassinate a *king* quick as breathing. But the gods frowned on killing queens. He wasn't certain how much weight the tradition would have against all that gold. But he was certain it wouldn't be none. This was a layer of protection he could give her *now*.

If she would have him.

Julia's hand drifted lazily across his chest and he caught it in his own, stilling it. He ought to give her the choice. He knew that. But what other choice did she have? Any other option would be a death sentence, and he would not—*would not*—stand by quietly and let her choose her own doom. Surely marriage to him was a better option than death.

He would sit her down and explain it. Very calmly and rationally. She was an intelligent woman; she'd see sense.

"Well. Isn't this a heartwarming tableau." It was Riga, leaning in the doorway, the sun pouring in behind him. "You're wanted at the main gate. They're burying the dead."

"They don't need me for that."

"Calthrax does. We need you to sing his *paeon*."

Brisca stood by the gate with Black Nathan; she gave Alaric a wry, tired grin as he approached. "Black Nathan was just pledging to lend us his strength in the passes."

Alaric grinned. "I thank you, Black Nathan."

Nathan inclined his head as far as his pride would let him. "The redheaded girl was right. Allying with the Romans is its own form of slavery. We will not be owned."

"Nor will I be, Nathan," Brisca said pointedly.

"That is another matter entirely." Nathan frowned. "I never agreed for large swaths of our territory to be ruled by a woman. It's against custom."

Alaric interjected smoothly. "Brisca is a trusted ally in these hills. She is also well trusted by my chieftains. Any king who takes place beside her would have to start again in earning that trust. In periods of war, I cannot afford the time that takes. Besides," he said quietly, "she showed more courage than a dozen hardened warriors last night. She needs no husband to rule her."

Brisca seemed to grow taller at his words. "These are my people, Nathan, and *I* am their queen." She turned to Alaric, slipping into the lilting mountain language of her people. "I shall endeavor to live up to your good opinion of me."

He answered quietly, in the same language. "It will take no endeavor."

"Well. Aren't the two of you knives in the same scabbard?" Nathan looked between them, glowering. "I'm going to find my breakfast."

And he stumped off, muttering to himself.

The *paeons* to the dead would be sung until sunset. To fail to sing the ancient songs would be to risk the spirits staying where they died, sickening the living and killing the crops.

Calthrax's body lay atop a pyre among dozens of others. Alaric stared at his white-lipped corpse, the red mouth he'd opened in his throat, and thought of that *rhomphaia* raised to Julia. "Wait. Not him."

Thorismund stood by the pyre, a torch aloft in his hand. "I wouldn't do that," he said quietly. "The gods are saying his spirit is still here."

Alaric could see that well enough. Calthrax was standing among those gathered by the pyre, his neck still bleeding where Alaric had slit it with a broken-off sword.

"I don't give a damn where his spirit is."

"Do you wish his shade to wander the earth forever?" Thorismund frowned. "I hope this isn't how you treat *me* when I fall in battle."

An old memory surfaced. He and Calthrax at seventeen, on the roof of Stilicho's officers' school, looking at the stars. *Do you suppose they're watching us from up there?* Calthrax had asked. *Your parents and mine. Do they hate us for what they see?*

Alaric knew what he meant. Their sons in the lap of Rome. Back in the days when he'd believed he could change things from the inside, because Stilicho had led him to believe so.

No, he'd said. *They want us to live.*

Calthrax's shade was nothing but an outline now, the whole, bright living world shining through behind him.

Alaric didn't know where the dead went. He told himself he didn't care.

"Throw him over the cliff and let the birds have him," he said. Quietly, for the dead to hear, if the dead could. "He chose."

CHAPTER TWENTY-SIX

Julia woke alone a few hours later. There was food in the guesthouse—a loaf of bread warm from the oven, honey, and sweet wine—and she devoured everything.

Outside the guest hut, the sun was high. She'd slept until afternoon.

She stepped outside and breathed in the air. It still tasted of fire. She felt Alaric approach before she saw him; the earth shook and Hannibal loomed before her, his hooves splitting the ground, Alaric astride in his battle-torn cloak. He halted before her, a slow, wild grin playing across his mouth, beautiful enough to wreck her world.

"Come with me." He held out a hand. "I owe you an apology, Julia."

Golden light sliced through the trees as they galloped into a field of flowers. Alaric let Hannibal run and then slowed to an easy amble.

It was so *large* up here, Julia thought as her gaze followed a bird circling high among a rise of black spires. She had lived all her life in cities and palaces, hemmed in and carefully constrained. She felt both exhilarated and unsettled under such a huge sky.

"That's an ibex." Alaric pointed far up a mountain slope. "They're rare here."

Julia squinted. "How can you tell it's not a rock?"

"Because of the giant horns." The man had eyes like a hawk. "That bird above it is a vulture. No doubt it found a meal up on that slope."

He knew the names of all the wildlife in these hills, and could tell a kite from a merlin on sight. The heat of Alaric's body surrounded her, one arm slung around her waist as he guided the horse one-handed through meadows of waving grass lit to gold by the blazing sun. It felt so good—the drugging heat of his body pressed close to hers, the strength of his arms around her, and the fluid power of the horse.

This was a seduction, as masterful as any she'd seen.

The path dropped and ran along a cliff. Alaric whispered in her ear. "Feel like a gallop?"

"A *gallop*?" Julia eyed the cliff edge. "Are you mad?"

But Hannibal was already leaping forward, Alaric's arm closing around her like steel as the speed threw her back against his chest. Julia gripped the pommel as Hannibal's great body stretched out beneath them, the gulf dropping beside her. Ahead she saw eagles rising, circling up to a world far above. For a moment Julia believed they too were flying. Fast in the wake of the eagles.

The meadow was breathtaking. The sun flung its light across the grass, making each blade glitter. Not ten paces before her a cliff dropped off, the whole of the wild, shining *campagna* below.

Julia wrapped Alaric's cloak around herself as she walked closer to the edge of the cliff. The gulf was irresistible, and for an instant she stared at the shreds of cloud drifting far below.

She'd never been so high in her life. A frightened thrill shot through her.

"Don't get so close, Julia."

Alaric was sitting in the grass behind her, long legs stretched in front of him, while Hannibal grazed peacefully nearby. He was watching her intently, as if she was the most precious thing in the world. A terrifying mix of longing and fear. Julia felt suddenly shy.

"Why did you bring me here?"

"I owe you an apology."

He was so *serious*. Julia gave him a light, teasing smile. "I suppose you do," she mused. "If only for your outrageous behavior at parties. At the first one we attended together, you put a knife to my neck. And at the second, you threw axes at my head—"

He roared with laughter. "You *asked* me to kidnap you. You handed me the knife." She wanted to sink into that laugh, wrap herself in it forever.

"You certainly seem capable of civil behavior when it comes to *Brisca*." But her lips curved in a teasing smile. "But your seat was above hers at the party. I rather think that's outrageous, considering this is *her* territory. Will you ever set a woman above you, Alaric of the Goths?"

"Only time will tell about that." He rose to his feet and closed the distance between them. "But you are right. I have treated you badly," he said. "I would make up for it now."

Julia stared up at him, struck utterly silent by the raw tenderness in his voice. "Do you know what my problem with you is?" she asked quietly. "I honestly can't tell whether you are the most earnest person I have ever met, or the most manipulative." For an instant his eyes held hers. Sun-warmed sea. Endless blue summer. A wide, inviting path to ruin and rending death, and Julia saw herself skipping right down it like a fool. "Well? Are you going to apologize?"

His gaze lifted to a spot behind her. "This is my apology."

Julia glanced behind to see an eagle spiraling down toward the cliff, the sun glinting off each individual feather. It descended in an effortless spiral. "What on earth—"

"They nest in the cliffs below. They return to the same place every year, so I'm told."

This close, she could see how the wind buffeted its wings. What courage it must take, that first time, to spread their wings wide and believe that the air itself would catch them.

Julia glanced up at Alaric, and for a moment the stark, sunlit beauty of his profile made her catch her breath. He was *of* this place, just as harsh and spectacular.

He glanced down at her. "I had another reason for bringing you here. We must speak of your future."

Julia tensed. Suddenly she knew what he was going to say— that he'd changed his mind about sending her back. He *must* send her back—despite his promises, someday it would come down to her or his homeland. She was under no illusions about which he would choose.

Her heart was already broken. It didn't need to break more. "I don't want to talk."

"Don't be stubborn, Julia." He turned her to face him. "There are things between us that must be understood."

"Alaric." She laid her fingers on the side of his cheek. "I mean it. Stop talking."

And then she stood on her tiptoes and kissed him.

For a moment he tensed and she thought he might resist her. But then he hauled her to him and kissed her back with a fierce desperation that swept away every thought she'd had. Julia lost herself in a fury of hungry, open-mouthed kisses, their tongues tangling, her hands sinking into his hair as she pulled him closer.

At some point, they sank to their knees. Then he rolled her beneath him on top of the rough-spun cloak, his broad body blocking the wind. Julia pulled at his tunic and he drew back just long enough to pull it off. She barely had time to run her hands

over the scarred glory of his torso—mindful of his bruises—
before hers was gone as well and his naked chest was pressed
full-length against hers and his hands were on her, calloused
and strong, his mouth trailing a fiery path down to her breasts,
making her gasp with the lightning that shot down her spine
every time he sucked a nipple into his mouth.

She couldn't say when she lost her leggings, or he his trousers. All she knew was that she was naked now, and so was he,
and she wasn't cold at all. In fact she was *on fire* as he bent his
head to her, kissing and tasting and sucking her into a frenzy.
Only when she was sweat-soaked and writhing beneath him did
he back off, stretching his long, hard body over hers, bracing
himself on a forearm. Julia wound her arms around his neck.
"Please, Alaric," she whispered, not even sure what she was asking for. "Please."

"Patience, woman." His voice all banked thunder against her
throat. "Be still."

And then he brushed his thumb against her. Soft and slow.

Julia gasped. A brilliant heat arced through her, hot as *ealu*
down her throat. Alaric drew back, watching her with terrifying focus as he moved his hand again, stroking another bright,
hot shock straight through her. He stroked her again and again,
with devastating gentleness.

And when he slid a finger into her, slow and careful, explor-
ing her tightness, Julia arched her back and pressed up into his
hand. He knew all her secrets now, and he could have them.
He could have whatever he wanted.

But in the next moment, his hand was gone. Cool air pebbled
her skin. Julia opened her eyes to see him rearing up between
her thighs, distant as some pagan god, looking down at her as
if seeing her for the first time. "You've never done this before."

Was it that obvious? Suddenly she was crushingly aware that he
had been with other women—countless others. Women who

had known what they were doing. She forced herself to hold his gaze, to raise her chin defiantly. "Why? Do I displease you?"

"Ah, Julia." His legs at her thighs, parting them. "You fucking *ruin* me."

And when his mouth closed on her, in her most secret place, she almost screamed with the pleasure of it. Soft, warm. Liquid sin. He pressed her down with both hands on her hips and moved his mouth on her, his tongue, in an utterly wicked, delicious dance that undid her entirely. Moving on instinct, she wrapped her legs around his neck and pulled him closer, grinding her hips up into his mouth, gasping nonsensical things into the great blue dome of the sky. Another bright, fierce arc of pleasure shot through her, making her back arch and her fingers curl in the grass, her teeth clenching around his name.

When he kissed her mouth again, it was a new taste, a whole new country. Indescribably intimate. She felt his lean hips shift forward through the haze of her desire and suddenly the hard, naked length of him was pressed up against the slick heat between her thighs. Slowly he eased himself into her, pinning her hard to the ground.

Julia trembled. The fog lifted, and for a moment she was just on the edge of pain. She felt herself expanding deliciously to accommodate him and held still, unsure of these new sensations.

"Are you all right?" A low whisper against her neck.

She could have wept. "Yes."

He began to move in slow, sure strokes. Expanding his territory. She could *feel* the tension in his back and shoulders, the fierce control he was exerting just to hold himself in check.

"Alaric—" She locked her legs around his hips and tried to pull him closer, her nails scraping down his back, hoping he would not make her beg. "Just do it all at once."

The muscles in his back tightened convulsively. "I'm trying to be gentle."

It came out urgent, *agonized.* "Don't be."

"If this is how you want it, Julia." He braced himself over her and buried a hand in her hair, arched her head back and covered her mouth with his. Kissed her long and deep.

Then he thrust into her in one powerful stroke. Julia gasped against his mouth, white-hot stars exploding in the dark behind her eyelids, her nails digging into his shoulder blades.

After the first shock, it didn't hurt. Not like she'd been led to expect.

Alaric held himself utterly still, cradling her in his arms, enormous and pulsing inside her. His heartbeat was everywhere under her skin. "Julia. My Julia." His lips brushed her forehead, her eyelids. The line of her cheekbone. "Did I hurt you?"

"No." Nothing could hurt her when he was holding her like this. Kissing her like this. Saying her name like she was the only good thing in the world. Julia pressed her mouth to his skin and tasted his sweat. "Finish what you started."

He made a sound deep in his throat, a choked-out groan that nearly undid her. Then he started to move again, cords of muscle standing out in his neck, flexing into her with ferocious discipline. It began to feel—not good, exactly. Complicated.

Then he shifted his hips. Just slightly, but it made *all* the difference. "There," Julia whispered. "Just—*there*." He was *killing* her with it now, his hips grinding up against the white-hot pinpoint of her desire. Erasing the discomfort entirely, moving in slow circles that were absolutely exquisite. Julia wrapped her legs tighter around him and held on for dear life.

"Ah. *Gods*, you feel good." His voice sending shocks down her spine to her toes. "Marry me."

Her head spun. The words did not make sense. "What?"

"Marry me. Be my wife. Stay with me until the world crumbles into ash."

Julia let out a wordless gasp. *He cannot mean this.* Something was building. Like the pleasure she had felt before but bigger, an ocean current next to a river. It made her wild. Made her want to claw his back to ribbons and then climb out of her own skin.

"Anything," she moaned. *"Please."*

He kissed her, tongue plunging deep, an act of raw possession. "Say the words."

Julia moaned, her breasts scouring the rough skin of his chest. Her nipples screamingly sensitive. *"Yes.* I swear. Only please—" She was writhing beneath him now, her legs tightening around him, her nails digging into his biceps.

He was so deep in her now. As deep as he could go.

"Gods, Julia. You feel so—" He hissed between his teeth. Flexed inside her in a way that made the world go black. "I'll be your shield and fight your battles. I'll lay the wealth of cities at your feet."

"What?" What sorcery was this? Nobody meant what they said to lovers; she knew that well enough. What diabolical game was he playing? Outrage built in her as she realized he might *not* give her what she wanted, not until she did what he said. She arched her back; a moan built deep in her throat. "Just—just *please*—"

His mouth at her neck. Desperate. "Say yes."

Anything. She'd have agreed to anything. *"Yes."*

His movements became more urgent, hard and merciless; giving her no quarter. Julia was beyond hearing now. She was beyond understanding. She could do nothing but dig her heels into his thighs and hang on. His hands clenched hard on her ass, hard enough to bruise as he took her ruthlessly, growling a litany of curses and love words into the curve of her throat. Heated praise and filthy encouragements and promises no one should make, not ever.

The pleasure this time tore her open, shattered her. She came apart in his arms, a raw, trembling mess, great arcs of pleasure ripping through her over and over. Only when she could take no more did he chase his own, wringing one more impossible cataclysm from her spent body with his deep, brutal thrusts, his own pleasure coming hard on the heels of hers.

CHAPTER TWENTY-SEVEN

For hours after they'd lain together, Julia believed—really believed—that Alaric meant what he said. They were engaged. Lying with her head pillowed on his bicep after the third time they made love, staring up at the clouds, Julia had closed her eyes and lived out an entire lifetime with him behind her shut lids.

They descended the mountain as the sun was setting to find a feast had been laid in the great hall. Everyone had gathered to celebrate. It was sheer, unimpeded joy being at Alaric's side, aware of his blue eyes on her, glowing with a warmth that made her dizzy. Julia had tried the most expensive opium that Egypt had to offer. She had never been so intoxicated.

But he did not mention that he'd asked her to marry him. She did not bring it up. And when he laughed with Brisca—seemed, in some moments, just as intimate with her—Julia held her sudden, *desperate* jealousy behind her teeth.

Nobody meant the things they said to lovers. Everyone knew that.

The next morning, in the cold light of dawn, Julia stood at the northern gate and watched Alaric at the center of the crowd, his smile flashing and his bronze hair glinting in the sun. Everyone had one last story to tell him or one last blessing to lay on his brow.

When Brisca threw her arms around Julia's neck, she silenced her poor, pathetic jealousy. "Take care of him. And remember to think of us when you are queen." She slipped her a slim, smooth object. It was a finger-bone flute, like Alaric's but not so ornate. "I had to make it quickly," she said with a wry grin. "Play it in the mountains if you have the need, and we will find you."

There was nothing else to say but *thank you*.

Julia shivered. A wind screamed down from the peaks, dragging a terrible cold with it. Brisca had gifted her thick leather leggings and high, lace-up boots; a fur-lined tunic; and a soft Phrygian cap with earflaps, but she wondered if it would be enough.

"Are you cold, Julia?" It was Alaric's voice in her ear, rough and warm.

"No," she said automatically, even as another burst of wind made her shiver.

"The hat is warmer if it covers your head, Julia." He pulled it low over her forehead, tied the strings on the earflaps, and then cast a critical eye on her coat. "No wonder you're shivering. You've done it up wrong."

Julia held herself still beneath his ministrations. It shouldn't feel so *good*, letting him fuss over her like this. "I can dress myself," she said tersely.

"It does not seem so." He pulled her cloak tight, then brushed his lips against her forehead for one single, transfixing moment. Lighting her up from the inside. "It's time to go."

Julia left the village as she had come, riding Hannibal with Alaric walking beside.

The days ran together in a blur. They climbed steep switchback trails, through forests of spearpoint pines and into vast fields. Mostly Alaric let her ride Hannibal; once, up a particularly treacherous slope, he carried her on his back. Julia shut her eyes and laid her cheek against the play of moving muscles beneath his skin.

As the days passed, the men fell into quiet; their stops were quick and efficient, only long enough to suck down water and check for stones in the horses' hooves. Alaric withdrew into himself more than the others; Julia recognized the fierce concentration that came over him when he was trying to keep them all alive. She tried not to distract. Instead she stewed in quiet.

She could not stop thinking about what he'd said to her on those cliffs.

In the days afterward, she was convinced only of her own foolishness. But then Alaric would be there at her elbow to offer food and a quiet word of encouragement, or a steady hand to stop her from stumbling. He always seemed to know when she was hungry or tired, and the way he looked at her sometimes—that ferocious tenderness, the same look he'd had on his face when she'd stood too near that cliff—made her question everything.

Surely he would at least try to lie with her again. But he did not. They slept in bare-bones shelters, shepherd's huts, and one shivering night, a cave full of howling wind. Julia fell into black, dreamless sleep, mindlessly seeking Alaric's warmth. And it was only there she felt his desire; pressed hard and heavy against hip or thigh as she lay in his arms. He still *wanted* her. But he did not reach for her in the dark.

Julia had never been so confused in her life. She did not understand him; that was the problem. She did not understand him, and she did not understand his customs.

After what could have been ten days, she found herself on a trail that rose to impossible steepness, wind scouring every inch of exposed skin. She had never been this cold or exhausted, and she almost wept with relief when the path turned a corner and wound behind a screen of sheltering, twisted pines.

Julia slumped against a boulder, sore and out of breath, as the men checked girths and sucked down water. She took two steps and nearly fell, her ankle giving way beneath her.

Alaric was by her side in seconds. "Are you all right?" His eyes swept her from head to toe, taking a brisk inventory. "Is your ankle paining you?"

"They should—put a proper road—up this mountain."

To her surprise he leaned down and kissed her; a slow, sweet kiss that drove away the cold. "Get what rest you can. We will move within the hour."

Julia stared after him. Was he *trying* to drive her mad?

Alaric followed the sun, skirting vast gulfs, traversing impossible ridgelines, exhausting himself and his men in the endless steeps.

There was no choice but to pass through enemy territory. He was *very* aware of what Calthrax had told him. If word was already out about that ransom, then they were being hunted. He kept one eye on Julia to make sure she didn't die of exhaustion, and the other on Thorismund to ensure his stitches held his guts in his body.

Meanwhile, Horsa wouldn't meet his eyes. Horsa who had left the western gate unwatched.

Alaric often caught himself staring at his wife. When he rode with her, he lost himself in the feel of her body moving with his, the scent of her hair. The clean, graceful sweep of her neck. *His wife.* He was almost afraid to say it aloud. Afraid if he spoke of it, she would laugh in his face and take it all back.

He was under no illusions. She did not feel what he did, that fierce, tight feeling in his chest whenever he looked at her, or thought of her, or held her close. He told himself it did not matter. There would be time to show her that there was more between them than brute necessity.

Finally they arrived at a great pass, hacked into the rock as if from a giant's adze. Beyond it, sweeping grassland gave way to stunted forests. They rode all day, swift gallops followed by rest on steep, grassy slopes and sun-dappled groves. They were finally out of enemy territory.

The farmhouse was where he remembered. Its roof rose out of the trees, all rosy stone and timber. Alaric pulled Hannibal to an abrupt stop at the front door.

Calthrax stood in the doorway. Still bleeding from that wound he'd cut in the man's neck.

Alaric pulled Julia down. She was laughing, her eyes sparking, and he knew she did not see Calthrax. Not even Thorismund did. He looked up into Julia's breathtaking face and heard Calthrax's voice clear in his ear. *Everyone who loves you dies.*

How could he explain to her about Calthrax's ghost? Or the terror that gripped him at the thought of harm befalling her? He could not tell her these things. He could only spend his life sheltering her, from the dangers she could not see as well as those she could.

"Wait here, Julia."

Alaric walked softly with his blade drawn through vast, beamy spaces filled with midday sun and the smell of rot. There were scorch marks on the wall where vagrants had lit a fire, and some large animal had made a nest in the stables. But other than that, no signs of life.

When he and Ataulf had found this place on the way back from Milan, it had been recently deserted. Cups of mead tilted over on the table, a stewpot bubbling over coals. They'd had it outfitted as a place of refuge then, and promised to meet here on their way to Noricum.

But now the farmhouse stood empty, and Ataulf was not here. That did not bode well.

The first floor was one large room, dominated by a hearth of river stones and a scarred long table flanked by benches. Upstairs, there was a loft bedroom. A massive bed hulked in the corner, carved out of a single immense black tree trunk. The air had the stillness of a place long undisturbed.

When he came down from the loft, Thorismund was leaning in the doorway. Alaric halted on the stairs, struck by the gray tinge of his friend's face, his exhaustion as he sagged against the doorframe.

A terrible, sick dread settled in his stomach.

Thorismund frowned irritably. "Stop looking at me like I'm a corpse you've been meaning to bury. I've still got life in me yet."

"No food," Riga announced cheerfully, striding in from the larder. "I think it's been looted. There are barrels of mead in the cellars, though."

Thorismund winced. "How long do we wait for Ataulf?"

"A day." They did not have more time. Already Noricum might have dissolved into civil war.

"If you say so, *Reiks*," Riga said. Alaric felt a stab of foreboding. Riga never used his title unless he meant to cause trouble. "But if we ride tomorrow, we'll bury Thorismund the day after."

"The fuck you'll bury me. I'm fine."

"No, you're not. The ride last night opened your wound and you've been too proud to admit it." Riga was uncharacteristically grave. "And *you've* been letting him get away with it, Alaric. You won't prick his pride."

"I barely feel it," Thorismund grumbled. "I can go tonight. Just say the word."

"Thorismund, we can bury you on the way to Noricum, if Alaric would spare the time. Or we could burn you. Of course we all know how he feels about fire—"

Alaric sucked in a breath. The longer they waited, the more time those ransom rumors had to travel, the more time his enemies had to strengthen their position. Even so. He took in the dotted line of blood across Thorismund's tunic—his ashen complexion, the way he stood braced against the door. Alaric knew what he *ought* to do—put his friend's life in the balance to save the rest of them. Such decisions were a king's daily bread.

He thought of Julia's grief if he were to let Thorismund die.

"You're not going anywhere, Thorismund," Alaric said flatly. "What does he need, Riga?"

"New stitches, and five days of rest. At least."

Five days. He thought again of his chieftains in rebellion. Stilicho threatening to come before the snows. "I'll do the stitches." He'd done this before, for companions on the battlefield, and once, a deep gash in his own arm.

Thorismund shook his head. "I've seen your needlework. You couldn't sew a straight line in a corpse."

"So have the torturer do it. Fine." Alaric resisted the urge to feel insulted. "I'll go look for sign of Ataulf." He could tell where he wasn't needed.

Julia stood outside the farmhouse, holding Hannibal's reins while the horse snuffled at her hair. It had seemed the most natural thing in the world to lean down for Alaric's kiss—only to have him toss her Hannibal's reins and stalk off toward the house, his blade sliding out of its scabbard with a wicked hiss.

Something was bothering him. She wished he would confide in her.

Horsa approached her. "Has Alaric said anything about me?" He glanced behind, as if Alaric would leap out from the bushes. "I think he's going to kill me."

"Why would he do that?"

Nearby, Hengist's shoulders shook with soundless laughter.

"I was supposed to watch Brisca's western gate. It was my fault Calthrax came in. At Brisca's, Alaric told me *I'll deal with you later.* That's Alaric-speak. It means he intends to murder me at this farmhouse, and then bury me in the pig paddocks."

"This is outrageous." Julia fumed.

"Will you talk to him? He'll listen to you. You're his—"

"*Will* you stop saying that?" She was tired to death of it. "I'm not his woman. There has never been *anything* between us except—" Horsa was staring at her as if she had sprouted a third eye, and a humiliating heat scorched her face. "It wasn't—we didn't—*stop* looking at me like that."

Alaric came striding out of the farmhouse, his bronze hair loose and his long spear balanced over his shoulders. "I'll be back before dark," he told her tersely. "Do not leave the farmhouse."

Julia readied a sharp retort. Was she worth so little, then, as to only deserve a non-explanation of his absence followed by a brute order? But he was already past her, his attention on the boys. He said something to them in Gothic and Horsa turned to her with an expression of stark terror. "Too late. Pray for me." Then he disappeared into the woods with Alaric and his brother, sending one last, defeated look over his shoulder.

Julia turned back to Hannibal, who was busy ripping at the grass with his teeth.

Marry me. Be my wife. Stay with me until the world crumbles into ash. What a joke.

She had been turning those words over and over in her mind since he had said them, wearing them smooth like river stones. Trying to glean their meaning. Why not simply *ask* Alaric about what had passed between them? She tried to imagine how that conversation would go. *Are we now engaged to be married, or no? Did you really mean it when you made me swear to be your wife whilst inside me? Is that a Gothic custom, or—*

Julia laid her forehead against the horse's warm flank in mute agony.

The door swung open again and Riga stuck his head out. "Julia. Where is Alaric's salve? Tell me you did not drop it in a ditch." Riga did not look like himself, and it took Julia a moment to realize it was because he wasn't smiling. Julia's unease

grew. Riga had gone quiet and serious the way Alaric did when
something was very wrong. Was Thorismund dying?

"Of course not," she said, thrusting her hand into the leather
pouch that hung at her waist.

Inside the farmhouse, Thorismund sat in the light of a clay lamp,
stripped to the waist, a dense thicket of tattoos slashed through
by a long, livid line. Beside him, Riga was readying a thread
and needle.

His wound gaped like a vermillion mouth.

"Julia. The salve." Julia handed Riga the jar. She'd seen plenty
of wounds in Brisca's great hall; but it was different with someone she knew. Thorismund tensed as the needle pierced his
skin. He gripped the edge of his chair, muscles standing out in
sharp relief.

For long moments, there was no sound except his periodic
sharp intakes of breath. Then Riga started to whistle through
his teeth.

"Riga. Please stop whistling while you sew me together."

"I could, Thorismund. But when I stop, people die," Riga
said mildly. "I could wait for Alaric to come back—"

"*No.* Gods, no." Thorismund shut his eyes. "Whistle if you
must."

Riga glanced at her. "He will live, Julia. I've seen much worse
than this. Once I flayed a man alive and he lived. He lost an
eyelid, but—"

"Shut up, Riga," Thorismund growled. "She's going green
around the gills."

"I'm fine." She *had* to keep her hands busy.

They would need a bandage, and water set to boil. Horsa and
Hengist had taught her how to light a fire on the road. Julia remembered a particularly painful hour spent rubbing two sticks
together until her fingers bled. Now she lit a fire in the stone

grate with practiced efficiency, boiling water in an iron pot, ripping an old tunic of Riga's into strips for bandages.

Suddenly, without warning, she felt an urge to sob.

When had these people become so dear to her? Alaric could be next to take a wound like that. War was coming, and if any of these men died, it would be *her* fault.

Cornelius rose up in her mind. The howls of wolves. Red gore soaking into the sand.

After a time, Riga declared his work finished, and Thorismund grunted his thanks. Julia drew a breath and turned, wiping at her eyes. Foolish, to weep like this.

Riga missed nothing. "What have *you* to cry about? You're not the one with the stitches in your stomach."

"No. It's just—" Julia willed the tears gone. "Just not very pleasant to see."

For a moment he only looked at her, assessing, and she braced herself for some acerbic response. But Riga only grinned. "Come outside," he said. "I have something for you both."

Outside, Riga rummaged in his saddle pack and pulled out a length of red felt. Julia watched with curiosity as he retrieved a cluster of narrow poles piled on the ground and stuck them in the soft earth. Then he stretched the felt over the poles to make a little tent.

Inside Riga's tent, sun filtered through felt and turned everything a lavish red.

Riga tilted a handful of glowing coals onto the metal dish propped over a small fire. Then he took a generous pinch of seeds from a pouch at his waist and dropped it in the censer. "This will help ease Thorismund's pain. Yours too. I've seen how you favor that ankle."

Thorismund appeared in the doorway, his abdomen bandaged, holding up the tent flap with one burly arm. "This is a sacred ritual space. Women aren't allowed."

"Among your people, perhaps. Among mine, they're welcome," Riga said. "Although it is unorthodox to have men and women in a tent together." Smoke rose up in thin threads from the glowing coals. "This is the same smoke we used in the tower, Julia. It will be stronger in the tent, where the smoke won't be diluted. And you must excuse the quality, Thorismund. I bought it in Ravenna, and it's difficult to find good strains in Italy."

"So that's where you went when Alaric was off with Stilicho. Ataulf wanted you skinned."

Riga snorted. "Ataulf should watch who he makes that threat to."

Julia lay down, watching the light move on the tent walls. She'd come to *like* the throaty rhythms of Gothic, and this smoke smelled like the language sounded. Earth and pine, with a hint of flowers underneath, tickling the back of her throat.

Hours passed. Riga and Thorismund told stories that took shape on the tent walls—ferocious warriors, clever maidens, and gods who granted or took life on a whim. Somehow Julia felt she knew the stories even when she did not speak the language. She felt buoyantly warm—almost as if she'd drunk wine with the Blue Lotus in it, except her toes had gone numb. "I wish the two of you would speak in Latin so I can eavesdrop properly," she said.

Silence. "Julia, we've been speaking in Latin the whole time."

Julia rose up on one arm, which proved a mistake. Her head swam. "You have?"

"We were talking about the time Thorismund ran into a burning barn to save a mother cat and her kittens." Riga's voice had gone to gravel with the smoke.

Julia's eyes went round. "Did you save all the kittens?"

"Of course I did. Do I look like a monster?" Thorismund looked scandalized. "There were seven kittens and I had to make two trips."

Julia felt a sudden, debilitating fondness for him. She gave a light little laugh, exactly the way she would in Ravenna after some shallow witticism, and suddenly she wanted nothing to do with that laugh. That self. "You won't die, will you?"

"You forget who you're talking to, girl." Thorismund glowered fiercely. "I am a prince of the Batavi. Last scion of a line of kings. The trees in the forest that birthed my people are thick as a man is tall, and strong as iron. Such a little cut would not fell me."

"This conversation calls for drink as well as smoke," Riga announced, producing a wineskin. "The two of you are very entertaining."

Julia was thinking of Thorismund hurtling to his death while she galloped off in the dark. Suddenly, in an uncontrollable rush, she was weeping.

"Now, now, girl. This won't do. Come here." He opened his great arms to her, and it seemed the most natural thing in the world to sob into his battered vest. He smelled of old leather and the medicinal tang of the salve. "I promise I'll not leave you. I swear upon the ashes of my homeland!"

"Best watch yourself, Thorismund." Riga laughed. "I did quite a bit of work just now to keep your guts on the *inside*. If our esteemed leader were to hear of this nonsense—"

"Don't be crass. He'd have nothing to be angry about." Thorismund sounded deeply affronted. "Julia is—is Julia."

Julia cracked an eye open. "And what does *that* mean?"

"It means you're—" Thorismund's brow furrowed. "Not a *girl*, exactly."

"Is that an insult? I honestly can't tell."

In the corner, Riga laughed.

"I mean—I suppose you *are* a girl. To Alaric, for instance. But not to me. You're just sort of a—" He waved a hand at her helplessly. "Riga, what would *you* call her?"

"Alaric's," Riga said promptly, and then cackled.

Alaric's. Julia straightened. "How does Gothic marriage work? Exactly."

Thorismund peered at her through the smoke. "Why? You and Alaric having trouble?"

Julia tensed. Had Alaric told them about his fierce promises up on that cliff? And how credulously she'd believed it? A rush of shame twisted her gut. "Must there be a contract? A bride price? A ceremony?"

Thorismund scratched his stubbled cheek. "It's customary for the man to offer a dowry."

I will lay the wealth of cities at your feet. "Supposing there was a promise of one later."

"*That* makes you a concubine." Riga laughed.

"I'm not a concubine." She glared at them. "Not that this has anything to do with me."

"Anything could be a marriage vow among these barbarians," Riga said. "Take what Alaric said in the great hall, Julia. Just before the axes. That could have been a marriage vow, had that been his intention."

"What did Alaric say in the great hall?"

"Nobody translated for you?" Thorismund frowned. "*If I harm a hair on the woman's head, give me the honor of the threefold death, and scatter my ashes at the feet of the Roman army.* He tied his fate to yours, Julia."

When had the earth begun to spin this way? "What is the threefold death?"

"It's an ancient custom among our people," Thorismund said loftily. "It's secret."

"It's a way these uncivilized louts sacrifice their own kings to the gods." Riga's eyes glittered with laughter. "I saw it done once, in Crimea. First you remove the poor sod's trousers, and then you bring in a sacred goat, pure white with no markings—"

"Riga," Thorismund rumbled in warning.

"You smear the man's cock with honey," Riga went on gleefully. "And the goat—well, goats will eat anything, but they're particularly fond of honey—"

An angry flush came to Thorismund's face. *"That is enough."* He turned to Julia. "It is a sacred rite, and a secret one. We do it three ways, to appease three separate gods. Hanging, stabbing, and drowning."

"I thought it was burning, stabbing, and beating." Riga scratched his cheek. "Or is that slashing, stabbing, and—"

"*No*, Riga. Stabbing and slashing are the same thing."

"Oh, I disagree. A slash to the throat is a far different death than a stab to the heart, or the groin—"

And now they were arguing the semantics of murder. "Gentlemen. *If you please*," Julia interrupted. "I hereby declare that both of you owe me a drink. Riga?" She held out her hand imperiously. Riga passed his wineskin to her.

It was milk wine. Instantly the whole tent took on a fearsome spin.

"You know," Thorismund said. "I've decided I like you, Julia."

Julia took another sip of the milk wine. "That's terribly gratifying to hear."

"I cannot say she is a friend," Thorismund was saying, more to himself than to Riga. "Because she's Roman, and the daughter of Theodosius, and of course I couldn't be friends with such as that. My honor would never recover." He resembled a very conflicted, very blond bear. "I suppose since she and Alaric came together, she's family. But not a sister, because we've all agreed that she's not a girl."

"Since Alaric and I—" Julia blinked. "We've *agreed* I'm not a girl?"

"We have. Which makes her—" Thorismund's eyes lit up. "A brother!"

That sent Riga into another convulsion of mirth. "Thorismund," Julia said, trying to get her eyes to focus, "I am *extremely* certain we are not brothers. For one thing—"

"Not yet! But we will be!" A wild look came to his eyes. He rummaged through Riga's things and came out with a knife in one hand and a little golden cup in the other, studded with fiery garnets. *"Blood oaths all around!"* he bellowed. "Riga, you do the honors."

Riga sat up, blinking tears from his eyes. "And what will your men say, to find out you've made the blood oath with a Hun and a Roman woman?"

"They'll tread quietly or they'll feel the wrath of my spear," Thorismund growled. "You do the honors, I said. It's your custom."

Riga took the cup and the blade. "Listen well, ye gods," he intoned. "We are of the same blood, us three. Whatever is done to one of these is done to me. Should I break this oath, let me water the earth with my blood."

His voice seemed to rumble up from the earth itself. Riga took the razor-sharp blade and sketched lines into Thorismund's palm. Drops of blood fell into the golden cup. Then Thorismund did the same for Riga, whose grin didn't fade an inch as Thorismund cut the shape into Riga's palm.

Then Riga turned to Julia. "Your turn."

"Uh." Julia stared at the implements. "Are you actually expecting *me* to do this?"

"Yes!" Thorismund roared. "Do you want to be brothers, or not?"

They were both looking at her now as though she were one of *them*, fully capable of it, and she was astonished to realize she *did* want to. Julia held out a hand. *Better not to watch.* She shut her eyes tight, and held back a yelp as Riga's blade broke skin. For the length of three breaths, the pain made her head swim. Then it was over. Julia's eyes flew open, euphoric. "Is it done?" She squinted at her palm. Riga had drawn a little symbol there, abstract and unfamiliar.

She wanted to do it again, to swear a thousand oaths and live through every one.

"Not yet," Thorismund said solemnly. "There is one more thing."

He took Riga's wineskin from Julia's hands and poured the remaining liquid into the bowl. Then he held his hand over it and let his blood drip into the bowl, handed it to her and insisted she do the same. Riga took the bowl from her and passed it back to Thorismund when it contained all three of their blood.

The blond man raised it to his lips and took a sip. "Blood of my blood, us three," he intoned. "Whatever is done to each of you is done to me."

Riga drank next and made the same incantation, then passed the cup to Julia.

She peered into it, red threads swirling into white. *Do it now,* she thought to herself. *Do it quick.* She raised the golden vessel to her lips. "Blood of my blood, us three," Julia said, looking up at their faces. Thorismund's, so deeply solemn; Riga's, amused and knowing. "Whatever is done to each of you is done to me." She felt the words settle inside her and bind her heart.

Then she drank. Milk wine laced with blood. Salt and iron on her tongue.

CHAPTER TWENTY-EIGHT

There was no sign of Ataulf, not in the high valleys, not in the pine forests, not along the pathways coming or going. As the day wore on, Alaric forced himself to contend with the idea that Ataulf may not have made it out of Italy alive.

No. If it had been so, Calthrax would have thrown that in his teeth.

At last Alaric halted on a high ridge covered with alpine furze, an unlovely, spiky yellow. He scanned the far horizons for any plume of dust rising from horses' hooves, trying to ignore the tight feeling in his chest.

"I think I see something." Hengist pointed.

Alaric glanced down at the meadow. "Shepherds bringing their flocks home."

"How can you be sure?"

"A flock of sheep doesn't move the way a war band does, Hengist." Hengist looked at him skeptically. "Take a closer look if you don't believe me. Just to the ridge below."

Hengist hesitated, glancing between them. "Alaric, about that gate—"

"*Go.*" He said it in a voice that brooked no objection, and the boy went with a laconic shrug, slipping down the rocky slope. His brother moved to follow him and Alaric held out an arm to stop him. "Not you, Horsa."

The boy's shoulders stiffened. They'd both known this was coming. He turned, defensiveness set in every line of his body.

"The main gate was failing. I did it to save your life."

"I told you to watch that stretch of wall for a reason. If you gave a damn about *my* life, you'd have watched my back."

"I thought you were *losing*. Was I to hide myself at the western gate and let you die?"

"*Yes*, if I damn well tell you to."

"And what worth is my life if you are dead?" Horsa demanded. "You are my *chieftain*. If I leave you dead on the battlefield, I would never survive the shame." There were tears glinting in Horsa's eyes now, and Alaric's own heart rose up in his throat. Suddenly all he could see was Gaufrid, on his deathbed in the wreckage that followed the battle of Pollentia, demanding he take care of his sons.

He could not let this pass. Horsa was already too reckless.

Alaric picked up his spear. "Draw your weapon, if you care to defend yourself."

Horsa paled. "You cannot be serious."

"You almost got Julia killed." He wouldn't hurt the boy, but he'd put enough fear in him to make him think twice before disobeying again. "If you want to do this bare-handed, fine."

He raised his weapon.

"*Wait.*" Horsa raised his hands, palms out in self-defense. "Kill me if you must. But I have something to tell you before I die."

Alaric lowered his spear. The boy wouldn't get so wild around the eyes at a garden-variety sparring. "Out with it."

"I don't think Julia knows you're married."

It was past believing. She had said the words. So had he.

Alaric *ran* across the ridgeline, the boys barely keeping up, his dispute with Horsa forgotten. He had meant to have a rational, *reasoned* conversation, with all their clothes on, the day he'd taken her to the cliffs. Instead he'd lost his mind. His heart, in the grass beside her, beating its lifeblood onto the earth.

It hadn't gone as planned. But he'd been *elated* when she had said yes.

It was not unusual among his people for couples to disappear for a few days into the wilderness and come back hand in hand, promised. It was an old-fashioned way of doing things, but it was legitimate enough. He had descended that mountain as if floating on air; he'd wanted to shout their marriage to the stars. Of course, that would not be prudent. He didn't want rumors to reach Noricum before he did, and Brisca still needed the illusion of his favor to cement her position in these hills.

But he made it as clear as could be without words. The night they had come down from the mountains, he'd held Julia's hand as a signal to all. He'd seated her at his right hand, fed her from his own plate. He'd made sure everyone saw them go to his longhouse together. And in the days to follow on the road, he had shared his cloak with her and everything else he had. As a husband does.

The men had been ribbing him about it all the way from Brisca's village. Not in Latin, of course; it would be rude to subject Julia to that kind of teasing. Alaric had expressly forbidden it. But surely she *knew*. It would be impossible for her not to— wouldn't it? She had said the words.

A terrible, sick feeling settled in his gut.

Alaric strode out of the woods as the sun faded beyond the trees. The red light glinting from Riga's ritual tent made him grit his teeth in annoyance.

He thrust aside the felt tent flap. A hot, stinking wind billowed out. Thorismund sat with his head nodding onto his chest. Julia was cross-legged beside Riga, who was teaching her the harmony of a ribald Hunnic song. Alaric's hands clenched on the fabric of Riga's tent. It should have been *him* teaching her about the Hunnic leaf, *him* singing the goddamn song with her. He envied Riga so much he thought he might kill him.

Both Riga and Julia looked up when he entered. Two pairs of bloodshot eyes in two sweat-flushed faces. "Oh," Julia murmured huskily. "It's *you*."

"Yes, woman. It's me. Your *husband*." He said it pointedly. "The ritual's over."

She was looking at him like he'd grown three heads. Her eyes were very dilated.

"Gods. Have a seat, man." Riga slapped the ground beside him. "You'll give yourself a headache, glowering like that."

Thorismund's head jerked up. "Ah. *Fuck*. Seventeen heads at the foot of the Walls of Constantinople." He blinked blearily. "I'm awake."

His head fell immediately back to his chest and he emitted a loud snore.

Julia was blinking up at him, her gaze wide and unfocused, her lush little mouth parted as if begging to be devoured. "Would you like to see what we did while you were gone?"

She held up her hand to show a livid design in her palm, bleeding onto the ground. Hunnic writing of some kind. Alaric cursed that he could not read it.

"Riga. What the hell is this?" He came into the smoke and sat down. "*Fuck*, Julia. Come here." To his surprise, she slid over to him without objection, practically falling into his lap.

"It is a protective sigil," Riga said. "No Hunnic tribe will harm her now. She could walk into the middle of a battle and nobody would stir a hair on her head."

The thought of Julia in the midst of a Hunnic battle froze his blood. "Except the tribes *you* have disputes with. Which is most of them, I assume." Riga shrugged. Thorismund's loud snore broke the silence. "Can you get him to bed?"

"I can do anything after a smoke that I can stone sober." Riga sounded affronted. "Here. I'll show you. Let me see your axe."

"Not a chance." He gathered Julia closer. "Drop him and I'll skin you."

"No. I do the skinning." Riga laughed. "You always cock it up."

Alaric carried Julia to her rest while she murmured sleepy protestations against his chest.

They were out of enemy territory, but not entirely out of danger. He would keep watch through the night, since Riga and Thorismund were insensible and the twins dead on their feet. Alaric carried Julia up the stairs, laid her down on the vast wooden bed. He managed a whispered good-night.

But when she began to pull him down, he could not refuse her.

She was eager for him. Her mouth found his and her hands skimmed his shoulders, his chest. Each touch sent a jolt of white-hot lust through his body until he was out of his mind with it. "Ah, Julia." He gritted his teeth as her lips grazed his neck. "I cannot—"

"You smell nice." Her breath was hot on his skin, like fever. "Don't you still want me?"

Did he still want her? "Woman, I think of nothing else." And his hands were sinking into her hair now, his mouth opening over hers, and he *could not stop* as his brain screamed about bandits and assassins. But then her mouth opened under his and her fingers wound in his hair, and he tasted intoxication on her tongue.

"Did you really tell people to kill you three different ways in the great hall?" Her eyes shone up at him from out of the dark, her red hair spilling over the pillow. "Did you promise to die with me?"

"Yes."

"Then I suppose I shall be your wife after all." It was ridiculous, the sheer relief he felt. Her nails raked his back, beneath his shirt, and now all he felt was lust. "But first I have terms."

Terms? One of her legs had wrapped itself around his waist. "What terms?"

"First, you never throw axes at me again."

He laughed, his arms tightening around her, his lips finding the soft skin of her throat. "And second?"

"Second?" Her voice sounded dazed. He laid his mouth against the place beneath her jaw that always made her tremble. "I want gold and jewels. Piles of it. A dowry."

"Done." He was kissing and licking his way to her collarbone. Her skin tasted like earth and ash and his own ruin; *gods*, he could eat her alive.

"And third—" Her voice trailed off. It took him a moment to realize she'd gone still beneath him, her breathing even and deep. She was fast asleep.

Alaric cursed quietly. Her body lay soft and warm beneath his and he was so hard for her it *hurt*. He rolled over onto his back, taking her with him. Julia pillowed her cheek against his pectoral, her body molding to his, her red hair spilling over his chest.

He could rise from this bed. Go and keep watch in the night; keep them all safe until morning. It was what he *should* do.

She snuggled closer, her legs tangling with his, her arm flung across his torso. He'd stay here for a moment longer, he decided. Ten breaths.

He could stay awake that long. He wasn't tired—

CHAPTER TWENTY-NINE

Julia woke with a pounding head and a dry, dead-carcass taste in her mouth.

The bed was still warm from Alaric's body. *What had she said last night?* She remembered Alaric saying the word *husband*. Not *betrothed*, *husband*. That had to be some fever dream. She remembered demanding concessions. He'd laughed, and then drowned her in fire.

Her hand was bandaged. She remembered the brotherhood oath, Riga carving belonging into her palm. She had earned her place. They couldn't change their minds now. You couldn't take back a scar.

Julia rose and pulled Alaric's cloak over her shoulders, enveloping herself in the smell of him as she stumbled down the stairs.

The men were already awake, tending horses and sharpening weapons. Riga's tent was gone; she caught a glimpse of bright felt tucked away on the back of his saddle, resting across a fence. Last night, it had been a palace of myth; now it was only a scrap of cloth tied to a saddle. The sight of it made her feel oddly bereft.

The cut on her palm gave a tingling throb.

Julia leaned against the doorframe and watched Alaric walk out of the trees. *He* didn't look like he'd had a hard night. In fact, with his bronze hair tied off his shoulders and his skin glowing golden in the sun, it seemed he'd just come striding off Mount Olympus.

She'd declared herself his, hadn't she? And then demanded a dowry. *How embarrassing.*

Alaric stopped before her, his blue gaze more amused than concerned. "Are you ill?"

"No." Automatically she raised a hand to her hair, and winced. Small animals must have made a nest in it last night. "It's just that no one should be awake at such a cursed hour as this."

"It's two finger lengths past dawn, Julia." He held out a half-full waterskin. "You look like you need this."

Thank the gods. Julia took the waterskin gratefully, sucking down water so cold and sweet it could have been chilled wine. "Is there anything to eat?"

"As a matter of fact, there is."

Alaric spread out a feast before her on the grass. Brown bread, cheese from Brisca's village. Strips of smoked deer meat. Julia fell upon the food, forgoing manners entirely. It took her a moment to realize Alaric was sitting back, relaxed as a sunning cat. Watching her.

"Do you remember the way you acted on the first night, when I tried to give you food?"

Julia laughed. "In my defense, I thought you were trying to trick me into eating shoe leather. Why didn't you tell me it was delicious?"

"You wouldn't have listened to me if I told you the sun was hot."

Julia smiled ruefully. "I was an utter horror then, wasn't I?"

"So was I."

It held the weight of an apology. He put his arm around her, pulling the cloak up around them both; and it felt *so good* to be with him like this, warm and sated and safe. There had been many kinds of silences between them. Angry, vicious silences. Dangerous silences. But this one felt full of sunlight.

She took a deep breath and found her courage.

"Do you know," she said lightly, "for a few hours after we lay with each other the first time, I really believed we were pledged to be married? Isn't that ridiculous?"

Alaric said nothing, but she *felt* his muscles tense. Suddenly Julia wished she was anywhere else. In one of those trees, perhaps. Or under the ground.

"We are not pledged, Julia."

Shame. Horror. "Silly of me, isn't it? I blame the lack of sleep."

"We are married."

Now it was *her* turn to fall silent.

"No, we're not," Julia said in rising panic. "Marriage involves—it involves *trappings*, Alaric. An exchange of rings. *Witnesses.* Marriage is a matter of state for me—for both of us!"

He was looking down at her with his own kind of horror. "I swore to be your shield and fight your battles. What did you think that meant?"

"Just—just love words." Her heart would *not* stop racing. "Pretty promises such as men make in the throes of lust."

"I do not make promises I don't intend to keep, Julia."

Julia drew a breath. That was perhaps the truest thing about him.

Even so. "You don't actually intend to *hold* me to this travesty of a promise, do you?"

His blue eyes held hers. "Is it not what you want?"

She lowered her eyes. Her heart was hurling itself against her ribs now. "I don't know."

Alaric took her hand. His lips brushed her knuckles; his eyelids lowered, hiding his blue eyes behind a screen of blond lashes. "Among my people, all it takes to bind us together is for a man to pledge himself to a woman, and her to him in kind," he said. "We don't need ceremony. Our gods are everywhere. A dowry seals it, if the man's family has one to give." He looked at her solemnly. "I cannot make you empress of Rome, Julia. We would never win such a war, not on the Empire's own soil. Let me make you Queen of the Goths instead."

Julia could only stare. Was she dreaming? Was this some fever-born hallucination?

"There are strategic reasons for this marriage," he went on, the soul of rationality. "You are still hunted. No one else can assure your safety as I can." He paused; the silence multiplied. "*Fuck*, woman, say something."

Was that—*fear* behind his eyes? Julia stared up at him in bemused wonder. "Why would you *want* to marry me?"

Alaric threw back his head and laughed, and the next instant, she was in his arms, being kissed *very* thoroughly. "Is that answer enough?"

Her face went hot. "Nobody marries for *that*."

"Are you certain?" His thumb dragged across her cheekbone, achingly gentle. "My whole life I have been at war. Peace is not my strength. Perhaps you could help me with that."

He wanted her to be his Cleopatra. Her stupid heart nearly died in her stupid chest.

"You'll need a currency, of course. And a trade strategy," Julia said. Suddenly her mind was full of all the things that must be done. "A back channel for diplomacy to Rome. I can help with that. And then there's infrastructure. Roads, bridges, aqueducts—"

"Is that a yes?" he asked her quietly. "Considering I am not currently distracting you."

Julia's heart soared wildly. High above, an eagle had found an updraft and was spiraling up and up, dizzy and alive with the sheer joy of the open sky.

"I am not some peasant who will marry you in a field, Alaric," she said archly. It would not do to be *too* easy. "I require a dowry.

A palace, and a minimum of *one* very expensive party. I want my enemies in Ravenna to hear the rumors and weep."

"What an opportunistic little minx you are." And she was gathered back into his arms again, his lips on her temple, his laughter *thrumming* through her. "I should have given this to you on that day. I suppose I was also distracted."

He slid something on her finger. Her mother's opal ring.

Julia stared up at him, astounded. "It takes a special sort of spine to marry a girl with her *own* ring."

He laughed. "Never fear. There is no end to the riches I'll shower on you once we reach Noricum."

Her face was sore from smiling. He was hers too. And if he said nothing about love—which he hadn't—Julia decided she would take as much of him as she could have. She didn't expect a declaration of love—although, with every fiber of her being, she'd *hoped* for one. But it was foolish to fall in love with your spouse. Everyone knew that. Alaric was not foolish.

"You know," she whispered into his chest, "as a wife I have *needs*. You have been curiously remiss in fulfilling them."

"So I have." He rose to his feet, lifting her in his arms as if she weighed nothing. "Come, wife. I have a mind to make it up to you." And he carried her, despite the youth of the day, back to bed.

CHAPTER THIRTY

For five perfect days, there was not a cloud in the sky.

Five of the happiest days of Julia's life. Five perfect mornings in Alaric's arms. Sometimes in a haze of sex, skin against bare skin in the dim light before dawn. Sometimes just lying together, tangled in each other, not speaking. Julia never tired of watching him sleep.

Alaric always disappeared for some part of the day. He came back with game from the hunt, or armloads of wood for the fire. Sometimes he returned with nothing, his demeanor grave; he would brush off her questions then, hiding his worries behind a quicksilver grin and a change of subject that did little to quell her fears.

When Alaric was gone, she was happy to run with the twins through the overrun garden, weeds rising up to her eyebrows. Together they explored a barn with a ceiling like the underside of a great ship, lay in the grass and picked shapes out of the clouds. Thorismund improved with every day, the gray tinge to his skin fading; once she spent a pleasant afternoon watching him repair the grip on his ornate shield. She examined the rich detail of the great oak tree, sigil of his family, and he told her legends from a people long since vanished.

That had been the Romans' doing. Her own people. Julia understood why he could not stomach her before. Why she still didn't deserve his friendship, even now.

And one day, in the late afternoon, the three of them—Riga, Thorismund, and she—shared a clay pipe of Riga's smoke. The afternoon stretched endless, and when Alaric returned from across the field with the twins in tow, her heart lifted with joy. She thought he might be angry with her for smoking, but when Thorismund offered him the pipe, he took it. Nothing was more captivating than watching him lay back in the grass and exhale smoke in elaborate rings like a sunning dragon, the sleeves of his tunic rolled up to his forearms.

That night, Julia learned that lying with a man under the influence of Riga's smoke was eminently satisfying. They didn't even make it down for supper.

When Alaric wasn't gone, they were inseparable. He took her up into the hills to show her a breathtaking view from a nearby peak, or walking in pine-scented woods next to clear, cold streams. The angry tension between them had dissolved entirely, and Julia found him incredibly easy to talk to. Alaric listened with an intense, kinetic interest; soon she was sharing things about herself that nobody knew except Verina.

Julia wanted to know everything about him too. But he dodged her questions with his easy laugh. That was the only stain on her happiness—Alaric's refusal to speak of anything serious. He avoided her questions about his past and those about her future in Noricum, the possibility of coming war. Each time she brought it up, he deftly changed the subject or distracted her with kisses. And the men were equally closemouthed. He'd gotten to them first.

Alaric appeared to be trying to keep her in the present, and was very good at making the present a beguiling place to be.

He made her laugh, real, side-splitting laughter, the way people never laughed at court. He split a wineskin of *ealu* with her in the sunshine on a high, steep slope above the farmhouse, then laid her down in the grass and made love to her in a way that turned her bones to water.

She resolved not to think about the future. She would cling to the present as hard as she possibly could.

Alaric had always assumed he would one day die for his people.

In battle, most likely, his luck running out in some ambush or a desperate charge into a hail of arrows. Of course, there was also the chance of his own doing him in. Assassination, maybe. A few too many hungry months; too many lost battles and all his people might start to believe the gods were no longer behind him. When that happened, in the old days, the people made a sacrifice of their kings. He thought it just as likely his end might come with him giving his blood for the sake of his people. He'd even accepted it, in a way.

But now, with Julia's cheek pillowed on his shoulder, Alaric found that he wanted to *live*.

The morning of the fifth day dawned warm and full of sunshine. Alaric lay in the massive bed, one forearm flung up over his head, the other cradling Julia to him. They had made love twice last night in the great bed; she had been on top the last time, her red hair falling all around him. Now Julia was fast asleep, her breathing filling the quiet. Alaric had known little peace in his life; this was a rare kind of contentment.

In Noricum, there would be no peace. His chieftains had been on the edge of rebellion when he left, and that had been more than two months ago by his reckon. He had no idea what he would find when he returned. Julia's status as his wife would protect her, but it could also inflame tempers.

The last thing he wanted was for her to discover the vast size of the ransom, or how close the threat of Stilicho loomed, or

how precarious his situation in Noricum was. He wanted no
unpleasant thoughts to enter her mind. He never wanted to see
that far-off stare in her eyes again, like he'd seen in that cave.

She certainly made that part difficult, with all her incessant *asking.*

Julia snuggled closer. As always he felt his body rise to hers,
but he'd worn her out over the past few days. She was new to
all this. Better to let her rest.

He sighed. Perhaps he was doing this all wrong. Perhaps he
ought to stay here in this farmhouse and tell everyone in Noricum to go piss into a headwind.

If he did, he could make Julia his world. He'd spend a year
in bed, perfecting every possible way to bring her pleasure. He
could take her riding; show her the mountain's treasures and
play *latrones* with her by the fire. He could hunt and fish, husband those half-wild sheep while Julia replanted the garden.

It was a stupid dream, of course. He knew little of planting
or animal husbandry, and his woman knew even less. They'd
both starve.

Julia was awake, fingertips grazing his chest. He caught her
hand in his. "Hello, Julia."

"Hello." Her fingers laced through his. "I have a favor to ask."

A favor. He was ludicrously happy for the chance to give her
anything. "What is it?"

"I want a bath."

He rolled her over, burying his face in the junction between
neck and shoulder. "You had one yesterday. And you smell incredible." He nipped at her delicate skin. "Like roses."

Roses and sex. She was laughing, her hands tracing the contours of his muscles. Eyes bright with invitation. But the day
was blazing, and there was so much more he could give her.

"Get up." He rose from the bed. "I have something to show you."

Julia gazed up in wonder to where the mountain stream tumbled
down, cascading into pool after pool before streaming into the

one at her feet. The kind of pool druids might have gathered at, its waters black and mysterious, its bottom littered with broken swords and chalices. Alaric had a spectacular talent for surprises.

"You did say you wanted a bath—"

"I did." She eyed the water uncertainly. "But it looks cold."

"I'll keep you warm." He pulled her closer, his lips brushing her forehead. Then he was stripping out of his clothes, leaving Julia to gaze in open wonder at the sight of his naked body.

She raised a hand to trace a scar that ran along the ridged muscles of his abdomen. She didn't know its story, and she wanted it. She wanted all his stories.

Alaric caught her hand, raised it to his lips. The brush of his mouth against the tender skin of her inner wrist made her tremble. "You're wearing too many clothes."

She'd have done anything for him when he looked at her that way. Strip naked in a snowstorm. Anything. Julia let Alaric help her out of her tunic, then her leggings, his knuckles brushing her thighs. When it was done, she stood bare before him, gooseflesh rising on her skin. Not from the air. From the look in his eyes.

Julia's hands slid across the lean, strong muscles of his flanks, the weight of his arousal pressing against her stomach, but he pulled back, his lips grazing her throat. She made a sound of frustration. "If you want it," he whispered in her ear, "come and get it."

Then he went striding into the dark water.

Unfair. Naked, he could have been sculpted from marble, not an ounce of spare flesh on him. But he was also marked by scars—a distressing reminder of his mortality.

"You aren't *really* going to make me go into that water, are you?"

His mouth curved in an answering smile. Daring her. Then he dove into the rippling pool, emerging close to the waterfall. "Come here, Julia. Unless you'd rather I come out and drag you."

"You wouldn't dare!"

"Don't tempt me, woman."

He was striding toward her now, through water up to his chest. Sunlight gleamed on his bare shoulders. Julia's mouth went dry. She eyed the water. Large rocks loomed beneath the surface. They looked slippery. She dipped a toe in. "Are there eels in here?"

A stifled laugh. "No eels."

She put one foot into the water, gritting her teeth against the icy cold. Here was a rock she could stand on. Slippery—she curled her toes, gaining no purchase whatever. Risked putting her weight on it and slid.

"Careful!" came his laughing admonishment.

"I'm *trying!*" She found her balance, her other foot on a stony ledge. "How in *hell* did you run into this pool as if the bottom was smooth gravel?"

"I didn't think it to death." He gave a lazy shrug. "Jump in. I'll catch you." His smile lit up the whole sky. "Come, Julia. When have I ever let you fall?"

Oh, that wasn't fair. Using that smile on her, those words, and all that glorious nakedness. He held out a hand and there was nothing in the world she could do but reach out and take it.

He grinned. Then he pulled her forward, into the frigid black. Julia laughed as his arms came around her, pressing her to his chest. Hard muscle glazed in icy water. "You *beast!* Let go!"

"If you insist—" And then his arms opened and she sank like a stone, toes grazing the bottom, the frigid line of the water rising past her shoulders.

She gasped, held tight to him. "Don't let go."

Something fierce blazed in his eyes. "Never." He held her close. His skin so warm and she heat-starved. "Are you warm yet?"

"Almost." She drew him down to her. "I'll take the rest of my kiss now."

CHAPTER THIRTY-ONE

Making love to Julia beneath the waterfall was like making love to a naiad.

Alaric lost himself. Pressed her against the rock, his face buried in her neck and one hand tangled in the soaking weight of her hair as the water pounded his back and shoulders. She gave herself to him with intense abandon, her legs locking around his hips, dissolving into a trembling, glorious mess as he drove into her over and over. Every kiss, every caress, every thrust a message. *Stay with me. Stay.*

These were words he could not speak—not yet—but there were other ways to tell her.

Later Julia sat in the warming sun. Alaric lay beside her, watching her comb out her hair with her fingers. Julia had insisted on washing her clothes, and now she wore his tunic and nothing else, drowning in it as the daylight turned her unbound hair into shimmering fire.

She had a troubled look in her eyes. He didn't like it.

Alaric sat up and dropped a kiss on her bare shoulder. "What are you thinking of?"

"Nothing in particular."

She said it in that light, brittle tone that meant she *was* thinking of something, and it was eating at her. "I can tell when you're lying, you know." He moved her hair aside so he could kiss her neck. "Talk to me."

"I'm terrified," she said quietly. "When my brother finds out what we've done, he'll be furious. You managed to stay alive in the face of Stilicho's assassins, but what happens when he sends an army?" She was actually wringing her hands now, like a mourner at a funeral. "Have you thought about what will happen if he captures you?"

Alaric caught her hands in his to still them. "No. I haven't thought of it."

"Well, you *ought* to. My brother hates you already, but if he finds out you've married me—"

A broad grin spread across his face. That was more like it. Baseless worries for his welfare. He gathered her closer, breathing in the sun-warmed scent of her. "Let me worry about the Empire. Marrying you isn't the worst thing I've done, and it isn't the worst thing I will do."

"Yes, but I've *lived* with them. I've seen what they do to people." She looked up at him, stricken. "What if my brother does to you what he did to Cornelius? What *then*?"

"Let him try. I've survived the arena before."

He thought she knew that story. Everyone knew that story. Even so, blue-green eyes narrowed. "Tell me from the beginning."

Alaric sighed. That stubborn set to her jaw told him she would not let this go. He couldn't tell her about the Huns, about the camps by the river Danube. About being sold into slavery or the horrors of that time. The only place to start was in the arena.

"My parents had sold me into slavery," he said matter-offactly. "I killed my master and tried to run, but I didn't get very far. I was fourteen." He used her own trick, kept his voice light, as if it didn't matter at all. "They threw me into the arena to be devoured by a beast for the amusement of a Roman crowd. It was no grand celebration, only a small execution of petty criminals and escaped slaves."

He felt her breath catch beneath his hands. "What beast?"

"A bear."

Julia flinched. "You should be dead."

"You're right. I was never supposed to walk out of there." And he hadn't, not really. It was still all too real to him. The heat of that sand. The sun hammering down like a punishment from the gods.

The bear had been skinny and starved. But still, he recognized it. Bears like that once roamed the thick pine woods on the island of his childhood. The god of his tribe had been a bear god. There had been a story of a legendary hunter meeting his fate at the claws of such a bear, a story his own father once thrilled him and his siblings with around the fire.

Fires all gone to ashes. Family all up in smoke with the sacred groves. Only the bear still lived, kept in a cage beneath the arena and starved.

"I was never supposed to kill it. The Romans expected me to die. And my people would have called that courageous."

That bear was still sharp in his mind. The way it blinked in the sunlight, as if it had been in the dark a long time, hungry and blind, wanting only to eat and stretch its limbs in the light for a while, free of its cage.

In the beginning, Alaric had not known how to tell her this story. But once he started, he couldn't stop. Beneath the crowd's murmur, he heard the slaughtered gods of his people. The voices of his dead family. *Let the bear have you*, they whispered. *It is an honorable death. A right death. Go bravely toward it and join us here where you belong.*

Thorismund would have let the bear have him rather than harm it. But he'd been only fourteen, and he didn't know how to die.

And so he'd chosen the coward's way. His foot bumped something long and heavy under the sand and he'd picked it up. He'd lifted the spear and killed the bear so that he might live.

The story ended and Alaric felt as if he'd just fought some battle. Meanwhile, Julia had gone still in his arms. She was weeping openly, and a rush of tenderness filled him. "Ah, Julia," he whispered, moved beyond measure. "You mustn't fear. I am harder to kill than your Cornelius."

Julia hugged him fiercely. "I know. But I'd go back to Honorius a hundred times rather than give him the chance to hurt you."

She cared for him. Suddenly Alaric couldn't breathe around the elation rising in his chest.

He held her close. He understood this fear, the fierce, unending worry that someone would take her from him. If that was how she felt about him as well— "Don't think you can save me that way," he said hoarsely. "Stilicho will never stop coming, whether you return to them or not. The things I've done demand an answer. But I chose this. I made my choice in Ravenna."

Her answering smile was the sun coming up. "So did I."

When he kissed her he could almost believe there was nothing else to life than this—the mountains, the waterfall, and this woman who tasted of sunshine and roses.

"Alaric." She whispered it against his throat. "What is that?"

Down below, he saw a dust cloud rising up from the valley, high above the trees.

Chapter Thirty-Two

They rode down from the high mountain pools at a gallop and arrived at the farmhouse just as Ataulf and his men came barreling into the yard.

Through the dust, Alaric saw the horses' heaving flanks. Black and red and gleaming bay, old horned cavalry saddles from the Gothic Wars, and the flash of snaffle bits and scraps of bright cloth in flying manes of red and black and white.

He pulled Hannibal to a halt and helped Julia down, just as Ataulf came striding out of the swirling dust. "Fucking *hell*. What took you so long?"

"Negotiating with the tribes. Dodging Stilicho's assassins. Trying not to die." Ataulf wiped at the dust on his brow. "*You* look happy."

Happy. That was an understatement. Ataulf was alive, Julia was his, and all would be right. As always his gaze landed on Julia, standing apart from the crowd. At a glance, he could have mistaken her for a Tervingii girl. Crimson braid emerging from a Phrygian cap, holding the reins of her man's warhorse as he ripped up the grass, roots and all.

"So that is the little Roman princess. You could almost mistake her for one of us, if you didn't look too close." Ataulf grinned. "You'd best clean her up before we send her back, or the Romans may not believe it's her."

Alaric did not take his eyes from Julia. "She is my wife. She is not going back."

Julia tried to keep sight of Alaric amidst the crush of horses and men. She caught a glimpse of his brilliant grin, and an acute sense of loss shot through her.

He had been hers these past days. Now he belonged to everyone.

"Julia! Is that you?" A tall Gothic warrior stood before her, his bronze-brown hair brushing his shoulders. "What on earth are you wearing? By all the gods—are those *freckles*?"

Recognition came with a jolt. "Bromios! You're *alive*!"

"Of course *I'm* alive." Bromios swung her up in his arms. "You've landed on your feet, I see. Seducing the barbarian warlord into marrying you!" He laughed. "Perhaps you should introduce us. The two of us could work him to our advantage, I think."

Jealousy swept through her like a hot wind. "I'd rather not share."

"Don't tell me you've lost your head over him." Bromios glanced over his shoulder. "You realize that man has a whole army of lovers in Noricum. *Look* at him."

"*What?*" Julia seized Bromios's arm and pulled him to the side of the crowd, where they would not be heard. "Alaric has told me *nothing* of what to expect in Noricum. Clearly you know far more than I do," she hissed. "Including that my husband has *lovers*. *Talk*."

"It's only common sense, Julia. A man like that always has lovers. You must be slipping." He shrugged. "Ataulf says there were several attempts on Alaric's life before he left. His chieftains are always halfway to revolting. And *you* should be on your guard," he added. "Have you given any thought to how his people will react when he arrives in Noricum with a Roman wife in tow?"

"I have. But he won't *tell* me anything—"

They had drawn Alaric's attention. He was coming toward them, the crowd parting. Julia tensed.

"He doesn't like me. I think he might put a knife in my back," Bromios said quietly. "We must stick together, Julia. Ride into that city as his queen, with your head held high. How you begin is how you'll continue. And don't lose your head any more than you already have."

And then he was gone, slipping back into the crowd.

That night, Alaric presided at the head of the scarred table, Julia at his side, regaling his men with stories of her deeds—the way she'd stood straight and strong before his axes, her bravery in Brisca's village. The men devoured these stories, toasting her name. Golden mead flowed—sparkling honey in her cup. Julia had one large tankard full, and was pleasantly loose and happy— but the second hit her hard.

Suddenly, a few hours after the meal, she could barely keep her eyes open.

It was, generally speaking, strategic to retire at the height of one's good impression. So when Julia rose to her feet, Alaric only smiled and promised to wake her later.

She was almost to the stairs when a man came toward her.

"I know what you are." It was Ataulf, Alaric's right hand. A scar ran down his face, giving him a rakish handsomeness.

Julia laughed. Light and airy, from her days in Ravenna. "What am I, then? Is this a riddle?"

"You may have enspelled Alaric, but it doesn't work on me. I am immune."

Julia raised a brow. "I notice *you've* been feeding my friend

Bromios off your plate all night. Did you enspell him? Does that make you a sorcerer?"

"Bromios is not your friend. He is your erstwhile *slave*. I have freed him from that life."

"Rubbish." Her temper rose. The *nerve* of this man. "*I* freed him before he met you. And how free is he, *exactly*, if he is not free to choose where he sleeps? At least I never made him share my bed for protection."

Ataulf reddened furiously. "I will be watching you *very* closely. If you do anything to harm Alaric, I will make your life a hell."

"I cannot imagine how stupid you think I am," Julia said evenly. "My fortunes are tied to his, same as yours."

His lack of an answer was answer enough. She felt him staring holes in her back as she went up the stairs to bed.

CHAPTER THIRTY-THREE

The night was well on its way to morning and the men were still wide-awake. They filled the blazing hall, drunk on mead and homecoming, working off the hardship of weeks of difficult travel. Alaric was at the center of it, dicing and drinking with the rest of them.

Ataulf stayed on the periphery and resisted the urge to grit his teeth.

Ataulf loved Alaric like a brother. He'd lay down his life for Alaric, willingly, without an instant's thought. But Alaric in a crowd set his teeth on edge.

In crowds, Alaric's towering charisma burned so bright it was impossible to ignore. People behaved strangely around it. Grown men would start laying their weapons at his feet and swearing hundred-year oaths. Women schemed to tempt him into bed— even those who were happily married.

And Alaric in a crowd could turn on a knife-edge. Ataulf had seen him go from at his ease to lethal in a blink more times than could be counted. It was worse when he was drinking. But he did it sober too.

Ataulf held no love for throngs, especially those that gathered around Alaric. But the things he had to say to his brother-in-law now couldn't wait.

He drained his tankard and waded through the knot of men. Alaric was seated at the head of the plank table, rolling dice with the men. There was no way Alaric would be dragged away from his adoring public to have a conversation he didn't want—and he wouldn't want this one. So Ataulf would have to be strategic.

He slid onto the bench, shoving a bearded Sarmatian out of the way. "I thought you'd like to play a real game."

The men roared their objections, but Alaric held up a hand. A silence descended. Ataulf blinked. He knew these men. A diverse assortment from Riga's and Thorismund's own war bands, not to mention Ataulf's own. Ataulf had led them the past few weeks, suffered with them in the heat and the dust. They followed him readily enough, but *he* could not simply hold up a hand and expect a whole room to fall silent.

Alaric was leaning back in his chair as if he'd done nothing so unusual. "And what was it you had in mind?"

Ataulf unrolled his *latrones* board and tossed his little bag of counters on the table. Alaric's skill at this game was more than legendary, but he hadn't played since Milan. "Durostorum rules," Ataulf said, raising an eyebrow in challenge. "Unless you're too rusty."

"Why don't we find out?"

There was a puzzled silence as Ataulf shook out his stones and began to lay them out on the board. None of the others knew about Durostorum rules. This was the game as they'd played it in the refugee camps by the River Danube, Alaric a gangly boy of six or seven, all knees and elbows, Ataulf a youth not ten years older and already a widower.

Alaric had had an elder sister, Inna. She'd had bronze-gold hair like Alaric's, and a quick, ready laugh. Ataulf had been married to her not yet a week when the Huns had come and driven them all into the Danube, to swim for the safety of the Roman side. Inna had gone in with them, but she had not come out.

The Roman soldiers had been waiting on the opposite shore, housed the refugees in camps at the fort at Durostorum. Camps that rapidly became traps of starvation and death. Ataulf and Alaric had learned how to survive there, both ravaged by grief and hunger.

The cacophony grew again as the men jostled and shoved for a better look at the board.

"I have to talk to you." Ataulf let his gaze slide to the stairs where the copper-haired Roman princess had recently departed. "About your *wife*."

As he said it, Ataulf slipped into the language they'd both grown up with—an ancient tongue with no name, a dense thicket of inflections no one else in this room would understand. It was possible there was no one else alive who spoke the language of the pine-tree island.

Alaric's grin broadened as he switched easily to the same language. "Ah, I see. You've come to congratulate me."

"That isn't it and you know it, you smug bastard." Ataulf finished laying the stones. "I suppose you're going to take loser's privilege from the last time we played."

"No. By all means." Alaric made a magnanimous gesture to the board, smiling as if he hadn't dropped the mother of all problems in Ataulf's lap. "I'm not the one who will need it."

Durostorum rules made *latrones* a fast-paced game. Cutthroat. Most versions of *latrones* sprang from the formal rules of aristocratic Roman villas; this version had arisen among people who knew their days were numbered.

In the camps, there wasn't time for lengthy strategy. Ataulf and Alaric had played this game there, cheating ferociously, winning scraps from those guards who liked to gamble. Just enough to keep them both alive.

"I'm not surprised that you took her to bed," Ataulf said as they fell into a lightning dance of thrust and parry. "I'm not questioning your right to that. But we both know how this goes. You fuck her senseless. Make her fall in love with you, if that amuses you. Then you send her back to the Romans for a mountain of gold. You don't—"

"It is already done." The words were flat and cold and final.

So he doesn't want to be questioned, Ataulf thought to himself. *That's too bad.* "You're fooling yourself if you think you can keep her. Be realistic. One day we'll *need* that gold. Or an exchange of hostages. Or what we've been fighting for all along." He spotted an opening and launched his first serious attack. "Would you turn down a homeland for her?"

"I will not need to turn down a homeland for her, Ataulf."

Alaric brushed his attempt aside. His answering move—from the diagonal—drew blood. Three pieces, and suddenly it was all Ataulf could do to hold his line. The men cheered for Alaric, who took their admiration with his usual generosity.

The game continued, and it was clear Alaric wasn't giving it his full attention. The men were rowdy, boasting and jesting, and Alaric joined in, his gaze barely flicking across the board as he countered. That was to be expected. Alaric in a crowd belonged to everyone.

But Ataulf couldn't help noticing how often he glanced toward the stairs, where the bright-haired princess had departed. As if half hoping she'd descend again.

Ataulf felt himself go furiously tense, thinking of what she'd said about Bromios. *And how free is he, exactly, if he is not free to choose where he sleeps?*

The *insult*. As if a Roman woman had anything to teach *him* about coercion or slavery or *choosing where one sleeps*. As if she hadn't kept slaves of her own, as if she wasn't currently bewitching his brother-in-law for her own purposes.

Besides, Bromios had chosen him of his own will. *Hadn't* he?

He could never be quite sure of anything with Bromios. The other man guarded his heart and his speech carefully, and Ataulf hadn't minded at first; this was never meant to be more than a dalliance. Something to fill the long nights between Ravenna and Noricum.

But now he glanced across the room to see Bromios bend his head to jest and laugh with Riga and Thorismund, and angry jealousy flared in his chest. *What if he chose one of them next?*

He knew it was ridiculous. He and Bromios did not own each other.

Still. He would tell him to stay away from Julia. He hadn't liked how the two had been thick as thieves all night. Hadn't liked how friendly the twins were with her either. Even Thorismund! *That* was witchcraft.

He turned back to Alaric, putting a check on his fury. "What did she tell you, to make you agree to this lunacy? I hear you almost lost the hill tribes over her."

"I strengthened my hold on the hill tribes because of her." He looked positively *smug* about it too. "Was there anything else?"

"What you faced in the hills will be as nothing compared with what's ahead of you at Noricum. The chieftains were half in rebellion when you left. Have you given thought to what they'll do when you insist they be ruled over by a *Roman* queen? They may not even open the gates." Ataulf straightened. Suddenly he had it—the solution to both of their problems. "You're lucky you have me," he informed his brother-in-law. "I'm going to get you in that gate and have all the chieftains prostrating themselves at your feet."

"Oh?" The lightning-fast *click-click* of the stones continued. "And how is that?"

Ataulf's grin broadened. "A triumph."

That got his attention. Alaric *loved* a spectacle. "Go on."

"How many times have the Romans thrown these to celebrate grinding our people into the dirt? It's *our* turn," Ataulf said. "A *proper* triumph. First will come the carts of gold you extorted from Stilicho, overflowing their coffers and leaving glittering trails in the streets."

"I didn't extort gold from Stilicho."

"No matter. We'll plunder it from somewhere and spread rumors that you did." He warmed to his topic. "And then the gems will come. Everything the princess wore when she came to you, carried on silver platters by a troupe of beautiful youths, or something." He waved a hand. "And then, we'll send *her.*"

Alaric's eyes narrowed dangerously.

Ataulf paused. He would have to tread carefully here.

"We won't actually *hurt* her," he added hastily. "No need to flog her through the streets. It will be very humane. We'll just put her in chains and make her walk behind your horse." He smiled. "You'll be the great warlord who answered Stilicho's parlay and came back with a valuable war prisoner and a royal cache of jewels. The people will be eating out of your hand again, and the chieftains will *have* to welcome you with open arms. Your kingship will be secure." It was as easy as that. He'd solved all of it, because between the two of them, he'd always been the one with the brains.

Alaric's impassive expression didn't change. But Ataulf saw the lethal glint in his eyes just before he spoke.

"No." ·

Just one word. Soft and chilling; and for the first time, Ataulf felt a prickle of fear up his spine. Even he would be foolish to provoke him now.

Which was why he leaned forward, looked Alaric in the eye, and said, "Don't be a *fool.*"

A sudden hush fell over the room. The men could not understand the language they spoke, but they knew a building argument when they saw one, and they were men of violence too. The very air in the room seemed to hinge on Alaric's mood.

There was none who could do this but him. "You *know* I'm

right," Ataulf pressed into the silence. "You cannot simply ride up to the gates of Noricum with that woman at your side, in a place of honor, and expect to be let in. They'll skin us all alive."

"They'll let us in, Ataulf." Alaric spoke with quiet certainty. "We'll all keep our skins. Julia will ride at my side, and the people will call her queen."

"Oh, for certain they will. And I suppose they'll call me a *leek*." Ataulf repressed the urge to roll his eyes heavenward. "Look. There isn't a man in this room who wouldn't follow you into the mouth of hell if you asked it. And I'm no different. But I need to know your *plan*."

For a moment Alaric only regarded him from beneath hooded lids. To the men, he must've looked bored. *I knew it*, Ataulf thought angrily. *I knew there's no plan. There's just Alaric thinking with his cock, and—*

"Do you truly not see it, Ataulf?" Alaric said then, softly. "Julia is Theodosius's daughter. If I kill her useless brother, I'll have a legitimate claim to the Empire itself. And if she carries my son, no force on earth can stop us."

"Is *that* your plan?" This was worse than he could have imagined. "You cannot believe the Senate will honor that claim. Assuming they'd overlook your many and varied insults to the Empire—which *they won't*—you'll never inherit the throne from a woman. The rules don't—"

"Fuck the rules. If I played by their rules, I'd still be in chains. And so would you, and every man in this room." A slow, bloodthirsty grin spread across his face. "I'm going to obliterate the rules. And the chieftains won't just thank me for it. They'll worship me."

He said it in Gothic. The silence broke among the men; their approving laughter rang in the hall. Ataulf shook his head grimly. Their plan had always been to bleed concessions from the Empire, never to replace it entirely. He had sworn to follow his chieftain even unto death—but he hadn't envisioned it would be so soon.

"Fine words," he said quietly. "One day they won't stop what happens to you."

Alaric smiled. Suddenly the fierce god of war was gone, and he was only Ataulf's charismatic brother-in-law, lounging lazily in his chair. "Maybe so. But that day will not come outside the gates of Noricum." He nodded at the board. "Shall we continue, or will you concede?"

Ataulf glanced at the pieces and cursed. His position had been entirely surrounded, a dagger at his throat.

He'd lost.

CHAPTER THIRTY-FOUR

The next day, they departed early for Noricum.

All day, Julia's nerves were on edge. *Did* Alaric have concubines? Would the people hate her? The questions rattled in her mind.

Two weeks after they left the mountains behind, a little town came into view, nestled behind high walls along the coast. Alaric set up his red chieftain's tent outside the city walls and sent for the magistrates. His brilliant smile dazzled as he bought all their grain out from under them with a bare handful of Julia's jewels, the magistrates sweating beneath the threatening demeanor of his men.

Their leader was a statuesque middle-aged woman in an elaborate dress made of stiff folds of crimson. "You can't simply buy up every scrap of grain in our storehouses," she informed Alaric indignantly. "What will we eat?"

"That isn't my problem." The magistrates' shock at Alaric's princely Latin was almost audible. "You can sell it to me, at a price you name. Or I can take it." His eyes fell to the magistrate's finery. "And I'll take that dress too."

The dress was too short, the chest too tight and the shoulders too constricted; Julia could barely raise her arms. The armholes dug painfully into her armpits, and the stiff fabric itched. And red was not her color. But it was a rich dress. Even queenly.

At least Alaric had been amenable to letting her ride into the city by his side, as his queen. She was gratified for that.

They moved faster after that. The days flew by in a blur of black-and-earth-brown landscape. Julia noticed the burned-down farmsteads, the overgrown fields. The landscape had been ravaged and emptied. Sometimes she saw ragged bands of men in the fields, dressed in animal skins atop swayback nags. *Bandits.* Riga informed her cheerfully that they'd take everything she owned and leave her bleeding in a ditch if she was alone out here.

During the daytime, she barely saw Alaric. He rode at the head of the column, surrounded by a knot of warriors, Ataulf ever at his side. Sometimes he rode up and down the lines, and when he did, he'd always stop to ask if she was well, to make her laugh. His presence was brief and bright, all-encompassing and all too short.

But at night, they came together. Julia spent each night in hedonistic splendor in his arms.

She knew she should try to get more information from him about what she would be walking into. But she'd tried it the direct way, and he had deflected. She could only gather what information she could from others—and most did not want to speak to her. Even Bromios avoided her now.

She *dreaded* Noricum.

Finally, after another week of travel, the city came into sight.

The entire column fell quiet as they rode through a plain strewn with the discarded detritus of battle. Burned husks of overturned war machines lay on the ground, wheels spinning slowly in the wind. Scraps of armor lay rusting in the summer sun. Julia watched a large vulture land on a helmet and lower its pink, wrinkly head to pick at something. It took her a moment to realize the helmet wasn't empty. Suddenly she and her stomach were at war.

Noricum towered above the plain—sand-colored stone walls and immense black gates. At the top of the wall were ten desiccated corpses tied to stakes. A few scrawny crows perched on their shoulders; one dipped its beak and tugged a piece of tendon from a weathered neck.

Her stomach defeated her. Bile rose hot in her throat. Julia slid off her horse, knelt in the road in her fine dress, and retched, shattering the oppressive silence of the valley. She retched until everything in her stomach lay in a little puddle in the dust.

"Get up, Julia." Alaric stood before her, golden and terrible, every inch the barbarian king. He raised her to her feet. "Look at me. Everything depends upon you riding through those gates with your back straight and your head held high. Look at me and nothing else."

Julia took a deep breath and nodded, her throat gone dry as parchment.

Then he was cantering up to the big black gates. Alaric halted before them and called out in his own language, rough and deep and powerful, the echo reverberating.

As his voice fell silent, an eerie stillness filled the valley. The sun pounded down and Julia sweated beneath her brocade. Horses stamped flies off their flanks and men murmured among themselves. Julia wondered if the entire city was empty. If everyone in it was dead.

The whole valley held its breath as they waited for the gates to open.

"Well. If it isn't your own vultures, coming home to roost," Ataulf said drily. "We could have had a triumph. We *could* have had them at your feet." He glanced at Alaric, frowning. "Do you really think a few meager wagonfuls of grain will get you into this city?"

"The people are hungry, Ataulf," Alaric replied, with a quiet certainty he did not feel. "They will let us in."

Alaric watched the black gates as if he could will them open. This had been his greatest fear—that his city would be barred to his return.

"You know there's only one way you'll get into Noricum without the crowd tearing her limb from limb." Ataulf glanced behind to where Julia nervously sat her horse, swathed in heavy fabric. Alaric held an air of unshakable calm. He must never let his confidence slip, especially not now, with his men at his back, drawing their courage from him.

Even so, he could not stop his own thoughts.

What would his fate be if the gates would not open? Torn to pieces outside his own damn city, no doubt. But it wasn't *his* fate that concerned him most. He'd considered sneaking Julia in under cover of dark. But showing weakness was its own mistake. The only way was to swagger up to these gates, with Julia riding proud in his retinue, and tell anyone who objected to take it up with his clenched fist.

A creaking and grinding split the earth. The great doors cracked open. Alaric let out a breath he hadn't realized he'd been holding.

Ahead, a paved road cut through a warren of houses, rich marble crumbling, doors broken and roofs falling in from when Alaric had taken the city months ago. The road went straight before cutting west and climbing the hill to the citadel. A hot wind stirred the dust at his feet like a demon's exhale. And then—

"Get back," Ataulf hissed at the sight of the angry crowd that was gathering in the road, hungry and angry and calling for blood. *His* people. "Get *back*."

"No." Alaric raised an arm, signaling for the grain wagons.

"They're still mine, Ataulf." He could not have Julia ride in with him now. But he *would* bring her in as his queen, as soon as he calmed the crowd. "Hold Julia back until my signal. Then send her in under close guard. Keep her *absolutely* safe."

Then he spurred his horse forward, into the hot demon wind.

Julia stood at the city gate, her throat clenched with fear as Alaric rode straight into a raging crowd. A multitude of faces, brown and tanned and sunburned, everyone dressed out of a fevered fantasy—worn animal skins thrown over ragged silk, long Greek stockings made of animal hair, mud-smeared calves flashing under brilliant Egyptian linen. Here a bloodstained peacock-blue veil; there a cloak of Tyrian purple with a deep knife slash in the back. Long, tangled hair adorned with bits of flashing mirror or animal teeth. There was a tense, febrile current beneath everything that set Julia on edge.

The carts had started to roll, overflowing with golden wheat. Alaric was handing loaves into the crowd, his great voice echoing off the ruined walls.

Don't lose sight of me, he'd said.

Julia glanced up at Ataulf, sitting his gray horse. "We have to go in. *Now.*"

His face hardened to a look of flat distaste. "Oh, you'll go in, Princess." He gave an order to one of the men behind him—a big, round-shouldered man with a russet beard.

The next instant, she was being lifted out of her saddle. The man stood before her with a length of rope. She held her ground. "Just what do you think you're doing?"

"Do you honestly think the people *want* a Roman queen?" Ataulf demanded. "They will rip you to shreds."

"So I must ride in as a prisoner?" Julia jerked her hands out of the man's grip. "Alaric will never allow it."

"Alaric told me to protect you. This is how. And it protects him too. What do you think the people will do to *him*, once they realize he intends *you* to rule over them?" The russet-bearded warrior seized Julia's hands and tied them quickly. Then he handed the other end of the rope to Ataulf.

Outrage choked her throat. "He will have you on the walls for this. I am his *wife*."

"Are you sure?" Ataulf's tone was silken, vicious. "What proof can you offer? Any witnesses? Any grand ceremony? Did he even grant you a dowry?"

"We pledged beneath the sky, with the gods as our witnesses. We did not need a ceremony—"

"Oh, Julia." Ataulf's expression turned *pitying*. "Is that what he told you?"

Fury and fear crashed in on her as she realized what a fool she'd been.

"I'm simply following Alaric's orders. Take it up with him," Ataulf said. Then he raised an arm in signal to the column and urged his horse forward.

Rage and humiliation burned in her throat.

The rope was too taut. It jerked at her wrists with the horse's every step. The horse cocked his tail and took a shit in the street, and she barely avoided the steaming pile.

Alaric had ordered this. Julia walked with her spine straight and her eyes fixed ahead, ignoring the shouts and curses as Ataulf's men struggled to hold back the furious crowd.

Did she believe that? It seemed past believing.

She had watched two triumphs in her life, both for generals returning from war. One had a rebel leader in a cage, who had been summarily strangled after the procession. She had never dreamed she would be in his place herself. And now she would never have a chance to prove herself to these people. This memory would remain in their minds each time she appeared before them. *Prisoner. Enemy. Whore.*

"I don't like this," said a voice in her ear.

It was Horsa, walking in the inner circle of her guard. Hengist was on the other side, just beyond the guards, leading Bura, who didn't like the crowd any more than she did. Her eyes rolled to whites and her feet were light with panic.

"Ataulf says Alaric ordered it," Julia whispered.

"Alaric has been up my back since Ravenna. I might as well add something else to the pile." Metal glinted in Horsa's hand. A dagger. He nodded at Hengist, who walked with one hand flat on Bura's neck, soothing her. "She'll run right through this crowd."

Julia sucked in a breath. If this failed, she'd be ripped apart. But she would *not* go into this city like a prisoner.

Horsa's knife flashed and the rope fell from her wrists, and then he turned without warning and shoved the nearest guard. Suddenly there was a brawl in the street.

Hengist reached for her, his hands going around her waist, and the next instant, she was clinging, one leg half-over the mare's bare back. Bura sidled nervously, ears flat. For a moment it seemed she would slip off and land in a pitiable heap.

"*Go!*" Hengist roared, slapping Bura's back. The horse surged forward, hindquarters gathering beneath her, and Julia caught a glimpse of Ataulf's surprised face before they went barreling past him and through the crowd with a speed born of abject fear. A woman grabbed a child and jerked it out of the way; the horse veered to avoid a barrel of grain spilled in the road. Bura had the bit in her teeth now, and Julia let the reins fall, clinging to the horse's mane as she clattered down the street, hooves striking sparks off the cobblestones.

Only when they rounded the corner did Julia see a hill rising ahead, a path snaking up a steep outcrop to a walled citadel. Bura lunged up the switchback path, no check on her fear. Now they were through the gate, and rushing toward a marble mansion that rose up gleaming before them at the top of a tower of marble stairs. A deafening roar rose up behind them—a roar that only spurred Bura into a panicked gallop up the steps.

A casual arm threw itself up and caught the horse's reins as if this had all been planned.

Bura slid to a trembling halt, her lungs heaving like a bellows, and there was Alaric, laying a hand on the horse's cheek, whispering. Julia *felt* the horse go calm beneath his touch. Then his pale eyes lighted on her, the crowd's roar fading into the distance. Her heart was racing, her borrowed dress raked up to her knees. She'd lost a shoe. Alaric lifted her down, beaming with pride. The moment her feet hit the marble paving stones she sank to her knees, the red dress billowing out around her, and the crowd's roar filled the world.

Alaric raised her to her feet. "You did well," he murmured.

Alaric stood on the landing midway up the steps that led to the mansion's entrance, amidst the snap of banners and the rattling of shields and voices swelling all around him. He would bet his own skin that the chieftains had worked the people up to their earlier furor.

That rage at the gate had been no accident. Noricum was a city of vicious joys and daggers in the dark, and the mobs of Noricum could turn on the edge of a knife. Alaric had a strong feeling the chieftains had warred among each other fiercely before giving the order to open the gates. Wouldn't it be convenient for *them* if he was ripped limb from limb before even making it to the citadel.

But the chieftains were playing a losing game. The people of Noricum were many: runaway slaves and farmers and refugees, Sarmatians and Greuthungi, Gauls and Getae and Parthians, Taifals and Alans and Huns. Those pushed to the margins of existence from every corner of the Empire. They walked around in a rage that the Roman aristocracy could only dimly comprehend, and that made them dangerous. That made them *his*.

Even so. The crowd would need persuading. It was this that made him give the order for Ataulf to hold Julia back. He had meant to shelter her from this; to gentle the crowd first with gifts and grain. But he was also keenly aware that the people needed to see her, to accept her presence as soon as possible. Their love would protect her most from the chieftains' wrath.

He never would have allowed Julia to go galloping through the city as she'd done, hair loose and streaming like a Gothic queen straight out of legend. But it appeared to be a stroke of brilliance. The people were cheering for *her* now. Their cheers had not abated even as he lifted Julia down from the horse. The people *loved* her. And that was a powerful force.

Perfectly attuned to the crowd, Julia gazed up at him with a flawless adoration that he knew damn well was an act. *She's performing*, he realized. He felt a fierce, savage surge of pride in her. He had chosen well.

At his raised hand, the cheers fell silent.

"My people. I have brought you gold, and grain, and a chance for victory." His voice filled the square, ricocheting off the yellow plaster and crumbling wood of the buildings. "With only fifty I walked into the city where the emperor cowers out of fear of us. I put my boot on his neck and my knife to his throat and brought back a great prize. The princess Julia, only child of the Imperator himself."

Silence fell over the crowd as they turned their attention to Julia. She stood straight, an expression of calm on her face, the mask of her royalty never faltering.

"This woman is my wife." He said it in his own language; Julia stared out at the crowd as if she were in perfect agreement. "I have their princess now; she's *mine*. She will bear me a son who will stand as the first in line for the throne of Rome. Soon *we*, my people, will have as much right to the Empire as the boy Honorius himself. And when we cross the mountains again, there'll be no one to stop us from ripping its bloody heart out of its body."

Around him, the city screamed its assent. He had never lost them. They were *his*, as they had always been.

The chieftains would be sweating in their boots right now.

Wearing their plaids and rings and great war brooches, they stood at the mansion's columned entrance, eyeing him the way they might a viper in their path. Behind him, Thorismund mounted the stairs with a dozen men at his back. Alaric glanced behind to give him a wordless order. *Hold back unless I signal.* Thorismund halted just at the top of the steps, his expression grim.

Alaric turned back to the chieftains with an easy smile, as if he'd come from a pleasant ride rather than having to placate a murderous crowd. "Hello, my brave companions. Have you missed me?"

Sigeric stepped forward first. He had lately taken on Roman ways, trimming his beard like a Roman. "King Alaric, you are well met. We had not had word in months. Some among us thought you dead."

And some among you would have me dead. Alaric held out a hand to Julia, who stood a few paces behind. "May I present the princess Julia. Daughter of Theodosius, Augustus of the Romans, and my wife."

A strangled quiet fell over the knot of chieftains.

Julia came forward, her lips lifted in a gentle smile. "It is a great pleasure to meet you all. I hope very much we will be friends."

"I hope that as well, my queen," Sigeric responded in kind, his Latin edged with the flavor of the war front.

"You sang another song this morning, Sigeric." It was Sarus, Sigeric's younger brother; dumber than a bag of hair. "You may all call that Roman whore a queen. But I never will."

Alaric stepped forward and drove his fist straight into Sarus's face.

The force of the blow skinned his knuckle. Blood sprayed; teeth scattered on the floor.

"You'll call her *queen*," he said flatly. "And you'll kneel, if only because you're gathering your teeth off the ground." Alaric raked his gaze over the shocked faces of his chieftains. "You'll all keep a civil tongue in your heads when you talk about my wife."

CHAPTER THIRTY-FIVE

Julia swayed on her feet. She felt like *she'd* been the one to take that punch.

Alaric turned to her, coolly distant. "Go with Thorismund's men. I will come for you later." He couldn't get rid of her fast enough.

Before she could object, a knot of Gothic warriors closed around her.

They escorted her through airy halls scorched by fire, past marble statues and overgrown gardens. Hardly a palace, but after all this time sleeping in caves and hovels, it seemed like one.

At last they arrived at a pair of doors painted blue and gold. Julia was ushered inside, and the doors shut behind her. She heard a bolt being drawn.

I have their princess now; she's mine.

Julia was hardly fluent in Gothic. It was a difficult, confounding language. But she'd managed to pick up a few things. She knew *son* and *throne* and *Empire.* Enough to put together that Alaric had introduced her to his people as *spoils.* A means to an end. After he'd ordered her tied and marched through the city like a slave. And now he was treating her like a prisoner.

What had she done? A cold dread settled in her stomach.

Perhaps as Ataulf had insinuated, Alaric hadn't married her at all. Perhaps he'd only lied to her, seduced her into being a model prisoner and a willing concubine. And what an excellent way to keep her docile. Before he'd even finished with her, she'd been crouched in a doorway, watching him fight Stilicho's rescue party, a blade pointed at her own chest.

Julia drew a shaking breath. *Think.* This was only her fear, crowding in and making her question everything. Of course Alaric wanted sons for strategic reasons. Was that not what a wife was *for*? Besides, Alaric had put his life at risk for hers countless times, promised to lay cities at her feet. He was *hers*. Was he not? He would never—

He would *never*.

Wouldn't he?

She was simply shaken, that was all. Galloping a horse through a murderous mob was enough to make anyone rattled. That brigand Ataulf had probably been lying too. Had he not declared himself her enemy the night they met? She would not let him and his *pity* rob her of her faith in her husband.

She would have strong words with Alaric tonight, though, about that language he'd used.

Julia straightened. Absently she began to take in her surroundings. It appeared to be a wealthy woman's apartments; the ornate room had an air of rotting glory. It was lined with murals, marred by long cracks in the walls, and stained by torch smoke. Couches were piled high with water-stained silken cushions. One wall was entirely open, beyond it a weed-choked garden surrounding a drained *piscina*, with a delicate fountain in the center in the shape of an arching naiad. Algae streaked her breasts.

There were four rooms, all arranged around the garden. A bedroom with a crumbling mural of yellow flowers and a large, iron bed. In another room, she found chests of clothes, all cut for a woman shorter than Julia was, with more generous curves.

She did not want to think of what had happened to that woman. Nor of the Roman corpses on the city's wall.

Julia distracted herself by delving into the chests. In one, she discovered a box of perfumes in glass bottles and a cedarwood container that held blush and kohl and colored eyeshadows. She dressed in a gray linen that set off her fiery hair. The cosmetics turned her eyes a startling sea green. Alaric had his weapons, his armor; these were hers.

When he came to her tonight, she would be ready.

Hours passed. A guard came in to light the lamps. Supper arrived, meat in a red wine sauce. Bread warm from the oven. Julia barely ate. Only wine would steady her stomach. She remembered this feeling—half-wild, cornered, *caged*—that had driven her to drink in Ravenna.

Bromios's words echoed in her head. *That man has lovers in Noricum.* Lovers who now knew that Alaric had tried to have her dragged into the city behind Ataulf's horse. Julia paced, vivid images of Alaric naked with other women burning across her eyelids.

From the north window, she could see fires blazing in the city. Whether from celebration or rebellion, she could not tell. *Supposing rebellion. Supposing he'd been assassinated.*

She reeled between fury and fear.

The hours bled together. Julia finished the wine, then fell into a fitful sleep. When she woke, it was well into night. The torches had burned down and the walls disappeared into darkness. Alaric still wasn't back.

She slept. In her dreams, everything burned.

For a night and a day, Alaric had been trying to get back to Julia. And all night and day, things had been blowing up in his face.

The first thing he did was drive Sarus and his followers out of the city. That was merciful; he was well within his rights to cut the man's throat and hang him on the wall. But his mercy did not calm dissent.

The chieftains' arguing had gone on all night. Then, just as he was leaving the damn endless meeting—dawn streaking the sky—a man lunged at him in the street, armed with a rusty knife. It had been Sigeric who stopped him; he'd have killed the assassin if Alaric had not stayed his hand.

He hadn't wanted to bring this violence back to Julia. He could only thank the gods that Thorismund had his most trusted men guarding her. He had tried to snatch sleep in one of the guardhouses while he waited for Riga to torture answers out of the man. But in the end, the assassin hanged himself in his cell before he could be broken. And Alaric was roused after barely an hour to put down a grain riot.

The next morning, he realized the walls had been left to rot since he'd left. It took all day to assess the damage.

It was well into the second night before Alaric could return to Julia.

Finally Alaric made his way through the airy, moon-streaked hallways in the stolen mansion he had set aside for Julia. He preferred to sleep in the open, or in the breathing shelter of a tent. He'd had his own war tent set up on the parade grounds at the highest point in the city, but for Julia, he needed something more defendable.

She'd be angry at him for taking so long to come to her. He would make it up to her. He imagined waking her slowly, teasing her with kisses. Outside, all was war and violence. But in here, he would make a safe, sheltered place for her, free of all hardship until he could remake the city into a place she could live in.

He slipped past the guards and through the doors to Julia's

quarters. Fires burned in the iron braziers; a cool breeze billowed the gauzy, floor-to-ceiling curtains like sails.

He took a step into the room. Pottery crunched beneath his feet. "Julia?"

One moment she wasn't there; the next she was—materializing in the bedroom doorway, a wine cup in her hand. She was wearing a silk robe over a dress the soft yellow of alpine primroses. Shadows gathered beneath her cheekbones. Kohl lined her lids; streaked her face.

Alaric felt a flash of remorse. *He'd* done that. Thinned her down on the road, put that haunted look in her eyes. All his violent protectiveness rose up in him at once. He wanted to pull her into his embrace, to torch the whole world to keep her safe.

"Julia." *Gods*, he wanted her. How had he gone a day without her? "Come here."

She stayed, maddeningly, across the room. "Am I your wife, Alaric? Or am I *spoils*?"

"What in hell are you talking about?" He could smell the wine on her from here. "Woman, you're drunk."

Blue-green eyes sparked at him and he took a step toward her, then another. Warily, as he'd approach a wildcat.

"I'm *not* drunk," she lied straight to his face. "I'm *spoils*. Is that not why you ordered me dragged through the streets behind Ataulf's horse?"

What on earth did she mean by *that*? "Julia—"

"*You stay over there.*" She screamed it at him, a wild panic about her eyes. "How *could* you?"

And then she winged her metal wine cup at his head.

Alaric swatted it out of the air and stalked toward her. She backed up, grabbing a second cup from a table as she did. "Put it down."

"*I am putting it down!*" She hurled the second cup at him. He dodged. It clattered against the wall and rolled onto the floor. "You treated me like a slave in a triumph—you refused me pride of place beside you—you locked me in these rooms like a war prize." As she spoke she hurled a flurry of objects at him with increasing fury—a terra-cotta vase. A silver mirror. A discarded sandal. He managed to dodge them, cursing.

"Your aim is goddamn awful." This was really starting to annoy him. "Julia, you are not a *war prize*." The very words made him incandescent with fury. "As for whether you are my wife in truth—I swore to be your shield and fight your battles, woman. What the hell do you think that means?"

"How would I know?" Somehow she had managed to maneuver so a heavy couch was between them. They circled each other around it. "Explain why you refused to let me ride into the city at your side."

"Because the crowd was like to rip you limb from limb, Julia. Have you eyes?"

"That is exactly what Ataulf said." She hissed it like a curse. "I am nothing but a prisoner to you, am I? You are a violent, uncivilized *barbarian* who forcibly kidnapped me—"

"You asked me to kidnap you." His temper—his *lust*—roared through him. "You threw yourself at me. What do you expect me to do when presented with an opportunity—"

"So now I'm an *opportunity*. A brood mare. A pawn to legitimize your next invasion." Tears shimmered in her eyes. "If you *did* marry me in truth, you manipulated me into it."

It shocked him, how much those words hurt.

Julia took advantage of his stillness—darting to his left, toward the bedroom. He caught her robe in his fist and Julia shrugged out of it, leaving him with a handful of cloth. He threw it to the floor and stalked after her as she backed into the bedroom, snatching a large pitcher from a table as she went.

"I broke a man's face in payment for an insult to you," he growled. "I spent all night bending the chieftains to my will so they'll bend knee to *you*. Would I have done any of that for a prisoner?"

For a moment she stood utterly silent. Alaric sucked in a breath. Julia in any mood was beautiful enough to inspire lust and poetry. Julia in a fury was magnificent. Her skin flushed to a pinkish glow, from her cheeks into the valley of her breasts. Her chest rose and fell, and her eyes snapped righteous fire at him, and his groin tightened at the sight of her.

"You always have convenient explanations for doing exactly what you want to do." Her grip tightened on the jug. "But perhaps you could explain to me why you told your people you'd *get me with child and use me to take the Empire.*"

She switched to Gothic for that one phrase. The words were slurred with drink, and broken, but better than he'd expected.

"Is that not what you wanted?" he snarled. "Julia, you *demanded* I bring you the Empire on a plate. How else do you think I will do it?"

But Julia only arched a brow and spoke with cool, clinical calm. "If all I am is a womb, Alaric, then send me back to my brother once you get your child out of me. Use me for a child *and* a bargaining chip. That was your plan all along, was it not?"

"And *your* plan was to use me for my army." He drew a shaking breath. "Rage at me all you wish," he bit out. "Hate me if you must. But I will never, *ever* let you go."

"Fuck you." She said it with sincere feeling. Then she hurled the pitcher at his head.

There was wine in the pitcher. A lot of wine.

Alaric dodged the pitcher like he had everything else she'd thrown at him, moving with a fluid speed that was almost supernatural. But he couldn't dodge the wine. It rained down, splattering his tunic and the floor around him with glittering red. For a moment he just stood there. Ice-blue eyes widening in shock.

Then a chilling smile curved his mouth, promised mayhem.

He reached up and unfastened his cloak. "Is marriage to me so reprehensible?" His voice deadly soft.

Reprehensible? "Er—" It wasn't the word she would use.

He dropped the cloak on the floor and stalked inexorably toward her. "Do you wish me to send you back to your own ruin? Is that what you want?"

Julia licked her lips. "No."

"Smart girl."

Then he yanked off his stained tunic.

He was bare to the waist now, and *oh gods*, his chest. Beautiful and battle-scarred and ridged with muscle. Torques twining about his throat and biceps. Julia caught her breath. He was magnificent. Golden and glorious and *hers*, hers by vow.

And suddenly he was *right there*, hands planted on the wall on either side of her head. The heat of his skin rolled into her like a burning tide.

"You are my wife, Julia. Not my prisoner. Anyone who says differently is a liar." He tilted her chin up to face him. "I told you that you were mine outside Brisca's longhouse. You should have considered yourself married then." He leaned down and tasted her; growled it against her skin. "Tell me you don't want me." A command, his voice grating harshly in her ear. "Tell me you don't and I'll spend this night with anyone else."

"Oh, fuck you." If he truly was her husband, all his nights were hers. All of them. Julia reached up, locking her arms around his neck. *"I'm* the one you married. If you even *think* to deny me my rights as a wife—"

She didn't get the rest of her sentence out.

She wanted him. She didn't love him—didn't want his name or his protection—but she wanted him in her bed.

It wasn't enough. But in this moment, he would take whatever he could get.

Alaric devoured her mouth, lost himself, pressing the hard length of his body to the soft, maddening curves of her. Her nails dug into his bare back; tiny pinpricks, breaking skin.

He could not stop himself. He lifted her easily, felt her legs lock around his waist as her fingers dug hungrily into his scalp, shooting sparks of pain down his spine. She answered his plundering kisses with matching ferocity, his hands gripping the perfect curve of her ass, feeling as if he were falling into her until he realized he *was* falling. She laughed in his ear as they both hit the mattress. He rolled her beneath him, kissing her deeply as he rid her of her dress. Her perfect breasts spilled free and with a helpless groan he filled his hands with them, sucked her nipples into his mouth, tasting her sweat, her heartbeat.

"Tell me you won't have me as your husband." He growled it against her skin. "Tell me you'd deny me what's mine."

"*No.*" Her fingers tightened in his hair.

"Why not?" He *needed* to hear her say it. "Why not, Julia?"

"I can't." Julia hissed through her teeth. "I won't lie to you."

She could lie or tell the gods' plain truth, he didn't care. Not in the state he was in. He laughed and moved lower, dragging his tongue down the silky heat of her skin until his mouth closed over the hot little center of her pleasure.

Julia gasped as Alaric took her with his mouth, used his tongue and the heat of his breath. Before he had drawn this out, unspooled her pleasure to last entire sunny afternoons. Now he brought her to orgasm hard and fast, once and then twice, showing her no mercy.

She might not love him, but no other man could give her this.

Julia was visibly trembling when he rose above her, barely pausing to strip off his breeches before stretching himself over her. His mouth seized hers; she wrapped her legs around his waist, pulling him in, and he could *smell* her arousal, hot and musky in the summer air. He had to be inside her—had to *show* her, once and for all, just who she belonged to. Alaric grasped the sweet curve of her ass in one palm and angled her up to meet him.

Julia bit his neck hard and punched him in the shoulder. "Let me on top."

The pain of the bite only added to the inferno of his lust, and the effort it took not to thrust himself inside her was *unbearable*. He held himself still, every muscle in his body taut and trembling, wanting more than anything to dominate her utterly. But Julia's sea-green eyes flashed at him from out of the dark, passion and temper combined.

It was wordless, this struggle for control. But in the end, he could deny her nothing. He gripped her tight and rolled himself onto his back, taking her with him.

Julia reared up above him and the sight of her took his breath. She was *perfect*, every inch of her—her hair falling wild all around her, the flawless globes of her breasts glowing in the moonlight, a fierce desire lighting her from within. Alaric could only feast on her with his eyes as she gave him a languid smile that made his groin tighten savagely.

Then, her eyes never leaving his, she reached down and guided him into her. Alaric had to grasp the iron bedrail, his muscles clenching as his woman slid down the length of him inch by excruciating inch until she was impaled on him completely.

"I don't forgive you," she murmured.

Ah, *fuck*. He could barely breathe, could barely *speak* through his lust, and here she was, coolly discussing forgiveness. "You'll be the death of me, woman," he growled.

"No doubt I will." Her hips began to move and his blood pounded fiercely in the place where they were joined. "If you want me as your wife," she haughtily informed him, "you must let me be your wife in truth."

Her walls fluttered around him in a way that made stars explode behind his eyes. He'd never *been* so at a woman's mercy before. "Yes," he breathed.

"When you must make a decision that affects me, you will *tell* me." She rolled her hips and his fists clenched reflexively on the bedrail. "We'll *discuss* it."

There was nothing he would not agree to. "Yes."

"You'll do anything I say, Alaric. Won't you." Her hand caressed a burning line down his chest; her lips curving in a knowing smile. "Because you're mine."

"*Yes.*" He would. He was. He always had been. "I'd burn the world down for you."

It was the truth. Ripped from the depths of him and he didn't even mind. Her eyes widened, filled his sight with glorious ocean green, and he could stand no more of this. He let go of the bedrail and grasped her hips hard enough to bruise. "And you?" he demanded, thrusting hard up into her. "Will you stay with me of your own will?"

"Yes," she gasped, even as her hips moved to meet his, thrust for thrust. "I'll stay."

"Why?" His hands in her hair. His lips on her throat. Undone. "Tell me."

"Because I love you," she whispered, and there were tears standing in her eyes. "I *love you*, Alaric."

A fierce, exultant joy rose up in his chest as Julia began to shudder all around him. Alaric could hold himself back no longer; he shouted his pleasure as he exploded inside her, not once but many times as Julia sobbed her own trembling climax, her heartbeat thundering through them both.

Alaric rolled over on his side and crushed her to his chest. *She loved him.*

He'd never let her go. Never.

"When did you first know?" Alaric lay on his back, one arm draped casually around her. Dawn was just barely beginning to slant through the window. "Was it when you ran off naked on the old battlefield and I pulled you out of that stream?"

"*Stop*. I wasn't *in* the stream. And I wasn't naked." Julia bit back a mortified laugh. He knew her secret now—that she loved him. He'd ripped it out of her in the throes of earth-shattering pleasure, and now he wouldn't stop torturing her over it.

"Perhaps it was when you left the nettles in my bed," he mused. "If I'd known then that it was your idea of a love offering—"

"It was no such thing!" Julia buried her burning face in his chest. "You were being *rude*, if you'll recall."

"Perhaps it was the first time I took off my shirt for you. You seemed to like that."

His thumb dragged idly over her shoulder and, *oh God*, she wanted to die. "Sometimes I wonder how you can move under the weight of that enormous self-regard of yours."

He laughed. Rich and warm and better than wine, better than baths. And then in one swift movement he flipped her beneath him. "Perhaps it was the first time I did this?" His mouth at her throat now. Pressed to that one spot that made her toes curl. "Or this—" His hand sliding between her legs. Julia gasped. It was impossible to *think* when he did that.

She pushed at his shoulders and he let her roll him over and rise up to straddle his hips. "Stop," she said, laughing. "I want to talk."

Alaric took her breath from this vantage, his sculpted arms folded behind his head, regarding her indolently from beneath gold-tipped lashes. "We've spent all morning talking."

She *felt* her face heat. "That wasn't talking."

"Wasn't it? You were quite vocal, this last time." He looked so pleased with himself that she couldn't resist punching him on the arm. "Such violence, little wife."

Little wife. "About that," Julia said drily. Her heart was hammering in her chest. She was loath to break the golden spell of this mood. "Alaric, if I *am* your wife, why on earth did you not let me ride in as your queen?"

"I've already told you why. The crowd would not have borne it, not until I pacified them." His fingers twined with hers; he raised one of her hands to his lips, his kiss brushing her knuckles. "I am sorry for what I said."

"You said what you had to." Her fears felt so silly now. Of *course* Alaric wanted a son from her; and of *course* he would think strategically about that. He would be a fool not to, and so would she to expect anything different. She had been *embarrassingly* sentimental, thinking he had married her purely out of passion. "If it was to make it easier for the crowd to accept a Roman as your wife, I don't mind. If only you'd *told* me first, rather than simply have Ataulf give the order for me to walk behind his horse. And bind my hands while doing it," she added with no small amount of affront.

Alaric's tone was deceptively mild. "What's this about Ataulf giving an order?"

She *knew* it. Ataulf had lied about that too! She recounted the story as best she could, and at the end of it, his expression did not change. But his gaze had gone wintry cold. "I gave no such orders. You must know that," he said finally. "As for Ataulf, I will handle him."

The look in his eyes sent a chill of foreboding down her spine. Origenes in the cave, his throat cut, rose before her sight. "Do not kill him, Alaric. Please."

He smiled faintly—and in the next instant, the cold left his eyes. "I was proud of you, when you rode through those streets like a warrior queen." His thumb dragged idly over her hip bone. "You did well, Julia."

This time, when he pulled her down to him, she did not stop him. She loved being pressed full-length against his warm, naked body, feeling his muscles move beneath his skin as he kissed her. She loved him. There was no part of her that would deny it now.

"I'd have walked through the streets behind Hannibal, if that's what you needed," Julia whispered fervently. "I'd have done anything, if you'd only *told* me first—"

"Enough." The look in his eyes raised goosebumps on her arms. "There are other ways to keep my kingship."

"Are there? What is your plan, then?" Julia sat up again, her hands flat on his chest. "It seems to *me* you'd have done better to keep me as your concubine. Marrying me seems bound to antagonize your chieftains."

"You wouldn't have me that way. Besides, it is done now. I'll put in the ground any who try to come between us." He trailed burning kisses along her collarbone; his strong arms closed around her and she felt her body giving in.

He was doing it again. Distracting her.

"I'm serious, Alaric." She curled her hands in his hair and tugged. "That is exactly what I mean by being your wife in truth. I want to be part of what you're planning—I can help!" The way his lips grazed her skin *tickled*. "I was raised in the Imperial Court—I drank intrigue with my mother's milk!" He bit down gently, making her gasp. "I'm—I'm *good* at this." He was making her *laugh* now, damn him, his warm breath tickling her skin. "I *am*! If you'd just let me charm the chieftains—use my talents! In Brisca's village I made friends—"

"Yes. And I made mistakes," he said gently. "If I hadn't been so open about my feelings there, perhaps I could have forestalled the rumors. And if I hadn't let you among the people, I never would have had to perform that ridiculous ritual with the axes. Berig would not have targeted you. You could have avoided Calthrax altogether." Rage flashed in his eyes. "Let me make this place safe for you. Trust me just a little longer."

Julia sighed. *Trust me*—she knew what that meant. Trust him to throw axes at her head and not miss. Perhaps that was what it meant, to be his wife.

"If we continue like this, I will never leave," he whispered in her ear. "And I must."

Julia watched with regret as he gently disentangled himself and slid, naked, out of bed. "When will I see you again?"

"I will return tonight. As soon as I can, but it may be a while after dark." He traced the line of her cheekbone with his knuckle. Julia felt herself blush ferociously.

"Go on, then. Go sack a city and bring me back a real dowry." That brought another gorgeous laugh out of him, and then he was gone.

Chapter Thirty-Six

Alaric stood at the crumbling wall and watched the dust rise to mark Ataulf's passing across the wreckage-strewn plain with his followers. An upwelling of grief rose in his chest and he forced it down. He could not afford such feelings now.

He'd gone straight from Julia's bed to roust Ataulf out of his own. Memories rose up in the back of his mind—he and Ataulf in the camps, their people starving all around them, their bodies churning into the deep mud that came with the rains. He barely remembered his elder sister now, but Ataulf had been a living connection to her, and a world vanished. No one else spoke the tongue of the pine-tree island. Losing Ataulf was like losing his own right arm.

But the way Ataulf had treated Julia, there was no place for him in this city. Alaric thought of Ataulf's efforts to convince him to drag Julia through the streets like a war prize. He'd refused, and Ataulf had done so anyway. The thought of it hardened his heart.

His mind turned to Julia. She'd wrung a promise out of him this morning to let her rule at his side, but it would be long before she was safe here. His own siege had wreaked havoc on these walls, and he'd left orders for their repair while he was in Ravenna. But the walls had not been tended to. The plain below was crawling with marauders, and all they had to do was look up to realize this place was an easy target. Already it was midsummer, and the seasons would turn in a blink. Soon the autumn would come, and so would Stilicho.

"What we need is building stone," Sigeric was saying. "The only mine within a three-day ride is Roman-controlled. If we attack it—"

Alaric shook his head grimly. "The last thing we need is a war on our doorstep. Not with Stilicho threatening."

"If we cannot win against their single legion, how will we win against Stilicho?" Sigeric sighed heavily. "I know this advice is not welcome, King Alaric. But I think you ought to reconsider negotiating with Rome. If we do that, we can halt this coming war. Perhaps even gain access to that quarry." He paused. "Surely one woman is not worth—"

Rage rose up in his chest. He would *not* use Julia as coin for his future. "Sigeric, if we ally with the Romans again, there won't *be* a people." The fact that he even had to *explain* this set his teeth on edge.

Sigeric frowned. "I followed you faithfully when you broke with the Romans. But if Stilicho comes over the mountain now—" His voice trailed off. He was staring at some point over Alaric's shoulder. *"Fuck."*

Alaric turned. A pack of dogs had gathered in an alley, the size of small ponies. He recognized those dogs. There had been plenty of their kind in the camps. Corpse dogs.

"They've multiplied since we took this city." Sigeric picked up a stone and threw it; the dogs danced out of the way, red tongues lolling between sharp teeth. "I heard a rumor that a pack of them took down a cow yesterday. It's only a matter of time before one of them kills a person."

Hoofbeats rang off the cobblestones. Sigeric muttered a curse beneath his breath.

It was Riga, galloping up the wide road. He pulled his horse to a halt and swung off. "I have news," he said quietly. "For your ears only, Alaric."

"Do not send me away." Sigeric spoke in cavalry Vandal so Riga would not understand. "You need someone at your back to weigh his words. You cannot trust mercenaries."

Riga fixed Sigeric with a cool, dead-eyed stare that had the man backing up a step.

"Enough." Alaric bit back a curse. Sigeric had proven his loyalty with that assassin, but that did not mean he would take the man's orders. "Go, Sigeric."

"The Huns are moving," Riga said when he had gone. "They've plundered Pannonia and burned the Roman fort at Carnuntum." Riga glanced down at the gathering refugees, moving like ants across the plain. "Those are fleeing the violence. The Huns will be here in ten days or less."

Huns. In the back of his mind flashed a scene from old nightmares. An oak tree, set ablaze. Smell of corpses burning. Ash coating his throat. "So it will be a siege, then."

"My men are restless. I doubt I can keep them behind walls for a siege."

Alaric's chest tightened. If he lost Riga's Huns, they'd never survive the coming war with Stilicho.

"You won't find plunder to match what I pay."

"If we stay within Pannonia. But there are other hunting grounds." Riga grinned. "Come with us. Pillage and burn where the plunder is thickest and become a bandit king. You'd excel at it."

Alaric shook his head grimly. "My responsibilities are not only to the warriors and their plunder."

He heard running feet behind him and turned to see Hengist slide to a panicked stop. "Come quickly," he said, gasping for breath. "It's the grain."

CHAPTER THIRTY-SEVEN

The moment Alaric left, exhaustion hit Julia hard. She slept again; when she woke, it was full-on day. A tray of food was sitting on the table by the bed: fruit and soft cheese, bread and honey; a pitcher of thick, cold milk and one of sweet wine. Not long after, a large wooden tub was hauled into the room—large enough to fit a man and full of steaming water. Julia sank down in the tub, the heated water closing over her head.

She loved him. And he knew it now. He had not said it back, not in so many words, but—*I'll put in the ground any who try to come between us.* Surely that meant what she thought it did?

She leaned her head against the edge of the tub. It was far too easy to lose such happiness—and then where would she be? She tried to force away her fears. That Alaric might die. That the Romans might come for her at last. That he might forswear her, betray her. Take another to his bed. Was this what happiness meant? Living in endless fear that she might lose it?

Carefully, with the ruthlessness born of the high court in Ravenna, she considered how to hold on to this love.

Let me make this place safe for you. He had not said he loved her, but that was something he *had* said. Julia understood there was danger. But surely not *so* much danger? He did not trust her or take her seriously. Perhaps if she *showed* Alaric that she understood the problems his people faced—she could change that.

She was about to sink back into the water when a sound arrested her attention. A thrown stone, striking the wall of the building. Someone outside was trying to get her attention.

Julia hauled herself out of the bath, pulled on a robe, and went to the window. A man stood staring up at her, his face hidden in the hood of a cloak. Even so, she knew him.

"Bromios! What are you doing here?"

"I've nowhere else to go. Your husband rousted Ataulf out of bed like a common thief and cast him outside the walls." He held up both hands, prayer-like. "Julia, I am asking as a friend. Shelter me. Protect me. Speak well of me to your husband."

"You don't have to ask." Julia cast her eyes over the fallen-in rooftops, to the great aqueduct, its crumbling arches looming over the labyrinth of streets. "But first I need your help."

"He's going to kill me," Bromios muttered, for perhaps the twelfth time since he'd helped her climb down from the window. "He's going to carve out my liver with a dull knife."

"No, he won't," Julia soothed. "I'll handle him."

She could practically *hear* his eyes rolling. "I'd be better off in the wilderness."

Julia drew the hood of her cloak over her head, praying no one would recognize her. The citadel gate rose up before them. Guards leaned on their spears, looking bored. They barely flicked her a glance before they were out and through.

The road down from the fortress took several careening hairpin turns to the city below. The cobblestones were uneven and slippery, worn smooth by centuries of traffic. Julia wondered how on earth she'd survived that gallop.

The buildings inside the citadel had been in relatively good repair. But beyond the protective fortress walls, the city had been badly damaged. The houses were hollowed shells, cloth stretched across walls to give some semblance of shelter. Filthy water trickled sluggishly through piles of trash. Everything smelled of rot and sickness. There were few people in the streets—those she saw had a starving, desperate look to them.

As they reached the bottom of the hill, Julia paused. A child stood at the mouth of an alleyway. She'd never seen anyone look that hungry.

Bromios sounded peevish. "Just where are we going?"

"There." Over the roofs of the ruined buildings, on the other side of the city, the aqueduct loomed.

The sun had risen high in the sky by the time they managed to reach it. Past houses rotting on their foundations. Soaring marble homes stood next to charred wrecks with missing roofs, sodden cloth strung across teetering walls, barely keeping out rain. All the fountains had stopped running. Trash was piled high in the gutters and alleys, no cleansing streams to carry it away.

Even so, up close, the aqueduct was breathtaking. Julia loved its perfect symmetry—a man-made river encased in soaring arches in the sky, supplying the city's lifeblood of fountains and wells. It was dry now, arches crumbling. Broken rock piled up at the structure's base. Julia thought of its roots in the far-off hills, the pipes and the drop-shafts and settlement tanks. No doubt it was all badly damaged and in need of repair.

"I wonder what shape the higher levels are in." Before Bromios could stop her, she was clambering up to the first archway, finding footholds in the rough stone.

"Julia, come down from there *at once*, or I'll—"

She ignored him. The structure was rotten in places; several times her handhold crumbled and showers of rocks clattered to the broken cobblestones. It was not as dry as she'd thought—water dripped down from the heights above, dark and rusty.

Even so, Julia was able to clamber up one level and stand under the first row of great arches. Bracing her arms against the stone, she stared out over the city.

It was breathtaking. As ruined as it was, this was *her* city now. From here she could see the broken rooftops, the warrens of streets, the great marble mansions all clustered beneath the far wall. Among the squares and plazas there were dry cisterns and fountains, laid out in lines over the city's underground pipes. This was fixable. It was a thing she could *do*.

And if she succeeded, maybe she could prove herself to him.

"It's not so bad up here," she called down. "Come up and look for yourself."

"Absolutely not," Bromios said.

She turned back, glancing up to see whether it was feasible to try going up another level. But her attention was caught by a rising, agitated shouting in the next square over, beyond a line of crumbled buildings.

A seething riot.

CHAPTER THIRTY-EIGHT

A full-on brawl had erupted in the market square. Horsa stood at the top of the stairs that led into the mercantile building where the grain was stored, looking flat-out terrified.

Alaric waded into the churning mass. There was a bare-fisted battle roiling, and Alaric shoved through, reached an arm in and yanked one of the brawlers out by the scruff of his neck.

Her neck. It was a woman, heavily pregnant. She landed a punch directly on Alaric's jaw. His head snapped back. He saw stars.

Fuck. He couldn't punch a pregnant woman. Alaric restrained her with his grip on the back of her tunic and caught hold of her opponent, a boy no older than ten. They both fought like alley cats; the woman landed another blow to the side of his face and the boy scored a sharp, painful kick to his shin. Alaric gritted his teeth. He couldn't punch a ten-year-old boy either.

"*Enough,*" he roared. He gave the boy and the woman a hard shake for emphasis. "What the hell is this about?"

"It was the last sack of grain." The boy pointed. "And *she* cut ahead of me in the line."

Alaric caught sight of the sack they'd been fighting over, ripped and spilled across the cobblestones, and he felt a bolt of recognition.

He'd been this boy once, skinny and starving, fighting for his life over grain kernels spilled on the ground. And this woman could have been his mother. "I have three starving children to feed—"

"I have *nine brothers and sisters!*" the boy hollered, and Alaric had to yank him off his feet to keep him from attacking the woman again. *"I was ahead in the line!"*

"All of you *be calm.*" That silenced them. "Is this what we've come to? Everyone is hungry. We did not come this far to kill one another over grain."

"The grain ran out," someone shouted from the back. "We have nothing to eat."

That was impossible. He'd brought enough to see the city through a month. The angry muttering grew louder as he made his way up the steps.

"There will be no starving time. I ask you to go to your homes—" the anger of the crowd intensified "—and come back tomorrow. I will be here at dawn, passing out provisions with my own hands. I promise you, on my life, that you will not be hungry tomorrow."

It wasn't what the crowd wanted to hear. But after a string of promises, they dispersed, hungry and shivering. Alaric thought of a hundred bellies going empty tonight because he hadn't kept the supply safe.

He turned to Horsa, who looked visibly pale. "Where is the rest of the grain?"

"There is no more grain. It's all gone."

"What the fuck do you mean, it's all gone?" He knew down to the ounce exactly how much he'd brought. "That much provision doesn't simply disappear into the air."

"See for yourself."

The mercantile building had once been where they auctioned slaves. Now it stood vast and empty. Alaric threw the doors open, stirring dust in the broad shafts of light that slanted down from the high, grated windows. The place was empty of grain.

"You just told a murderous crowd they wouldn't go hungry," Riga drawled, leaning against the doorframe behind him. "What do you plan on feeding them?"

"We can raid," Horsa said. "There must be something out there."

"You'll need the chieftains for that." Sigeric strolled in behind. "You're late for the war council. Wallia is hosting it."

Wallia. Suddenly Alaric had a strong suspicion of where the grain was.

On his way to the merchants' quarter, Alaric could see the bodies on the wall.

There were ten. The city's richest merchants, and the governor and magistrates who'd enriched themselves from the slave trade. Noricum had specialized in selling *his* people, war captives from north of the Danube, valiant, strong-backed Goths preferred for the brutal Roman mines. The sight of the bodies calmed him. This was *justice*. Alaric normally did not sanction indiscriminate slaughter, but when he'd taken Noricum, he'd slipped his army's leash—and for once, the slavers had gotten exactly what they deserved.

It was an ugly irony that some of his chieftains had chosen to live here, in gleaming mansions paid for in his people's misery.

"Alaric, *think*." Sigeric was at his ear. "*If* Wallia took the grain, you cannot simply take it back in front of his warriors. You must allow him to save his honor."

"If this was *my* army," Riga said in a bored drawl, "I'd haul them out of their fancy houses and hang them on the wall with the slavers. Among my people, we deal with dissent severely.

Otherwise you're cleaning up a rebellion every other week, and you never get anything done."

"Don't listen to the honorless mercenary, King Alaric—"

"Better than listening to fools who follow their honor to the grave."

"Enough," Alaric snarled. Riga's strategy tempted him. But he needed the warriors badly. He'd already lost many who'd followed Ataulf and Sarus. Stilicho was coming in scant months, and the Huns would be here sooner than that. If he lost Wallia, he lost everything.

They'd arrived at the finest of the marble houses now.

"You cannot simply walk in there like a lit torch and start setting things on fire," Sigeric said. "What is your *plan*?"

"They've forgotten who they are," he answered, setting his shoulder to the great brass doors. "I'm going to remind them."

The doors swung open and the man guarding them fell off his chair, wine jug smashing on the marble floor. "Hey!" he slurred. "You can't go in there!"

Alaric ignored him. He stepped over the amphora fragments and the spreading stain of wine, and the others followed.

Inside was chaos. Drunken warriors sprawled on every piece of furniture. Belligerent Gauls with their hair limed straight up, tattooed Huns blowing smoke rings in the soaring atrium, a Gepid and a Thracian fighting shin-deep in the *impluvium*. They were staggeringly drunk, but that didn't stop them from waving *spatha* and *seax* at each other while a wild crowd took bets and roared encouragement.

Here, a group of Hunnic warrior women tried to outdo each other with knife tricks. There, a couple fucked furiously against a wall. Alaric stepped over broken furniture and snoring bodies, past a lush formal garden where goats roamed untended, ripping up the expensive flowers. *Goats.* The refugees were starving and these people had *goats* in the gardens.

By the time he reached the inner sanctum, he could barely breathe through his fury.

The columned dining room was packed to the gills. The chieftains and their retinues lounged on Roman couches inlaid in pearl and ivory. Along one wall, a low table groaned with food, and Wallia presided over everything like a king out of legend.

The din cut off abruptly at Alaric's entrance; a hundred heads swiveled in his direction. Laughter died in a hundred throats.

Alaric spoke into the sudden silence. "Hello, Wallia."

"King Alaric! Where have you been? We've been expecting you for hours!" His smile was half grimace. "Drink and be merry. Tomorrow may be our last on earth, eh?"

There was much laughing and raising of goblets. Alaric thought of the boy in the square. The pregnant woman, desperate enough to punch through anything. "Would you like to hear why I'm late?" he asked mildly. "I was breaking up a brawl between Wulfric's wife and a ten-year-old boy over grain." The man named Wulfric was sprawled on the stairs. There was a woman in his lap, not his wife—blonde with her tits half-out, a string of rubies hanging between them. "Your wife throws a mean punch, Wulfric."

"Aye, that she does!" Wulfric answered merrily, raising a cup of wine and spilling a good portion down his front. "I shall beat her for her disrespect."

Rage made his vision go red. *"The hell you will!"* Alaric roared, and a room full of hardened warriors flinched. "She *was justified*. Eight months pregnant and going to battle for the last sack of grain in the city, while you sit on your arse with your hero's portion and your *concubine*."

Wulfric was drunk enough to answer back. "I'll wager your *Roman* wife eats well in her fine mansion," he sneered.

"Aye, she does. And it's her rubies hanging around your woman's neck, Wulfric." Suddenly Wulfric looked like he'd swallowed a turd. "Her money paid, by the way, for the grain that will keep our people alive over the winter. The way I see it, she's done more for our people in a week than any of *you* have done in months." His gaze turned to Wallia, and his voice went dangerously soft. "Speaking of grain. Where is it, Wallia?"

"I took a measure for my warriors. I didn't want to bother you with such dull administrative matters," Wallia said, in the unctuous tone of a drunk man arguing law. "The fighting class needs to keep their strength up. Supposing we were attacked?"

"Supposing we *are*." Alaric thought of the Huns sweeping down from the eastern plains. "The walls are disintegrating, and this city makes an easy target. I'm surprised you all aren't dead already."

"You insult my honor," Wallia growled. "A homeland is a fool's errand. We will never have anything in this world we don't simply *take*. You can talk until you grow hoarse, but the truth is you are hanging by a thread." He quaffed his drink. "Let us be done with all this talk. I challenge you. Man to man. Winner takes the kingship."

The crowd's laughter grew to a roar, and suddenly it was Wallia's name they were shouting. They just wanted to see blood; they didn't care about the consequences.

Alaric smiled, razor-sharp. "No."

Wallia frowned. "You refuse to fight me?"

"I refuse to gut you like a fish in front of your own kin." The crowd laughed as Wallia fumbled his sword out of his scabbard. "Sit down before you cut yourself with that. You're drunk."

Wallia's face reddened furiously as his warriors roared with laughter, at him this time, pounding the tables. Alaric walked up to the dais and poured himself wine, sitting down in an ivory-inlaid chair with his feet on Wallia's table as if this was his own war tent. "I have just received news of Huns coming down from the north," he said, letting his voice carry. "They've ravaged Pannonia, and they carry all its riches with them. I say we go and take it."

Wallia stared. "The Huns are coming and you want to ride out to meet them? Insanity."

"Insanity would be hiding behind these crumbling walls that will do nothing to shelter us. Better to meet them long before they arrive. If we ride fast enough, we could pick our ground." Nothing united his people like a common enemy. And whatever battle came with the Huns, he could keep Julia out of a siege. "Drink as if tonight is your last, men," he said, voice booming over the heads of the cheering crowd. "For tomorrow, we ride."

Julia pulled herself over the windowsill with Bromios's help and without alerting the guards. She was still shaken by what she had seen that day—the starving children, the ravaged city. The violent riot over the grain. She'd heard of such riots in Rome, in the days of the grain dole, but had never seen one up close. And Alaric had plunged right into the center of it.

She thought of the food that had been brought to her in the days since she'd come here. Beef and wine and bread. Simple food, but filling. Where had it come from? Who was going hungry while she ate well?

She felt even more determined now to help Alaric fix the city's problems.

The guards were willing enough to bring her maps of the aqueduct from the library. Hours later, she sat on the marble floor, maps and scrolls scattered around her.

The maps showed miles of siphons and catchment tanks and high arching bridges. She could trace the path the water took from the mountain lake at its source, flying over valleys and beneath the ground until it reached the city. There were maps of the pipes and passages beneath the city streets too; at her fingertips was the plan for how every city cistern and fountain was fed. Apparently there were tunnels in the rock beneath the fortress that led to underground cisterns and passageways. Julia laid everything out on the marbled floor and poured herself wine, considering where the breaks in the aqueduct might be.

She'd seen water dripping from the structure when she'd climbed it. That meant the water was still running, although not at full strength. She suspected the damage had been done close by, during the siege. But it would take an engineering team to know for sure.

Julia was still poring over the plans when Alaric stepped into the room.

He looked—*exhausted*. He wore a dusty tunic and trousers, and his bronze hair was pulled back from his face, leaving his features in sharp relief. Julia rose, forgetting the plans at her feet. She ran to him, and he pulled her roughly into his arms. "I missed you, wife."

"I thought you'd be *days*." Her arms tightened until she felt his ribs creak.

"I like this greeting better than the last one." He tilted her face up and kissed her. "I suppose I should ask why the floor is strewn with scrolls."

Julia felt a slash of unease as she pulled him over to look at the maps. She expected him to glance cursorily at the scrolls, and then take her in his arms and end the conversation in bed. It wasn't that she *minded*—but she did. She thought of her father, patting her head and calling her beautiful.

But instead he sat on the floor and listened, one elbow up on a knee, fiercely quiet.

Julia explained how the aqueduct worked. The infrastructure beneath the ground, reaching forty miles east to a lake in the hills. The damage taken in the siege, where it likely was, and what it would take to repair. Alaric's gaze was intent, following her fingers as she showed him the lines on the map that represented siphons and water bridges and settling tanks. How many and where they were.

"I saw things when I rode through your city." He didn't need

to know about her outing to the aqueduct. "Bad sanitation is one of your problems. It makes you vulnerable to plague. Your people are surviving on water in stagnant fountains. If we don't repair the aqueduct soon, it's only a matter of time before sickness comes within these walls. And if we're ever under siege, we won't last a week without fresh water."

He was silent for what seemed an interminable time as she came to the end of her words. What if he laughed at her? What if he hated her idea? What if—*oh gods*—what if he patted her on the head as her father had and told her how beautiful she was?

He was looking at her thoughtfully. "There's ink on your cheek," he murmured, his thumb skating gently over her cheekbone. "What do you need to accomplish these repairs?"

"Building materials to make the concrete, and stone for the facings. And manpower, of course. A team of engineers. Armed guards to protect them when they go out into the hills. It will take a week, maybe two, once we have the stone." She drew a breath. "It will be worth it, Alaric. The benefit to our people—"

He leaned over and kissed her. Slow and achingly gentle.

"*Our* people. I like when you say that." Julia's breath hitched.

"You can have your aqueduct," he said, smiling. "Meet with Sigeric tomorrow. He'll be leading the reconstruction of the walls in my absence."

Julia frowned. "Where are you going?"

"I have to lead a raid. I'll be gone for a week, maybe two. It's nothing to concern you."

Nothing to concern her? "Alaric. What if there's an insurrection? I cannot believe you'd leave the city in this state when you barely entered in one piece last time."

"Thorismund and Sigeric will be here. You can trust them. In the meantime, I'll keep a battle far away from you, and you won't have to live through a siege." He pulled her closer, scrolls crumpling beneath them. "If anything happened to you—"

Julia felt a strange sense of foreboding as she gave herself to

the kiss. She told herself she had gotten what she wanted. And when he returned, it would be to a new, gleaming aqueduct. He would see what an effective queen she was.

The kiss deepened. Became hot and demanding. "The bed would be more comfortable—" Julia murmured.

He rose to his feet, lifting her easily in his arms. They didn't make it to the bed—only to the couch, mere steps away. Julia didn't mind in the slightest.

Alaric took his time with Julia, lingering over her.

She'd called his people *ours*.

Someday, when he had brought the chieftains to heel, he would have endless time to listen to his brilliant wife tell him everything she knew about aqueducts, or road engineering, or the economics of piracy. Anything, really. He didn't care *what* she told him about, as long as it was in exhaustive detail. He loved listening to her, loved watching the passion flash across her face as she spoke.

He left before she woke. Better not to draw out a long good-bye. Better to leave her with a project to occupy her restless mind.

He'd promised to hand out food to the refugees himself, at dawn. But dawn was almost risen, and he was late. It would be no small feat to marshal the warriors after.

Horsa was waiting for him on the mansion steps, sharpening his *seax*.

"Horsa. I'm very glad to see you." Alaric drew an arm over the boy's shoulders and led him down the stairs. "I need you to lead the grain distribution for me. The sun is almost risen, and the crowd will be fractious if—"

"I thought we were going raiding. Hengist is going raiding."

Alaric sighed. This conversation was unavoidable. Even so, he'd been dreading it.

"Yes, Hengist is going with me," he said, as gently as he could. "You will stay here, Horsa. I need someone I trust at my back."

Horsa halted on the stairs. "But—why?"

"Both of you must lead in battle *and* rule a city if you're to become chieftains. Hengist must strengthen his leadership on the battlefield. He's levelheaded in a fight, but isn't a leader of men. You, Horsa—you must strengthen your skills here. Help Julia build her aqueduct. Watch her back."

Horsa's face scrunched, hurt clouding his features. "It isn't fair."

"Nothing is fair," Alaric said. "You should have learned that by now."

Julia woke to the sound of voices at her door. Alaric was gone, without even a goodbye. She scrambled out of bed, snatching up a robe, with every intention of catching him and upbraiding him for daring to leave her so abruptly. Outside she heard impassioned arguing, and then the thud of the door swinging against the marble doorframe.

Julia halted in the bedroom doorway to see Horsa burst into her atrium. She watched him pace a tight circle on the marble, and winced when he kicked a couch across the room. He put a hand on a rather large iron candelabra next, clearly itching to do something violent with it.

"Horsa." His eyes snapped to her, radiating fury. "What on earth did the furniture do to you?" The boy gave a vicious scowl. Julia regarded him impassively, arms crossed over her chest. "Well?"

"Alaric took Hengist raiding and left me here behind."

"That makes two of us," Julia said drily, and for a moment the two of them stood in silence, both stewing in their own hurt. "You might as well sit down," she said, waving at the couch he had kicked.

Horsa's idea of sitting seemed to be the one thing he had in common with her younger brother. He threw himself on the couch, adopting a loose-limbed lounge, his eyes half-closed. Julia lowered herself onto a chair, trailing one toe on the marble.

"I cannot be angry with him. But I am angry."

"Hengist said something similar once." Julia rolled her eyes. "I don't understand the difficulty of being angry with Alaric. The man can be absolutely insufferable sometimes. All the more so because people are afraid to be angry with him."

"Alaric is my chieftain. If he died on the battlefield and I walked away alive, I would never live down the shame." Horsa gave an exaggerated sigh, as if to express his frustration that she did not understand something so painfully obvious. "Now if he does die on the battlefield, I won't be there. Hengist will get to die with him, and I *won't*."

"And so you feel—jealous for not having the opportunity to die with him." Suddenly she was outraged. "You're fifteen, Horsa. Dying on the battlefield *indeed*. What a load of—" She paused, her outrage suddenly eclipsed by her curiosity. Alaric hardly ever told her anything about his past, including his relationship with the twins. "He saved your lives, you said? How?"

It was a long story, and Horsa was feeling talkative. He lay on his back on the couch, one leg dangling over the back, and recounted the story of two children who'd grown up following in the path of an army, playing amidst the detritus of war. Or perhaps *playing* was the wrong word. The only play the twins had known was the deadly kind.

Horsa had been fighting battles since he was ten, and trailing after armies his whole life. He'd been bringing trouble down on his head for just as long. He told her of the time Alaric had sent the boys out to forage for supplies and Horsa had found a group of bandits to pick a fight with—Alaric had had to ransom him back in the midst of a siege.

'I can see how Alaric would be driven to distraction, trying to keep you alive," Julia said.

"I remind the great lady that she also got herself kidnapped." Horsa drawled, mimicking her palace Latin. "Although Alaric didn't bother with ransom then."

Julia laughed. "I suppose he got sick of paying ransoms for hooligans such as us."

"He thinks I'm stupid," Horsa said bitterly, sitting up and sliding to the floor, long legs spread out on the marble, his back to the couch. "Hengist doesn't even want to raid. He wants to be a farmer. Have you ever heard something so foolish? Alaric thinks I'm impulsive."

"Well. That's not exactly untrue." Horsa glared at her. "But you've been quite heroic, Horsa. Do you remember how you fought in the cave when I was kidnapped? You were first into the gap behind Alaric, if I recall."

Horsa had taken his knife out of his belt and was now tossing it from hand to hand in an intricate pattern. The knife flashed in the sunlight. "You should have seen me fight at the ruined temple," he said contemplatively. "I filled a ravine with the dead."

"If you hadn't, I might be dead myself. You saved my life!"

"I did, didn't I?" His smile was like a sunrise.

"You are only as reckless as he is. Surely he can understand that." Julia couldn't stop staring at the knife. Sharp enough to slice a finger off, if he got it wrong. "Where did you learn to do that?"

"Alaric taught me." Horsa caught the knife with a little flourish and a showman's grin. "Want to learn?"

"No," Julia shuddered. "Alaric would be angry if you did. Thorismund gave me a knife and he took it away because he thought I would hurt myself." Suddenly she felt a bit forlorn. "You're not the only one he believes to be incompetent."

Horsa was staring at her, the knife gone still in his hand. "He

took your knife away?" He looked outraged. "But what if you have to defend yourself?"

"That's what I said. He insisted he would defend me himself, but as you can see, he is currently nowhere to be seen and I rather think we'd kill each other if we were always together anyway."

Horsa rose to his feet. "This is insanity," he muttered, as he stalked over and yanked Julia abruptly to her feet. "Go change into your trousers. I'm going to show you how to use this." He held the knife out to her, hilt-first. "I'm in a mood to make him mad."

Horsa started by looking Julia's body up and down, criticism written all over his face. "You stand all wrong." He turned her so that her right shoulder and foot came forward. "Stand on the front of your feet. Light. Like this." He demonstrated. "Make yourself as small a target as you can. The less for your enemy to catch with his blade." He adjusted her again, stepped back to judge his work. "There."

"Now what?"

Horsa looked up at her, a flat, feral grin on his face. "Now we try to kill each other."

In the next hours, Julia got an education in the many ways to put a man in the ground. Horsa taught her how to hold a knife, how to move quickly, and where to aim. He howled with laughter at her grip and told her that if Alaric had seen him hold a knife like that, he'd be beaten senseless.

"You'll never win in combat with a full-grown man who's battle trained," Horsa told her. "You must rely on surprise. If he knows you have the knife before you use it, it's too late."

He showed her several places to hide a knife on her body. In her trouser leg, in her boot, up a sleeve. "This one is designed to hide in a boot," he told her, showing her how to draw it quickly, how to strike with deadly accuracy. "Right here, just beneath the rib cage." He demonstrated the angle on his own

rib cage with his two thumbs. "Or the neck, here, where the pulse is." He tapped the side of his throat. "You cut this place, and you will be rewarded with a river of blood. But don't hesitate. If you fail, you'll only make him mad."

More than mad. Julia understood Alaric's hesitation. If she failed to kill a man when she needed to, she could end up dead herself. Or raped, or maimed. She could not slip up, even once. But she *needed* this knowledge. Alaric couldn't be by her side all the time, couldn't protect her every moment. She knew that, even if he refused to admit it.

Julia practiced all day. Practiced until she was exhausted, and reasonably sure she could slice a man's throat from sheer muscle memory. Horsa was a demanding teacher, exacting and precise, refusing to let mistakes pass. She had a feeling he'd learned it from Alaric.

That night, she didn't need wine to fall asleep.

CHAPTER THIRTY-NINE

The next day, Julia met with Alaric's chieftain Sigeric about repairing the aqueduct. She quickly realized he would be an obstacle.

"It *won't* take weeks to seek out repairs in these hills," she said for perhaps the dozenth time. "The main reservoir is only ten miles outside the city."

"You're not listening, my queen." Meticulously polite, Sigeric wore a Roman toga and a clipped Roman beard and even affected an irritatingly correct version of palace Latin. "Even if we knew exactly where the break in the piping is, the dangers outside the walls mean we will need an armed escort. There are bandits and Roman patrols—" He paused. "We do know where the damage is, incidentally. I sent men to destroy the aqueduct when we invaded Noricum. It was Alaric's orders."

Alaric had not told her that.

"Well. Now Alaric's orders are that the aqueduct be repaired," Julia said briskly. "And since you know where the damage is, you can lead the engineers in repairing it."

"That's what I keep telling you. We don't *have* engineers."

Sigeric shook his head mulishly. "Besides, perhaps you misunderstand King Alaric's priorities. Before he left, Alaric ordered *me* to shore up the walls before he returned. There isn't enough stone in this city for both." He tapped a hand on the table. "Our orders conflict, my queen. I will simply tell Alaric when he returns that he cannot have both."

Julia hid her irritation behind a genial smile. "Is that who you want to be? The man who tells Alaric that his orders are impossible?" Sigeric frowned. "Suit yourself if you'd rather not repair the aqueduct. But this city will descend into plague if you don't. I'll make certain my husband knows who to thank when it happens."

"The stone for both is simply *not here*, my queen."

Julia glanced down at the maps she'd spread out on the table. One trimmed nail tapped at a spot just under the crosshatched mountains. "Here is a quarry, fifty miles away."

"That quarry is defended by a Roman legion. The last thing Alaric needs is a war behind as well as before him."

Julia glanced up sharply, a sudden suspicion building. "Who did you say controlled that quarry?"

"A prominent family from Ravenna."

A prominent family at odds with her brother, if they hadn't already gone to war with the Goths on their doorstep. Julia smiled. "We won't have to fight them. In fact, they'll offer us engineers and stone as a gesture of friendship. Perhaps enough to repair the city walls, as well."

A week later, Julia stood on the citadel wall, watching a long procession snake up the hill.

"Her guard is rather excessive," Thorismund said, the wind from the plain whipping his blond hair around his face.

"She did have to travel fifty miles over bandit-infested terrain. Of course she would bring a small army."

The line of soldiers marched in unison through the gate.

Broad-shouldered slaves lowered the litter and a silken-gloved hand emerged, and then the rest of Lucretia, swathed in pale blue linen, her toes perfectly dustless in her silver-studded sandals.

Julia came down from the wall to greet her friend. It was surprisingly wonderful to see a friendly face from Ravenna, rare as those were. Even so, it made something constrict in her chest, how much Lucretia resembled Cornelius.

"My poor darling. *Look* at you." Lucretia grasped her arms familiarly. "You look like a sunburned Spartan maiden. What on earth have you been doing in this utter pile?"

"Let us retire out of this dreadful heat, and I will tell you all about it."

Julia watched Lucretia's face as she led her through the mansion. The older woman's eyes fell upon the withered garden, the green-slicked statues, the fire stains. Julia could just see her thinking about the siege, and who this manor once belonged to, and what had happened to them.

She judiciously did not mention the bodies on the wall.

Finally Julia settled her guest on silken cushions and poured her wine with her own hand. Lucretia took a careful sip. "For Boeotian red, this is quite good."

My husband only pillages the best. It would be a tasteless joke.

Julia only smiled.

"Darling, I didn't know *what* to think when you disappeared. Nobody did. My spies told only the most outrageous lies."

Lucretia's face went perfectly smooth. "You are a queen now, as you wanted. Cornelius would be happy for you."

For a moment the ghost of Cornelius hung between them. Julia drew a breath. "He has not left my thoughts since the day I escaped Ravenna." The words stuck in her throat. "Lucretia—"

"You must not blame yourself," Lucretia said immediately. "He would be glad that you managed to escape a treason sen-

tence. What incredible talent for survival." She shook her head, wondering, "Do you love this Alaric?"

Julia hesitated. It would be an innocent question about her well-being, from anyone else. But from Lucretia, it had had the semblance of a trap. Lucretia often laughed at married couples who seemed to dote on each other too much. *Only fools fall in love with their husbands.* Julia had taken those words for deepest truth, once.

But—her eyes fell to Thorismund and Horsa, each leaning casually on either side of the door, her honor guard. They had both insisted on watching her back, as they did not trust this new Roman in their midst. And the last thing she wanted was to deride her own feelings for Alaric before them.

"He would die for me," she said simply, raising her cup to her lips. "And I for him."

"Well. Isn't that theatrical?" Lucretia smirked. "I cannot fault you for enjoying yourself. These barbarians are quite breathtaking." She cast an assessing eye toward Thorismund.

Julia held a tart reply behind her teeth. Had Lucretia always been like this—all veiled insults and sly glances? Had *she* been like this? No wonder Alaric had found her insufferable.

She rose to her feet. "Come. Let me show you why you're here."

Not an hour later, Julia stood in the shadow of the aqueduct, gazing up at its high arches.

"My. What a ruin," Lucretia remarked. Julia gritted her teeth. All the way down from the citadel, Lucretia had been ostentatiously noticing the city's failings—shuddering in disgust at the sight of hungry children, casting a critical eye on crumbling walls.

At least Thorismund was here. He made her feel safe. He stood close by now, silent and discreet as a palace guard, having led a contingent of his men to watch their backs in the streets.

Julia exchanged a muted look with him; she read in his glance that he would have *plenty* to say later.

"Only the higher levels are damaged," Julia said to Lucretia. "The supporting structure remains unharmed. I believe your men could repair it within days if we had a ready supply of stone."

Lucretia's own men stood close, holding up a pair of parasols to shield them; but the parasols could do nothing to protect from the hot, sluggish wind. "It really is incredible, how great the destruction your husband wrought here."

Julia felt a sudden need to defend Alaric. "He wants to make a better life for his people. That is what I hope to accomplish, with your help."

Lucretia looked at her from beneath hooded eyes, unsmiling.

A sudden roar of pain split the sky. Thorismund was crumpling, a sword biting into his side where his wound had been. Julia stared. For a moment she could not comprehend what was happening. The next, she stood in the middle of a battle.

Lucretia's men had tossed their parasols aside, swords gleaming in their hands; there were suddenly twice the men in the square as there had been.

Thorismund's guards were outnumbered.

Julia could not move. Her feet were frozen to the ground. *Thorismund*. She thought of him rushing to her rescue at the temple, his axe held over his head as he barreled toward a battle he could not possibly survive.

"Run," Thorismund bellowed from the center of the melee, fighting for his life. "Go."

Lucretia seized her hand, breaking her trance. "This way. Hurry!"

The freeze of fear gave way to utter panic as she fled with Lucretia up the hill to the citadel, their feet slipping on the worn cobblestones.

Julia strode inside the citadel gates, calling for her own men. A great crash behind her as the huge citadel gate swung shut.

Lucretia stood behind her, a sharp-edged smile on her face. And there was Sigeric, coming down from the walls. "Sigeric!" Julia cried. "Thorismund is under attack. We must—"

But Sigeric passed without a glance at her, and Julia watched him stroll up to Lucretia as she took his hands firmly in her own. "Dear Sigeric. Well done. It all unfolded just as you said it would."

Sigeric laughed. "It was easy to gain Alaric's trust. All I had to do was stop my own assassin from killing him."

Julia froze. *Assassin?* "Lucretia, what have you done?"

"Dear Julia. You've always been only half as clever as you thought you were, and twice as entitled." Lucretia's smile was vicious. "How does it feel to lose everything you have?"

CHAPTER FORTY

Alaric halted on the ridgeline, eyes tracing the plains and valleys to the shimmering horizon. They'd been chasing the Huns for a week through a blasted land. Empty villages dotted the plains below, like corpses on an abandoned battlefield. Dead crops rattled in their fields and vultures watched from the trees.

"Vultures are a sign of death to come," Riga said, reining his horse in next to him. "The question is, whose death?"

"We cannot go much further. This feels like a trap."

Riga glanced at him, unsmiling. "The gods help you though, if you don't deliver."

Alaric knew. At his back, Wallia's men spread out across the slope below. He had promised them plunder and victory; if he delivered, the warriors would see those spoils flow from *his* hands. He didn't like to think what would happen if he failed. At least Julia was safe with Thorismund and Horsa.

Just then, something caught Alaric's eye. Dust, thick and white, churned up from horses' hooves. He recognized that dust cloud.

He raised his voice and called his men to him.

* * *

Alaric galloped into the valley with his army at his back. The Huns had sighted them; they were running for the high ground. Riga's mercenaries would flank them from the west, and to-gether they would grind the enemy to meat. And then he could go back to Noricum, to Julia, with Wallia's men united under him. The city would be just a little safer for her.

A prickle started in the center of Alaric's shoulder blades. Then he felt it—the change in the air. The shift in the earth; drumming up from his horse's hooves.

Movement in the trees that was not the wind.

Ambush. He tried to signal the men. But his army was starv-ing and dust-blind, the enemy drawing them on like a mirage in the desert. Then Wallia emerged from the cloud, raising his spear as if to signal the men. Alaric glanced up, and there—up on the ridgeline—he saw Riga and his men sweeping down the opposite ridgeline. To the east.

It took him a moment to realize what he was seeing. They were riding in the wrong direction. Riga had betrayed him. It was the last thought he had before a heavy spear haft sent him crashing off his horse.

An old war rose up in his sight, one long over.

Your enemy is down there. The ghost of Eugenius pointed with a rusty gladius down into the canyon at Frigidus. Alaric tightened his grip on the reins and twenty thousand voices rose up at his back. Then he lunged forward into the canyon's gullet.

His spear was death spinning in his hands, cutting through breathing bodies. Arrows rained down without mercy. Stilicho never warned him that the enemy was in the walls.

Down where the canyon narrowed to a cut, there was a black-clad man standing still against the chaos, a wicked spear dripping blood onto the sand. It was Calthrax, the throat-cut demon who rode in Alaric's wake. It was Eugenius, the bright red line bisecting his head from his

body. It was the bear, great teeth bared. Alaric stepped over the bodies of living and dead to meet his enemy.

He fought as his father taught him long ago, his weapon a black slash in the filmy curtain between life and death. There was too much blood in the earth. Alaric's feet slipped in it. He tightened his grip on the spear and drove it into his enemy's heart.

The spear is in your heart, brother. Alaric looked down and saw the spear lodged in his own chest. The bear flashed bloody teeth. *It is a good death. A right death.*

He knew he was supposed to accept his death. But Julia stood before him now, her red-gold hair spilling over her breasts, tears glinting in her eyes like diamonds. He could not die here.

Alaric ripped his own blood-soaked spear out of his chest. The bear rose snarling out of every shadow.

Death was not as he expected.

Alaric lay on his back on the battlefield, on earth sodden with blood. A sharp pain stabbed him in the ribs.

You still live, brother. I should know.

Alaric turned. The voice came from the corpse that lay next to him. It was Calthrax. Blood leaking out of the slash Alaric had put in his throat.

What a battle, eh? Almost like those of old that we fought together. What I wouldn't kill to live those days again.

Thorismund would know some spell to send the dead away. Alaric didn't know any goddamn spells. So he used plain words.

"Go away, Calthrax. Go back to wherever the dead go."

Battlefields are where the dead go, brother. You should know. You're halfway one of us. The corpse's terrible smile broadened. *But not all the way. Not yet. Now get up.*

Now the corpse was a gray-bearded warrior, eyes already milking over, Alaric's own axe rising from his forehead. Alaric rose to his feet and jerked his axe out of the man's skull, then looked across the charnel floor of the valley. Corpses littered

the battlefield, already bloating in the hot sun. Vultures picked at the dead, their great black wings spread over their meals.

A shape was coming toward him through the carnage, leading an exhausted horse.

Another ghost. He had killed Ataulf, had he not? Killed him in his heart, at least.

"You look like shit," Ataulf said, halting before him. The horse he led was Hannibal, his black coat sweat-soaked and throwing off the sun. "I think you know this old soldier. I found him skulking on the edges of the battlefield, harrying deserters."

Alaric felt a hitch of relief in his chest. *Hannibal.* He braced his hand on Hannibal's shoulder and the horse reached around to run his teeth across his back. "I sent you away for a reason, Ataulf."

"It figures I would rescue you from being hacked to death by your own army, only to have you tell me to make myself scarce. You're welcome, you tyrant."

Alaric wiped sweat and blood off his brow with a forearm. It was too damn hot to think straight. His head was still ringing. "I think Riga ambushed me."

"You think *Riga* ambushed you?" Ataulf was looking at him in bewildered disgust. "Riga saved your miserable life. Ask him yourself."

Ataulf pointed with his sword across the battlefield. Riga and Hengist were riding toward him, their horses picking their way among the corpses.

With Riga's help, the story began to piece together. Riga had seen the ambush through the trees when he'd swung west with his men. He'd planned to flank the ambushers, but there had been too many. Luckily Ataulf had been pillaging in the next valley.

"There were Goths amidst the Huns," Hengist told him. "I think it was Sarus, working with Wallia to lead us into this trap."

Alaric rubbed the bruise along his jaw. "Wallia was the one who knocked me off my horse." Suddenly the true size of what had happened crashed in on him. Wallia had lured him out of the city and worked with the rebels and Huns to assassinate him. None would question it if he died in battle. And if Wallia still had allies in Noricum—

Ataulf was thinking the same thought. "Who did you say you left in charge in Noricum?"

Julia. Stark fear rose in his chest.

"I will handle it myself," Alaric said to Ataulf. "Your help is not needed. What you did to Julia is *not* forgiven."

"I didn't offer," Ataulf snapped. "But if you love your wife, you'll let me ride to Noricum at your back. You're out of men, and Wallia *must* have an ally behind those walls. You need me."

Alaric cursed. Ataulf was right.

It took four days of hard riding to get back to Noricum, fear for Julia crowding Alaric's head. He worried for Horsa too, and Thorismund. But it was Julia's fate that had him waking up in cold sweats.

When the walls of Noricum rose on the horizon, Alaric felt an immediate sense of foreboding. The city was too silent. A wind snapped the flags to tautness and ripped at the tattered clothes of the dead on the wall. Julia was not among those bodies. Thank the gods.

They halted at the ridgeline above the valley at dusk, and Hengist pointed across the plain. A figure was moving toward them at a panicked gallop. Riga raised his bow and nocked an arrow to it. Sighted down the line.

"Lower your weapon, Riga," Alaric said, nudging Hannibal into a ground-eating canter toward the other rider.

Alaric slid off Hannibal just as the rider near fell off his own horse and into Alaric's arms. Horsa's eyes were wild, rimmed with fear as he said the words Alaric dreaded most in the world. "It's the Romans. They've taken the city."

They approached from the east, where trees gave cover and there were holes in the walls large enough to drive a chariot through. But whoever had invaded was not posting guards. Their entrance was not challenged.

Inside, the city held a haunted quiet. Alaric led his men through narrow, sloping streets toward the citadel. Halfway up, they crossed a large square. The alleyways leading out of it had been blocked by street rubble. Alaric didn't like those blocked alleyways. It had the feeling of a trap. But to go around would mean losing hours.

There was an old Roman bathhouse that ran the length of the square—a way to cross without being seen. The door was rotted off its hinges. Inside it smelled of mildew and death. With his men at his back, Alaric moved through shafts of filthy light, over layers of dust that covered bright mosaics. Archways yawned into blackness and empty pools opened at their feet.

And then he heard a cough. And then a low, guttural groan.

They found Thorismund lying on a couch beside a drained pool. There were black stains on the cushions that stank of blood. Alaric knelt and grasped Thorismund's hand.

"The Romans hold the citadel," Thorismund whispered. A long, livid cut ran across his torso. The old one opened anew. "I couldn't stop it."

Fear gripped Alaric's heart. "Is Julia alive?"

"Last I saw—" he gave a great hacking cough "—she was fleeing toward the citadel with the Roman woman. I do not know whether she lives now."

Alaric stilled. "What Roman woman?"

"She was trying to secure stone to repair the aqueduct. She knew the Roman woman from Ravenna. A friend, she said."

Ataulf spoke behind him. Cold and factual. "She let Romans in, under the pretext of repairing the aqueduct. She did this."

"It wasn't like that." Thorismund let out a low growl. "She never betrayed you, Alaric."

Noises on the roof. Hobnailed boots on the tile.

"Leave me here," Thorismund grated. "I'll only slow you down."

But already Alaric was helping Thorismund to his feet. "Not a chance." Not a chance Julia had betrayed him either. Even so—doubt nagged at his mind.

There would be time later to determine where Julia's allegiances lay.

The citadel loomed high and forbidding, atop a rock that rose up from the center of town. But that rock was not as solid as it looked. Alaric knew from Julia's maps that it was riddled with caves, ancient and damp, used as sepulchers and sewers.

That night with Julia was burned into his mind. Sitting on the floor with her, the maps spread between them and her red hair gleaming in the lamplight as she explained to him the inner workings of the aqueduct. He could not tear his eyes away.

But he'd also studied the maps. They hadn't only detailed the aqueduct—they'd also shown a network of branching passageways beneath the citadel. He'd committed them to memory, knowing he might need them someday. He'd never thought it would be this soon.

The map, unfortunately, failed to tell him which of the passages were flooded.

They slipped into the tunnels under cover of dark, Alaric and the twins and some ten of his own. The first three channels had been flooded, the last only half-flooded. This one had been a sepulcher once. There were rock-cut tombs lining the walls, their contents shrouded in darkness; Alaric shuddered to think what was rotting below the waterline.

A muffled cry from behind him. Horsa. "Something brushed my ankle."

"It's probably a corpse," Hengist answered. "It wants to devour you and throw out the husk to preserve its youth."

"Quiet, both of you," Alaric growled.

"Are you lost, Alaric?" came Hengist's too-casual question.

Alaric gritted his teeth. He didn't want to admit it.

This passage *should* connect to another, branching off to the west. From there, they would reach a vertical shaft that connected to the citadel courtyard. He could only hope there would be some way to climb it. Then all they had to do was kill the guards and open the gate to let Riga and Ataulf in with the rest of the men. Easy.

"Fuck," Horsa whispered. "I think something bit me."

"Coward," Hengist muttered. "Don't tell me you're afraid of a little fish."

"It was a *big* fish," Horsa said. "I felt it brush my—"

"It was probably a minnow." Hengist laughed, and some of the men started laughing too, and heckling Horsa, as if they were fucking invincible. As if *he* was fucking invincible and could keep them from any harm they brought on themselves with their noise.

The passage ended at a fork, neither pointing in the right direction.

"North," said Horsa immediately.

"How do you know?"

"I don't. But it's dry up there. No fish."

It was as good a reason as any. "North, then," Alaric said, and pushed forward, feeling his way in the dark.

Four days after Lucretia took the citadel, she summoned Julia in the middle of the night.

Lucretia was sitting in the atrium of Julia's former quarters, wearing the same linen robe Julia had worn on her first night. Her dark hair tumbled down her back. For an instant Julia had a disorienting vision—Lucretia stepping into her life, into Alaric's bed like some life-stealing ghost. Herself banished.

"Julia. *Darling.* Come in. Have some wine."

Wordlessly, Julia went to the table and poured. She handed Lucretia a cup and looked at her expectantly. "You don't mind, do you? Out of an abundance of caution."

"If I wanted you dead, I hardly have to go to the effort of poisoning you." Julia held quiet and Lucretia gave an elaborate sigh and took a sip. "Happy?"

"Delighted," Julia said flatly. "I suppose there is a reason you summoned me here in the middle of the night?"

"I haven't been able to sleep properly since wolves ripped my son's throat out before my eyes. If I cannot sleep, neither can you." Lucretia regarded her contemplatively. "Do you remember what the problem is with love, Julia?"

The answer came readily to her tongue. It had been her sacrament. The one holy rule of Ravenna. "Love ruins you."

"Precisely. When you love someone like I loved Cornelius, losing them *ruins* you. I was ruined. The only thing to do is destroy that which destroyed the thing you love." Lucretia took a sip of her wine. "Imagine my surprise when I found *you* had landed on your feet. Not fifty miles from my own home, the beloved wife and queen of another man you'd beguiled into marrying you, after doing the same to my son and leaving him dead in the dust."

A flash of rage crossed her face like a storm.

Julia drew a breath. Her own grief over Cornelius, her own self-hatred and blame, her own nightmares in the dark, rose up and choked her throat.

Lucretia would not care. She had suffered more. Julia would not insult her by appealing to her sympathy.

"What do you plan to do with me, then? Considering my

husband will arrive soon," Julia said mildly, affecting an attitude of bored indifference that would have been perfectly at home in Ravenna. "I don't wish to scare you, Lucretia, but he *is* as vicious as the rumors say. Have you seen the bodies on the wall? Those were people my husband didn't like." There was a smell of smoke in the air. Battle. "He is here now, is he not?" She carefully hid the overwhelming surge of hope, said it as if it were all the same if he was or was not.

"Yes. In fact I believe he will join us any minute," Lucretia said. "The maps of the citadel tunnels you left strewn about this house were *very* helpful in determining where to place our defenses. And when *my* husband arrives, with reinforcements, I will send you both to Honorius."

"Really," Julia said incuriously. "I thought you'd have something more interesting in mind than running back to Honorius like a dog to its master. I suppose not all of us can be credited with imagination."

"It would seem your brother's power base is stronger than I thought. The future is with him." A heavy knock sounded at the door. Lucretia smiled. "Ah. There he is now."

Two centurions entered, a man's limp body braced between them, bronze-blond hair falling forward. It took Julia a shocked moment to realize it was Alaric.

"Did you enjoy watching Cornelius get devoured?" Lucretia asked, tapping her manicured nails lightly against the table. "It would amuse me to see you watch someone you love die screaming, as I did."

One of the centurions gripped Alaric's hair with a mailed fist and hauled his head up. His face was streaked with blood; but he was alive. His blue eyes blazed with rage.

He was alive. Julia nearly fainted in relief.

Lucretia's eyes were on her, missing nothing. Julia knew this game. She had played it as a child, when her father had a favorite tutor whipped in punishment for her transgressions. She had done it as an adult too, to protect those who depended on her.

She understood with riveting clarity that if she betrayed any feeling for Alaric, Lucretia would torture him to death in front of her. She must *not* fail him.

She examined her nails. Every inch the bored, dissolute princess. "I'm afraid you misconstrue me, Lucretia. I do not love him."

Lucretia laughed. "That is a lie, my dear. I could see it in the way your face heated and your voice trembled with awe when you spoke of him the day I came. Like a lovestruck, green girl." She smirked. "You said you would die for him."

Julia shrugged indifferently. "Then my act was good enough to fool even you. Did you see how close his men were listening? There has never been a moment when I was not surveilled." She took a languid sip of her wine. "Don't be naive, Lucretia. I used him. That's all. I seduced him and made him love me. I had to."

"Well then, my dear. You won't mind if I rearrange his features, will you?" Lucretia raised a finger. "Verinus, bring the hot metal. I think we'll start with his eyes." The centurion reached for a long piece of metal that had been warming in a brazier, and brought it up to Alaric's face. He didn't even flinch at the heat.

Julia tensed. *"Wait."*

"Is that sentiment I see, my dear?" Lucretia's razor-sharp tone raised every hair on Julia's arms. "Surely not."

"No. Don't be ridiculous." Julia rolled her eyes. "If you want to gain my brother's favor, you won't send him back blinded. Find him a doctor, give him food and water, and bring him back to health. My brother will hardly want him ruined when he could do the ruining himself."

"A compelling argument," Lucretia murmured. "But I was *so* looking forward to seeing your husband tortured. I hate to be robbed of my simple pleasures."

"Domina?" The centurion held up the hot poker. "I'd love to blind this bastard."

Alaric stared past the poker as if it didn't exist. His eyes were on her.

Julia drummed her fingers on the arm of her couch as if bored. Alaric had adopted just this affectation at that banquet in Ravenna, all that time ago. Surely he would recognize it. "Let me do it. I know exactly how far to go without incurring my brother's displeasure. This brute would go too far."

"Hmm. I had never imagined you shared your brother's *proclivities*." Lucretia raised a brow. "Well? Go on."

Julia rose to her feet and approached her husband. The seething rage in his blue eyes nearly scorched her to the floor. *He knows it's an act*, she thought wildly. *Surely he does.*

But she wasn't so sure.

She halted in front of him and held his burning gaze. "Do you trust me?" she asked him quietly. "Now you must."

Then she took the iron and laid it against his chest.

Alaric did not scream; he did not even flinch.

"Oh, darling," Lucretia spoke from behind her. "That was pathetic. Let me show you how." She grasped Julia's hand and drove the iron hard into Alaric's chest.

The sizzle of burning flesh filled the room and nausea clawed up her throat. Alaric's jaw clenched; his body went rigid with pain. It was long minutes before she finally let go.

"There," she said. "A fitting punishment for a man who ravaged all of Italy, is it not?" Alaric's gaze was only on Julia, with so much blazing hatred that she took a step back. Lucretia flicked her fingers at the guards. "This game has ceased to be amusing," she murmured. "Send him away."

Alaric fainted on the way to the prisons beneath the citadel. He came to himself lying on his back on hard stone. Every inch of him hurt.

The Roman soldiers had been waiting when they'd emerged from the tunnels. It was almost as if they'd been warned.

Alaric's had been vastly outnumbered, corralled in a narrow space; he'd lost sight of the twins. He'd taken a vicious beating. Blood still covered his face from a cut to the scalp.

He thought of Julia with her maps. She knew exactly where those tunnels were too. *She* could have warned Lucretia's men.

The hole in his chest hurt the most. It screamed from even the barest contact with his shredded shirt. He shut his eyes and it didn't make a damn difference in the blackness.

Julia. With his eyes closed he could still see her, lounging on that satin couch, every inch the Roman princess he'd first met with her red-gold curls spilling down her back, that cruel little smile lifting her red lips. What she'd said had been seared into his mind as if with hot metal.

I used him. That's all. I seduced him and made him love me. I had to.

Fuck. He'd been right about her in the beginning. After everything they'd been through, after the war he had fought with his own heart. In truth, she was only another child of Theodosius. Ataulf had been right. She'd made him mistrust and drive away his best friend and chieftains. She'd made him risk his kingship. *Fuck.*

The darkness pushed in on him as if it had its own weight. Somewhere water dripped and rodents scurried in secret places. The rats would come for him soon, if he continued to give a credible impression of a corpse.

She enspelled you, Calthrax whispered. So quiet and sibilant it could have been the rats. *She cast a spell, just as Ataulf said.*

"Superstitious horseshit." But the rage—the *hurt*—that rose up in him this time created a new pain that rivaled the burn in his chest. It drove him to try to stand just to escape it.

The moment he did, the black rushed in on him and pain filled his world.

The next time Alaric opened his eyes, there was light in the room. Smell of burning lamp oil. He forced himself to sit up. The effort didn't make him faint this time.

Between the bars of his cell, he could see two guards sitting at a table with a single dim lamp between them, staring at a *latrones* board and muttering to each other in broken Dacian-inflected Latin. One man barrel-chested and potbellied like an aging gladiator; the other wiry and dark with a skinny neck. A pile of coin gleamed between them.

Beyond, Horsa and Hengist stood watching the game from behind the bars of the other cell. Alaric nearly fainted in relief. *They lived.* There was a purpling bruise extending down Hengist's neck, and he didn't like how Horsa was holding his arm. But they lived.

Somewhere, something was burning. Ataulf had likely set fire to the houses outside the citadel. If he could get himself and the twins out of this place, perhaps the original plan could still work.

But first he had unfinished business with his *wife*.

Alaric leaned against the bars, watching the guards in their oily circle of light. They drank from a clay jug of wine—rotgut stuff like they had in the army, barely more than vinegar. He could smell it. They were bored and drunk. That could easily be channeled into belligerence.

Alaric raised his eyes to the twins and laid a finger to his throat, drawing it across. The boys did not have to be told twice.

"Hey. Ugly," Hengist whispered, in the same bastard Latin the guards used. Both of the guards' heads snapped up. "He's cheating."

The wiry one narrowed his eyes to slits. "You cheating, Raskus?"

"No. Not him." Horsa gave him a jagged smile. "You, my friend."

The aging gladiator, Raskus, glanced up. "If you're cheating me, Dagomar, I'll kill you."

"Don't listen to him," Dagomar said. "They're just trying to rile you up."

"We're not," Hengist said, yawning widely. "I saw him slip

a piece in his sleeve. We used to cheat like that when we besieged Verona."

"How do you think he won all that gold?" Horsa added. "He's
not the better player."

Carefully, so as not to attract notice, Alaric ripped a piece of
cloth off his tunic and wrapped one end around his fist.

"Fuck you," spat Dagomar. "I never cheated."

"Let me see your sleeve, Dag."

"You calling me a liar?"

In an instant they were shoving each other across the table, the
jug of wine shattering on the floor. The big one hit the bars of
Alaric's cell with a *thud*. Alaric was ready. He looped the length
of cloth around the man's neck and jerked back.

The sound of gruesome choking echoed off the close walls.

Dagomar hurled himself at his friend, trying to pull him out
of Alaric's grip. He only succeeded in making the strangulation
go quicker. Raskus flailed, knocking over a chair, then kicking
Dagomar in the stomach. The man went staggering, his back
hitting the bars on the opposite side. Horsa caught him, choking him out, using the weight of his own forearm. He slumped
lifeless to the ground and Hengist had his hands through the
bars, rummaging in Dagomar's pocket for the key.

"The other one must have it," Hengist muttered. "Hurry and
kill him, will you?"

Easier said than done. Dagomar had a skinny neck, but
Raskus's was meaty and full of muscle. Alaric got one hand to
the side of the man's head—Raskus tried to *bite* him, almost
took a chunk out of his forearm—and it was all he could do
to get the leverage to snap the man's neck. It was not a pretty
death. When he was finally slumped against the bars with his
head twisted nearly all the way around, Alaric turned the corpse
over to rifle through his clothes.

Raskus did not have the keys either. He drove a fist into the
stone wall. *Fuck.*

"You'll break your hand," Hengist said mildly.

Horsa gripped the bars and rattled them savagely, cursing. "There must be a way out. There *must* be."

"Keep calm, Horsa."

"He says *keep calm* as if he didn't just break his own fist."

Alaric gritted his teeth. "Get me that dagger off the Dacian's belt." Maybe he could dig one of these bars out of its socket.

The door swung open and a cloaked figure stepped into the room. It was Bromios, Ataulf's shifty-eyed lover. He stopped on the threshold and cast an eye over the two corpses in the wrecked room, a disreputable grin on his lips.

"What a mess you three made. I suppose you were looking for this?" He held up his hand, a ring of keys swinging from his fingers. "You wouldn't believe what I had to do to get it."

CHAPTER FORTY-ONE

Julia huddled on the floor of her cell and listened to the battle raging outside. By now the sounds should be familiar—the screams and shouts of men. The clash of weapons and the whirring *hiss* of arrows. But she was still not used to it. Sometimes it seemed as if the battle might be going on right outside her door. Julia did not dare look out the windows.

The guards outside were Lucretia's. The way they'd looked at her when they'd shoved her into the cell—the disgusting things they'd said—Julia shuddered to think what they'd do to her if Lucretia won this battle. Somehow Julia doubted the other woman would stop them from acting on their worst impulses.

But if Alaric won, perhaps her fate would be worse.

Julia pressed her hands to her eyes. She had never *seen* him look at her with such menace—such scorching contempt. *He's been angry with me before,* she told herself. *Surely he'll see that I was only trying to save his life.*

The light stretched long and red across the flagstone floor.

Somehow she slept, her back to the cold stone wall.

She woke to a massive crash outside her cell. Metal clashing against metal. Something hit the door with a *thud* that seemed to shake the building. Then—a muffled groan. A red pool spread beneath the door.

Julia scrambled to her feet just as the door banged open. A dark figure stood framed in the low light, his sword held low and bare, blood dripping from its tip. Blue eyes blazing out of the dark.

"Hello, wife."

Alaric stepped over the still-warm corpses of the guards and halted on the threshold, shoving his sword back into its scabbard. Julia stood in the center of the room, red hair loose down her back, her nightdress slipping off one pale, silken shoulder.

The hole in his chest still burned.

Even now, knowing how she'd betrayed him, she still held that supernatural pull over him. He ached to hold her, to protect her. To lose himself in her. The air tasted of ash and murder. A distance away, by the gate, he could hear the sounds of battle. He didn't give a damn. The whole citadel could go up in flames around him and he would let it burn.

"Alaric. You're hurt." Her eyes traveled, with a credible impression of horror, from his battered face to the rest of him, and now she was rushing toward him, the consummate actress, her hands flat on his stomach. Burning their own shape into his skin. "Let me—"

He curled a hand around her throat and backed her up against the wall.

"Give me one good reason to let you live."

A defiant half smile lifted her lips and suddenly the pretense of concern was gone. "You think I haven't been ready to die? Whatever you do to me, it would be a mercy compared to what my brother would do."

"Don't be so sure." His hand tightened convulsively around

her neck, his eyes fixed on her mouth, on the racing butterfly pulse at the base of her throat. He wanted to crush her tight in his arms and howl like an animal. To send her so far from him that not even the stars could find her. He'd lost his bleeding *mind*.

"I never turned on you. Do you not see that? I was trying to save your *life*."

"Did you let the Romans into the city to save my life as well?" His thumb traced the outline of her red lips; he felt her pulse accelerate under his hands. "Lie to me, Julia."

"*I'm not lying*. I let Lucretia in to help with the aqueduct. I did it for *you*, Alaric—"

He leaned in, close enough to smell roses and sweat and beneath it the riot of her fear. Already he'd had enough of her lies. "I changed my mind," he muttered. "Shut up."

Then he took her mouth. The force of his kiss drove her against the wall. He felt her grunt, felt the shock of her collision with the hard stone at her back. He kissed her savagely, plundering her mouth like he'd plunder a city, his other hand clenched hard in the wealth of her hair.

Julia met him in his rage. This was not love; it was *war*. She ripped at his shirt, unmindful of his wounds, tearing at his skin in her rush to get it off him. When she bit down on his lip, lust and rage ripped through him, made his vision go black with it. He needed her fast. Needed her *now*, up against this wall. His control rode on a knife edge, but if he let her go, he'd drown.

She was cursing him now. In Latin and Hunnic and Gothic, everything she'd learned on the road, her nails digging into his scalp. He laughed darkly and pulled down the neck of her dress; took her breasts until she was arching up into his mouth, her head thrown back and gasping his name. When he rose to his full height and lifted her up against the wall, her thighs in his hard grip, she was wet as a river.

He drove all the way into her in one single, brutal thrust. Her back arched, her eyelids fluttering, and her hot little mouth kept up its cursing. *Gods*, he couldn't get enough of her; he'd *never* get enough of her even as he knew—some detached, dark part of him knew—that she would destroy him. He didn't care about that, only about battering down every defense she had until she was gasping and shuddering. "*Harder*, you bastard," she whispered, all smoke and sex, earth and ash and his own ruin. He answered her with everything, all he had entirely until she was trembling around him, her nails digging convulsively into the skin of his shoulders as he drove himself over and over into her hot, shuddering tightness.

When he came in her, it nearly killed him. The pleasure nearly blacked out the world.

When it was over, he stood holding her against the wall for a long moment, their foreheads pressed together, their breaths mingling in the dim light of the siege fire. His trousers were barely undone in his terrible, world-wrecking haste. A ruinous urge filled him to lean in and kiss her long and sweet and soft. To swear his own life for hers.

This woman was poison.

Abruptly he let her down. He turned to arrange himself, and when he turned back, she was watching him with green eyes gleaming like a trapped animal.

"Can we talk?"

"No, woman. I will talk and you will listen," he said. "In the next few hours, I *will* have this city back. You are my wife and you will stay my wife. Once I get a child out of you, I'll put you in the furthest tower I can find and forget you ever existed."

A calm, cold mask descended over her, sleek as marble. "Suit yourself," she said, with perfect, chilling indifference. "Better there be no lies about what is between us, don't you think?"

Of course I acted like I loved him. Did you see how close his men were listening?

Alaric drew a breath. She knew exactly how to play on his emotions. Even now, if he took her again, he'd be lost.

He didn't have to belong to her. He would make of his heart a walled city. "Yes. Far better." He stepped over the threshold, over the bodies of the two men he'd killed to get to her, shutting the door behind him. Then he walked into the burning citadel.

Anywhere was safer than in here.

When the sun rose, Julia knew that Alaric had taken back the citadel.

From the single window she saw the sunrise over the ravaged rooftops, over a new line of bodies high on the outer wall. Ten or so Roman centurions, still wearing their gleaming armor. And the one on the end was Lucretia. She had been hoisted up on a pole with the others, bare feet dangling above stone, staring bent-necked and blind up at the sky. Someone had cut her throat.

There was no question who Noricum belonged to now. The dread barbarian who had paced the battle line outside Milan, outside Verona, catapulting corpses into the Roman cities. The man he had been all along. Alaric of the Goths.

Her legs gave out beneath her and she sank to the cold floor. Lucretia could have been a hostage, used to barter their way out of a siege. Instead Alaric had simply cut her throat and hung her up there, facing the west, the direction Roman reinforcements would come from. A dare, thrown in the Romans' teeth.

She had a terrible suspicion he would do the same to her when Stilicho came for her.

Julia let her fingertips graze the tender skin of her throat and a dark thrill shot down her spine. Alaric had fucked her hard against the wall, with a violence she'd barely withstood. Her orgasm had come like a world-ending cataclysm. Her calves were still viciously sore from the cramping.

Wine and opium held no grip on her like he did. He was an addiction, a dark thing in her blood she could not root out.

Lucretia had been right. Love ruined her. *That* was ruin.

Julia let out a low sob. She had thought she could prove herself to him and make him love her, make him trust her. She'd forgotten what he was. A barbarian to the core, as brutal as he'd always been. He'd never loved her, had never *thought* to love her.

Once I get a child out of you, I'll put you in the furthest tower I can find and forget you ever existed.

So he had meant those harsh words after all, in his speech on the first day they'd arrived. She *was* simply a means to an end for him. Her greatest fears had come true—to be shunted to the side, forced to live a stilted, proscribed life, cut off from joy or freedom. Imprisoned. It had been exactly why she hadn't wanted Olympius. What difference between that life and this one?

I love him. That's what's different. Loving Alaric made everything so much worse.

All day, Julia waited in agony, pacing ruts into the floor of her cell. Alaric didn't come.

It was night before the door opened. She turned from the window, her stomach flipping convulsively, her knees suddenly weak with longing and fear and need.

But it wasn't Alaric. Bromios stood in the doorway, dark circles under his eyes. "Julia. Thank the gods you're still alive. Listen, the city is back under Alaric's control. They're celebrating on the parade grounds. The gates are unwatched and refugees are streaming out in droves. If you're going to go, it must be *now*."

"I can't just leave—this is *my* kingdom." She sucked in a breath. "Where would I go?"

"Are you really this foolish?" Bromios cursed. "I watched Alaric cut Lucretia's throat himself. How long do you think it'll be before it's *you* up on that wall?"

He was looking at her with pity. *Pity.* It was this that broke her.

Briefly Bromios touched her face. She had always known, deep down, what he was; there was no relationship with him that was not transactional. But there was fondness in his eyes now, even affection. "I am sorry that this did not turn out as you hoped."

She shut her eyes. Behind her lids, she throttled her love until it was dead.

"Me too," she said quietly. "Thank you. You have been a good friend."

He thrust a bundle into her arms. Clothes—a man's tunic and trousers, sturdy boots and—by the gods—Alaric's old cloak. There was a sack of food and a waterskin, the pouch Julia had carried all this way, with Calthrax's finger-bone flute in it. Here was even the small knife Horsa had given her, shoved into one of the boots.

"I raided your old bedroom. Change your clothes and hurry," Bromios said grimly. "I will cause a distraction."

Alaric slept badly—*badly* meaning *not at all*. There was violence in him when he went to sleep, and he woke at war with himself. The air in his war tent was hot and close; the place had become a torture chamber.

He *ached* for her.

Alaric rose, pulled on trousers, and thrust aside the hide flap, striding into the airless night. He turned his eye toward the west, the direction where Lucretia had assured him her husband would come, just before he'd cut her throat. He and the Roman settlement had lived in uneasy coexistence for too long. Now the first thing that Roman general saw would be his wife up on that wall. Let there be no pretense of coexistence now.

Alaric knew he should be watching for the dust that would rise from five thousand horses striking hooves to the bare earth. But instead his gaze kept going toward the rooftop of Julia's manor house. Of course she'd betrayed him. She was Theodosius's daughter, after all. She had only done what was in her nature to do.

His body was tight with need. Healers had put salve to his burn, but it did nothing to ease the vicious sting of it. And there could be no salve for Julia's betrayal. No salve to ease a lifetime of sleepless nights, wracked with guilt and hate and reckless want. No salve but her.

He could stand this no longer. He needed her again.

It didn't have to be more than sex. It *wasn't* more than sex, he told himself. He'd get her with child, and then he'd be done with her. It wasn't love; it was pure utilitarian need.

He needed to know if it was making her mad too.

Of course not, said Calthrax, the dark shadow dogging his steps. *She enspelled you.*

"I don't give a fuck if she did." He hadn't stopped feeling her nails digging into his skin. Her little white teeth at his throat. He hadn't stopped feeling her hot clenching passage closing around him, drawing him deeper, even as she cursed him out. In bed there were no walls between them. At least there was that.

His hands clenched into fists. What need had he for a kingdom? He could put her before him on Hannibal's back and ride out of here now. Before dawn. Go quickly, before anyone knew they were gone. And then he could sate his addiction for her in peace.

He was halfway down the hill before he saw the flames rising from the roof of Julia's prison.

By the time he got to the building, flames had swallowed the roof and billowed out of every window. One of the guards ran out of the smoke, his face red from the heat. "We could not get to her," he said hoarsely. "The fire grew too fast, and—"

Alaric barely heard him. *He had locked her in there.* He'd shut the door himself.

A roaring sound filled his ears.

His mind was full of Julia. Julia red-haired and laughing, dancing with Berig at Brisca's fire. Julia standing proud and fierce before his axes. Julia in the mountains, lying flushed beneath him as he begged her never to leave him. Julia with ink smudges on her cheeks and her eyes bright, entrusting him with her grand vision for his city. Their people. *His* woman. He could not let it end like this. Not when the last words he'd said to her were full of hate.

Ataulf was at his back, pulling him away from his headlong plunge toward the fire. "You fucking idiot. She's dead already," he was screaming. "Do you want to die with her?"

Alaric jerked himself out of Ataulf's grip and ran forward into all that heat and light, his *seax* drawn as if he could beat back death with it.

CHAPTER FORTY-TWO

Julia was long through the gates and down onto the wreckage-strewn plain before she dared look back.

She'd slipped in with the crowds pouring out of the city, the hood of her cloak concealing her face and hair. Nobody stopped her; no one even looked at her twice. Now she walked amidst hundreds of blank-faced refugees. None of them spared her a glance. Why would they? She was just one of many fleeing the destruction Alaric had wrought.

Behind her, she could still see the city looming over the blasted valley. A column of smoke rose thick from the walls as if breathed from the mouth of hell. Somewhere far above, a hawk screamed and shattered the eerie quiet, carrying all the way to the low, parched hills.

Alaric had taught her how to be on the road. He'd taught her to set one foot in front of the other, to go on through grinding hunger and thirst. How to sleep on the ground, without fearing the bugs and the dirt.

Hundreds had fled Noricum once war erupted in the streets;

hundreds more came from the north and east, fleeing the Huns. Everywhere, on the vast scorched plain haunted by broken war machines, wandered refugees alone and in groups, trudging through the dust with their meager belongings on their backs, all of them with that empty stare that spoke of the terrible things they'd seen.

She had a stare like that now. But she was not the same. The ransom was still out there. Her life depended on not being noticed. Everyone seemed to be part of some group, but Julia avoided those. She no longer trusted anyone, most especially men.

In the first week, she ran out of food.

Hunger was a gnawing thing, the feeling of her stomach devouring itself because it had nothing else. All she could think about was food. All the decadent feasts she'd been subjected to in Ravenna, when she'd lounged and yawned and eaten nothing—she should have devoured everything. As she walked, her imagination filled with delicacies. Baked swan stuffed with sea urchins. Eel in cream sauce. She'd always hated eel. Now she would eat one alive and squirming.

In the second week, she saw her first dead body by the side of the road. It was a child, his eyes open and flies crawling on his face. Others came after that—an old man in a ditch, a few others in a copse where Julia went to find water. One wrong step and that would be her, lying by the roadside with no kin to bury her.

Sometimes she took refuge in memories of being in Alaric's arms. Julia found that her imagination was vivid; she could half close her eyes and imagine his arms around her, his mouth on her, what he felt like deep inside her. The tenderness in his eyes when he'd told her she should have been a general.

I've never seen anything so brave and wonderful as you. Those words kept her alive.

Some days she hoped—*believed*—he would come riding after

her. How could he not, after all that had passed between them? But the days went by and he did not come. *It's just your love for him dying*, she told herself when the old longing flared up. Eventually it subsided to a dull ache, eclipsed by hunger, which faded but would not go away.

Love was nothing but a lie after all. She'd been unforgivably foolish to believe anything else.

The hunger was bad, but the thirst was worse.

In the second week, she ran out of water and could not find more. The thirst dwarfed the hunger, devoured it. All the rivers were dry or fouled by the dead. Finally—after three weeks on the road—Julia sat on a low stone wall, her flask dry as dust, her tongue swollen in her mouth, her head pounding viciously—from thirst, not wine. If she did not drink, she would die.

If I die out here, nobody will know. Alaric wouldn't know.

She pulled his cloak up over her head. It still smelled of him, somehow: leather and pine trees and wide-open spaces. She shut her eyes and imagined him riding up on Hannibal, reaching down and pulling her to safety, to shelter, to some world-wrecking adventure. She imagined the Alaric who had offered her food on the road, which she had refused. This had been his first act of caring, before he could express it in any other way.

No. He had never cared for her. Keeping her alive was a means to an end.

Maybe it's easier if I just lie down here in the shadow of this wall.

As soon as she had the thought, another came fast on its heels. *Get up, Julia.* Alaric's voice. She raised her head—it felt like a monumental effort—and something caught her eye, up the slope. A green cluster of trees amidst a slope of brown.

Where there was green, there was water.

The spring burst from beneath a birch tree—sweeter, more intoxicating than the finest Caecuban. How had she given her allegiance to wine? Water had been here all along. The best and only drink. She filled her flask, then washed the back of her neck, shivered as ice-cold springwater ran down her spine.

When she raised her eyes, a man was watching her. Tall and broad at the chest, his hair dark and curling at his sunburned neck. He took a step toward her as one might approach a nervous horse.

In an instant she had Horsa's knife out of her boot.

"Easy, girl. I won't hurt you." He spoke in gutter Latin. "Are you alone?"

Men were always asking if she was alone. By answer, Julia shifted her stance, her knife held low and businesslike, as Horsa had taught her.

Touch me and you'll lose a finger. That was what her stance said.

The man halted. "Come with me if your belly is empty. I have food and a warm fire." He held out a hand. "You have a husband? He's no worry of mine. A man only keeps what he can hold in this world." He took another step toward her, and Julia felt a dizzying surge of fear. All Horsa's directions—*do it before he sees the knife; press here at the throat; don't let him see, don't make him mad*—cascaded in her mind.

Julia raised the knife and held it to her own throat.

The man frowned. His eyes fell to her blade, and for a minute Julia dared not breathe.

Finally, after interminable time, he took a step back. "Too skinny to be this much trouble," he muttered. "By Cernunnos, woman. I meant you no harm."

He stamped off down the slope. Julia breathed a sigh of relief.

"Now, why did you do that?"

A voice at her back. Julia turned, her knife up, but this time it was a woman—dark hair cut short, cheekbones hollow. The woman gave a strange, ironic half smile that would not have been out of place in the court at Ravenna. "You can put it away. I won't attack."

Warily, Julia slid the knife back in her boot.

"Why did you drive him off?" The woman knelt and filled her waterskin. "It's dangerous to walk these roads without protection. And you have none."

"I don't like men."

"No one likes men. Most don't get to forswear them entirely. Have you taken vows?"

Julia did not answer. Her throat felt dry. Speaking felt like an alien act.

The woman stood and started back down the slope. "You can come with us if you want," she said without turning around. "We're all women. No men to talk to."

There was a donkey cart at the bottom of the hill. The donkey stood in the stays, eyes at half-mast, one back foot cocked as if sleeping where he stood. A group of women were making a camp around him. One of them—a tall, red-haired Thracian— took one assessing look at Julia and pressed a leather flask into her hand. "You look like you need this."

It was liquor—not quite as strong as *ealu*, but with a fierce, fiery bite. As night fell, Julia joined the women around a fire, passing the flask at the end of days.

There were about twenty of them. Some were Roman women who had lived in Noricum when Alaric besieged the city. They spoke of how they had run to the rooftops, throwing down anything on the attacking Goths—heavy roof tiles, pottery, torches—until the Goths started setting the houses on fire.

The Thracian woman told a tale of fleeing from the Huns, who had killed everyone in her village in their inexorable sweep west. And others had followed Alaric's army for years, until the Romans took Noricum. They hadn't wanted to be enslaved, and had lost hope of ever finding a homeland.

"Alaric doesn't want a homeland," Julia said quietly. "No—

that's not true. He wants a homeland, but he doesn't know how to live in one. All he knows is war."

The women's eyes were all on her now. "And what is your story, then?"

"She doesn't owe anyone her story," the Thracian said harshly.

"No. It's all right." They had shared their food and drink; she had little else to offer in return. "I'm Roman. From Ravenna, although I was born in Rome." She stuck scrupulously to her gutter Latin; the palace accent would require explanation. "I followed Alaric, and I did it of my own will. I—I fell in love." It hurt to admit it. That love was still there, aching under her skin, of no use at all. She had not truly killed it, only buried it alive like a misbehaving vestal.

"You remind me of someone." The Thracian woman's eyes narrowed. "King Alaric's bride. The Roman princess."

Silence fell. That old, brittle laugh came easily to Julia's lips, her first weapon. "I've never been confused with a princess. That is flattering."

Suddenly the women were all talking at once. *I heard that she rode through the city like a queen out of legend. I heard she was the one who let the Romans in. And then King Alaric locked her in the palace. Maybe she's dead. Probably better off. I shouldn't like to be married to him.*

Julia took another sip of the Thracian liquor. "I suppose she got what she deserved. Good riddance."

Her old self *had* died in that city. It was time she put that foolish girl to rest.

A week went by and Julia traveled with the women. They foraged together and shared a fire at night, swapping stories of siege and war. There was a sameness to these days that felt strangely comforting, but Julia knew they would soon end.

They were coming to the foothills. Eventually she would have to make a decision.

At first she'd barely been able to consider beyond the present. But as the mountains drew closer, Julia began to give thought to her future. She had no blessed idea where she was going. And who would have her? Who would willingly stand against Honorius's wrath? Only Alaric could have done it, and Alaric was lost to her now. There was no one else.

But of course that was not true. Brisca would not turn her away; nor would she sell her back to Honorius. But getting there would not be simple. The mountains were vast and treacherous. She would need a guide. But Julia recoiled from the thought of trusting anyone, especially a man. *You could seduce one*, said the Cleopatra voice. *Make him love you.* Julia recoiled at the thought. She had played that game and lost badly.

One night, as the women lay sleeping, Julia walked off by herself toward the rising hills. She slipped her hand into the bag at her waist, and her fingers closed around Calthrax's finger bone.

Play it in the mountains if you have the need, and we will find you.

She raised the flute to her lips and blew. What emerged was a thin, pathetic whistle; nothing like the oscillating birdsong that Alaric had played. Pathetic.

Julia shoved the flute back in her bag, feeling ridiculous. She was doomed after all.

CHAPTER FORTY-THREE

In the weeks after Julia died, Alaric had to kill two of his own chieftains. One who challenged his rule, calling down the ancient tradition of *holmgang*. Another after an assassin came for him at dinner and he almost took a blade in the ribs. This time, the assassin didn't die before Riga tortured his employer out of him. Now there were two more bodies on the wall.

In his heart, he hoped one of them would kill him. It would end the horrible torment his life had become. Some days, when his mood was darkest—when the dead called loudest from out of the shadows—he considered ending it himself. It would be easy enough; he wasn't the boy he'd been in the arena. He knew now how to die.

Even so. Alaric was a warrior. His own pride *demanded* that he find his death at the end of a spear. So he took every challenge as far as he could; escalated every confrontation to a war; led his men on the most dangerous raids.

The wound on his chest was healing, but it still burned painfully. It was a vicious reminder of Julia's treachery. In his mind, she was Theodosius's child, the betraying enemy; the copper-haired goddess in his arms; the excitable girl whose eyes lit like stars as she explained aqueducts to him. He reeled between love and hate, and could not answer what she was to him.

He could not resolve this war within himself. So he would rain down fire on the world. He would burn it to its foundations. In a scant few months, Stilicho would come down from the mountains and put him out of his misery, but Alaric did not want to give the old man the satisfaction.

So he went seeking his own death.

One night out of all the other nights, Alaric lounged in the chair Wallia had once occupied. The warriors were in an uproar, drinking and bellowing their war songs as a man was dragged from the room, a long crimson streak of blood gleaming on the white marble. Another challenger. This one only a little older than the twins, and doing it for the glory. Alaric didn't *think* he'd killed him. But he'd not been as careful with his blade as he would have been, once.

He raised his horn to his lips, his eyes hooded, legs stretched out lazily before him. To any watching, he might appear bored.

In reality he was thinking of Julia. He could not stop imagining what she might have gone through, shut in that burning building. How the smoke must have filled her lungs. The despair of knowing there was no way out—hoping for his rescue, and he had never come for her. When he thought of how it had been him to lock her in—

He replaced that memory with one of her from life, and that was almost more painful. Still, he could not look away. Julia rising from the river, her hair streaming down her back, all of it in meticulous detail. He should have taken her in his arms right then and tried his hardest to make her love him. He'd wanted to remake the city, the world, into a place she could be safe in. He'd thought they had so much more *time*.

Then he remembered the way she'd laughed with that Roman

woman who now decorated his wall. Sharp as broken glass, mocking him for loving her in the first place. Fury rose and burned the grief to ash.

Riga sat beside him, laughing at the carnage. A ruby of obscene size gleamed on his chest; gold glinted in his ears and winked on his hands. Two women draped themselves in his lap, a blonde and a brunette, kissing each other with furious abandon. Riga didn't seem to mind; he rested a hand casually on the brunette's thigh. "Continue as you are, ladies," he said merrily. "When I'm ready, prepare yourselves." He turned to Alaric, one dark eyebrow smugly raised. "Where's your wench?"

Alaric's hand tightened convulsively on his drinking horn. "Where did you get that fucking ruby?"

"I rifled through your things. I take my plunder wherever I can."

"It's Julia's."

"She would want me to have it." Riga laughed easily. "Cheer up. Isn't my way a vast improvement?" He swept a hand to indicate the chaos before them, nearly dislodging the women from his lap. "The warriors *love* you. And the ones who'd deny your rule are dead or driven off, which certainly makes things easier."

Alaric raised the horn to his lips. "Damned if I'll ever understand men or women."

"It's very simple, my friend. *You* lead the raids. *You* find the plunder. All their wealth, their honor, their glory comes from you now. You are the ring-giver. It's far more effective than banning plunder and insisting on taking only grain."

Riga was right. It was dark irony that to truly seize power in Noricum, he'd had to become everything he had fought against. He'd even let the walls lie unrepaired. He could hear Julia's voice in his mind. *You were just a barbarian after all. Never capable of anything better. My father and I were right about you.*

The potent mead pounded through him. He understood why Julia drank so much now—to make herself forget the death of her old lover in the arena. Perhaps he was the one Julia had truly loved. It was good he was dead, or Alaric would have to find him and kill him on principle.

"Alaric." Ataulf stood before him, looking exhausted. "We must discuss the grain. We're running low—"

"Later."

"No, *now*. Three days you've been ignoring me. If Thorismund was here—"

"Thorismund *isn't* here," Alaric growled. Thorismund had gone in the night, after a fierce raging argument, in which he'd blamed Alaric for Julia's death. *Fuck* him. If Thorismund ever darkened his threshold again, Alaric would put him in the ground. As far as he was concerned, Thorismund was already dead. "I forbid the mention of his name within these walls."

Riga looked up from nuzzling the neck of one of the women. "I never liked that hulking lout anyway. Too full of himself and his gods."

"Alaric. The grain." Ataulf said it with a kind of tight-lipped persistence. "You've taken the bulk of it to feed the warriors and now the refugees are starving. The riots are worse than ever. A whole neighborhood burned down last night."

Alaric laughed. Thank the gods, an easy problem. "Let them eat the corpse dogs. There are more than enough of those." *One child for the slaver's block, one dog for the roasting spit.* "We'll set bowmen on the dogs, and then distribute their meat among the people."

"You'd waste arrows on dogs?"

"What else would you have me do? The land is ravaged. There is nothing in a fifty-mile radius to eat. Let the people eat the dogs. It solves two problems."

"If people wanted to eat the dogs, they don't need your permission. You cannot simply order them to—"

"And why not?" Several people glanced over at his tone.

"Back in the camps, we were *lucky* if we had dog meat. When I was a boy—"

"You don't have to describe it to me. I was there, you pathetic drunkard." Ataulf seized his shoulders. "*Will* you snap out of it? We fought the Empire so we'd never be in that position again. If your people are reduced to eating dogs, we've failed. We've *failed*, Alaric."

"Touch me again, Ataulf, and I'll let Riga cut off your hands," Alaric said coldly. "Get out."

"Out of this room or out of this city?" Ataulf snapped. "Seems to me you're bleeding allies."

"This is the only ally I need." His hand strayed to his knife.

"Not even your thrice-cursed Roman *wife* would have approved of this," Ataulf said in a low voice. And then he was gone.

Much later, Alaric stalked the hallways, stepping over snoring bodies. He wasn't drunk enough to fall asleep in this manor house that stank of beer and sweat.

Maybe he would take a woman to his bed tonight. There were plenty; even some of the warriors' wives had made overtures. He didn't fool himself that they wanted *him*—it was proximity to power they wanted, or safety, or both. But that was what Julia had wanted too, and he hadn't given a fuck. He'd been happy enough to have her, no matter her reasons.

He *should* have a new woman. He should have a dozen.

Outside the manor, the city stank of death and open sewage and he thought again of Julia's aqueduct. Its crumbling bones stood black against the sky. He wanted to tear it down.

A dark shape stood in the moon-drowned street, amidst the cracked cobblestones. For a moment his heart leaped and he hoped—he *hoped*—it was Julia's ghost. Since she died, he'd believed she would haunt him. But she hadn't. He'd have paid a kingdom for Julia to haunt him.

But it wasn't her. Fucking Calthrax again.

Was Theodosius's slut of a daughter really so good that you'll stay celibate all your life out of grief for her? Blood glinted in the wound Alaric had put in Calthrax's neck. *Perhaps I should have tried her before I died.*

"You'd have only died quicker."

Calthrax laughed. *You really are as big a fool as the rumors say. Willing to be led around on a leash for a chance to get between her legs. You didn't care how many lives it cost.*

"I risk no life save my own."

That's a lie and you know it. Thousands of our own are enslaved in Italy. Hostages, all of them. Goths. What do you think her brother will do to them when his sister isn't returned?

"The Romans need no pretext for what they do."

And neither do you. Calthrax laughed. *You did not have to kill me, for example. With very little persuasion—and the woman—I'd have told Stilicho you slipped through my fingers. He wanted that, you know. Even if he would not say it.*

"And you could have thrown off the Roman yoke and come with me at Frigidus." Alaric threw it back in his face. "You wanted to. You hated them more than I did."

Not all of us had the luxury of rebellion, Alaric. His bared teeth gleamed. *All of us were painted with your brush after you turned. I had a brother. A wife. A son—*

"You think I would not have welcomed them?" An old anger rose in his chest. "Half my army goes to war with their families trailing after. Your own would have found a place with us."

They would have found slavery and death with you, Calthrax snarled. *Everyone who follows you dies. That Roman princess was no exception.*

What the hell was he doing? Standing in the middle of the street and arguing with a ghost. "Go away," he growled, his hand on his sword, for all the fucking good it would do. "Or I'll send you back where you came from."

"Alaric?"

The world shifted beneath his feet. It was the same moon-drenched street, empty windows gaping at him like eye sockets in a line of skulls. But the shape standing before him was Horsa, pale hair spiked up silver in the moonlight.

Alaric took his hand off his sword hilt. "How long have you been there?"

"Long enough," Horsa said. "Who were you talking to?"

"Nobody." He said it in a tone that forbid further questions.

Horsa was staring as if he'd sprouted an extra eye. "Where is Hengist?"

"Out raiding." He'd told the boy already. Days ago. "Go to bed, Horsa."

Horsa smirked bitterly. "Hengist gone. Thorismund gone. Soon you'll have no one."

Alaric felt his jaw clench. He was too tired and drunk for this fucking conversation. "Do you know why I didn't send you out to raid with your brother, Horsa? You're impulsive. You put yourself in danger. You put *Julia* in danger." Grief rose up and gripped his throat. "If you'd stuck close to her when that Roman legion came, she never would have—"

"If *I'd* stayed with her? *You* were the one who left!" Horsa was in his face now. Teeth bared. Feral. "You left us both behind. I was there; I saw everything. She never betrayed you, she *loved* you."

Alaric grabbed the boy and shoved him against the nearest wall, gripping his tunic in one fist. His envy nearly crippled him. "How the fuck do you know? Is she talking to you?"

"No. She isn't *talking* to me," Horsa snarled. "Why would she talk to either one of us? I couldn't keep her safe, and you're the one who killed her."

Violence ripped through him. The argument with Thorismund thundered in his mind. *Your fault. All your fault.* He could kill Horsa out of sheer envy for having been with Julia when he had not.

Even as he had the thought, Gaufrid screamed at him from out of the dark, an arrow buried in his belly. What the fuck was he doing? His *life* had been protecting the twins.

"Get out of my sight," he growled, giving the boy a violent shove. Horsa ran off into the night, his footsteps echoing against the buildings, not looking back.

He's right, you know, came Calthrax's laughing voice, out of the shadows that gathered in the alleys. Redolent with the voices of all the dead who'd come before him.

Alaric stared down the empty street. "I know."

Chapter Forty-Four

In Julia's dream, she lay in Alaric's arms, her head on his chest, listening to the strength of his heartbeat. Their legs tangled beneath the blankets. She felt warm and protected and utterly safe.

You must wake, Julia.

"No." She breathed in, tightened her arms around him as if she could hold him there forever. "Don't go."

Wake up.

She opened her eyes and the warmth of the dream bled away. It was still night. By the faint glow of the kicked-out fires, she saw shapes running, shouting in a dozen languages. Somewhere in the dark she saw a flash—polished metal, armor.

Then all dissolved into screaming chaos.

She tried to run but didn't get ten steps.

Roman soldiers flooded the camp, rousing people from sleep, dragging them from their ragged blankets. Julia sprinted for the trees and a man leaped at her and drove her to the ground, his metal breastplate digging into her back. She hit the dirt so hard the breath was forced from her lungs. She was still heaving—

struggling to breathe—when the faceless soldier hauled her up by one arm and dragged her back.

Not an hour later, Julia sat huddled under guard amidst a group of freezing refugees. There were maybe fifty, all rounded up from the camp and the surrounding hills. The sun was just starting to rise, casting a metal-gray light over everything, and it had begun to rain. The Roman soldiers stood stoic beneath their heavy helmets.

One of the guards spoke. He was young, with a clean-shaven, square-jawed face. "You have been taken under the protection of the Empire," he said, in blade-crisp Imperial Latin. "You will not be harmed."

Beside her, a man rose to his feet. "Where will we be going?" he asked, in polite, lawyerly tones. "Where, exactly."

"To a place where you will be given food and shelter, and will work in return." The man's tone turned sardonic. "Surely none of you can object to that, given the state you are in."

Julia felt her hands clench into fists. *Slavery.* Her first instinct was to rise to her feet herself, to flash her mother's opal ring and demand to be taken to their commander.

She was halfway to her feet when the polite, lawyerly man spoke again.

"Wait! I'm a Roman citizen. A citizen! Send word to the family of Titus Publius Barius in Verona. Ask *anyone* in that town—"

The soldier glanced at a burly subordinate, who waded into the crowd and dragged the man forward. "What family is it that you come from?"

"Titus Publius Barius. In Verona. A very respected family."

But the soldier only laughed, and his subordinates stripped the man to the waist and tied his arms to a wagon. "Let *this* be the message sent to the family of Titus Publius Barius."

Then the guard shook out a scourge. The whip hit the man's back with a wet, meaty *thunk*. It seemed to go on endlessly. Julia sat very still, the sight of the man's torture burned into her eyes. The man had all but stopped screaming by the time the Roman soldiers untied his arms. He fell to the ground, his back flayed to ribbons.

Alaric's voice was all she could hear. *There are no princesses in these woods. Only predators and prey.*

All night they walked, through rain that pounded the bone-dry grass, pressing Julia's hair flat to her head. She huddled under Alaric's soaking cloak; freezing water squelched in her boots. The Romans on their horses were rain-slicked shadows, glinting with menace. She wanted to fall to her knees and give up, but she knew what happened to those who stumbled. The Romans hauled them to their feet and whipped them along, and if they fell again, they were trampled into the mud beneath the horses' hooves.

Her father never would have allowed his soldiers to treat people like this. Never would have allowed—*he would, though.* Alaric could have told her.

It was another day before they reached the mines.

Exhausted and terrified, she was herded amidst a crowd of refugees through the heavily guarded gates of a wooden enclosure. Beyond, the ground dropped into a vast pit. Watery light illuminated walls scarred and cracked; at the bottom, the condemned moved in sluggish lines, staggering under the weight of woven baskets piled high with stones. Sparkling dust filled the air. Marble dust. The air tasted dry and sharp. It hurt to breathe.

They were led into a long, low building. The woman to Julia's left had a bleeding cut on her head from a soldier's club. One of the guards—a tall, hulking man with a protuberant belly—told them that they were in a marble mine, they were to work hard, and they would be fed.

There was only one mine this close to Noricum. Lucretia's mine. Lucretia was dead but her husband was still alive. Of course, there could be no rescue by revealing herself. Lucretia's husband would be just as likely to kill her as look at her.

The guards confiscated all their belongings. Gone was the pouch with Alaric's salve and the finger-bone flute; gone was the cloak and her mother's ring. Julia stood dry-eyed as they shackled her by the ankle to the woman with the bleeding cut. The slaves—for that was what she was now, a slave in a marble mine; how Lucretia would laugh—were led from one low building into another. In the second building, a line of massive cauldrons belched steam into the air. Rough wooden benches lined the walls. They were each given a bowl and a tin cup. Julia sniffed the drink and flinched. It was *posca*, a drink made from sour wine, unwatered and foul and very, very strong. A drink for soldiers and slaves.

She took an experimental sip. The *posca* was pure fire, harsh and fierce. Scouring away all that had come before.

The scarred walls of the mining pit told a story of enslaved workers hammering pins into the weak seams in the marble, shearing it off in heavy sheets that were used to clothe the great buildings of Rome's many cities. Now the pit walls were stripped clean and the slaves were sent into tunnels, chasing veins of marble deep into the earth.

The children went the deepest. Most were between the ages of five and ten, none more than bones under translucent-thin skin. They moved with unnatural silence, their eyes huge with hunger, their skin red with welts and fleabites.

The enslaved men looked no better than the children. Their shoulders slumped; their ribs pushed at their ravaged skin. They shuffled down into the tunnels with haunted eyes, carrying wicker baskets on their backs and iron pickaxes, but there was no hint in their faces of even thinking of using them as weapons.

The tunnels were kept from flooding by a number of impressive screws, many times taller than a man, that twisted the water up and out. *Archimedes* screws. Julia had studied them as a child. She remembered sitting in a scented garden, a fountain trickling merrily nearby, dressed in the finest linen. Her nails perfect, her hair wound in flowers, her tutor droning on and *on* as she traced the line of the twisting screw on the parchment that spilled across her lap.

Now, under the overseer's gaze, Julia grasped the smooth shaft and pushed, her feet slipping on the damp stone. The *posca* gave her strength.

There was more than rotten wine in the *posca*. Long after the effect of the drink should have worn off, her thoughts had a slow, feverish cast. There was a buzzing in her head; it blended into that memory, of tracing the image of the screw on the parchment, the buzz of insects at the height of summer. Now that summer day bled into nightmare. The guards leered from out of the dark, whips in their hands; whenever someone's feet faltered, they felt the lash at their back. Julia felt it only once— a bright red fire lancing across her shoulders—and she did not falter again.

Night fell. The prisoners were herded up through the tunnels and into the uneven ground at the bottom of the pit, where marble dust hovered in the air like snow. In the long, low hall, everyone received their bowl of gristly stew and a cup of *posca*. Julia drank it greedily. Suddenly all her aches and pains diminished as fire pounded through her veins.

After, the prisoners were all brought to a dimly lit barracks that smelled of smoke and the rot of unchanged rushes. The beds were rickety towers of cots, with barely room to sleep between them. Julia and the curly-haired woman slept chained together on one cot.

Julia slept little; all night the woman next to her was gripped by ripping, convulsing coughs. That morning, Julia woke up to find she was chained to a corpse.

She needed the *posca* after that.

★ ★ ★

Time passed. Julia woke every day with a vicious headache, her tongue thick and furry in her mouth. Only the *posca* calmed the headache; only the *posca* made the world bearable.

It kept her standing when she should have collapsed. It made her mind eerily absent, so she didn't notice the hours she spent pushing the shaft that turned the screw that passaged the water up and out of the tunnels. It dulled her pain, so that she didn't notice the iron shackle digging her skin raw above the ankle. And it kept her numb to the violence around her.

People dropped like flies in this place. Some under the guards' whips; other times, the dead would be found in the night, when guards would prod those who did not rise and drag them off to be burned outside the walls.

Julia understood that she would die here.

Sometimes she thought of Alaric. He had been a child in the mines. How long had he lived like this? In moments of lucidity, she wondered. But those moments were few—and she tried to forget Alaric ever existed. It was better—kinder—to forget.

Even so, she could not. She had little willpower now, and thoughts of him rose when she was shuffling with the others down into the mines or lying on the cot, trying to sleep. She spent hours lost inside those memories—Alaric driving her to ecstasy in the warm waters of that cave, or by the cliff with eagles circling in the air, or under the driving waterfall. Whenever someone dropped dead in front of her, she could close her eyes, summon his memory, and disappear.

He was an escape. No—he was an addiction, always had been. Worse than the *posca*.

Julia understood in a kind of detached way that the Roman guards would round up refugees and bring them in to replace the dead. Some fought; once a large, muscled man put down several guards before he was whipped within an inch of his life. The guards made everyone watch. Somewhere, vaguely as if through glass, Julia remembered being made to watch such things before.

Days later, the man was shuffling down into the earth, blank-faced, open wounds glistening on his back.

Sometimes, in the hard, vicious mornings before her first drink of *posca*, Julia felt a crushing shame that *she* had not fought. She had not tried to attack the guards, not tried to escape the forced march in the rain although she'd *known* where they were heading.

The guards watched the women. It was not uncommon for one of them to stroll up to a shackled line, select one of the slaves, and take them to a shed near the enclosure gate. It was obvious enough what went on in that shed.

Julia kept her eyes down under that predatory gaze. Eventually it would be her turn. Her old self, she was certain, would at least have fought *that*; but now she felt only a profound indifference. It would be just another thing to survive.

But she could not survive forever. Every day she grew weaker; the air grew harder to breathe. Those who had been here longest had a dry, hacking cough that brought up blood, and breathing the air in this place felt like inhaling knives. Once that cough took root in the lungs, death was not long after.

She could not summon the energy to care.

One day—which one she could not tell; the days all bled into each other now—a new woman came to share her shackle.

Julia barely looked at her. It was breakfast time. She'd already devoured her bowl of gray slop. Any minute now, the guards would come with the *posca* and then she could drink, and everything wouldn't hurt so much.

One of them at last put a cup in her hands and she raised it to her lips. *Oh God, thank God.*

A hand stayed hers. "Don't drink it."

It was the woman she was now chained to. Black hair, matted and braided. Dark eyes. Somewhere in her mind, a bell was clamoring. Recognition.

"Fuck. I thought it was you, but now I know for sure. *Don't drink that.* It's drugged."

"I know it's drugged," Julia said dully. "I need it."

"That's how they keep you enslaved." The woman glanced over her shoulder at the guards. "Watch." She raised her own cup to her lips and waited until the guard glanced away. Then she spit it surreptitiously onto the floor. "Now you do it. Unless you *want* to die here."

Maybe I do.

Julia took a measured sip of the *posca* and felt an immediate urge to swallow. The pain would go. Her mind would stop its ceaseless circling. But the other woman's nails were digging hard into her knuckles, and she felt a sudden flush of shame. She'd *never* fought. Not once.

"Spit it out *now*," Ehre hissed. "Quickly."

Julia spit the *posca* into the dirt.

So the finger-bone flute *had* worked. She had summoned help, and help had appeared. Too late, though. Curse her life.

That night, they lay in their wood-plank cot, in whispered conversation. Julia hadn't had any of the *posca* since morning. Her body throbbed with pain, but she felt *awake*.

The line of Ehre's body stood out in sharp relief, turned toward her in the dark. "I was coming down the mountains to find Alaric. I wanted to get out from under my sister's shadow. They rounded me up in the foothills." Her strong, calloused fingers interlaced with Julia's. "How did this happen to you? Why are you not with him?"

Easily ruined and easily led, none more than her. "It's rather a long story."

"I don't believe he let you go," Ehre said, quietly. "I remember how he looked at you."

Julia shut her eyes. If she wasn't so wrung out—so broken and empty—she would sob. Better the *posca* than love. Better oblivion.

"Compose yourself," Ehre hissed. "This is not the Julia who stood tall and brave before the axes. I'm here to rescue *that* Julia. Not a sad corpse of a girl who thinks she's already dead."

Julia drew a breath. To think of herself as still alive felt like climbing a mountain. "But how will we escape?"

Ehre grinned and pulled a long, slender knife out of her boot. "The guards missed this."

There were no guards in the barracks, never had been. The *posca* was guard enough.

They picked the lock on the shackles using the knife. Then they snuck out of the barracks. Julia stood blinking in the moonlight, everything cast into sharp light and shadow.

She knew this place inside and out. She knew its routines, knew when its guards came and went, knew when the corpse cart did its hideous cycle. Always they burned the dead at night, and always outside the mine—it wouldn't do to rile the workers unnecessarily. That stench clung to everything.

Julia crouched in the shadows of one of the rough-hewn buildings with these thoughts piling up in her head, more than she'd had in days.

Hastily, in whispered scraps, she and Ehre worked out their plan.

At the gate, three guards passed a wineskin. Ehre and Julia hid themselves in the shadows between buildings, waiting for the terrible cart to trundle into view.

The cart stopped at each barracks, the driver looking for the dead. The plan was to wait until it came to the last, and hide themselves among the corpses while the driver was inside. Then, once they were outside the wall, Ehre was confident she could kill the cart driver, and they could both escape. Julia thought this a tenuous plan. But at least she would die *trying*.

But when the cart arrived, its load of bodies was fewer than usual. It would not hide them both. Julia cursed. "We must go back."

"You'll not live another week if we go back, Julia. *Look* at you."

Julia knew Ehre was right. She was hardly more than bones now, and this morning she'd coughed up blood. "So what will we do instead?"

"I'll rush the gate and kill them all."

"No." Somehow Julia held the other woman back. At the gate she could hear guards laughing and telling ribald stories. "Listen," she hissed. "Only one of us can hide in that cart. You go and get Alaric. I will distract them."

Ehre nodded. "Take this," she whispered, pushing her knife into Julia's hands. "You may need it."

Julia objected, but Ehre was already gone, darting between buildings. Julia strode out into the moonlight, in full view of the guards, to cause the biggest scene she ever had in her life.

The three guards were drinking *posca*. She could smell it—the soldiers usually got their own wine, but if the supply ran low, they would pilfer the *posca* rather than go sober.

Ehre would not find Alaric. Not in time to save her life. Julia knew that well enough. And even if she did find him, there was no guarantee he would come. He had not come to her rescue before; why would he now?

Julia was certain this would end in her death. But securing Ehre's freedom seemed a good enough reason to die. Better than dying in the tunnels, of use to no one.

From somewhere she summoned the old self—the woman

who had beguiled a man to his death, who had won the heart of Alaric of the Goths for a little while. She knew how the *posca* would put a nimbus behind her, how it would make her glow in the torchlight. When she stepped out from the shadows—at just the right angle for the light to be favorable—all three guards looked up and stared, their mouths falling open. "Is she real?" the shortest one asked, the one with the crooked helmet. It was the *posca*, erasing her flaws.

One of them seemed less drunk than the others. He was tall, wiry. "She's out of her barracks, where she shouldn't be." His eyes narrowed. "How'd you get out?"

"Does it matter?" She adopted a throaty purr. "I seek a protector in this place. One of you will do, I suppose." Her eyes fell to the least drunk one. "You, perhaps."

His mouth turned down suspiciously. "What for?"

"For special treatment. Extra food. Protection. Is that not how this works?"

The man raised an eyebrow. "It *could* be how it works."

The third guard lurched to his feet. "Why'd you choose *his* skinny arse?"

The cart driver had drawn up to the gate, and even he was staring at her, dumbfounded. From the corner of her eye, Julia saw a shadow flitting under the cart. Ehre, leveraging herself up beneath it, muscles standing in her arms. *How long could she hold herself like that?*

Julia licked her lips and the men's stares turned glassy. "Send that cart through." It was the tone of command that had come so easily in Ravenna. "It's spoiling the mood."

"Open the gate," the wiry one barked. The others scrambled to do his bidding. The cart rattled through the open gates. *Thank the gods.* Now all Ehre had to do was kill the man driving the cart—somehow without a weapon—and escape.

The wiry man approached her, his eyes hard in the torchlight. "Now then. Why don't we get to know each other better?"

★ ★ ★

Julia entered the hut knowing she was already dead. The guards would kill her, or this place would. It did not matter which. Even so, she could not bear this man to touch her.

The shed stank of unwashed bodies. It was a guard's living quarters, with a narrow, stained cot in the corner and piles of belongings everywhere, confiscated from the slaves.

The man's breath was hot in her ear. "You want special treatment, do you?"

Despite knowing she was already dead, Julia recoiled instinctively. *You have to do it. You have to.* Outside, it had seemed simply like a thing she would have to endure. But now, in this stinking place—she should have drunk a barrel of *posca* before trying this.

"So shy?" His eyes narrowed pugnaciously. "Go sit on the bed." He gave her a shove onto the cot. The man lowered himself next to her. "Be good, now." He leaned in to kiss her, his lips cold and wet like garden slugs. He rolled on top of her, pressing her onto the bed.

Ehre's knife was in her palm.

Julia did not hesitate. She thrust it into the side of his throat, just as Horsa had shown her. The man made a horrific choking sound. Blood gushed warm over her hands.

Julia lay still, the dead man on top of her, and fought back an eternity of screams.

Her tunic was covered in hot blood.

She rifled through the dead man's belongings until she found another, stinking but *not* bloodstained, and pulled it over her head. Something fell off the pile of rags; it was a cloth bag she recognized. It was *hers*. Calthrax's bone flute, her mother's ring. She tied it under her tunic.

If she wasn't guaranteed to die before, she was now. Even so, she refused to do it in this hut. Somehow, on shaking legs, she slipped outside. The men by the gate had slumped into a dazed half sleep brought on by the *posca*, and Julia slipped back into her barracks with no one noticing. Not even the other slaves noticed; if they did, they didn't care.

It didn't matter. Soon someone would find the guard's corpse. She'd be dead by dawn.

Just kill me, then, she thought wearily, turning on her side. *Get it over with.* Her bones dug into the hard cot and she felt like an empty amphora. A home for ghosts and wind.

Julia was jerked out of sleep by the sound of a horse screaming. There was a great crash. A cacophony of shouting.

Battle sounds.

She rose from her bed. All around her the other slaves were stirring, but they were still drugged and chained. Julia was not chained. There was nothing to stop her from going outside, from shading her eyes against a sky lit up with fire.

The gate hung on its hinges, and through it streamed a crowd of wild men on horses. Bandits. A wind stirred her cheek. Behind her, a guard dropped like a stone, an arrow sprouting from his eye. Someone had lit the sheds on fire, and it had already spread to the enclosure walls. And through the smoke that bellowed up at the gate galloped a woman, hair jet-black, wielding a Hunnic axe. Ehre.

Horsa followed close behind, blond hair spiked up and eyes blackened with campfire-black, a wolf-tooth necklace gleaming about his neck.

CHAPTER FORTY-FIVE

The bandits who followed Horsa were escaped slaves and impoverished farmers and ex-*foederati*, rounded up by the Romans and later freed by their own hand or the luck of a raid. Horsa had been close by, raiding villages for food when Ehre found him.

They rode all day to be free of the mines, Julia riding with Horsa, her arms wrapped tight around his waist and her face pressed into his back. As night fell, the bandits halted at a deserted village and raided homes, dragging furniture out of ruined houses, lighting a bonfire that towered over the rooftops. Then they drank and danced, the deserted village ringing with songs and battle cries.

Julia drank from any flask handed to her—Hunnic milk wine and fiery barbarian liquor that boiled her blood and old cavalry wine that was half gone to vinegar. And she danced, in the ruined village on the great ravaged plain of howling winds, her bones barely hanging together in her skin. She danced amidst a crowd of wild men and women, all fierce and sharp as the edge of a blade, all with the same look in their eyes. Feral. Wild. Devoid of pity.

Surely this was the last bonfire, burning at the end of the world.

The next morning, Julia woke wrapped in her cloak on the hard ground.

The air had a chill that had not been there before. How long had she been in the mines? Had summer passed already?

The bonfire still burned, and a crowd of bandits sat around it, sipping from flasks. In this light, they looked far younger than they had last night. Practically children.

She reached for her flask and the taste of the wine made her sick to death. She retched it out onto the ground and then poured out the rest, watching the red liquid sink into the earth.

Where was Horsa? She sat up, her head pounding viciously. Her eyes caught on a crowd beyond the fire—a group of people in filthy clothes, chained together at the ankle. Slaves from the mine.

Horsa was by the bonfire amidst a crowd, a pirate grin flashing that could have been Alaric's grin, Alaric's way with a crowd. Julia shoved through on shaking legs, her head pounding. She *hated* being sober.

"We must have words, Horsa. Alone."

Horsa waved a lazy hand. Alaric's hand, Alaric's gesture. "I am King of the Bandits, Julia. Whatever you would say to me can be said to my followers."

Julia reached down and twisted his ear. Hard.

"*Ow!* Stop! *Harpy!*" His followers laughed uproariously. "Fine," he grumbled, and rose to his feet.

Julia dragged him to the edge of the crowd. "What do you intend to do with them?" she demanded, gesturing to where the slaves were huddled. "You'll let them go, will you not?"

"They're *spoils*, Julia. How do you think I persuaded the others to help me trash that mine? We're going to sell them."

"No respectable slave merchant would buy stolen slaves from a *bandit*. You'll only get yourself crucified."

"You'd be surprised what *respectable* slave merchants will do." Horsa crossed his arms over his chest. "I have to sell them, Julia. The only way to *stay* Bandit King is to provide my followers with plunder."

"Well. If that's the case, then I'd say plunder is the Bandit King. Not you." Julia arched a brow. "Alaric would have let them go, don't you think? And he'd have kept the loyalty of his bandits anyway."

"Alaric would have—" Horsa reddened. "Fuck him," he grumbled. But then he turned, and Julia watched him swagger over to the group of slaves and fall into conversation with two men who'd been standing guard. They were older than Horsa, maybe Alaric's age.

They didn't like what Horsa was saying. One of them growled something murderous and the other put his hand on his sword.

Julia thought of the mines, the burning *posca*, the bodies on the cart. If this did not work, she would intervene. She had no idea how she'd keep from getting skewered, but over her dead fucking corpse would these people stay enslaved.

Horsa said something else, eyes heavy-lidded and insolent. After long moments, the two men backed down. One of them moved forward to undo the chains. Then Horsa came sauntering back to her, the expression on his face forbidding in its blankness. Only when he reached her did he break into a broad grin. "I *am* the King of the Bandits. Told you."

That night, they sat together by the fire.

In the mine, Horsa had practically hurled himself off his horse and come running up to Julia, staring as if she were a ghost come to life. Then he'd pulled her into his arms and hugged her hard enough to break ribs. Now she knew why he had been so terribly glad to see her.

"He thinks you're dead, you know," Horsa said, poking at the fire with a broken chair leg. "We all did."

He told her about the fire. Julia remembered seeing smoke rising from the city at her back, but now she was starting to realize that Bromios had set that fire. He had promised to cause a distraction. She hadn't stayed long enough to see what it was.

Julia caught her breath. She did not know what to feel at that news. All she felt was numb. "I wasn't dead. I *fled*." She tried to say something else, but her throat closed and the words would not come. Horsa put an arm around her and she leaned into his shoulder.

"Alaric went insane after you went." He spoke as if the same grip was on his own throat. "Fighting *holmgangs*, hanging his own chieftains on stakes. He talks to the *dead* now, Julia. Talks to Calthrax all the time. Thorismund said he refused the man a proper burial, and now his ghost walks the earth without rest. But I think he's just mad now." He glanced at her from beneath ash-pale lashes. "He asked if I had seen *your* ghost."

"And what did you say?"

"I told him he'd been the one to kill you. Then he cast me out." Horsa shoved the chair leg into the fire. "He'll murder me if I set foot back in that city."

His face was impassive in the firelight, underneath ravaged by grief. She took his hand and squeezed it. "That makes two of us," she whispered.

They sat there for an instant, staring into the dying fire, both broken by the same man and not remotely sure where to begin picking up the pieces.

"What is *wrong* with you two! The sour faces!" Ehre came barreling into their silence, sliding down the bench, wine sloshing in her cup. "We should be celebrating!" She launched into a highly exaggerated narrative of how she had escaped the mine.

Julia closed her eyes and thought of the long, bleak road laid out before her now. "Ehre," she said, interrupting the other woman's gruesome description of what she'd done to the cart driver. "Will you take me back to Brisca?"

Horsa turned to her abruptly. "Why not stay with me?"

"I can't be Queen of the Bandits, Horsa. I'm already Queen of the Goths."

"Maybe I'll be Queen of the Bandits. I'd be good at it." Ehre grinned. "No, Julia. I am sorry. I came over the mountains to get out from under my sister's shadow. The only direction I'll not go is backward."

Julia understood. All three had that in common; they could not go back where they'd come from. She felt the weight of the little finger-bone flute in the bag at her waist and shut her eyes. Her last lifeline. She watched it dissolve before her eyes.

"I have an idea," Horsa said quietly.

It took three days to locate Thorismund. He and his followers had chained a circle of wagons together on a hilltop—a movable fort, visible for miles, bonfires blazing. It must have been a quarter of Alaric's army. Julia had no idea so many followed him.

It was easy enough to gain entry; the sentries saw three ragtag, refugee bandits as no threat. Once inside, Thorismund's tent was obvious. Above it fluttered a green flag with an oak tree blazoned on it; Julia had seen the same symbol on his shield.

When she walked into his tent, he rose to his feet with eyes wide, as if he'd seen a ghost.

His face was thinner than it had been before. He'd grown a length of blond beard, glinting over his jaw; he looked grimmer and more barbaric than she had ever seen him. It was only after he'd embraced her—held her at arm's length as if to ascertain she was real—and then embraced her again that he allowed himself to break into a broad grin.

"Alaric used to see the dead, real as the ground beneath his feet," he breathed. "I never thought I would."

Julia wasn't prepared for the emotions that flooded her upon seeing Thorismund again. She dissolved into sobs, her face pressed to his leather vest. His arms went around her, his embrace driving the air from her lungs, and for a moment they wordlessly clung to each other.

When she'd finished crying—it took an embarrassingly long time—Thorismund led her to one of the camp stools set up around a pit of glowing coals dug into the earth. He produced a flask and pressed it into her hands.

Julia laughed through her tears. "Is this the last of the batch?"

"The last of the batch isn't wasted on you."

But she could not drink. Even the *smell* of alcohol made her nauseous now.

"I never thought I'd see the day the princess Julia refused a drink. You must truly be a ghost." Thorismund replaced it with cold water in a tin cup. "Welcome back to the living, girl. Where have you been?"

It was easy to talk to Thorismund. The story had been gnawing at her guts the whole time, and Julia found herself pouring it out, telling him of the mines, the *posca*. The man she'd killed. Julia talked until her throat was hoarse, and Thorismund listened with solemn attention. By the time she had finished, he took her hand in his.

"Julia, if I'd known, I'd have come for you myself." He looked as though she had hit him with a brick.

"You thought me dead. How could you know?" She drew a shaking breath. "Why—why did you leave him?" She could not imagine Thorismund turning his back on Alaric. But then, she could not have imagined herself doing it either.

His brow clouded. "When I joined with Alaric, I believed he wanted what I did. A homeland, and safety for our people. In the beginning, he tried to rein in the chieftains and keep us from devolving into banditry, although these past three years we've had to plunder to survive." He drew a breath, his great shoulders rising and falling. "But after you left, something broke in him. He stopped caring about the people. He let them starve and drove out chieftains who had been with him since the beginning. No king who neglects to feed his people will keep his right to rule." He glanced down at their entwined hands, his brow heavy. "We fought the night I left. I accused him of causing your death, and he told me that if he ever saw me again in his city, he would kill me where I stood. I could not stay after that. I had my own to look to, and I still cared to protect them. So I left. I had to."

"He would kill me too if I returned," she whispered, thinking of the way his eyes had blazed with hatred the last time she saw him. "He hates me too."

"No." Thorismund shook his head. "Alaric loved you. He went mad because he thought *he* was the one at fault for killing you. That's why he threw me and Horsa out—we both struck the same nerve."

Julia's hands clenched convulsively on his. Horsa had said much the same thing to Alaric, and had been driven out too. Could it be that Alaric's madness was driven by guilt over *her* fate? She shut her eyes tight. *What did it matter?* There was nothing between them now but a blasted battlefield.

"Perhaps if I could just return for a little while and show him that I'm alive—" she sniffled loudly "—he would come back to himself."

"I doubt he'd even recognize you," Thorismund said gently. "But that is not the only reason you shouldn't try. Julia, I just received word this morning. Lucretia's husband has finally brought his revenge. Noricum is under siege."

Julia's head snapped up. "Then, you're—going to ride to his rescue?"

"No." Thorismund's face was grave. "I'm not."

"What do you mean, *no*?" Julia gripped his huge, battle-scarred hands. "Thorismund, he's *always* come back for us. He didn't leave you when you were in the farmhouse with your guts out. He didn't leave me with those bandits. If he knew one of us was in such dire straits, he'd break down city walls to get to us. We cannot just *leave* him there."

Thorismund sighed heavily. Then he rose to light the braziers; when he turned back, grief was etched into his face.

"It would most likely do no good. Alaric was probably in Roman custody before that message reached me. He was in no sound mind to defend against a siege, and Noricum's walls were in no state to withstand one. But even if I *thought* I could do any good, I couldn't reach him now if I wanted. There are Huns between us and Noricum. Not even I can fight my way through." He wiped his forearm against his forehead and she could see his exhaustion, his pain. "There are a thousand people outside this tent, relying on me. Not all are warriors. I will not lead them to their ruin."

Julia remembered what Horsa had said. *If he died on the battlefield and I walked away alive, I would never live down the shame.* "You'll be leaving him dead on the battlefield."

"I know," Thorismund said, and she knew what it cost him. Behind his haggard stoicism, he was as wild with grief as she was. "It is what he would do, if he were in his right mind. We must let him go. We must." He came to sit by her again, gripped her hands tightly. "Ask anything else of me. Ask me to give you refuge. Ask me to send you back to Brisca with protection. You can start a new life. Only do not ask me to send you to your own death. He would never forgive me if I did."

Julia was given a tent at the edge of camp, away from the bonfires. She lay for hours, wrestling with herself. Horsa had told her Alaric had gone insane. But she hadn't quite grasped the reality until she'd spoken with Thorismund.

She drew her knees up to her chest beneath the piled furs, Thorismund's words pressing down on her like a mile of earth. Alaric was under siege in Noricum, if not in Roman custody already. If captured, his death would be a spectacle in Ravenna. He would die as Cornelius had. And it would all be her fault. If he'd never met her—if she'd never made him love her, if she hadn't *insisted*—none of this would have happened.

Love had ruined him, just as it had ruined her. Perhaps it had ruined him *worse*.

Let him go, Thorismund had said. For a moment Julia let herself imagine it. Stilicho would not look for her in Brisca's village. She could lose herself in the highlands. Perhaps she could apprentice herself to the healers. And there would come another love, in a few seasons, who would help her forget—and whenever she closed her eyes, she would see Alaric dying alone and in pain, because of *her*.

She could not live in a world where she had ruined him with her love, and then left him to die alone. She could not.

Thorismund had set guards. But she still had her knife. It was short work to cut a hole in the back of the tent.

Outside, the camp was quiet. The bonfires had burned down to embers, and it was still hours before dawn. Carefully she made her way to the horses.

"And where do you think you're going?"

Julia nearly jumped out of her skin. Ehre and Horsa stood behind her, their breath coalescing into cool steam in the moonlight.

"I'm going to Alaric," she said, raising her chin defiantly.

"Is that so?" Horsa grinned crookedly. "How will you avoid the Huns?"

"How will you find food and shelter?" Ehre added.

"And keep away from the bandits? They'll take a horse from a lone traveler unless you're very good with a sword."

"I suppose I'll figure it out," Julia said. "Don't try stopping me. If you tell Thorismund, I'll only escape again."

"You misunderstand," Horsa said solemnly. "I cannot leave Alaric alone on the battlefield, Julia. We're coming with you."

Chapter Forty-Six

As they rode south, the land only became more ravaged.

Roving bands of Goths had pillaged this country, as had bandits and Roman slavers. Julia and her friends hid during the day in burned-out villages and moved at night to avoid the Huns, riding toward a horizon streaked by lightning. Once they rode past a village that was entirely on fire. The road south was increasingly strewn with corpses.

Horsa told her that the Romans and Goths were both brutal—both prone to pillage and murder. But the Romans took slaves, and the Goths sometimes left people alive to weep over the glowing coals of their homes. The Huns, though—they did not take slaves, and they did not leave survivors.

Julia's plan for Noricum was hazy. Her hope was that Alaric was neither captured nor dead, but still under siege. In her mind, she would somehow evade capture and sneak into the city, and her presence would snap him back to sanity. In her most fevered imaginings, he would fall to his knees and swear his undying devotion. It was a fantasy, of course. But she ignored her looming doubts. She would rescue Alaric, as he had rescued her so many times in the past. Somehow.

They were almost to Noricum when they fell into the hands of the Huns.

Julia lay in a pile of straw in a burned-out barn, somewhere between sleep and waking. She couldn't say what made her lurch out of sleep—perhaps it was the silence. No birds chattering, no lone rooster crowing at the dawn. Not even any breathing. Horsa and Ehre were gone. Instantly she was filled with foreboding.

The door to the barn hung open. Movement caught her eye. She froze.

Across the yard, a black-clad rider held the reins of a bay horse, a wicked curved blade at his hips, a quiver of arrows bristling from his back. She recognized that bow, those blades, the hard-nosed silhouette of that horse.

Riga. Her first thought. But then he turned his face toward her and she realized he wasn't.

A Hun.

Julia held perfectly still. The moment she moved, he would see her. *They don't take slaves,* Horsa had told her, *and they do not leave survivors.*

Better death, then. Better than being a slave.

The man's gaze snapped toward her as if she'd spoken aloud. He had his bow out and an arrow nocked to it in one smooth motion.

Julia raised an arm on instinct, flinching from the arrow that would send her into death.

Moments later, Julia found herself dragged out of the barn and into the ruined village square. There were more than twenty Huns scattered among the outbuildings, bristling with weapons. Ehre and Horsa were brought at sword point out of one of the houses, where they'd been pilfering supplies.

"What did you tell them?" Horsa whispered. "They should have killed us already."

"Nothing! I haven't spoken a word."

"Keep your silence," Ehre said grimly. "If you can escape, do it. Do not worry about us."

Julia barely got a chance to object. They were separated, her hands tied with rough rope, and she was shoved up on the back of a horse.

The Hunnic camp was close by. It smelled of supple leather and fresh hay, mud turned over by a hundred hooves, and over that, a scent of spices and cooking meat that made Julia's stomach turn over. *How long had it been since she'd eaten?*

She had always thought of the Huns as a single group and culture. But those here appeared to be from dozens of nations, speaking a multiplicity of languages. Men and women looked up as she passed, their curious gazes following. Julia knew what they saw: a stranger. A captive. She had a feeling they were all wondering why she was not already dead.

The largest tent was made of white cowhide. Julia was ushered in and found herself standing before a tall, imposing woman who wore cowhide leggings and a colorfully dyed tunic, fur stitched into the wrists. Her hair was very dark and straight, wound into a meticulous braid.

She spoke one word in military Latin: "Kneel."

Julia knelt immediately. Forehead to floor. She wasn't so foolish as to disobey.

Above her, the woman spoke again in rapid Hunnic to the men who had brought her. There were many languages in this camp, but Julia recognized this one. She'd sung ribald songs in it one night, in a tent full of smoke. It was Riga's language.

She was jerked roughly back to her feet. Someone cut the ropes at her wrists, then held out her arm toward the woman, shoving her sleeve up to the elbow.

The woman's eyes widened. She was looking at the mark Riga had cut into her palm.

"Where did a Roman slave come by that? I ought to cut it off you."

Roman slave. Her pride rebelled. But was it not true? Had she not been a slave? "Cut it off if you like. I am in your power." Julia did not flinch from the woman's gaze. "But the one who gave me this mark promised it would grant me safety here."

"Who are you? You do not drop your gaze like a slave." The woman's eyes narrowed suspiciously. "Who is this person making promises on our behalf?"

"The mercenary leader Riga. He rides with Alaric of the Goths."

The woman hissed through her teeth. She grasped her wrist harder, examining the sigil. After a breath of silence, she spoke again. "Do you know what this is?" She tapped Julia's wrist with the point of her dagger. "It's the same mark he would put on a pet. Or a beast of burden, like a donkey."

"A *donkey*?" Julia stared in outrage. "Cut it off, then! I *insist.*"

"I decide what limbs are cut off in my own tent." The woman looked down at her coldly. "Your *friend* spoke the truth. I have my honor. I will not harm you." She hardly looked pleased about it. "In return for my generosity, you will tell me where Riga is now. I have unfinished business with my elder brother."

Riga's sister's name was Kreka.

There was little resemblance between them. Where Riga was smiling and mischievous, she was stern and straight-backed with a kind of gracefully lethal self-possession. Not a strand of her hair was out of place. Julia had a feeling she stayed up late polishing and honing her weapons to flawless, obsessive sharpness.

Julia sat cross-legged on a pile of rugs by the hearth, sipping a cup of warm milk wine. Her stomach still rebelled at the smell and taste of alcohol, but she was not so foolish as to refuse hospitality. "Before I answer your questions," she said, "I must know that Riga's protection extends to my friends."

Kreka frowned. "My brother's mark does not extend to your entourage."

"That may be. But those with me are dear to him too," Julia said quietly. "I ask you to honor the spirit of his mark, not the letter of it."

Kreka's eyes narrowed, and Julia held her breath. In another life, she'd be terrified. But she had lived through the mines; she knew there were worse things than death. She met the other woman's gaze and waited.

Finally Kreka inclined her head. "Upon my honor."

"He is still with Alaric of the Goths," Julia said, taking a slow sip of the steaming drink. "I was on my way to them when you found me."

Kreka considered this. "You must have wanted to get back to my brother very much."

Julia considered her next move, masking her delay with a thoughtful sip of the milk wine. Would it go harder or easier on her if Kreka believed she had shared Riga's bed? Whichever she chose, it seemed unwise to disclose her identity, or her relationship with Alaric. She had a feeling the moment a word of it passed her lips, Kreka would turn her mind to ransom. Any rational person would.

She kept her story simple, the lies mainly by omission. "I come from Ravenna. My family were seeking a marriage not to my liking, so I ran away and found refuge with Alaric. Riga and I—became close."

It was not a lie. It seemed better, safer to let Kreka assume she'd been Riga's lover than Alaric's.

But a mocking smile lifted Kreka's lips. "So close that he marked you his *donkey*."

Temper rose in her throat. Suddenly she didn't care how Kreka saw her. What did it matter what happened to her? The worst had already happened, several times over, and seeing Alaric again was vanishingly unlikely.

Julia downed her milk wine in a single long gulp. "If I ever see Riga again, I will take that transgression out of his hide."

She meant it. Horsa had shown her what to do with a knife. She'd already killed a man. There seemed nothing left to her now but recklessness, and when she glanced back at Kreka, the other woman was looking at her with a kind of fierce recognition. "If there is any hide left when I am through with him," she said with chilling finality.

Julia could not help her curiosity. "If I may ask, what insult did Riga deliver his chieftainess?"

"I am not the chieftainess." Kreka took a long sip from her cup, and looked at the fire. "It is tradition that the oldest son inherit the leadership of our tribe. But my older brother, Riga, ran off to make his fortune in the west. I was the one who stayed. And when my father fell sick, *I* ruled the people. I found the best pastures and the richest plunder. Now my father is dead and the augurers are demanding I step down until my brother can be found. The only way I can rule my people is to prove that he is dead—or find him and wrestle him into submission before the augurers to demonstrate *I* am the better to rule."

Julia fumed. "That is the way of the world, is it not? For a woman to be accepted as a leader, she must be twice as clever and strong as any man." It was infuriating. She glanced up at Kreka, and the opportunity was right there. Clear as a rope to a drowning man. *Get your own army.* "I know exactly where he is," Julia said. "And I'll help you get to him."

CHAPTER FORTY-SEVEN

By the end, Alaric was too exhausted, too hollowed out from killing to know dream from reality. The night in Noricum bled into day, burning projectiles filling the sky, lightning streaking the horizon, and army fires dotting the plains beyond.

Weeks ago, his people had been many thousands strong. Now there was only a few hundred left, mostly in the citadel. Much of the lower city had been taken. The granaries were still on fire; Alaric had tried hard to preserve those, in three nights of vicious hand-to-hand fighting in the narrow streets. In the end, he could not. He'd done all he could.

Now he stood on the wall of the citadel and contemplated the drop from there.

Do it, Calthrax whispered at his back. *Join us.*

No. It was not a good end. Not a warrior's end.

Better than being dragged back to Ravenna and tortured to death before a screaming crowd.

The drop pulled at him. Alaric looked out across the plain, and instead of Roman fires, he saw a vast army of ghosts; those he'd killed and who'd died following him.

All but Julia. She would have none of him even in death.

"Alaric." It was Hengist behind him, dead on his feet, smudges of dark beneath his eyes. Hengist had been leading raids into the city, dangerous raids to find food. For a moment Alaric's heart clenched, thinking of the danger he'd subjected Hengist to, and his brother fatherless and alone in the wilderness. He'd betrayed Gaufrid's deathbed promise in a fit of temper. Self-loathing choked his throat.

"What."

What he answered was not to be believed.

Alaric followed the boy at a run to the top of the parapet. Beyond the ruined walls, beyond the Roman army, he saw a wave of men and horses rolling in like a terrible tide.

Riga was waiting for him at the top of the wall, and he turned, the lightning flashing behind him in a sky that was black on black. "It's the Huns," he said, testing the tautness of his bow. "Either they've come to join the Romans in picking over our corpses, or they've come to our rescue."

Alaric found pessimism more rational than optimism. It was easier to believe that the Huns were coming to feast on the Romans' leavings. He knew his own would not last more than two days under the assault of both.

So he stood on the walls with Riga and Hengist, watching the Huns thunder through the Roman camp and hit their undefended flank. He had seen this happen to *his* people, driving them far from the pine-tree island in the middle of the Danube—the Huns riding in on their ferocious little ponies, arrows flying farther and faster than any had thought possible. Even his stalwart father had fled before them.

Which was why it shocked him to the core when, hours later, it was clear the Huns were harrying the Romans. Even Riga could not say why.

With the Romans outside the walls fighting off the Huns, it was up to him to drive the occupiers out of the city. It was easier said than done.

Alaric's warriors were exhausted and starving, their numbers dwindled.

He led raid after raid. The fighting was vicious and their margin for error nonexistent.

Alaric lived only in the present, each moment a tapestry of blood and pain and fear, his steps haunted by the throat-cut ghost of Calthrax. Somehow he and his survivors beat the Romans back street by street, snatching sleep in scraps that felt stolen from death.

And as the bloody days passed, Alaric caught wind of a rumor. At first he did not believe it. In the daytime, he dismissed it. At night, he could not let it go.

Rumor said that a redheaded woman rode among the Huns.

By the end of three days, the streets were piled high with corpses, the buildings half-burned and the walls little more than rubble. But when the sun finally rose on the fourth day, the Romans had pulled out of the city.

That morning, Alaric walked to the southern gate, Ataulf following behind, both of them exhausted almost to the point of hallucination. Ahead there was laughter and shouting, a raucous ricochet off the walls as survivors came out of the ruined buildings where they had taken refuge. And down at the demolished western gate, a contingent of Hunnic warriors was spilling into the city, their shouts of victory mingling with those of his own.

What they wanted was still not clear. It was time he found out.

A tall warrior woman he did not recognize strode through

the crowd, a bow slung over her shoulder. She halted in front
of Ataulf. "Are you Alaric of the Goths?" She looked him up
and down, her lips curving into a mocking grin. "They said
you would be taller."

Alaric stepped forward. "I am Alaric. Are you the chieftain
I owe my thanks to?"

"I am no chieftain yet. I've come to take that title out of my
brother's hide." Her gaze rose over his head and she shouted in
a voice that ricocheted off the walls. *"Riga!"*

Alaric glanced behind to see Riga on the rooftop, his face
pale beneath his tan. The woman took off running after him,
furious. She looked ready to scale a building.

"Am I to believe," Ataulf said quietly, "that Riga's kin just
fought through a Roman legion to settle some family dispute?"

Alaric bit back a laugh. It seemed past believing. "I didn't
know he had a sister."

He was too damn tired to sort it out. And Ataulf seemed dead
on his feet. There was more to do—no doubt nests of Roman
survivors to rout out before the city would be fully safe.

Alaric and Ataulf had just turned back up the hill when a
tumult arose at their backs. Shouting at the gate. He turned to
see another woman fighting her way through the crowd—two
curved blades at her hips, her black braided hair trailing down
from beneath her helmet.

He recognized her at once. Brisca's little sister.

"Ehre? What the hell are you doing here?"

She rushed forward, her face flushed. "Thank the gods I've
found you. The Romans are attacking the hill to the west, where
the Huns had their camp."

"And what are we to do about it?" Ataulf frowned. "We barely
won this battle in the streets. Anyone who goes out in defense
of that hill will be going to their own death."

"You do not understand." She turned fierce, reddened eyes
to Alaric. "Julia is there. She lives."

According to the lore, the Huns moved fast—sweeping in to shower their opponents with a deadly barrage of arrows, then galloping off into the dust, outriding and outshooting their opponents at every turn. There was no room for the slow, for the weak. For noncombatants. That was why they did not take prisoners.

Julia found that was not entirely true.

Kreka's people traveled in wagons, pulled by sturdy little ponies. There were healers and children and craftspeople, and although everyone could ride a horse and handle a weapon, not everyone was a warrior.

Since she had not been killed immediately, Kreka's people welcomed Julia and her friends readily enough. Ehre and Horsa fit in as if born among them, both proficient with their own horses and weapons. There was little room for anyone who could not hold their own. Julia was far more uneasy about her own place—but she quickly found her riding skills were better than she thought.

There would be no sharing a horse here. Kreka allowed her a mount of her own—a tough, rawboned little mare who barely came up to Julia's waist. After months riding before Alaric, Julia found her body moved with her horse like water moving downstream. It was easy enough when the group was galloping across the plains; all she had to do was hang on. The horse would not leave its kin. Her thighs had built up a kind of iron-hard strength, and instead of fear, Julia felt an intense exhilaration, the wind whipping her hair and the entire plain spread out before her. This was *freedom*—a freedom she had never felt in her constrained life in Ravenna.

This, too, was a kind of home.

Long before Noricum came into view, the wind brought the smell of it over the plains. Stink of battle and ash; fire and siege smell. They made camp behind a ridgeline out of sight of the Roman army, and the warriors prepared for battle.

That night, Ehre and Horsa took her aside.

"There will be no noncombatants if the Romans come over that rise," Horsa told her, grimly. "You will need to defend yourself."

Julia already had a knife snug in her boot. To that, Ehre added a lightweight Hunnic axe. "Its weight is in its head, so it adds strength to your swings," Ehre said. "Your arm will be as strong as a man wielding a sword."

And then he and Ehre spent several hours—until the day fled before the dark—making sure she could keep herself alive. They showed her how to stab and where to slice, the weak points in an infantryman's armor, a handful of underhanded tactics.

Julia ended that day more convinced than ever that if she ever stepped foot on a battlefield, she would be the first to die on the end of a Roman pike.

But that was not the only possibility. The others included being captured and sent back to her brother, or killed by Alaric himself. It seemed the more likely scenario than all her fantasies about him falling to his knees before her.

Maybe it was better to be killed in the first seconds of battle. It would save her the humiliation of whatever would inevitably happen next.

The next day, Julia watched Horsa and Ehre ride off with the Huns in their hundreds, galloping down the rise toward the great, glinting Roman army spread out on the plain.

There was no time to wait or worry. The camp was a hive of activity. A group of wizened women marshalled those remaining to set up a field hospital, and everyone—even the children—fell into what seemed like well-worn roles. Julia kept herself busy boiling water and preparing bandages, making poultices and mixing medications for pain.

Then the wounded came streaming in, and now she was busy

in earnest, helping hold thrashing men and women down as arrows were removed and broken bones set. Julia kept moving, never letting her eyes linger too long on the horrors she saw, never allowing herself to think of her friends. Only a few times did she withdraw to a private place to void the contents of her stomach, and once, after the death of a young woman with a sword cut in her neck, to weep.

For two days, Julia helped with the wounded and listened desperately for news of the battle. She worked until she was too exhausted to stand and snatched sleep anywhere she could get it, wrapped in her cloak under whatever shelter she could find.

News trickled in with the wounded. Julia heard that the walls were about to fall, that the Romans had slaughtered all the Hunnic warriors, that both sides were near overwhelmed, the balance of the battle turning in the space of hours. At the dawn of the third day, the news swept the camp that the Huns had made it into the city and the Goths had come down from the citadel.

News of Alaric was wild and contradictory. Some said he was dead, his body hanging from the walls of Noricum. Others said he was fully mad, holed up in his citadel, that none had seen him in weeks. Still others said that he was in the city, fighting as though he were the embodiment of battle fury come down to earth. There was no consensus.

Julia took refuge in the frantic activity and chaos of the medical tent. She was helping to stitch up a gash on a man's forehead when shouts rose up at her back.

Her hope rose wildly. But it was not Alaric. A contingent of Romans had broken away from the retreating legion and was riding toward the rise with all speed.

Within the space of an hour, this place would be a battlefield.

Not an hour later, Julia lay on her stomach on the ridgeline, just one in a line of defenders, gripping a recurve bow as she stared down the slope at the approaching Roman soldiers. She was floating above herself with fear.

Two fingers on the string, one of the wizened old women who'd led the camp had told her. She had the cool gaze of a warrior decades younger. *Do not waste time trying to aim. Point your arrow into the line of men and shoot.*

Julia would die here; she knew that. A hot, fierce ache kindled in her chest. She would never see Alaric again.

The Romans were close now. Julia could see their breastplates sparking in the hot sun as they ran up the hill. The woman next to her loosed her arrow in one fluid motion and Julia followed suit, a cold, vast place inside her where her fear should be.

Her first arrow went high over the Romans' heads. Her second went higher. Her third hit a man in his chest and sent him tumbling into his fellows.

Julia bit back a gasp. *She'd killed a man.* A Roman soldier. How her father would— But there was barely time to think as her hands scrabbled for another arrow. Draw; loose; load. Over and over, she fired into the ever-approaching line.

The Romans crested the hill anyway.

Now the enemy was in the camp, cutting down anyone they came across.

Somehow Julia survived the initial rush, fleeing before the enemy, barely avoiding being trampled. But the Romans were everywhere now, the noncombatants fighting with anything they had—weapons, shovels, broken-off chair legs. There was no refuge.

A centurion loomed grinning out of the chaos, his red horsehair helmet a ridiculous embellishment. He stared at her and his eyes widened. "Princess?"

Shit. Shit shit shit. He reached for her and Julia swung her axe wildly, sending his hand flying in a gleaming arc of blood. The man screamed and Julia *ran*, ducking behind an overturned cart just as an arrow slammed into the wood by her head.

They knew her.

Something blocked the sun above her. She glanced up to see the shadow of a man, no centurion this time—some infantry-man who wouldn't know her from a camp follower. There was no offer for safety as his sword swung down to split her from neck to pelvis.

In the next instant, a thrown axe split the man's skull with a wet *thunk*. The man's knees gave out and Julia just barely scram-bled out of the way as a huge black horse trampled his still-twitching body beneath dinner plate–sized hooves. She raised her eyes to see a rider whose shadow blocked out the sun, the horse's bloodied hooves lashing at the air, encrusted with brains and bits of skull, the rider's blue eyes blazing with the light of a thousand siege fires.

Hannibal came back to all fours and shoved his nose into her chest.

Well. At least *someone* was happy to see her. "Hello, Hanni-bal." Julia petted the snuffling warhorse awkwardly.

She could *feel* the weight of that gaze on her.

She was afraid to look at him. Afraid to even acknowledge him. But when she finally did, the force of his gaze stopped the breath in her lungs. He was beautiful and terrible as a heathen god of war, come down to ravage the earth.

"Get under that cart," he commanded, his words murder-ously soft. "And stay there."

Then he whirled Hannibal and plunged back into the battle.

As soon as it was safe, Julia crept out from under the cart.

Alaric's men had flooded into the camp, fighting alongside the Hunnic defenders, trampling the Roman infantry and sending heads flying with their axes and skewering the deserters with their spears. Now the hilltop was piled high with the dead and she could not see Alaric—not anywhere. She did not want to run to him like a lovesick fool and hurl herself into his arms. He was still angry at her—or perhaps still insane. She had no idea what to do.

The medic tent was in chaos, half-collapsed, the surviving wounded huddled behind a makeshift wall of cots. Julia threw herself into helping the healers. *He* could come to *her*. Hadn't he treated her like war spoils the last time they'd been together? Hadn't he refused to believe her when she'd told him she'd burned a hole in his chest only to save his life?

Fuck. What if he was injured? Dead?

A heavy hand landed on her shoulder and she nearly started right out of her skin. She turned, ready to bite his head off and hurl herself into his arms all at once. But it wasn't Alaric. It was Ehre, eyes narrowed against the glare.

Relief and joy flooded through her and suddenly the two women were in each other's arms. "I thought I'd never see you again!" Julia cried.

"I thought the same of you!" And then for a moment they just screamed like wild animals and clung to each other, Julia half-insensible with relief as the story tumbled out of Ehre in a torrent of vulgar Latin, of how she'd convinced Alaric to come with her on a battle-mad chase through enemy territory to stop the Romans from taking the ridgeline.

Just then Julia caught sight of Alaric across a bloody field strewn with bodies, his red cloak snapping about his heels. He was turned away from her, the Hunnic warriors and his own men crowded around him, all of them staring down the slope.

Something was wrong. The earth seemed to tilt beneath her feet.

"That first wave was only a scouting party," Ehre said beside her. She understood the situation at a glance—much faster than Julia did. "No doubt they also heard rumors of the red-haired woman who rides with the Huns."

As she spoke, Julia realized what she was looking at. The entire legion had changed direction and was swinging toward them at a gallop.

She thought of that handless soldier.

For a moment Julia stood staring down into the juggernaut. "There's no way we can fight that. No possible way."

Horror rose in her throat as the enormity of what Alaric had done hit her. He could have stayed behind his walls, and let the ridgeline go. She would have died or gone back with the Romans—to her brother—but he would have lived.

"Damn him." She strode toward Alaric, ready to give him a piece of her mind. She didn't come all this way only to watch him die. How *dare* he?

She'd only managed a few steps when Ehre caught her arm again. She pointed out across the battlefield, over the bodies and broken siege engines, above the glittering threat of the Roman army, to the great plume of dust that rose like smoke just beyond the horizon. *"Look."*

A second army. And above it, a great flag with a green oak tree shining in the sun. Thorismund's army.

CHAPTER FORTY-EIGHT

Once more, Alaric rallied the Hunnic defenders and his own men. He ordered barriers built around the top of the hill, dragging broken wagons and freshly dead corpses to impede the coming charge. Anyone not engaged in building the barriers was to gather up arrows and stones for slings. Let the Romans fall before their arrows, pile up before the makeshift barriers and be ground down by Thorismund's army behind them.

When it was over, he could not find Julia.

He hadn't known what he'd find when he went off against everyone else's better judgment, including his own, chasing her redheaded ghost on the battlefield. His words had died in his throat when he'd found her alive, rising to her feet cool and unruffled as she watched Hannibal trample her enemy beneath his hooves. She'd showered attention on his horse and ignored him, until the moment she met his eyes and he couldn't get a damn word out.

If she'd fallen this time, his sword would find its home buried in his own heart.

He rushed to the medical tent and could not find her there.

He stepped into the path of one of the healers as she passed—a slight woman who wielded a wicked hatchet.

"Where is my wife?" He asked it in Hunnic. "The red-haired one."

"Don't know. Maybe that way." She pointed in a random direction and darted around him, clearly displeased at his interruption.

Alaric went stalking off the way she pointed, to the east where people were piling bodies up for the burning. *What if Julia was among the dead?* Or only half-dead, unconscious and about to be lit on fire? He broke into a ground-eating run.

"*Alaric.* You fucking *bastard.* Don't you dare run away from me, you thrice-cursed dog."

Alaric slid to a stop. Thorismund had planted himself in his path like a wall.

"Get the fuck out of my way, Thorismund."

"Oh no. Don't try that *quiet-threat-of-blood-and-beheading* tone on me. I'm fucking *immune.*" Thorismund's face had gone red. "You *stupid* man, do you comprehend what you've done?"

Maybe killed the woman he loved. Again. "I don't have time for this."

"You'll damn well make time!" Thorismund roared, gripping his arm as he tried to brush by. "I cut a path through a Roman legion just to give you a piece of my mind and I fully intend to do it. I offered to take Julia to Brisca's and I think she'd be mad not to take me up on it. If you *ever* hurt that woman again I'll take that spear of yours and ram it up your—"

Alaric jerked his arm out of Thorismund's grasp. That was *it.* He was tired and battered and worried to death over Julia and he had had *enough.* "Why don't you try it," he gritted. "Right now."

Thorismund drew his axe and Alaric raised his war spear and shifted his stance. *Good.* Whatever was between him and Thorismund, he was ready to put it to bed forever.

"Are the two of you insane?" A voice behind him. Incredulity mixed with *laughter*. "Really. *Are* you insane? Have you not had enough of war?"

He turned to see Julia behind him just as Thorismund swung his axe.

Alaric didn't have to look to block that blow. Thorismund announced every move with his stance and his feet and the tilt of his shoulders, and the blunted flat of the axe bounced off the hard cured wood of his spear. Even so, it sent a shock up his arm that numbed it to the shoulder. He didn't give a damn. He could not take his eyes off Julia. She was staring at him, those blue-green eyes glinting in the sunlight, every inch the aristocrat despite her barbarian trousers and dusty boots and her red hair braided beneath a Phrygian cap, pulled low around her ears.

Alive. Alive and safe and *his*.

He acted on instinct. Seizing the reins of the nearest horse and swinging up onto its back, he pulled Julia up before him. She gave a startled gasp as he urged the horse to a gallop, then a flat-out run down the steep pitch of the hill, dodging corpses and hillocks and discarded steel. Behind him, he could still hear Thorismund roaring his outrage at his back.

Julia's nails dug into his forearm as he urged the horse on faster. Her cap was gone; her hair came loose and whipped in his face. "You could have *asked* before kidnapping me."

He tightened his arms around her. "I didn't the first time, and I won't now."

Because her answer might be *no*. Because she might not have him. Because now—even now—she might disappear like smoke from his arms.

They galloped down the ridge and through the ruined citadel gates, attracting a laughing, cheering crowd that followed them all the way up to the place where his war tent still stood. Alaric pulled Julia down from the sweating horse and dragged her into his tent, with a look of death for any who'd dare interrupt them.

When they were finally alone, he let himself look at her—really *look*.

She was standing in the middle of his war tent, her hair coming loose from its braid and hanging down her back in a glory of sunset tangles. She wore a borrowed Hunnic tunic and leggings embroidered with rich geometric designs, and riding boots that rose nearly up to her knees. She looked like a barbarian warrior woman, with a Hunnic hatchet at her waist and the hilt of a knife sticking out of her boot. There was a hollowness to her cheeks and a haunted darkness around her eyes that said she had seen things she should never have had to see.

That was his fault. Suddenly it was hard to breathe around his own self-hatred. He had tried to protect her and failed. In the reflection of her ocean-green eyes, he saw a double image of himself, wild-eyed and half-mad with feelings far too huge to give voice to.

How could she just stand there? Cool as marble when he was wrecked by the very sight of her. He'd believed he had lost her.

"Are you alive?" It came out like he was choking on gravel. "Or is it your spirit I see before me?"

It was the worst thing he could possibly say. She thought him mad enough already.

"Yes, I've heard you've been having a little problem with—spirits." Her tone was dry as Imperial wine; completely incongruous with the redheaded barbarian woman who stood before him. She raised a red-gold brow; entirely unimpressed. It was such a *Julia* expression. Grief and terror and *longing* washed over him and suddenly he was drowning. Unsteady on his feet. "Well? We lived through the battle, Alaric. Now what?"

"Thorismund said that he offered to take you to Brisca." He could hardly bear to say it. "Will you go?"

She held quiet and every muscle in his body went tense. *What would he do if she said yes?* Tie her to the bed. Refuse to let her go. Spend the entirety of his life convincing her to stay.

Finally she spoke; her tone only mildly curious. "Would you want me to stay? After everything that has passed between us?"

Alaric caught his breath. She was *necessary* to him; could she not see that? He was suddenly acutely aware that Julia was perfectly fine without him; whereas he had unwound into madness without her. She was air to him. Water in the desert.

He managed a broken *yes*.

"Then, you must change," she said quietly. "I will be a queen in *truth*, or not at all."

All his terror rose up and threatened to overwhelm him. Julia on the battlefield, rushing recklessly everywhere. Calthrax raising his *rhomphaia* against her. The axes, flashing in the dark of Brisca's great hall. This world was not safe for her, would never be safe for her. He would lose her again; she would hasten it. And then he would lose himself.

Suddenly *she* was the enemy of everything he held dear.

"Am I to let you wander unprotected on the battlefield?" *Fuck.* He heard his voice rise to an ungainly bellow, but there was nothing he could do to rein it in. His grief—his rage—seemed to explode out of his chest. "I was nearly assassinated *twice* after you left and once before. Am I to let you deal with chieftains who would just as soon murder you as exchange words?"

It took *ferocious* willpower not to haul her into his arms. His body screamed to hold tight to her with everything he had. He was still fighting a fierce war with himself when she crossed her arms over her chest as if to put a barrier between them.

"Are you going to tell me I must depend on *you* to keep me safe?" She regarded him skeptically. "Alaric, you'd be dead now if not for me. I brought two armies to save your hide. Not one— *two*. And what do I find when I arrive here? Ten more bodies on that wall. I counted." Her lips pursed disapprovingly. "Perhaps I should be the one locking *you* away, for everyone else's safety if not your own. Is this the kind of king you will be?"

His temper roared. *Who was she to tell him how to handle threats?*

"If they challenge your place with me, yes." His jaw tightened defensively. "I will kill or drive off any whose loyalty to you I cannot trust. I will not apologize for that. And I will *not* apologize for trying to keep you alive."

Tears glinted in her eyes. "That's my answer, then," she said with quiet dignity. "You will not change. You won't."

And now she was walking away from him. She was almost out the door.

Anguish threatened to choke him. He crossed the distance between them in two strides, and he heard her give a surprised little squeak as he pulled her into a bone-crushing embrace. It was not enough to hold him up. He slid to his knees, his arms still around her, his face buried in her stomach, desperation filling his lungs. He was drowning in it.

"Don't go."

Julia held quiet, standing rigid in his arms. Alaric had been in more battles than he could count; and never, in all the times his life had been in mortal danger, had he felt terror like he did now, waiting for his wife to speak.

Her hand curled gently in his hair.

"If my choice is between freedom and prison, Alaric, I will not choose prison." But it was not abject refusal. Hope flared in his chest. "If you lock me away, I will escape. I escaped you before. I escaped Thorismund. I escaped my own brother. I *will* leave you."

His arms tightened until her ribs creaked. If he let go, she would vanish and his life would be worth less than nothing. He breathed in, his heart thudding hard in his chest, inhaling as if he could take her into his lungs whole.

"Then, I surrender." He said it roughly. "I surrender, Julia, to whatever terms you set. *I love you.*" He would rip his own heart out of his chest before he let her walk away again.

"Is that so?" Was it his imagination, or did she *purr* those words? He glanced up to see her smiling through glinting tears. "What will you give me if I stay, Alaric?"

What would he give her? His life. His heart. His fucking *bones.* "What is it you want?"

"What I've always wanted. An army at my back. An Empire laid at my feet."

"Done." He didn't even have to think about it.

"And a wedding. A public one, with vows and a priest and *gifts.* It's the man who gives the dowry, after all. That's one of the first things you ever said to me." Humor tugged at her voice. "I suppose you knew you were mine, even then."

"Yes." Even then. Without fucking question. He rose to his feet, his arms still tight around her, to see she was smiling up at him with all the warmth of a stolen afternoon shining in her eyes. Still, she was not making any promises. "So you'll stay?" He *needed* to hear her say it. "I am not above begging, woman—"

"Oh, Alaric." She laughed, warm and rich and unaffected. Pressing a hand against his cheek, she murmured, "I can think of much better things you can do with your mouth."

Then she kissed him, and the walls around his heart crumbled forever.

Julia drifted between dreams and waking for what seemed like years. She felt warm and protected and utterly safe. She didn't want it to end.

When she woke, it was past dawn. Alaric was sitting by her bed, watching her with ferocious intensity. He was dressed as a warlord, golden torques encircling the strong swell of his arms. He would have looked positively fearsome, if his blue eyes were not lit with concern.

"Don't get up." He pressed her gently back down on the furs. "Is it water you want? Food?"

The memory of their lovemaking the night before crowded

in on her mind. The aching, almost *pained* tenderness of it. "Water." It was brought to her immediately, cold and faintly metallic-tasting. "I must look frightful."

"You are beautiful," he said with a fierce honesty that made her face heat, and she realized he had never called her so before. She remembered his impassioned confessions last night. *I love you.* He had said it many times in her arms. Seemed not to be able to stop saying it. Suddenly she was wracked by sobs. His arms were around her. His lips at her forehead, at her throat. Anguished. "I cannot stand to see you cry."

"I'm not crying." She let out another sob. More of a *snort* really. And then she was laughing, and he was laughing too, his forehead against hers.

"I am sorry. For everything."

"Please stop apologizing." For a moment she just let him hold her. It felt so, *so* good. She'd thought she had lost him. And then, yesterday, there had been a moment when she was certain she would have to leave him. Julia pulled back, searching his face. The pain in his eyes had not abated. "Did you sleep?"

He smiled faintly. "Very little."

"Is it Horsa?"

Horsa had not come through the gates with the others; Julia heard later that he had left after the battle, gone to reunite with his bandits.

Alaric did not have to speak. The answer was there in the pain in his eyes.

"We will find him again. We'll bring him home." Julia laid her palm against his face. "And Calthrax? Do you still see him?"

She felt him tense beneath her hand.

"I see him all the time." Blond-tipped eyelashes screened his eyes. "I thought he would go once I found you again. But he kept me awake most of the night, once you slept." A long, pained silence. "He says everyone who loves me dies. He is right."

Julia drew a breath. She understood now why Alaric was so

terrified of harm coming to her. He had been unable to safe-guard so many. His fierce protectiveness led him to do terrible things, made him the villain. But it was terrifying to love any-one in a world like this.

Alaric refused the man a proper burial. Now his ghost walks the earth without rest.

"I have an idea." Her clothes were piled at the end of the bed and it was still there, in the little pouch, smooth and cool against her palm. She held it up in the dim sunlight. Calthrax's finger-bone flute. "We can give him a proper burial."

CHAPTER FORTY-NINE

That day, the Huns lit a fire on the parade grounds and slaughtered a cow for feasting.

Julia watched from the steps of the burned-up manor house, Thorismund beside her, the two of them passing a wineskin as they watched the festivities. Below, Riga stood with his shirt off, tattoos twining across his chest and down his arms, his sister standing before him as all around them, people cheered and shouted. They were all Riga's family—his many siblings, his nieces and nephews. The elderly women who'd overseen the healing and led the defensive line during the battle had also delivered him as a baby.

As she watched, Riga and his sister began to engage in what looked more like a dance than combat.

Julia held up her hand, showing the mark Riga had carved on her palm. "How should I murder him for this? Poison?"

"You'll have to beat me to him, Julia. If his *other* sibling doesn't kill him first." Thorismund glanced at his own palm and shook his head, more amused than angry. Then he looked at her, gray eyes glinting in the fading afternoon light. "Have you decided to stay?"

"I have." She raised her chin. Thorismund had never stopped offering her other roads. "I know you disapprove."

"You're a grown woman. You can make your own decisions."

"At least *someone* thinks so." Julia took another sip from the wineskin. Disappointingly watered. "Have you made yours?"

Below, Riga's hair whipped around his face as he and Kreka clashed and came apart, both of them laughing in savage joy. Thorismund glowered down at them. "I meant what I said."

"And yet here you are."

"You are my blood brother. I swore an oath." He looked none too pleased about it. "I cannot forswear my oaths."

Julia glanced at him, his wheat-blond hair pulled back from his face and tied with a leather thong, frowning down at the combat as if there was some kind of mortal insult to him in it. She could see what went unsaid—his all-consuming love for Alaric. His refusal to abandon his chieftain on the battlefield. His resentment at being bound by such things, even as he refused to live any other way.

"He needs you, you know. He won't say it, but he does." She paused. "As do I. You were the only one among the chieftains who cared about the refugees."

"And Alaric let them rot. With the slightest setback he became a warlord like any other."

"I should like to think my supposed death was more than the *slightest* setback." Julia took a sip from the wineskin. "I have no intention of letting them rot, Thorismund. I will need allies who carry influence with Alaric. You and I could do a great deal of good here, if we work together."

"Hmm." Thorismund was silent for a bit, mulling this over. "He isn't better, you know. It might seem like he is, but he's not. He won't be until Horsa comes back."

Julia sighed, watching the crowd below. Hengist was there,

and Ehre, cheering. Both had placed bets, and they weren't on
Riga. Ataulf and Bromios sat close together at the edge of the
audience. Alaric had promised not to throw Bromios out on his
ear; there was a story about how he had freed Alaric and the
twins from prison. Perhaps he had earned his place. Bromios
always landed on his feet, eventually.

But Horsa's absence was palpable. It ate at *her*; she could only
imagine what Alaric felt. "I promised Alaric we'll bring him
back," she said in a low voice. "Call it my oath."

"Perhaps it's better for the boy to spread his wings on his
own."

Julia didn't know what to say to that. It pained her to think he
was right. The two of them watched the wrestling for a while,
and Julia winced as Kreka flipped Riga over and slammed him
onto his back, her boot on his chest.

"Do you think Riga let Kreka win?" Julia mused. "Or is he
really just *that* bad at wrestling?"

"I think I'll go and find out." In the next instant, Thorismund pulled his shirt over his head and was striding down the
slope, bellowing Riga's name.

CHAPTER FIFTY

They buried Calthrax as the leaves turned, in a copse of trees in the shadow of Noricum's walls, along with all the bodies Alaric had hung on stakes. Alaric sang the *paeon* he'd denied before, in a clear, rich baritone; Thorismund joined him in a deep bass, the song raw and rich as deep earth.

Alaric did not see Calthrax again.

The days passed. Alaric and Julia marshalled their forces to repair the walls. By the time summer faded into fall, the walls were rebuilt and the aqueduct restored, cool water flowing in from the mountains. The city was now as ready for a siege as it would ever be. Alaric set guards on the newly repaired walls, and for a while, Julia was ready to wake to the sight of a new army on the horizon. Calthrax had promised Stilicho would come over the mountains before winter, and now summer had fully turned. Word would come from the hill tribes any moment that he was on his way, and even Alaric believed the hill tribes could hold him back for only so long.

But word did not come.

They had an explanation when Alaric's spy in Ravenna rode into Noricum at a gallop.

Caius was a man of middling height and indeterminate age, the sort who easily passed unnoticed. He bowed before Alaric in his war tent, his cloak dusty from the road.

"I'm sorry, my King. Stilicho is dead."

Julia thought immediately of Verina, alone in court without Stilicho's power to shield her. Alaric's blue eyes narrowed. "How?"

Caius told them. When Honorius heard the rumors of Julia's marriage, he had fallen into a rage. Olympius had used the opportunity to resurrect old accusations of Stilicho plotting with Alaric, and Honorius had ordered Stilicho executed. Stilicho had taken refuge in a Christian church and Honorius's men had told the bishop that they had come only to arrest Stilicho, not to execute him. As soon as the general crossed the sanctuary's threshold, they cut him down.

Then, after Stilicho was executed, Honorius had ordered thirty thousand Gothic *foederati* and their families in Italy slaughtered.

After hearing this story, Alaric ordered everyone from his tent except Julia.

"This is war," he told her flatly. She could *feel* his rage. The kind that burned down cities. Even leashed, it filled the tent, sucked up all the air in the room. "This deserves an answer."

His eyes were on her, direct and level, and she bristled at the question he was asking. She was no longer the Roman princess, could he not see that? Julia thought of the great marble buildings of Rome, and where that marble came from. She wanted to tear it all down. She never wanted to look at marble again.

"This is my wedding gift to you." She straightened her spine and met his level, determined gaze with her own. A sacred oath. Thorismund would be proud. "I will give you the keys to the kingdom. All my alliances, all my wealth, are yours. We'll burn it down together."

She laughed as Alaric lifted her by the waist, spun her in the smoke-scented cavern of the tent. She didn't want to be empress. She just wanted to see it burn.

A week later—the day before her wedding—the princess received a visitor.

Alaric had been up for hours. But Julia had slept long into the morning, and jerked awake to find Horsa sitting by her bed. He was every inch the Bandit King, a gold hoop earring glinting in one ear. But he ruined the impression by pulling her close in a tight embrace.

"I had to see you before your wedding," he said quietly. "I brought you this. Seeing as you keep losing them."

It was a dagger. Small enough to fit in a boot or up a sleeve. The hilt glinted with emeralds. "It's beautiful," Julia breathed. Almost *jewelry*. "Where did you get it?"

"Stole it." He shrugged, and grinned. "You can always come with me. Be Queen of the Bandits instead."

"Horsa, you and I would never work out." People were always offering her ways to run away from Alaric. Julia sighed. "Will you stay for the wedding?"

"No."

She'd known this would be his answer and it still broke her heart. "He misses you," she said quietly. "Will you ever come back?"

Horsa shook his head. "I cannot say."

"Then, come to *me* sometimes. Rome is stirring against us and I need my own spies." She took his hands in hers. "I'm sure you've heard the news about the Goths in Rome slaughtered."

"Yes. And I hear you go to war." He regarded her solemnly. "I wish I could go too."

She put her arms around him and held him tight. For all the

times she knew she wouldn't be able to. "I will always be a safe haven, Horsa. Even if you cannot return to Alaric."

She drew back to memorize his face. His eyes glinted in the fading light. Blue, paler than Alaric's. Almost gray. Soft and steel. "I know."

She could not hold him. He was gone between one breath and the next.

The wedding of Alaric of the Goths and Julia Augusta, daughter of Theodosius, took place in the fall. Tribal leaders came from far and wide, and Alaric and his men slaughtered wild sheep and goats. The feasting lasted for days.

It's said that the couple was married by Thorismund, last scion of the Batavi, who joined the couple in the eyes of the gods. Alaric was a barbarian warlord, and she the only daughter of the emperor of Rome—natural enemies, but those who were there only saw how the bride and groom looked at each other, with such breathtaking tenderness that it was easy to forget this marriage was a kick in the Empire's teeth.

It's said that according to custom, at the height of the feasting, the King of the Goths gifted his wife with jewels and gold from plundering the richest cities in the west, carried in by a parade of handsome youths. It's said that he set her on a throne above his own, and gazed up at her with an expression of love that outshone all those riches.

And when they went to war against the Empire, the whole earth shook at their coming.

★ ★ ★ ★ ★

ACKNOWLEDGMENTS

It took me eight years to write this book. Through that time, my life changed completely. I started writing it in the midst of a breakup, and continued through a year-long health crisis, years of terrifying political upheaval, and my mom's death of pancreatic cancer. I read her early chapters in the hospital. I don't know how much she heard, but I like to think that now, maybe, she knows all of it. Like Alaric, I don't know where the dead go. I wish, desperately, that I did.

Through it all, this book was my refuge and my escape hatch. But all is not grim. There is joy in this book, and so many helped me bring it into existence.

My parents are the first I have to thank. They were the kind of people who camped out on Civil War battlefields for their honeymoon, who loved history and lived immersed in it. My mom was the librarian in the small town where I grew up, and I spent hours among the shelves, reading books about ancient history and mythology from all over the world. My dad taught me that battlefield history is so much more than dates and numbers; it's gripping and visceral. And my mom encouraged my reading, no matter where it led.

So thank you, Mom and Dad, for instilling in me all I needed to do this work. Thank you to Dad for your endless support and love, and for never flagging in your belief that I can do whatever I set my mind to. Thank you to Mom for ordering every book I ever wanted on interlibrary loan, no matter how obscure, and for turning a blind eye when I checked out the smutty books. I thought I was fooling you at the age of fourteen; of course I wasn't. I love you both so much. Also: libraries are life. Thank you to local libraries.

Thank you to Jenny and Luna for your wonderful early support. I dearly love you both.

Thank you to Juliet, for all the long, still writing days with tea and cat cuddles, and the soup dumplings, and for Wales. And for wandering around the Met with me while I went on and on about axe-throwing. I was obsessed then; I am obsessed forever.

Thank you to Erin, for the epic drag brunch brainstorming session that broke my eight-year block about my title. You are magic.

Thank you to Brittney, for all your support and creativity and supreme event-organizing skills. Without you I would not have met my wonderful agent. I am grateful always.

Thank you to Minet, for sitting me down and writing out Alaric's memorable quotes in the original Latin on a napkin, and then translating. I didn't think I could fall in love that fast.

Thank you to Heloise, for coming into my life when you did. I wish so much you didn't have to go.

Thank you to Liv, whose friendship and love have made all good things possible. Thank you for Rome, and for Greece, and for cocktails overlooking two-thousand-year ruins. Your friendship has changed my life.

Thank you to Sarah from Three Little Words Romance Editing, for giving me the road map that took this book from a very rough diamond into something you might propose with.

Thank you to my incredible agent, Ellen, for believing in this book and in me. Thank you for your wit and your wisdom and for keeping me grounded, and for every opened door.

Thank you to my copy editor, Jerri Gallagher, for the confidence boost when I needed one, and helping break me of my intractable semicolon addiction.

Thank you to my wonderful editor, Cat, for loving this book as much as I do. Thank you so much for helping me shape it into its highest form and bring it to the world. I hope the world loves it as much as we do.

Thank you to the listeners and supporters of *Ancient History Fangirl*, the podcast I co-created (with Genn) because I needed a place to talk about all the wild research I was doing. Thank you for loving ancient history like I do, for your endless support and encouragement, and for those of you who signed up to the Patreon: thank you a hundred times. I am so excited for all of you to read this. It's been a long time coming.

And finally, thank you to Genn. My three-eyed raven, my all-seeing eye, my redheaded portent of disaster. Thank you for hauling my carcass across the Alps twenty-two times and midwifing this thing into existence, for sweating and bleeding right along with me. Thank you for keeping me in it when I asked, for going all in with me on *Ancient History Fangirl*, for coming into my world and deciding to stay. It always amazes and humbles me what the two of us can accomplish when we do it together. Thank you.